IBIZA BLUES

By Gary Culver

ISBN: 979-8-9880259-1-7 print
ISBN: 979-8-9880259-0-0 eBook

To all my Hawaii peeps, without whom I could never have written this.
You know who you are.
And to my beloved Sunny, who's always been there for me.

***

"Movin' ahead so life don't pass me by!"
— Jim Croce

Chapter 1

France—Late 1970s

Jake had managed to reach the middle of France about 260 kilometers south of Paris, in the midst of the Loire Valley, when disaster struck. He was just outside a city aptly named Nevers as his wounded 1972 Simca limped off the highway and headed into town. The car was making a sound like an old man clearing his throat, and smoke was leaking out from underneath the hood. He kept an eye out for a garage that might still be open even though it was already Saturday afternoon. His fear was that in France, everything tended to shut down on Saturday after lunch and not reopen again until Monday morning. "Please, God," he said through gritted teeth, "if you're listening, please, please help me find a place where I can get this damned jalopy looked at so I can get back out on the road again."

As if in answer to his prayer, he spotted what looked to be a garage further on down the street. A mechanic in oil-stained blue overalls was in the process of rolling a Michelin tire display inside the garage. He turned to look at the Simca as it rolled noisily toward him. He was clean-shaven with greased back black hair, a hawklike beak, flared nostrils, and a filter-less cigarette glued to his lower lip which stayed attached even as his jaw dropped an inch at the car's approach.

Jake rolled up to within a few feet of the man, pulled up the emergency brake, left the motor running, threw the door open, and ran out to meet the mechanic.

"Are you still open?" he queried in French.

"Can't you see I'm closing up?"

"Yes, yes, I can see that. But I have an emergency here."

"I wouldn't call it an emergency," said the man, inhaling the stench of the car with distaste. "I'd call that a disaster."

"But can't you at least tell me what's wrong with it?" asked Jake. "I need to know what kind of damage I'm looking at here and what it's going to cost me."

"I can look at it," he said. "But I won't be able to do anything until Monday at the earliest."

"Fine," said Jake. "That would be a great help."

The man directed Jake to drive his car inside the shop and turn off the ignition. Then he opened the hood and started sniffing around. His manner was gruff, but it seemed like he knew what he was doing. He reminded Jake of the kids he'd grown up with back home in upstate New York, who'd been working on cars since childhood.

"I'm not going to lie to you," he said at last. "This engine is a piece of shit. If I were you, I wouldn't spend another franc on it. Just put it up for sale, get whatever you can, and cut your losses."

"But I just bought it," moaned Jake. "In Paris. And I paid good money for it too. I mean, just look at it. It's beautiful."

"So are the whores in the Hôtel du Lion … from a distance," said the mechanic leering at Jake. "Especially at night after a few glasses of wine when the lights are down low. But at least when they fuck you, you know you're getting fucked. Whoever sold you this piece of trash was counting on you not knowing much about cars. On top of that, you're a foreigner, right? Just a sucker in their eyes."

Jake felt his heart sink. He knew the mechanic was right. What was he going to do now? He'd spent about half of his hard-earned savings on this car, money he'd gathered working at a ski resort in the Swiss Alps. Now he was planning on driving down to Ibiza, where he hoped to live for as long as possible, enjoying the sun, the beaches, and the island's promise of pleasure. Jake had been on the road for a good while now, and he just couldn't seem to stop, nor could he think of a reason why he should.

"Look," said Jake, his voice quavering with anxiety. "I need to drive this car to Barcelona, which is a full day's drive, and then take it over to Ibiza on the ferry. Can't you at least fix it up enough to get me that far? I have a friend on the island who's good with cars. He can help me fix it once I'm there."

The mechanic plucked the cigarette from his lip, spat out some paper, and took a deep drag, exhaling a thick cloud of smoke. He looked hard at the car, coughed a few times, and puckered his brow in concentration. A thick vein was throbbing at his temple.

"Well," he said, "if that's what you want to do, even though I advise strongly against it. There are a few things I can do to get you up and running again, but I can't guarantee how long it'll last. Probably to Barcelona, though."

"Great, thanks!" said Jake. "And can you recommend some place for me to stay in town while I'm waiting for you to fix the car?"

"Sure," he said. "The Hôtel du Paix. It's clean, cheap, and right across the street from the only adult cinema in town. You can spend your time in there if you want," he said dismissively with just the trace of a smile. Jake noticed the dark, puffy circles under the mechanic's eyes and wondered how well he knew the inside of that cinema.

"C'mon, I'll drive you over," said the man abruptly as he flicked his cigarette into a barrel full of foul-smelling liquid.

Chapter 2

Jake sat on the edge of the bed in his hotel room, feeling like a fool. This trip was not going according to plan, and his budget did not include much wiggle room for things not going according to plan. Even spending these few days in a hotel and paying for meals in a restaurant made him exceedingly nervous. He was supposed to be traveling as cheaply as possible, sleeping in his car, and buying food in stores and gas stations to eat along the way. He'd gotten used to living on the cheap from the first moment he'd arrived in Paris from New York with only a few hundred dollars in his pocket. He'd just scraped by washing dishes in a restaurant and helping to paint an old château near the end of the Metro line, and staying rent-free with friends. He'd studied French every chance he'd got, and it had paid off, giving him the confidence to work for French-speaking bosses later on at a ski resort in Switzerland, enabling him to save up for this journey. It would be his third trip to Ibiza in the past year, but his first with the intention of actually living there. Spain was notoriously cheap, and he knew that once he got there, he could live on a shoestring budget, cashing in his valuable Swiss francs for pesetas and enjoy an extended stay in the sun.

He chastised himself for not choosing a more practical car like a *Citroën deux chevaux*. With an unusually high suspension, it had become the car of choice on the island, especially adaptable to the rough roads on Ibiza. Instead, he'd been seduced by a brightly painted car which he knew nothing about. In fact, he'd never even heard of a Simca before.

The Parisian who owned it figured that a fresh paint job might entice some fool into buying it, and she was right.

As his thoughts on the subject became more and more self-critical, he found himself starting to panic. He could feel his blood pressure rising and a tightening sensation taking hold in his chest. Forcing himself to focus on his breathing, he gradually began to calm down and relax. The calmer he got, the more he was able to glimpse the irony in his situation. The town where the breakdown occurred, after all, was called Nevers. "I should *ne-vair* have come here," he mused aloud, with an exaggerated accent. "It is *ne-vair* a good idea to come to Nevers," he continued, chuckling aloud. Nevers soon led to nowhere in his Beatle-loving brain, which cued up John Lennon's voice plaintively crooning about a nowhere man in his nowhere land, making plans for nobody. "That would be me," Jake conceded, getting up off the bed and going to the window. *Yessiree. Thank you, Mr. Lennon. Now I know who I am at last!* Peering out the hotel window, he noticed the day was growing dark and gloomy. *What difference does it make, ultimately,* he asked himself, *if I am stuck here in Nevers. It's not like I'm on some important humanitarian mission.*

But his cynicism was short-lived. It had triggered another voice in his head—"Who the fuck are you kidding? Of course, it makes a difference, to my own life at the very least, which is only just getting started." He viewed the shadowy profiles of dreary-looking buildings looming against a sad city backdrop. Red neon lights flashed, and headlights swept the streets below. A tired and tawdry urban scene for sure. *Nothing for tourists here,* he thought, chuckling to himself. Although he was a foreigner in Europe, he'd never considered himself a tourist. A tourist, he reminded himself, being someone who visits for a short time, sees the sites recommended in a guidebook, and leaves. *I'm not doing that. I could give two shits about the Eiffel Tower or Napoleon's tomb.*

He could not stop berating himself for buying a lemon, though. His mind, like an unstoppable windup toy, kept repeating "What an idiot" over and over as he beat his head gingerly against the wall. *I'd better go downstairs to the bar for a drink,* he finally decided, *before I throw myself out the fucking window.*

Chapter 3

Seated at the bar, Jake ordered a glass of house red wine and regarded himself in the mirror. He was wearing his best outfit—a clean pair of well-worn jeans, a white long-sleeved cotton shirt, a brown leather belt with a brass buckle, and laceless brown shoes scraped painstakingly clean after surviving his château-painting days in Paris. His brown hair fell below his shoulders, and he sported a full reddish-brown beard. Studying his reflection, he wondered for the umpteenth time if shaving it off might not make a difference in his life.

Halfway down the bar, a middle-aged woman with thick black mascara, an unnaturally pale complexion, and black hair in a short pageboy cut, ground out her cigarette in an ashtray, picked up her drink, and moved to the empty bar stool next to Jake. She scanned her reflection indifferently until she finally caught Jake's eye in the mirror.

"*Bonsoir*," she said.

"*Bonsoir.*"

"Are you just passing through Nevers?" she asked in a husky voice.

"Yes," said Jake, relishing the opportunity to speak French. "I hope so."

"You hope so? You mean you might stay?"

"Oh no," said Jake. "I'm just waiting till my car gets repaired."

"Oh," she said. "Well, that sounds terribly boring."

"It is boring," he admitted.

"Are you by yourself?"

"Yes," he said, turning to look at her directly for the first time. "I'm afraid I am."

"Well," she said with a suggestive glance, "what's wrong with that? I'm by myself as well."

"I think you'd be wasting your time with me," said Jake.

She gave him an appraising glance. "Why do you say that?"

"I'm afraid I have nothing to offer you. I'm broke."

"*Salaud,*" she said. "What are you trying to say? Do you think I'm a prostitute?"

"I ... well ... guess ... not?"

"Have you ever even been with a prostitute?"

"To be honest, no, I haven't."

"Oh, so now we're being honest, are we?"

She frowned, plucked a fresh cigarette from her pack of Gauloises, lit up, and blew smoke out toward the mirror, turning her head to check out the other patrons at the bar. Jake drained his glass, reached in his pocket, and threw down some francs on the counter. Just as he stood up to leave, the woman turned her head and glared at him.

"Where are you going?" she queried.

"Up to my room, I suppose."

"You guess ... you suppose? Aren't you sure of anything?"

"You mean philosophically?"

"I mean in your life, right now."

"About the only thing I'm sure of right now is that I'm standing at a bar in Nevers talking to you."

"Good," she said, straightening her posture. "Then we've found something we can agree on. Now sit down, please."

Jake complied. It would have seemed impolite not to. And something about this woman intrigued him.

"Well, monsieur," said the woman, "now that we've broken the ice, what shall we talk about?"

"How about a name?" asked Jake.

"A name? Fine. Mine's Muriel. A good Jewish name, except that I'm not Jewish."

"Of course not," said Jake. "Why would you be?"

"I could be, of course," she said. "There still are some Jews left in France."

"Some," agreed Jake. "Just not you."

"That's correct," she said, studying her nails. "And you? What's your name?"

"Gaston," he replied, as his high school French class moniker inexplicably popped into his head.

"Gaston? Really? Did you just make that up? Never mind, I already know the answer."

"It's a good French name, isn't it?"

"What happened to you being honest?"

"Honestly . . . ? It's Jake."

"Ah," she said. "That's more like it…*un Amerloque!*"

"Do you have to call me that?"

"Well, it's what you are, isn't it?"

"No," he said. "I'm an American. *Un Américain. Amerloque* sounds, I don't know, insulting … like something you'd call Richard Nixon."

"Oh," she said, relighting her cigarette. "I'm so sorry, *Jake*. I didn't realize you were such a sensitive young man."

"And I didn't realize you were so sarcastic."

"Fair enough," said the woman exhaling smoke through her nostrils. "I think we're getting off on the wrong foot, *mon ami*. I have an idea, though, which may remedy that."

"All right," said Jake. "I'm game. What do you have in mind?"

"What do you say we just go up to your room and have sex?"

"Wait a minute. I thought you said you're not a prostitute."

"I never said any such thing," she replied.

"But I already told you I don't have any money."

"Well then, in that case, I am *not* a prostitute. Now, can we please go up to your room and make love? Or perhaps you prefer to call it fucking? Or should I pick up my drink and go and sit at the other end of the bar?"

"Hold on," said Jake enjoying the banter, "don't be so impatient. Haven't you ever heard of foreplay?"

"I've heard of it, yes."

"Only *heard* of it?"

"Look around you, Jake. Do you think that these sorts of men have any interest in that kind of thing?"

Jake gave the other bar patrons a perfunctory glance. He saw a decidedly desultory crowd of slack-jawed, mostly overweight men with sallow complexions wreathed in a dingy cloud of tobacco fumes. "Hmmm, probably not," he conceded, extracting a cigarette from Muriel's pack and lighting it. He took his time inhaling and slowly blew out a large cloud of smoke.

"You're not in too much of a hurry to go upstairs, I hope," said Jake, catching the bartender's eye and signaling him for another round.

"Not at all," she said, flashing a crooked grin. "I'm enjoying the foreplay."

"I'll drink to that," said Jake as fresh drinks arrived on the counter.

"Me too," she said, downing her wine. "You know what, Jake? It occurs to me that you aren't like most of the men who come here."

"Well, I'm not French," he said, "if that's what you mean."

"No, that's not what I mean. *Pas du tout*," she continued, "they're … ordinary. Extremely ordinary."

Jake had to laugh. "Well, there's nothing special about me. I can assure you of that."

"I beg to differ," she said, exhaling smoke and suppressing a slight rattle in her chest. "Most of these men are, well, very predictable. In their behavior, I mean. I can tell you exactly what they will be like tomorrow or next month or even ten years from now. They are not going to change. But with you, I get a different feeling. You are still in flux. I can sense that. You could still be anything you want to be."

Jake felt a shudder pass through him. Her words had stirred up something inside him, something which lay coiled up and ready to spring loose. A sense of hope, perhaps? She's right, he reminded himself. I could still be anything I want to be. The fact was, except for the vague idea of being a writer, he had no idea what he wanted to be. "Thank you for saying that, Muriel. As it happens, that's just what I needed to hear right now."

Muriel nodded, her eyes glistening in the low-lit room.

"Hey," said Jake, more out of loneliness than any real desire. "What do you say we order a bottle of wine and take it up to my room?"

"For some foreplay?"

"I thought that's what *this* was," said Jake. "Let's just continue our conversation up there. Your description of the men here has gotten me depressed. Why not go somewhere where we don't have to look at them for the rest of the evening?"

Muriel turned her head to give the men at the bar a final appraisal. "Okay," she agreed. "But let's not leave together. Someone might get the idea I'm a prostitute."

Chapter 4

Once upstairs in Jake's room, Muriel fell apart rather quickly. She propped herself up against some pillows on the bed and quickly downed two more glasses of wine. With her skirt hiked up on her thighs, she took out her lipstick, clumsily tracing a red line around her mouth.

"Wyntcha sit here?" she asked, tapping the bed beside her.

"And do what?" asked Jake, trying to hide his growing revulsion.

"What you said … foreplay."

"It's okay," said Jake.

"Wuzzat s'posed ta mean?"

"I mean … I think this was a mistake."

"Mistake?" she said. "Wuddja mean by that?"

"I mean, Muriel, I probably should not have invited you up to my room."

"Oooh," she said, slopping wine onto her dress. "Is that how it is? *Vraiment?* Really? Well, lemme tell you something, Gaston, or whoever the hell you are. This may be your room for the moment, but this is not … your … town! It's *mine*," she said, stabbing her chest with a sodden finger. "My … town!"

Jake reached over and managed to dislodge the glass from her hand. He was fearful she'd spill wine on the bedspread, and he'd end up having to pay to have it cleaned. "You're right," he agreed. "It *is* your town. And

11

I'm very sorry to have intruded. But look, Muriel, the bottle's almost empty, and there's really nothing for you here."

"Are you kicking me out of your room?" she asked, giving Jake a reproachful look. "Izzat what's happening here? Before we even get started?"

"No, I'm not kicking you out. You can stay for a little while and take a nap," he said, giving her leg a light slap. "Then, after you've had a little rest, we'll see, okay?"

Muriel didn't answer. Jake realized she'd suddenly fallen asleep sitting up on the bed. To his dismay, her hair seemed to be sliding downward over her forehead. He gingerly readjusted her wig, squeezed her legs together, and took off her shoes. In no time at all, her facial muscles slackened, and she began to snore.

Feeling tipsy from the wine, Jake collapsed into an armchair in the corner of the room and reached for a yellow legal pad on the table beside him. The sight of Muriel, drunk and disheveled, sleeping on his bed in the sterile hotel room, filled him with a profound sense of loneliness. A deep sigh escaped his chest as he balanced the pad on his thighs and contemplated a letter to his girlfriend back in the States. In his heart, Jake knew that the idea of her still being his girlfriend was an illusion he needed to let go of. Nonetheless, putting his feet up on a stool and leaning back in the chair, he picked up his pen and began to write:

"Dear Joan,

I'm totally alone now in a place I don't want to be with nothing to do but think. My thoughts are mostly about how stupid I am or how unfair life can be. They are not good thoughts at all. Every one I have is like an indictment against myself. To live this type of life I've chosen—full of spontaneity, discovery, and adventure, and real learning from the book of life itself, not the kind you get in a classroom—requires a certain level of clarity and confidence. I always assumed I had that, but it's been sadly lacking in my life of late. I've discovered that my judgment may leave something to be desired and that scares me a little. No, actually a lot! If I could make the kind of mistake I just made by buying a pretty but fucked-up car in Paris—blowing a big wad of cash on a junk heap that's already broken down here in Nevers after less than a single day of travel—what other avoidable mistakes are waiting in the wings to jump out and betray me in the future? It's a real blow to my self-confidence, Joan. I've gotta tell you. But I will get through this if for no other reason than there is no other alternative. I've committed myself, but I'm not sure to what."

He paused, having been interrupted by some loud snorts from the bed. Then there was a long silent pause, and Jake waited anxiously until her breathing started up again.

"The hard part now is that at this moment, I no longer have any clear idea of what I am or where I'm going. There is just a part of me inside that says, 'Don't overthink this, just GO! The meaning of all this will become clear later on.'

Joan, you still are very much a part of my thoughts, and you always will be. Many's the time I've been tempted to give up here and rush back to be with you, assuming you would even still want me. But I know that I'm not ready. I still feel a deep restlessness inside, like my journey here has hardly even begun, and were I to come back, there's a good chance I'd make you miserable all over again by deciding not to stay. I know you love me, or at least that you once did. That has helped to sustain me during many difficult moments on this journey. There are times when I'm feeling really lost, and all I have to do is remember the look of love in your eyes whenever we'd meet, and that helps me to believe in myself again." Jake looked up again at his eerily quiet guest. For one ghastly moment, he wondered if she'd died. Then another loud snort revived her, and he turned back to his writing.

"Our time together was good, very good, easily the best time of my life. Doing construction jobs to save up money, coming home filthy and exhausted, and you bathing me so tenderly at night in that old, clawfoot bathtub in that rundown old house we shared. Then taking you to bed, making sweet love long into the night. You touched my soul, Joan, like no one before … And I'm so grateful for that … but the truth is I've put off my return for too long. I think we both know that. I know in my heart that I've forfeited any rightful claim to your love. It should now be open to all comers, for I no longer deserve it, and you have so much to give. There is ambiguity in my heart still, and there's nothing I can do about that. But that should be my torment, not yours. Letter writing is futile because nothing I write could possibly satisfy you anymore. I know that, but still, I'd rather send you this than nothing at all …

Love,

Jake"

As Jake finished writing, he looked up and noticed that Muriel was peering at him through slitted mascara-smeared eyes. Apparently, nap time was over.

"Writing to a lady friend?" she asked.

"Wha—? How did you know?" asked Jake.

"I've been watching your face for the last few minutes. You look troubled. The way a man looks when he's thinking about a woman. A woman who is stirring up his heart."

"It's not that," he objected. "It's just that …"

"Just what?"

"Just … I don't know what. I guess I'm trying to come to terms with the fact that she's no longer in my life, and that was my decision, and part of me thinks that I might have made a big mistake."

Muriel reached inside her purse and rummaged around for her cigarettes. Her face had softened after her brief nap, and she looked more tired than dissolute.

"You're right," she said, lighting her Gauloise. "It probably is."

"What?"

"A big mistake."

"How can you say that? You barely even know me."

"Oh, I know you well enough, Jake. All men are the same, you know, in certain ways. Trust me. I have been studying this subject for many years."

"What do you mean, 'all men are the same'? That sounds rather facile, don't you think?"

"Exactly," she said. "Facile is a good word. It has to do with facility. And when it comes to love, men simply don't have the same facility as women."

Jake put his letter aside and sat up straight in his armchair, eyeing her warily.

"Go on," he said. "I'm listening."

Muriel pushed herself up against her pillow, adjusted her wig in a clumsy attempt to make it sit right, and pulled her skirt down over her thighs. "You may have misunderstood me earlier when I said that you were different from other men," she said.

"How so?"

"I said that you were different from the other men at the bar because you are young and still adaptable to change. But in another way, you are the same."

"I suppose you're right," said Jake.

"Don't pretend to be so humble," she snapped. "Listen to me! You probably think that you've written this woman an extraordinarily sensitive letter, and because of your no doubt exceptional honesty and humility, she is going to understand you and forgive you for whatever it is that you think you've done to her. Am I right?"

"It would be great if she did," he admitted, "but I have my doubts."

"Well, you should have your doubts. Because she is never going to forgive you for this."

"Forgive me for what? You don't even know—"

"Yes," she interrupted. "I do know. I know that you are here and she is there. Somewhere very far away. And you are trying to justify this separation from her while her heart is bleeding. Bleeding, do you hear me? And you have no concept of that because you are only thinking of yourself. You say you're waiting for your car to get repaired? For what? To take you even farther away from her, am I right? And she has not stopped thinking of you at all. Not even for one minute. The whole time you've been gone."

Jake felt the blood drain from his face. Her accusation was unfair and unjust. So why did it feel like she'd just plunged a knife in his gut?

"What's the matter, mon ami," she said, wheezing slightly. "Cat got your tongue?"

"I ... well, I guess I don't know what to say," he stammered.

"Of course you don't, Jake. If you said anything right now, you would just be condemning yourself. Because you know that everything I've said is absolutely true. Now go ahead. Tell me that I'm wrong."

Jake rose up from the armchair then and walked to the window. The clouds had opened up, and the window was streaked with rain. Staring at the blurred lights outside, he said softly, "I have to give you credit, Muriel. Perhaps I underestimated you."

"What is that supposed to mean?"

"It means you really have studied men, and what you're saying is almost certainly true, which makes me a fool at best. I know that, and I'm trying to deal with it, but there's nothing I can do about it. I'm kind of learning as I go along here, at least as far as women are concerned."

"You're right," she said, nodding in agreement. "There is nothing you can do about it. That doesn't make you a fool, though. It's just your nature, and you must follow it. Of course," she said, shifting her tone, "one could also make the argument that it is very courageous of you to do this."

"To do what?"

"To be yourself, of course," she said. "You can break her heart, which is always a nasty business, but also be brave, Jake. To be otherwise would lead to, well, the kind of life that those men at the bar downstairs are leading. One that is safe, predictable, and ultimately full of regrets."

"But I feel regret already," said Jake.

"I assure you, *mon ami*, that the regret you are feeling now will pass quickly. Only because you are still so young, and life still has so much to offer you. But don't think this won't leave a scar. *Une toute petite cicatrice.* It will, and it should. For the rest of your life, there will be times when you ask yourself, 'Did I do the right thing with her?' That is the price you pay when love is right there in front of you, ripe for the asking, and you turn your heart away."

Jake turned then to look at her, surprised to find that her eyes were glistening with tears.

"This insight that you're sharing with me, Muriel … it also came at a price, did it not?" he asked.

"*Putain!*" she replied angrily. "Look at me, Jake! Do you think I don't realize what I've become? Do you think I'm not aware of the price that I've paid? Look at me … my wig, my makeup, my swollen liver? Do you think this is what I dreamt of becoming when I was your age?"

Jake just stood there feeling pity for her, but also envying her hard-won wisdom.

"Look at me, Jake," she pleaded again. "This is what love has done to me. I am a living example of its perils. I've been in your shoes before, and I've been in her shoes as well. You can trust me on this. So get your car fixed, mon ami, and drive away as far from her as you can. What's your destination anyway?" she asked. "Do you even have one?"

"Ibiza."

"Ibiza? Well, that's just perfect. The perfect place for someone not serious, like you. Have a good time there. You deserve it."

He paused to take her in once again. Despite her sarcasm, he felt profoundly grateful for the reality check she'd provided. "Can I help you back down to the bar?"

Muriel slid off the bed, swaying slightly, and looked up at Jake. "No, *merci*," she said, sighing deeply. "Not necessary. I'll be fine on my own. It's what I'm used to. And you'd better get used to it also, Jake." She reached up then and suddenly threw both thin arms around his neck, drawing his face down to her lips. They kissed briefly until Jake gently pulled away.

"*Au revoir*, Muriel," he said, leading her to the door. "And thank you for your sage advice."

"*Au revoir*, Jake," she said, stumbling out into the hallway. Closing the door softly behind her, he continued to feel the sensation of being stabbed in the belly after she'd confronted him about Joan. Her confident assertion that Joan had loved him more than he would ever know, or was even capable of understanding, was a painful reminder that his irrepressible urge to lead a vagabond existence had already cost him in ways he was reluctant to acknowledge. He walked back to the armchair, picked up the yellow legal pad that lay there, and tore off the letter to Joan. Folding it, he stuck it inside a journal he kept, knowing now he would never send it.

Chapter 5

Lying back on his bed, resting his head on a pillow, his hands cradling the back of his head as he stared at the rain-streaked window, an image of himself and Joan playing Frisbee rose up in Jake's mind. They were both on quaaludes which were trendy at the time. Drug use was pretty widespread at the school in upstate New York where Jake had gone to college and where he and Joan had met in the early seventies. They'd smoked pot, in fact, almost every time they got together. They liked the sensuousness of it and the easy access to what felt like a higher realm of consciousness, more all-inclusive, more boundary-breaking, and euphoric than one's ordinary state of mind. But this lude was on a whole other level. The intensity of it far outstripped the pot experience.

They were both barefoot, and each step on the grass felt like an intimate embrace with Gaia herself. Jake felt himself entering a world where time slowed to a crawl, and each individual moment came clearly into focus, filled with an intensity of sensual pleasure that remained mysteriously out of reach in everyday life. Each time he dove for one of Joan's Frisbee tosses, he bounced along the ground in delight, feeling the earth rise up to meet him like a child on a trampoline enjoying a delightful foray with gravity.

"I'm starting to come on," he called to Joan. "Are you?"

"Oh yeah," said Joan, walking toward him. "I sure am." Her body appeared to Jake to be shimmering as she approached, and the fluid rhythm of her movements was mesmerizing to watch. Her smile was stretched to the limit, and her deep black eyes were glowing with pleasure. Jake felt bathed in liquid joy. She was more beautiful than he'd ever seen her before. Even her slightly buck teeth, which she normally tried to conceal, were framed in her irrepressible smile like protruding ivory gems.

"D'you wanna stay here?" she asked, squatting down in front of him. "Or do you wanna go back to my place?"

Jake pushed himself up to face her and placed a hand on each of her bare knees. Looking into her dark, unblinking eyes, he felt the presence of an unseen bridge between them, allowing for an unprecedented flow of perception and enjoyment. He moved his hands forward so that his fingers slid under the frayed hem of her cut-off jeans, giving her thighs an exploratory squeeze and registering the jump of pleasure in her eyes.

"I think going back to your place is an excellent idea," he agreed, aware that his mouth felt uncommonly dry.

They held hands as they floated the few blocks to Joan's apartment, each enjoying a sense of unaccustomed weightlessness. Once inside the apartment, mercifully devoid of her annoying roommate, they retreated to Joan's bedroom and closed the door behind them. She moved quickly to the stereo, dropping the needle on an Otis Redding LP already on the turntable. "Try a Little Tenderness" began flowing from the speakers. They responded to Redding's soulful crooning with an intimate embrace, kissing and squeezing and gradually removing each item of clothing until they stood naked and trembling slightly, gazing at each other in amazement. Joan's breasts were a revelation to Jake. Her light brown areola ended in perfect erect nipples—little brown gummi bears screaming "Suck me." He did his best to comply, even as the wave of sensual stimuli was threatening to overwhelm him. Feeling compelled to suck her breast while at the same time squeezing her ass and alternately plying her mouth with his tongue, he moved his lips from her nipple to her mouth and back again with the unimpeded joy of a musician who's just been presented with the perfect instrument to play on, one responding ardently to his ministrations with no possibility of being off-key. He was tempted to stay with her tongue, exploring that quivering, juicy organ that had taken on a vibrant life of its own: its muscular form wrestling with his own until their conjoined mouths were a single pool of lust. Then her breasts would beckon once more, and his head would bob again downward, his tongue flicking out like that of a lascivious serpent, intent on gathering every last morsel of pleasure. The intensity of their embrace was escalating at a dizzying pace, expanding beyond any semblance of control. They had entered a realm where time no longer held sway, and in an infinitely expanded instant, his prick, as stiff and unyielding as an iron bar, had feistily nuzzled its way inside the damp, sizzling recess of her lust-soaked inner walls.

"Uhmuhgod," said Joan, groaning. "Yes, yes, yes!"

She'd wrapped both legs around Jake where they stood, and he strode with her to the bed, where he eased her down, bracing himself with one arm while holding the other beneath her. Joan's closed eyes and ragged breathing told him that she'd already crossed over to another dimension. Feeling like a passenger now in his own body, Jake experienced himself experiencing rapture. He felt the walls of her vagina spasmodically gripping his shaft until they were both pulsing with the energy and light of a shattering star, lost in the vastness of unrelenting bliss, as he emptied into her, again and again, feeling the glory of inexhaustible union.

***

The weekend passed slowly in Nevers. Jake's life was on hold, and there wasn't a damned thing he could do about it. The weather was wet and rainy, and he spent his time hunkered down in the hotel room sipping cheap wine, studying the newspaper with his dictionary to bone up on his French, making notes in his journal, and rereading Kerouac's *On the Road,* one of the seminal books which had inspired his journey. Jake had been reading intensively since high school, becoming a great admirer of the heroes of the Beat Generation. Kerouac, Allen Ginsberg, Gary Snyder, Henry Miller, William Burroughs, and others held a fascination for him with their love of freedom and adventure and truth and their clear defiance of authority, which was always threatening to suppress the full possibilities of whatever experience life had to offer. He had tolerated what he considered to be the faux wisdom of college professors whose knowledge of the real world seemed limited at best, taking advantage of his time with them to study languages and read more widely, all the time champing at the bit to get out into the world and gauge what life had to offer for himself. An innate urge to be able to transform his wanderings into art in the form of writing drove him much in the way he imagined it drove his Beat heroes, and he prayed for the discipline to be able to write even when he felt he had nothing much to say.

He wondered what Dean Moriarty, the quixotic hero of Kerouac's epic novel, would do in his situation. Probably, he decided, Dean would sneak out of the hotel room without paying, hot-wire someone else's car, and continue on to Barcelona. Alas, Jake possessed neither Dean's street smarts nor his fearless disregard for the law and ended up paying both his hotel bill and the mechanic promptly on Monday with his dwindling funds as soon as the car was ready to go. Once again seated behind the wheel of his patched-together Simca, the surly mechanic's parting words, "Good luck. You'll need it!" rang inauspiciously in his ears.

Chapter 6

IBIZA

True to his word, the mechanic had managed to do a cheap stopgap repair that allowed Jake to reach Barcelona, but the engine was already making an ominous tapping sound by the time he arrived. He suspected a valve job was in order and prayed the car would hang on for at least another few weeks until Carl would be there to help him do some repair work. Carl was an American friend and fellow adventurer who hadn't yet arrived on the island when Jake drove his car off the ferry near Ciudad de Ibiza.

The island known as Eivissa in the local Catalan dialect was originally founded by the Phoenicians. Its name stemmed from the Phoenician word "Iboshim," a derivative of Bes, the Egyptian god of music and dance. That fact, when Jake discovered it seemed uncannily prescient to him. How did they know, he wondered, what Ibiza was destined to become a few thousand years later? Or did the name already preordain its fate? In any case, music and dance were certainly alluring aspects of the island, eventually developing into a massive draw for tourists from all over the world as the fame of Ibiza's discos and trance music spread far and wide. But Jake was there in the early days, and the commercial success of the entertainment industry had not yet overwhelmed the bucolic, sun-drenched island off the northeastern coast of Spain, which for some time had been attracting discontented misfits and foreigners in search of relief from the stress and rigors of modern civilization.

Two letters awaited Jake care of lista de correos at the main post office in town. The first was from Carl, letting Jake know he'd been delayed by an unexpected side trip to Germany to do some repair work on his Mercedes van. He planned to join Jake on the island in about two weeks, and would Jake please do whatever he could to find a place for them to live, perhaps an old finca, with stone walls thick enough to shut out the heat in summer and the cold in winter, preferably far out in the campo?

The second letter was from Joan:

"Babe,

I can't believe I'm still holding out some hope for you. It's been what? Sixteen months now? That's a lot of time in our young lives. A lot of lost passion, lovemaking, and tenderness together. I should just give you up. That's what everybody says. My sister Anne tells me I'm the biggest fool that ever fell in love. She says I don't understand what's as obvious as the mole on my cheek, namely that you are not coming back to me ever. It feels so sad to write that. And I don't really believe it still. That's what makes me the biggest fool, I guess. I'm still here, Jake. In the same place you left me. Did you remember that I'm gonna graduate soon? Wish you could be here to celebrate with. But my sister disagrees. She says if you showed up, she'd pull your hair out by the roots! And you know she'd do it too. Guess that's the difference between us. She's not a sucker like me. Will you write me from Ibiza? I'm going to stop now, or I'm afraid I won't send this.

Love,

Joan"

Jake sighed and walked outside the building allowing the bright sun to shower him with its withering rays. As usual, the thought of Joan filled him with yearning and regret. What were they doing? Why were they even still writing to each other? Why was he still torturing her with his indecisive words, still leaving open the possibility of his long-awaited return? The whole thing demanded resolution, but he simply couldn't bring himself to deal with it. Not now. He was too excited to be back in Ibiza to think about the past. Getting back here had been a long and arduous journey, and any regret he still had about leaving Joan was eclipsed by the growing sense of elation he was feeling since arriving on the island, lifting his spirits like the high from some new and exotic drug.

It was still early morning but already oppressively hot. Jake felt uncomfortable in his long-sleeved shirt and jeans, remnants of his sojourn in Switzerland, and made a mental note to get hold of some lighter clothing pronto. He drove the Simca from the post office to the Vara del Rey plaza in the very heart of town, parking as close as he could to the Hotel Montesol, with its extensive awning-covered café which spilled out onto the sidewalk. It was a favorite haunt for locals and foreigners alike, and although the hotel itself was expensive, the waiters would invariably tolerate young indigent travelers who ordered nothing but coffee or a single beer as long as they didn't overstay their welcome. Jake hoped to run into some friends he'd met the previous winter when he'd come down for a visit from Switzerland, where he'd been working at a ski resort. They were already living the kind of lifestyle he wished to emulate, and he was hoping to reconnect with them now. He was especially keen to find Jacqueline, a French woman who, together with her German boyfriend, lived in an old, outwardly rundown finca near Santa Gertrudis, a centrally located town on the island. They'd managed to renovate the finca sufficiently to turn it into a tasteful cozy retreat. Most of the fincas on Ibiza were off-the-grid in modern parlance, and Jake had been impressed with how much they'd managed to accomplish with little or no money. The place was beautifully but simply decorated, thanks to Jacqueline's background in interior design and her penchant for acquiring castoff *objets d'art*. Car batteries ran their stereo, and a propane tank fueled a small fridge and stove in their tiny kitchen. They'd even managed to hook up a shower by running a long hose from the stone well behind the house.

The original meaning of finca was a kind of ranch, but for most foreigners on the island, the meaning had been reduced to a simple stone building, usually painted a blinding white to reflect the oppressive heat in summer. The ones that interested Jake and Carl, indeed the only ones they could afford to rent, were well off the beaten track without any modern conveniences, often reachable only by a rutted dirt road. For many locals, they symbolized the old way of life they were anxious to escape in their headlong rush to lead a more rewarding material existence in town. The concept that their abandoned fincas, handed down from one generation to the next, might be valuable rental properties, highly prized by foreigners, hadn't yet completely sunk in. They were catching on quickly, though, and Jake knew it was going to be an increasingly tricky task to find a suitable place that he and Carl could afford to rent.

Jake recalled that Jacqueline, who worked part-time at a fashion boutique in town, often came to the Montesol to enjoy a continental breakfast. When he and Carl had met her that winter, she'd promised to help them find a finca to rent should they ever return to the island to live, and Jake was determined to hold her to that promise. But first, he had to find her. Standing now on the sidewalk in front of his brightly painted car, he stretched his limbs and smiled. *Hallelujah*, he thought, *I've made it this far! Now I just have to find my friends….*

On his way to the Montesol, Jake paused frequently, meandering slowly, taking in the shops and restaurants bordering the vast plaza, many already bustling with early morning customers. He still felt stiff and sluggish from the time spent in his sleeping bag on the deck of the ferry from Barcelona the night before, and his body reveled in the movement. Shielding his eyes as he approached the hotel, he peered expectantly into the shadows of the awning-covered sidewalk, hoping to discover Jacqueline with her dimpled chin and sparkling blue eyes, undoubtedly wearing one of her colorful self-styled dresses. He'd almost given up when he finally spotted her seated in a far corner, at a table with her boyfriend, Klaus. Sporting a broad-brimmed straw hat, encircled by an iridescent red ribbon, she sipped coffee and stared into space while Klaus read the *Diario de Ibiza*, the local Spanish newspaper.

"*Hola amigos*," said Jake, beaming as he approached their table, "remember me?"

Jacqueline set down her coffee, tilting her head to get a better view.

"Jake?" she exclaimed. "For real? Is it you?"

Rising from their chairs, both she and Klaus stood up to greet their friend. Effusive by nature, Jacqueline offered Jake both cheeks to kiss before stretching out her arms to hug him. Klaus, the more stoic of the two, extended a limp well-manicured hand.

"When did you arrive, *mon ami?*" asked Jacqueline in her heavily accented English.

"Just now," said Jake. "On the ferry from Barcelona. Do you mind if I sit down?"

"But of course. If you can find a seat, that is!"

Jake quickly appropriated a chair from a nearby table and sat just as a waiter appeared.

"*Un café con leche,*" said Jake, "*con pan tostado, por favor.*"

"*Si, señor,*" said the waiter.

"Well," said Klaus, his erect posture contrasting sharply with Jake's more relaxed bearing. "This *is* a surprise. Are you planning to stay long? And where is Carl?"

"Carl's coming soon," said Jake, "and yes, I'm planning to stay for as long as possible. Assuming I can find a finca to rent."

"Well, you're always welcome to stay with us, you know, until you can find something," said Jacqueline. "I'm sure it won't take too long."

Jake smiled, appreciating her optimism and generosity, at the same time giving her boyfriend a sidelong glance. Pleasant enough but without much personal warmth, Klaus remained an enigmatic figure. He'd left the hubbub of industrial West Germany to try to create a more laid-back lifestyle for himself in the south of Europe, but his Teutonic mindset was still mired in the stringent work ethic of his homeland, and he came off as stiff and awkward as if some inner battle were raging to prevent him from feeling truly at ease. Tall and slim with a protruding forehead, he took immense pride in his immaculate grooming. Brown lustrous hair parted in the middle reached well below his shoulders, and his unblemished face with its high cheekbones and cleft chin shone almost blue from his closely shaven beard. He reeked of patchouli and wore John Lennon glasses over deep-set brown eyes. The colorful, almost foppish clothing he sported, Jake presumed, had been custom-made for him by his brilliant seamstress girlfriend.

"Would that be okay with you, Klaus?" asked Jake.

"Why not?" said Klaus, after a moment's hesitation. "If Jacqueline says so."

"I won't stay long, I promise," said Jake, feeling the need to reassure him as the waiter arrived with his order. "Just until we can get set up somewhere on our own."

"Don't worry," said Jacqueline. "I told you I'd help you find a place, and I meant it. We can start tomorrow. Looking for *fincas* for my friends is something I never get tired of doing. It's such a great way to see the island, and you never know what you might find."

"That's right," said Klaus. "And who knows, maybe we will even find a better place for ourselves."

"Better than your place?" said Jake, genuinely confounded. "I very much doubt that. But if you do decide to move out of the place you're in now, we'll take it! And what about your work here in town?" he asked, turning to Jacqueline.

"After today, I don't have to come in for a while. I have some new projects which I'll be designing from home. So it seems your timing is perfect, *mon ami*."

"In that case, I graciously accept your kind proposal. Now I hope you will at least allow me to repay you by buying some groceries for the next few days."

"We can go shopping right after breakfast," said Klaus. "I'll take you back to Santa Gertrudis with me. Jacqueline has to stay here today and work in the boutique. I'll come back this evening and pick her up. I hope you don't mind riding on the back of my moped, though!"

"Not necessary," said Jake. "I picked up a car in Paris. I'll follow behind you."

"I have an even better idea," said Klaus, ever the pragmatist. "I'll ride with you and leave the moped here for Jacqueline. She can ride it home herself after work. Right, *ma chérie?*"

"But of course, *mon amour*. Forget about the groceries, though. I'll pick up a few things and prepare a lovely meal for us tonight to celebrate Jake's arrival!"

Jake felt a surge of anticipatory delight. Jacqueline's cooking was legendary. She had mastered not only French cuisine but that of Morocco as well, where she had spent several years doing interior design work for wealthy French ex-pat clients. During his winter visit, she had served up a couscous royale, unlike anything his taste buds had ever known. The tender, juicy lamb, the chickpeas, and the vegetables dripping in cumin and coriander had revealed to Jake a whole new world of culinary delights. And cooking was just one of the many things he admired about Jacqueline. Her creativity was boundless. Apart from her skills in fashion and architectural design, she also painted beautiful watercolors of the Ibicencan landscape. Her life was a great reminder of how rich and creative existence could be. A true woman of the world, Jacqueline was quite unlike anyone Jake had ever encountered before. Giving Klaus an envious glance, Jake sipped his coffee, marveling at his luck. Running into Jacqueline like this was clearly an auspicious event. It cheered him greatly after the self-doubt he'd encountered during his troubled journey driving down from Paris.

Chapter 7

The next morning, after having feasted on Jacqueline's chicken specialty *pollo del campo* in a delicious wine sauce the night before, Jake opened his eyes to the glaring sunlight coming in through the open front door of the finca. Wriggling up out of his sleeping bag on the couch, he shoved his fists into his eye sockets, trying to massage out some of the wine he'd drunk the night before. David Bowie's *Station to Station* crooning about the search for love had begun blasting from loudspeakers which Klaus had strategically placed outside in the garden.

Out of the corner of his eye, Jake noticed Jacqueline gliding by wrapped in a blue and pink sarong just sheer enough to reveal that she was wearing nothing underneath it. She stirred up a little breeze in passing, and Jake sensed the seductive power of the gardenia-scented perfume she wore, not to mention the outline of her hips and buttocks through the flimsy sarong as the sunlight framed her momentarily in the doorway. *Ah,* he thought, *such a promising sight. It's going to be a wonderful day!*

He pulled on a pair of torn jeans and walked outside shirtless as Bowie continued crooning about a thin white duke who was throwing darts in lovers' eyes. Strong black coffee laced with chicory filled his nostrils with its pungent aroma. Klaus was stretched out on a kind of makeshift lounge chair with ragged yellow cushions, his eyes closed and a beatific smile on his face. A large, blue beach umbrella which had obviously seen better days, shaded him from the sun, and a long cone-shaped joint, partially smoked, rested next to a box of matches in a glass ashtray on his lap. Jacqueline was pouring a cup of coffee from a metal percolator perched on a nearby rickety tabletop.

"Good morning, Jake," she said in a welcoming tone. "Sleep well?"

"Sure did," said Jake, stretching. "I was out like a light. I think it's the first good night's sleep I've had since … well, I don't know when!"

"That's because you're back on Ibiza," interrupted Klaus. "It's such a relaxing, magical place. You'll see. I always get a good night's sleep here. Much better than in Germany."

"That's true," confirmed Jacqueline. "Once he's out, it's like sleeping with a . . . how do you say . . . corpse!"

"Is it even more magical when you're stoned?" asked Jake, eyeing the joint in Klaus's lap.

The German's smile widened, exposing flawless white teeth. "Of course," he said, straightening up. "Isn't everywhere? I'm glad you woke up now, Jake. Otherwise, I would probably have to finish smoking this by myself."

"Over my, how do you say again . . . corpse?" interrupted Jacqueline, her blue eyes sparkling, as she approached with two cups of coffee. "Here you are, chérie, just the way you like it. Two lumps of sugar and a little bit of leche from the can. And you, Jake? How do you like yours?"

"Black is fine, *gracias*," he said. "I'll just take it industrial strength if you don't mind. And by the way, Klaus, you didn't seriously think I could continue sleeping with Bowie blasting like that, did you?"

"Hmm," he said, grinning wickedly, "I suppose not. But isn't it great to wake up to?"

"And there is bread, too," interrupted Jacqueline. "Very fresh from the local *tienda. Pan del campo.* And butter and homemade marmalade … over there on the table. Please serve yourself."

"That's very kind," said Jake. "And, by the way, Klaus, I'm not complaining. I love Bowie!"

"I thought you would," said Klaus, handing over the joint. "Now, first things first. *Voilà!*"

Jake held it up to his nose and sniffed. "Mmmm," he said, "Moroccan hash?"

"Of course," said Klaus. "That's all you can get around here these days."

"Don't you ever get any grass?"

"Once in a while," said Klaus. "Of course some people try to grow it. But you have to be very careful. If the Guardia Civil finds out, they'll throw you in jail for sure."

"Unless you have enough money to bribe them," added Jacqueline as Jake held a flame to the end of the joint.

He tried inhaling gently, but it was no use. The second the harsh fumes from the burning hash, mixed with some of Jacqueline's strong Gitanes tobacco, entered his lungs, he erupted in a fit of jagged coughing. He held out the joint to Klaus, tears streaming down his face. "Whoa," he said, pressing a hand against his chest, "that stuff is strong!"

"Look at you, you're crying," said Jacqueline, her blue eyes twinkling as Bowie sang about love and cocaine. "Just try to relax, and I'll bring you some water."

Jake did as he was told, both touched and amused by this maternal side of Jacqueline, which he'd never seen on display before. *She's really very kind,* he thought, *and so lovely, too.* He looked over at Klaus, sitting tight-lipped, holding what was undoubtedly an enormous cloud of smoke in his lungs, and felt envy for this simple pastoral existence he and his girlfriend shared together, enjoying life at their own pace, for the most part shunning the material side of things and living in the moment.

"Jake," said Klaus, handing him the joint again. He reached for it and, this time, carefully took in tiny puffs little by little until his lungs were ready to burst.

"Jake, what are you doing?" asked Jacqueline. "You didn't drink your water yet." Just as he reached for the glass she was holding, the hash suddenly hit home with the force of a sledgehammer. His entire body simultaneously expanded and felt like it was floating as light as a helium balloon as a wave of euphoria engulfed him. Exhaling smoke, he laughed and coughed and laughed again. "Woo-wee," he said, taking a sip of water. "That is some good shit."

"I'm glad you like it, Jake," said Jacqueline helping herself to the remains of the joint. "And welcome to Ibiza. Now you have officially arrived!"

Chapter 8

Jacqueline, true to her word, decided to head out right after breakfast to help Jake find a finca. Klaus stayed home tinkering with a moped he'd been commissioned to repair, and Jacqueline and Jake got in her light blue 2CV with the roll-down top, feeling nicely toasted from the morning joint, and headed out toward San Mateo. They hadn't gone far on the paved road when Jacqueline suddenly swerved the car to the left and started bouncing down a nearly invisible dirt lane, heading toward a clump of carob trees in the distance.

"Where are we going?" asked Jake.

"There's someone I'd like you to meet," said Jacqueline. "She's a good friend of mine, and I've been meaning to stop by. You are the perfect excuse. I think you two will like each other. She's quite an . . . how shall I say . . . interesting person."

Jake said nothing but felt pleased by her announcement. The more people he met, he reasoned, the greater the chance that someone might know of a finca that had come up for rent. Word of mouth seemed to be the way that news traveled on the island, and he planned to advertise his search to as many people as possible.

Once past the clump of trees, a finca came into view. A very different kind of finca than Jacqueline's place. More spread out, more rundown and rough-hewn, it seemed like a real working farmyard. It didn't boast any of the aesthetic improvements or decorative quality that garnished Jacqueline's place with its sculpted ceramic and metal artwork and colorful pieces of macramé hanging outside on the walls. On the contrary, this finca's whitewash was already peeling off, exposing an earthen clay-like substance underneath. There were a lot of chickens and roosters running around, clucking and crowing, and a vast blue hammock stretched between two monkey pod trees in the courtyard. As Jake looked closer, he noticed two heads popping up from inside the hammock. Two sets of bare legs swung over the side, revealing a pair of towheaded boys with incredibly dirty faces, their mouths agape as Jacqueline brought the car to a halt inside the courtyard.

"Jacqueline!" they yelled, jumping from the hammock and running toward the car. As soon as they saw Jake, they hung back, suddenly shy, kicking up dust and staring.

"Who are you?" one of them asked.

"I'm Jake. A friend of Jacqueline. And who are you?"

"I'm Atif," said the taller, skinnier one.

"And I'm Johnnie," said the shorter one, whose plump face was covered with freckles. "Are you…" he said, twisting his hair, "are you here to see Cannelle?"

"Who's Cannelle?" asked Jake.

"That would be me," said a low voice from the finca's doorway.

Jake turned to see a tall, lanky woman with tightly muscled arms standing in the doorway to the finca. She had long black hair, streaked with gray with bangs covering her forehead, and scintillating green eyes. Jake noticed she was wearing what looked like a homemade pair of dirty white coveralls with large hand-carved wooden buttons holding the shoulder flaps in place. *Does everyone make their own clothes around here?* he wondered, just as Cannelle stepped barefoot out of the doorway and strode toward Jacqueline, extending her arms wide.

"*Bonjour* Jacqueline," said Cannelle as the two exchanged cheek kisses. "I'm so happy you stopped by. And who is this?" she asked in French, eyeing Jake with an openly lusty gaze.

"This is my friend, Jake," said Jacqueline. "He's staying with us for a few days. He's trying to find a finca to rent, so I'm taking him around."

"*Bonjour,*" said Jake extending his hand. "I'm very pleased to meet you. You have a lovely place here." He meant it too. Despite its rundown appearance, there was an earthiness and a sense of privacy about it that appealed to him.

"You speak French?" she asked in a surprised tone.

"Yes, if you prefer," said Jake.

"But you're not French," she said.

"American."

"Another American? Ooh, la la. There are a few of them nearby. I'll have to introduce you. Nice people too. But if you don't mind, I prefer to speak English. My husband is English, and I want my kids to learn it too in his absence."

"That's cool," said Jake wondering what she meant by "his absence." "So let me get this straight, though. Your native tongue is French, but your kids are learning English here on Ibiza. Do they speak Spanish, too? They must, right?"

"Of course, and Ibicenco also," chimed in another voice from the doorway. An impressive looking girl began walking toward them, wearing a white kerchief around her hair like the local peasant women did and a red knee-length peasant dress and blouse. She was shorter than Cannelle but powerfully built with a forceful presence. Her green eyes were curious, and she had a ready smile. Her white teeth stood out in marked contrast to her deeply tanned face.

"This is my daughter Isabelle," said Cannelle. "Did you feed the chickens yet, honey?"

"Mom," she whined, "Can't I say hi to Jacqueline first?"

"*Bonjour, ma petite*," said Jacqueline, eagerly embracing her. "Why don't we all have a cup of tea together. Then you can go and feed the chickens. I'm sure they can wait a little while longer. There are plenty of bugs for them to eat in the meantime."

"And Arabic, too," said Atif, running up and shoving Jake, narrowly missing his crotch.

"What do you mean?" asked Jake, reaching down to grab him.

"We speak Arabic, too. That's how I got my name, Atif."

"We lived for about a year and a half in Morocco," explained Cannelle, sucking on a hand-rolled cigarette, "with their father. Before he got arrested."

"Yeah," said Johnnie matter-of-factly. "Daddy's in jail now."

"He is," said Cannelle. "But he'll be out soon. Next year, we hope. Although you never know with these fucking Spanish judges. But we have to be ready for him when he does get out. That's why we're trying to make a nice home for him here."

Jacqueline gave Jake a look as if to say, "See, I told you she was an interesting person."

"Now you've got me curious," Jake confessed. "What's he in jail for?"

"Well, if you really want to know, you'll have to come inside with us for some tea, *n'est-ce pas?*" she said, winking slyly.

She and Isabelle turned then and began walking back toward the doorway, but Jake hung back a little, wanting to check in with Jacqueline first.

"It's okay," she assured him, looping her arm through his, "there are no secrets with Cannelle. She is very, how do you say, up-front? About everything. Just relax and enjoy your tea!"

Johnnie and Atif swarmed around Jake as they headed for the door.

"Hey, do you guys really speak Arabic?" asked Jake.

"Yeah," said Johnnie, clinging to his leg.

"I don't believe it," said Jake teasingly as he ruffled Johnnie's hair. "Let's hear you say something then."

"*Ibn Sharmuta*," said the little boy, pointing a chubby finger at Jake.

"Son of a bitch?" said Jake as both boys began laughing hysterically.

"That's right, that's what you are," said Atif, giggling. He suddenly punched Jake in the thigh and then jumped away just out of reach.

"Ow!" said Jake. "That really hurt! Oooh, I'm gonna get you for that! You wait and see!"

"Oh yeah? Go ahead, try it," said Atif, bouncing with excitement.

"Yeah," said Johnnie aping his older brother. "Go ahead and try it!"

"How did you know about *ibn sharmuta?*" asked Jacqueline as Jake fended off the two boys.

"I worked with some Egyptian guys on a farm in Switzerland," he explained. "I used to hear it a lot!"

Inside the kitchen, Cannelle set about making tea while her daughter Isabelle set the simple wooden table with small plates and tea mugs. She then set down a plate with sliced banana bread, all the while dancing with her brother Johnnie, who'd wrapped his arms around her waist from behind and was clinging to her like a freckled barnacle, his cheek pressed up against her butt.

"Get out, Johnnie!" she said at last. "Go in the other room and play with your brother! Right now. Shoo! Can't you see I'm busy in here?"

Just then, Atif appeared in the doorway between the kitchen and the main room of the house. "C'mon, Johnnie, let's play IT!" he said, disappearing back into the room.

"Okay!" said Johnnie screaming like a banshee as he let go of his sister and raced out of the kitchen.

"Jeesh!" said Jake, "talk about boundless energy."

There was a sound of furniture and bodies crashing, and Cannelle abruptly left her tea-making chore and swiftly crossed to the other room, a furious look on her face.

"That's it!" she yelled. Her exclamation was followed by the sound of slapping, crying, and bare feet rushing back out of the house and into the courtyard as far from their mother's reach as they could manage.

"No fair!" cried a sniveling Atif from somewhere outside. "It was Johnnie's fault too. How come you didn't hit Johnnie, Momma?"

"And now you guys can feed the chickens, too!" yelled Cannelle, ignoring them as she reentered the kitchen, her face still crimson with rage.

"How come? That's Isabelle's job!" cried Johnnie.

"Not anymore," yelled Cannelle, "and don't make me come out there, or you guys're really gonna get it!"

Cannelle grabbed the teapot then and carried it to the table, the anger in her expression fading quickly. "Those boys," she said, shaking her head, her eyes flashing amusement. Isabelle said nothing, her expression neutral, obviously used to such shenanigans. Jake sensed how thrilled she was, though, to sit down at the table and share in a grown-up conversation.

"So," said Cannelle, adding two cubes of sugar to her tea, "tell us about yourself, Jake."

Jake explained briefly about the journey he was on.

"So you must be on the road a long time now?" asked Cannelle.

"About a year and a half, I guess."

"And what made you want to come to Ibiza?"

"It's a long story," said Jake.

"Another long story?" said Cannelle. "I thought the story of my husband Colin, which you asked about, was going to be the long one. But I can make it pretty short for you. Do you still want to hear it?"

"Of course," said Jake. "I love a good story."

"There's nothing good about it," said Isabelle.

"Isabelle's right. It's a pretty stupid story when I think about it now," said Cannelle. "Colin and I met in Bordeaux, my hometown, and moved down here to raise our children, but we soon found ourselves running out of money. That's when Colin, who's always had contacts in the drug world, convinced me we should all move down to Morocco, where he said he knew some people who could help us to smuggle hashish back here to Ibiza. He said it would be a piece of cake, and that we'd make a lot of money, and I believed him."

"Because you were stupid, Mom!" interrupted Isabelle glaring insolently at her mother.

"Yes, perhaps," admitted Cannelle, rolling her eyes. "No, Isabelle, in fact, you are absolutely right. I was stupid. But I was also in love. Not just with Colin, but with the whole romantic notion of living in such an exotic place and figuring out how to do this deal and make a lot of money. Anyway, I knew that Colin had done something like this before and gotten away with it. So I trusted him. What can I say?"

"I know people who have smuggled hash out of Morocco. It can certainly be done," added Jacqueline.

"Anyway, it's so cheap down there. Even with the little money we had left, we managed to stay there for about a year and a half, living on almost nothing out in the countryside in the northeastern part of the country near a place called Chefchaouen, where there are plenty of kif growers."

"Kif?" asked Jake. "Is that the same as hashish?"

"Exactly," said Cannelle. "It's just the term they use over there. They say it comes from the Arabic word for pleasure," she said, looking Jake in the eyes again with that curiously seductive gaze he'd noticed when they'd first met. He had to admit there was some kind of energy happening between them. As he observed her skinny muscled body more closely and the large calloused hands, he kept thinking to himself, *This should not be happening. This is not the kind of woman I am attracted to at all!* And yet there it was—a kind of electrical charge running between them.

"*Tiens,*" said Jacqueline. "All this talk about kif has given me an appetite for some. Isn't there something you can do about that, Cannelle?"

"You know there is," she said, grinning. "In fact, I was going to suggest it myself."

Jake gave Jacqueline a look as if to say "Again? Already?" But Jacqueline was looking elsewhere: smiling at Cannelle, who was smiling back. It was clear that the two of them were very fond of each other and obviously quite dedicated to being stoned together. Moving her plate aside, Cannelle swept clean the space in front of her with the side of her hand and reached over to grab an ornate hand-carved Moroccan box made of ivory-colored stone. Opening it, she began pulling out various materials to build a joint. There were scissors, papers, a lighter, a piece of hash, cigarettes, and a strip of cardboard.

"Wow," said Jake, "that is quite a magical box you've got there."

Cannelle said nothing but tilted her head to look at Jake in that curious unsettling way again, almost obscenely blunt, as if she knew exactly what it was that he desired, even if Jake didn't yet know it himself. When she was done, she held the joint aloft, allowing everyone a chance to admire her handiwork. It was very neatly done. Nobody liked a messy joint, one that would burn unevenly or fall apart quickly, and everyone gave it an appreciative nod. All except for Isabelle, who seemed bored with the whole procedure. She was clearly waiting for this part to be over so she could hear what else the visitors had to say.

Cannelle handed the joint to Jake. "*Après toi,*" she said, her green eyes twinkling mischievously. Jake slid the joint between his lips and lit a match. Having learned his lesson at Jacqueline's that morning, he inhaled cautiously, bit by bit, eventually filling his lungs without having to cough it all out before passing the joint to Jacqueline. By the time she'd finished and passed it on to Cannelle, Jake's lungs were ready to burst, and he blew out a thick stream of smoke, coughing and pounding his fist on the table.

"Jesus," he said, his eyes watering, "I'll say it again. That is some strong shit."

"Did you think I would give you some weak shit to smoke?" asked Cannelle in a curiously threatening tone.

"Not at all," said Jake, momentarily taken aback. "Of course not, Cannelle." He was more unsure than ever what to make of this woman. She was clearly not someone to fuck with, though. Just as he was beginning to wonder if she was seriously giving him a hard time, her lips parted, and she smiled, revealing a gap where her lower front teeth used to be.

"I'm just fucking with you, Jake," she said, her eyes gleaming with undisguised mischief.

"She enjoys doing that, Jake," said Jacqueline, grinning at her friend. "You should know that about her."

"Mo-om," said Isabelle, sounding embarrassed. "Don't be mean."

"Who's being mean?" said Cannelle without taking her eyes off Jake. "Jake knows I'm just fucking with him, right Jake?"

"Yeah, sure," he said, shifting uncomfortably in his seat. "'Course I do. It's not like I've never been fucked with before." *But not like this*, he thought. *How does she do that? I thought only guys were supposed to do that with their eyes. Strip someone naked that is.* The more he looked at Cannelle, the more he became aware of how manly her energy was. Her aggressive nature, the long, wiry arms and calloused, muscular hands, the hint of a moustache on her upper lip, the flat chest and big, bare feet, and finally, the thick tufts of dark hair under her armpits, all suggesting masculinity. But the desire in her eyes had a feminine, softer quality. It was an unlikely chink in her armor, and Jake found himself, against all better judgment, attracted to this unusual person, unlike anyone he'd ever encountered before.

"So, anyway, what's the rest of the story?" asked Jake, forcing himself to break the spell she was weaving.

"Well, we finally made the right contacts," she continued. "We ended up buying two kilos of hash, drove to Tangier to get on the ferry, et voilà, they busted us when we were going through customs. Colin told them that he alone was responsible, that we didn't know anything about it, and took the blame for everything. We'd agreed on that beforehand, of course, just in case."

"I *didn't* know anything about it," moaned Isabelle, frowning.

"No, of course you didn't, chérie," said Cannelle. "You were only ten. Why should we tell you?"

"I get it, Mom," she replied. "To be honest, I was just happy to be coming back to Spain."

"Why? You didn't like it in Morocco?" asked Jacqueline.

"No," she said. "I didn't. The men there are weird. And I couldn't go to school there either."

"Isabelle loves school," said Cannelle proudly. "She gets As in all her courses."

"School here is so easy," she said, enjoying the attention.

"For a smart girl like you, it is," said Cannelle, pulling her daughter to her and kissing the top of her head.

"So wait a minute," said Jake. "Colin got busted in Morocco, but he's in jail here in Spain?"

"That's another long story," said Cannelle. "Let's just say some bribes were paid, and he ended up getting kicked out of Morocco to Spain. As soon as he got to Spain, though, they arrested him again."

"Hold on," said Jake, clearly fascinated, "you bought two kilos of hash and then paid bribes? Where did the money come from? I thought you were broke."

"It's all we had. Don't forget that two kilos down there costs next to nothing. The real way the growers make money when they sell to foreigners is by informing the police. When the police bust them, they are inevitably bribed by whomever they've arrested in order to get some kind of more favorable treatment, and then the cops split the bribe money with the growers who gave them the tip! We thought we were being really careful, only dealing with honest people, but *putain*, we did get screwed in the end after all."

"Then you and the kids ended up back here with no money?"

"Well, we had to stay with a friend in Barcelona for a while. I had to borrow some money from my family just to survive. Fortunately, I've always been a seamstress of sorts. I invested in some bolts of cloth, bought a used sewing machine, and started making clothes for kids, which I was selling to a shop there. It's something I'd been thinking about doing for a long time, anyway. But I couldn't wait to get back here, to the peace and quiet. So now I do the same thing here."

"She sells at the hippy market in Es Canar, Jake. Everyone loves her clothes there. We'll have to go together sometime," said Jacqueline.

"Please, do come," said Cannelle. "I'll show you how to make some money here on the island. Or don't you need to do that?"

"Oh, yes, I really do," said Jake. "I think I'll take you up on that offer."

"Good," said Cannelle, devouring him once again with her eyes. "It'd be my pleasure."

Chapter 9

Later that afternoon, after having driven around the center of the island for hours without finding a single finca for rent, Jake and Jacqueline drove back to Santa Gertrudis and parked in front of the popular Bar Costa. The town itself was small and typically Ibicencan, with an imposing whitewashed church, a post office, and several small stores or *tiendas* on either side of the road. There were also a few boutiques, restaurants, and cafes, occupied mostly by foreigners. Because it was centrally located and surrounded by beautiful countryside, the town was a natural tourist attraction for anyone wanting to explore the island. As they seated themselves on cane chairs at an outdoor table, Jake noticed that most of the men and women around them spoke a language other than Spanish or Catalan. He recognized English, French, Dutch, and a lot of German. They were mostly young with long hair and colorful clothing in contrast to the customers inside, who tended to be local men dressed in blue work smocks and berets. Many of them, both inside and out, were bent over backgammon games, studying the board intently.

After they'd each ordered a San Miguel beer, Jacqueline asked Jake what he thought about Cannelle.

"I think she's one of the toughest women I've ever met in my life," said Jake, "and I have to say, I feel tremendous admiration for her. I think a lot of women in her situation would have simply called it quits and gone back to an easier life in France, but she's doing exactly what she wants to do. You have to admire her for that."

"I agree," said Jacqueline, rummaging in her purse for a pack of Gitanes. "She is tough. Almost too tough sometimes."

"How do you mean?" asked Jake.

"I mean, she has, how do you say, rough edges?" she said, sighing. "It can sometimes be difficult to be around her because she has a short temper, and she's so blunt about her opinions. She doesn't suffer idiots happily; I think you say?"

"Yes. Doesn't suffer fools gladly. I get it. I can see that. But that's part of what I like about her."

"Sure," said Jacqueline. "Until you are the fool someday. And it will happen, I assure you."

"Funny," said Jake. "I thought you liked her?"

"Oh, I do. Of course I do. She is a good friend, in fact. You can always rely on Cannelle. Once she considers you to be a friend, she will never let you down."

"That's admirable," said Jake.

"Yes, it is. And good friends are not so easy to find, Jake. Especially here, believe me."

"Huh," said Jake. "I wouldn't have thought that."

"That's what I like about you, Jake. You have a certain innocence about you. And by the way, I think that Cannelle likes you too. A lot!"

"Yeah, I could see that. What's the deal with that? She's married, right?"

"Oh, c'mon, Jake," said Jacqueline, chortling. "Don't be so naive. Her husband is in prison, for God's sake. Has been for years now."

"I know. But she speaks so, I dunno, devotedly about him."

"Of course she is devoted to him, in her own way. He is, after all, the father of her children. Two of them, anyway. But she is a hot-blooded woman, Jake. I can assure you of that!"

Just then, a waiter arrived with their beers, and Jake decided to change the subject.

"Let me guess. The two boys are from Colin. But not Isabelle, right?"

"That's right. How did you guess?"

"Well, there's the difference in age, and Isabelle just looks so different from them. The boys are blond and pale and freckly, and she's so dark and, I don't know, kind of reserved, I guess?"

"Yes, I don't know much about her father except that he was also French, like Cannelle. But she's a very special girl, you know. Incredibly intelligent. In fact, Cannelle's sister offered to bring her back to France and put her into a private school, giving her the opportunity to have a classical education, but Cannelle wouldn't allow it."

"Why not? Seems like it would've been a great opportunity for her."

"I agree. But Cannelle is very possessive. She would never let go of Isabelle. It seems rather selfish of her when you think about it, but I can understand why. She's very attached to her daughter. And anyway, I don't think that Isabelle is unhappy here. She's like a second mother to the boys, and she already has a boyfriend, the son of a local farmer. She will probably spend her whole life here. She wasn't brought up to expect anything different. I can't say it's a bad choice for her."

"As long as she's happy. That's what really matters, right?"

"I can't disagree with that. I think that's what we're all trying to be, don't you?"

"That's why I'm here," said Jake, holding his bottle of beer aloft to toast Jacqueline. "On Ibiza, I mean. Let's drink to happiness!"

Chapter 10

A few days after their meeting with Cannelle, Jacqueline received word from a friend in Ibiza town that a bartender named Tony was looking to rent out his family's finca close to Santa Gertrudis. She arranged for herself and Jake to meet him in Bar Costa, and they followed him by car for a few kilometers out of town one morning down a long dirt road to his property. It was very remote, on a flat stretch of land with a stand of cedar trees behind it. There were no neighbors nearby, and a huge shady olive tree grew near the front entrance providing welcome relief from the sun. There was a sense of hiding out in plain sight, which appealed to Jake. The finca itself was very ordinary with a separate outdoor kitchen area, a large common room, and two smaller rooms inside the house. There was no bathroom, and the only water source was a well in the courtyard. There were some rudimentary furnishings, including a few cane chairs, a wooden table, and a metal bed frame without a mattress. The door to one room was locked, and Tony explained it was for his mother, who occasionally came out to visit and do some gardening.

"She won't be any problem," insisted Tony, a short, pudgy balding man with a fringe of blondish hair on an enormous round head. "She has a place with us in town, but she gets homesick for the finca sometimes. Every once in a while, she may turn up just to spend a few hours here."

Jacqueline and Jake exchanged worried glances.

"Are you sure, Tony?" Jacqueline asked him in Spanish. "She doesn't really live here anymore, right?"

"Like I say," said Tony, "she has a place with us in town. But I can't always control whether or not she comes out here to visit. She doesn't drive, but she knows how to take the bus, and she's used to having to walk for long distances. I'll let her know that we've rented the place to Senor Jake. Then she'll know not to come very often."

"Tell him," Jake said to Jacqueline, "that I would prefer if she didn't come at all."

Jacqueline translated, but Tony said nothing. He just smiled nervously and nodded his head. They agreed on a month-to-month rental. Jake gave him a handful of pesetas and accepted a huge iron key, and Tony got in his pick-up truck and drove away, leaving a cloud of dust in his wake.

"Well," said Jake. "What do you think?"

"What do *you* think?" she countered.

"I think it's a really nice place. It's cheap, peaceful, and not too far from the village or from you guys. I'm looking forward to spending some time here relaxing in *la vida del campo*. Until Carl gets here, I plan to bone up on my Spanish, plant some onions and tomatoes, and drive into the village every day to have a drink and meet the local gentry. I can't tell you how good it feels to be here in this sunny weather after the cold, snowy winter in Switzerland."

"Well," said Jacqueline cautiously, "it should be a good place for you. And for Carl, too, when he finally arrives. We'll have to see, though. I had the feeling that Tony wasn't being completely honest with us about his mother. Believe me, you don't want to share the place with an old, Ibicencan peasant woman."

"Why not?"

"Because she's not used to strangers. Especially young men. She'll be watching you like a hawk. She'll be very suspicious of why you've come here. She may think you're trying to take this place away from her. I guess the next few weeks will tell the story."

"I just gave Tony a month's rent. Now I'm invested in this place. We'll just have to hope for the best," said Jake. "But no matter what happens, *merci beaucoup*! You've been wonderful, and I'm very grateful."

"*De rien, mon ami*. There's nothing to thank me for, really. Let's just keep our fingers crossed that you and Carl will have a good home here on Ibiza."

Chapter 11

The very next morning, in the newly rented finca, Jake was hanging up his sleeping bag on a hook outside on the wall to air out when he noticed a dark-clad figure approaching at a slow but steady pace along the dirt road. She was still far off in the distance, but Jake could tell it was an old woman by the black headscarf and the dark puffed-out ankle-length dress she was wearing. *Oh shit*, he thought to himself. It was only 10 a.m., but the sun already loomed large. It was going to be another hot day, he told himself, as he stood naked in the courtyard, his hand held up to his brow, shielding his eyes from the bright light of the cloudless Mediterranean sky. He turned to go inside and emerged moments later, holding a bottle of water and wearing a pair of cut-off jeans. Seating himself on a small bench near the door, he sipped his water and waited.

"*Hola*," he said as she finally drew near.

"*Hola*," she said in a high-pitched, squeaky voice. Jake was struck by how tiny she was. She didn't even come up to his chest. Her face was wrinkled, having the same clay-colored hue as the ground they stood on. *She's the salt of the earth*, he thought, absorbing her presence. Her eyes were wide and suspicious as she stared at him intently. Soon she opened her mouth and let loose a long, high-pitched stream of invective.

"*Lo siento*," interrupted Jake. "I'm sorry. *No hablo Ibicenco. Habla usted español?*"

The woman shook her head. It dawned on Jake that, incredibly, this woman probably didn't speak Spanish. She was presumably an uneducated peasant who'd never roamed far from this very spot for her entire life and had never really needed to learn it. The local dialect, a subset of Catalan, the language spoken throughout Catalonia and the Balearic Islands, was all the farmers spoke amongst themselves. It was as different from Castilian Spanish as it was from Italian or French. A book he'd bought in Switzerland, *Learn Spanish in 30 Days,* had been Jake's bible for the last few months, and he'd found he could carry on a basic, uncomplicated conversation in that language, but he had no real grasp of Catalan.

"I'm glad to meet you," he said, half-smiling, in Spanish. "Juanita," he added, remembering the name her son had provided. *"Yo soy Jake."*

The old lady just blinked and brushed right past him, making her way inside the finca. Dropping her hand-woven basket on the floor, she fished out a large iron key and used it to open up the locked room where she kept her things. Once inside, she closed the door quickly behind her without even turning to glance at Jake, who stood in the main room watching her in disbelief. After a brief pause, he heard the key turning inside the lock.

What the fuck, thought Jake. *What's supposed to happen next?* He decided to go outside, lie down on a blanket in the sun and think about this for a while. This was exactly what he and Jacqueline had feared might happen, but they hadn't really made a contingency plan for it. Juanita was an old woman but decidedly not a pushover. She was clearly tough and strong and not someone to trifle with. Any fool could see that. How long she would give him the silent treatment was anyone's guess, but it was clear to Jake she could make his life hell.

Chapter 12

Lying in the sun with his eyes closed, unsure of what to do next, Jake soon began to feel woozy. He'd slept poorly the night before on the mattress-less bed, and the unaccustomed heat put him into a hypnotic state of drowsiness. He found himself drifting back in his mind to Paris, where his journey in Europe had begun more than a year earlier, right after he'd abandoned his life with Joan in upstate New York. He was back in a sixth-floor walk-up apartment in Pantin, a part of the city inhabited mostly by immigrants from North Africa and the Middle East. It was said to be unsafe, but Jake never felt at risk there. He'd made friends with the vegetable and fruit shopkeepers on the street below and felt drawn to the aliveness of the place teeming with children and laughter and exotic smells from the ubiquitous spicy food stalls, selling endless portions of falafels and couscous and technicolor ultra-sugary sweets. At night he was often unceremoniously woken by the sound of blows and arguments of unhappy people filtering through the thin walls of the apartment. Whenever nature called, he often had to stand in line outside in the hallway for the one and only toilet, which served three different families, some of them with numerous children. If, when it was his turn, the porcelain hole in the floor and the two concrete foot blocks to stand or squat on weren't too splattered with shit, he counted himself lucky. There was a large, rusty tin can on the floor, which you could fill with water from a tap in the wall to wash away the muck. He would drop his trousers, at the same time lifting his pant legs as far as he could off the floor, squat down, and do his business quickly, taking care that nothing splashed on his shoes. Returning to his lover Marie-Madeleine's narrow apartment, he'd wash his hands in the cold water from her sink.

Once inside the small room she rented, he would walk to the only window, often rain-streaked, and look out over the city, appreciating the one luxury the walk-up had to offer: a good view of Pantin, and further off in the distance, a shadowy hint of Paris itself. But mostly, he wasn't so concerned with what lay outside the window. She was always there with him, and Marie-Madeleine's loving presence was the one thing that kept him from going mad from loneliness, allowing him to stay in the game. The Game of Adventure, he liked to call it. It was a game you played when, against all common sense, you left what had become familiar and warm and predictable in your life and struck out for the unknown without having the least idea of what kind of reality you might encounter from one day to the next. It was a game of self-invention, and in playing the game, you began to discover what it was that you were made of, what you wanted in the world, and even more importantly, what you *didn't* want. Jake's reverie deepened as images of Marie-Madeleine formed more clearly in his mind.

"Jake?" she asked, "Are you coming to bed or not? It's cold, and I'm waiting."

"Just a moment, *ma chérie*," he said. "I'm finishing my tea."

"But why can't you drink it in bed?"

"You know why," said Jake, in a teasing voice.

"Jake, you are impossible."

"Yes," he said. "I am."

The challenge of the game, Jake mused, was that it had neither easily defined rules nor a time limit. You might end up doing anything, going anywhere, depending on how well you knew yourself or, in the absence of self-knowledge, at least on your ability to pay attention to clues as to which direction your fate might lie, which could present themselves at any moment, and then having the gumption to follow those clues to their logical conclusions. The only hard and fast rule was no self-pity. Ever. Having left the safe path of Joan's love behind in the States, which presumably would have led to a conventional, safe, American middle-class existence, Jake had felt equally lost and liberated almost since the moment of his arrival in Paris. He knew that he'd escaped a fate that would have weighed him down like a rock-filled straitjacket, but he also didn't yet know what the alternative to that fate might be. Except for this—the life he was living in the moment, with all of its uncertainty and lack of a cohesive vision for what to do with his life going forward. It was kind of like jumping off a cliff into a foggy pool of water and just hoping there were no rocks too close to the surface so that he could at least tread water while waiting for the fog to lift. It was the price he'd paid for obeying the strong inner voice which had told him, *If you want to be a writer, you must go to Paris.* He'd trusted that voice, which had sent him off in the footsteps of his heroes; Henry Miller, Anaïs Nin, Hemingway, Fitzgerald, and others who'd spent time in the City of Light and had found inspiration there.

"Marie-Madeleine," he said, loving the exotic sound of her name, "do you remember the first time we met?"

"*Mais oui,*" she replied. "Of course I do. You came into the restaurant with Agnes, the chef. You kept staring at me while I was waiting on tables. Did you notice that you made me blush?"

"Yes," said Jake. "I did. And I loved it!"

Agnes was a friend he'd stayed with when he'd first arrived in Paris. He'd first met her a few years before as a student, and they'd kept up a correspondence. When he wrote to her from the States and told her he wanted to try living in Europe, she enthusiastically invited him to stay with her and her new husband in Paris. She'd even arranged for him to take a dishwashing job at the restaurant where she worked as a vegetarian chef. It was in Château Rouge, another Arab quarter closer to the heart of Paris, and was run by devotees of an obese adolescent Indian guru who was all the rage in Europe at the time. A poster image of Guru Maharaji, as he was called, was on kiosks all over the city, pointing his finger like Uncle Sam with the caption, "I will bliss you out!"

Agnes and her husband Remy had only been married a few months, and Jake couldn't help but feel like an intruder, crashing in his sleeping bag every night on a thin rug in their tiny living room with barely any furniture at all. Their nightly pattern of fighting and making love was all too audible through the thin wall separating him from their bedroom. Jake couldn't wait to move out, but in the meantime, saw his stay there as a necessary step toward learning French and getting to know Paris. He took advantage of Remy's kindness and basic idleness, acquiring him as an unofficial guide and tutor in French. An effeminate man with a ponytail who got money from *chômage* or unemployment, Remy spent most of his time reading books of poetry in street cafes. His facility with his native tongue was a source of particular pride, and Jake prevailed upon him to share helpful linguistic hints whenever possible. He took special pleasure in teaching Jake euphemisms for sex, such as *faire une partie de quatre jambs en l'air* (have a party with four legs in the air).

"You know, Marie-Madeleine, you were the only person working in that restaurant who showed any sign of life," said Jake, still staring out the window. "Everyone else was pretty much a zombie."

"A zombie?" she asked.

"Yeah, you know, like a dead person walking. Afraid they might do or say something that could offend the guru. As if he had ears in the walls there."

"You're right about that," she said. "I never really could understand that obsession."

"And you were also very pretty."

"Did you really think so?"

"Of course. I still do. You know that," Jake assured her, bending down to kiss her eager lips. He'd become used to her constant need for validation. She was from a broken home where her existence was barely even recognized. But something about the strength of her spirit kept Jake from feeling sorry for her. She had moved out at age seventeen, barely out of high school, and worked hard to become an independent woman against all odds, and Jake admired her for that. She was bright-eyed with chestnut-colored hair, thin as a rail, and in possession of one of the most radiant smiles he'd ever seen. She didn't have the same level of self-awareness or political engagement that Jake had so often found in other French women he'd met. In fact, more than a few were reluctant to have anything to do with him based on his citizenship in what they referred to as "the most imperialist nation on earth." But Marie-Madeleine had no politics at all to speak of. She did have an inner flame of sweetness and joy, which spoke directly to Jake's heart and helped him to ward off a sense of bleakness and sadness which the combination of dreary winter weather, very little money, and his self-imposed exile inflicted on him daily.

"You know," said Jake, "from the moment I first met you, I felt a kind of bond between us as if this was meant to be. At least for a while."

"You probably say that to every girl," she said.

"I assure you I don't," said Jake.

"And what do you mean, 'for a while?'" she asked, her blue eyes suddenly sad. Jake set down his empty teacup and squeezed in next to her on the narrow bed, cradling her head on his chest. "You know I've never promised to stay," he said, bending down to kiss her. She responded instantly to his kiss, which mercifully for him swept away the need for further conversation.

Jake related to her as a fellow outsider. The other women working in the restaurant saw her as a kind of primitive child brought up in the countryside far from Paris, unable or unwilling to comprehend the complex patterns of political engagement and feminist ideology, which was the culture they thrived in. Like Jake, she also felt lonely and isolated and was more than happy to be wooed by the handsome young foreigner who'd appeared so suddenly and unexpectedly in her life. Jake was the first American she'd ever met, and his foreignness intrigued and excited her. He paid more attention to her than any man had done before, never tiring of trying out new and unexpected phrases in French, which she found endlessly amusing.

"*Comment est-ce qu'on dit ça?*" (How do you say that?) was a phrase she frequently heard from Jake, and she took pleasure in educating him in her native tongue. She wasn't used to being looked upon as someone with knowledge to impart, and his need for her assistance filled her with a newfound sense of importance.

The two of them started out just walking around the neighborhood together after work but soon found themselves taking the Metro to the Place Saint-Michel and walking along the banks of the Seine, just below the Notre Dame Cathedral, holding hands and disappearing into shadows where—her slim body shivering with desire—Jake would press her up against the wall, cup her pale, ruby-lipped face in his hands and kiss her with all the ardor that a young man momentarily rescued from a loveless life can muster.

"Oh Jake," she finally said one day, "you must come home with me. I can't stand this anymore."

"Me neither," said Jake. He didn't need to be asked twice and was soon gone from the living room of Agnes and Remy's uninviting tenement. Holed up in Marie-Madeleine's tiny apartment in Pantin, the two of them spent the remaining nights of that winter together; laughing, talking, warming up hot drinks on her electric burner, and making love like two starving fools with no idea where their next meal would come from.

Chapter 13

Jake's impassioned remembrance of Marie-Madeleine in Paris was suddenly interrupted by the sound of an unfamiliar song sung in a high-pitched, squeaky voice. He pushed up on his elbows and, blinking, looked around. He was surprised to see Juanita some distance away, down on her hands and knees, her dark dress billowing out around her. She wore a large straw hat and was pulling up weeds which she tossed into a hand-woven basket.

Jake blinked a few more times and shook his head, trying to escape the swoon he'd fallen into. *The crone is crooning,* he thought to himself. Forcing himself to stand, he spent a long moment stretching and yawning before pulling a T-shirt over his head and making his way toward the old woman, determined this time to have a little chat. He stood beside her for a moment, but she ignored him, continuing to sing and work in the dirt. At last, he knelt down beside her, and she finally looked up, her gray eyes clouded with suspicion. Reaching into the basket, Jake picked up one of the wilting weeds and held it in the air.

"What kind of plant is this?" he asked in Spanish.

She responded with a word Jake didn't understand, but looking more closely, he saw immediately that it was chamomile, recognizing the plant from pictures he'd seen on boxes of herbal tea. The yellow button in the middle was very distinctive.

"For sleeping?" he asked.

"*Si, si,*" she said, nodding. "*Mucho dormir.*" She was responding to him in a kind of pidgin Spanish, or perhaps it was pidgin Catalan which opened up at least some possibility of communication.

"Ah," said Jake, smiling. "*Que bueno!*"

"*No puedes dormir?*" she asked, pausing in her task to squint up at him.

"Sleep? Only with great difficulty," said Jake deciding to exaggerate his plight.

Juanita frowned then, and Jake thought he discerned a momentary flash of sympathy in her expression. "Here," she said, surprising Jake by reaching into the basket with both gnarled hands and offering him some plants.

"Gracias," said Jake. She cackled a bit to herself then as though enjoying some private joke. Jake couldn't help thinking it was a joke at his expense for not even knowing how to deal with something as simple as an inability to sleep. *Well,* thought Jake, as he retreated inside the finca, *at least I've been acknowledged.*

***

The next day Jake's friend Carl finally arrived on the island. After meeting with Jacqueline and being apprised of Jake's new living situation, he showed up at the finca one afternoon in his old Mercedes van. Juanita, who still had not returned to her son's apartment in town, was in the kitchen annex doing some cooking when the sound of his van first became audible in the distance. She looked up as the big vehicle approached the house, stirring up a large cloud of dust in its wake, finally coming to a halt in the driveway near the house. As she stood there watching, a troubled expression came over her face, growing more pronounced as a bearded man stepped out of the van. Carl was in full hippy attire with loose orange Indian clothing and beads strung around his neck. Ignoring the old woman, he enjoyed a languorous moment of full body stretching as Jake, who'd been taking refuge from the heat of the day, stepped outside the finca and waved to his friend.

"Carl!" he cried. "At last!"

"*Hola amigo,*" replied Carl, walking toward his friend and pulling on his beard as he took in the scene. "Looks like you've found yourself quite the place here."

"It is beautiful," said Jake, after giving Carl a hug. "But … well …"

"I heard," said Carl, tilting his head in Juanita's direction. "*Hola!*" he said, waving.

"*Hola* yourself is probably what she's thinking," said Jake. "She's not exactly thrilled that I'm here by myself. The idea of two of us probably freaks her out completely."

"Well," said Carl. "This is her place. And nothing we do or say is gonna change that."

"I'm afraid you're right," agreed Jake. "It wasn't supposed to be this way, though."

"I know," said Carl. "Jacqueline filled me in. Don't worry, amigo. We'll either make it work or we won't."

Carl's easy confidence was like a tonic to Jake. He suddenly felt some of the insecurity he'd been feeling about this new living arrangement lift off his shoulders.

"I'm so glad you're here, Carl. I feel like I've been in limbo, waiting for you. Wasn't really sure what to do about this."

"We'll figure it out," said Carl reassuringly. "Meanwhile, I'm starving. How about some pollo del campo? I bought some freshly dressed chicken on the way over at a local tienda. What say we cook ourselves up a meal?"

"Great," said Jake. "I'm starving too."

Carl went back to the van, brought out the chicken, and the two friends made their way toward the outdoor kitchen where Juanita was standing, both arms folded across her chest, watching them sourly as they approached. It occurred to Jake that she must feel doubly put upon now, and he could feel her resistance stiffen as they got closer.

"*Hola,*" said Carl. "*Yo soy* Carl."

Juanita said nothing, ignoring his outstretched hand. She just stood there glaring with both arms crossed on her chest.

"Well, now," said Carl, grinning broadly. "I think that what we have here is a failure to communicate. So you know what, Jake? Fuck it. Let's just cook our chicken. She can give us all the stink eye she wants. I don't give a damn."

Both men then looked around the open-air kitchen, trying to plan a cooking strategy. Unlike other fincas, which at least used propane tanks to power a stove, this one just had a firepit on a raised brick structure with an old metal grill on top. Juanita appeared to have finished her cooking, and there were still some glowing embers left in the pit. Carl, whose Spanish was much better than Jake's, asked the old woman politely, "Do you mind if we use your cooking area?" Juanita launched into one of her now familiar streams of unintelligible invective and then positioned herself in front of the pit so that there could be no question about her objection to the plan.

"Well," said Carl. "I wouldn't call this a failure to communicate. I would call this just bad juju on her part. It's okay, though. I've got a little Coleman stove inside the truck. We can cook in there. Let's go. All this confrontation has stoked my appetite."

Inside Carl's spacious van, an entire wall of which was covered with a reproduction of Hieronymus Bosch's *Garden of Earthly Delights*—the surrealistic quality of which seemed to exemplify the situation the two friends found themselves in—they began plotting their next move together, while frying up the chicken.

"Carl," said Jake settling into a cushion and leaning back against the wall of the van while Carl cooked. "I was beginning to wonder if you were really coming back to Ibiza."

"I said I would, didn't I, buddy?" said Carl as he reached into a small cabinet full of spices. "I just had stuff to do up north. Like turn in an insurance claim for a very expensive camera I had stolen from me."

"Really?" said Jake. "Stolen? I never heard about that."

"No?" said Carl pointing to a Nikon camera with a huge zoom lens on it lying on a bench in the corner. "I'm telling you, Jake, that camera was stolen from me."

"Oh, I see," said Jake nodding his head. "And it was no doubt quite a large insurance claim you made."

"Large enough," said Carl, slightly embarrassed. "You don't wanna be too greedy in these transactions. Could end up getting you in trouble. But definitely well worth the trip up north. Helped pay for a few needed repairs on my van as well."

"I thought you did all the repair work yourself."

"Well, yeah, I like to. But you still gotta pay for the parts. I'm telling you, man, Mercedes parts are *expensive*."

"Speaking of repairs, I've got a car I drove down from Paris that needs some work. I thought maybe you could help."

"That orange beauty out there?"

"That's the one."

"Can you still drive it, though?"

"Yeah, but probably not for much longer."

"Okay. We'll take a look at it. Together."

"Sounds good. Thanks."

"But first things first. We've gotta figure out if we can stay here or not," said Carl, dropping some sliced up onions and peppers into sizzling olive oil. "My gut says not."

"It is weird having her around. Definitely puts a cramp in our style, don't you think?"

"Well," said Carl. "Maybe not. We've just gotta put our 'style' to the test. Know what I mean? We can start right after lunch."

Chapter 14

Carl and Jake had first met in Valencia the year before while awaiting a ferry to Ibiza. It was springtime, and Jake had just hitchhiked down from Paris after leaving Marie-Madeleine and the City of Light behind. He'd only recently been alerted to the existence of Ibiza, which he'd never even heard of before, by a Frenchman who'd given him a lift and explained to him what a magical place it was.

"Nice to meet a fellow American," said Carl. The two of them had just met at the ticket counter for the ferry and had a few hours to kill before the boat took off for the island that evening. "We can hang out in my van while we're waiting," said Carl. "It's out there in the parking lot. I've got a joint, and we can listen to some music."

"Sounds good to me," said Jake, who was feeling lonely after hitching down from Paris by himself. The much-anticipated spring weather had triggered some instinct in Jake to head south. He'd spent four months in the great city learning conversational French and felt that was long enough, at least for now. He knew he would miss the friends he'd made there, but it seemed as though his life was on a trajectory that no longer allowed for sentimental attachments. Marie-Madeleine had been especially hard to leave behind, and he was still in correspondence with Joan. The possibility of a new friendship, however brief, was appealing. After checking to make sure there weren't any Guardia Civil in the vicinity, he and Carl got inside the van and lit up the joint. This was still Franco's Spain, and the penalty for drug possession, even small amounts, could be harsh. Carl, who was a few years older than Jake, told him he'd been traveling for the last three years and had just left a job teaching high school in Australia to earn money for the European leg of his journey.

"So you're a teacher then?" asked Jake exhaling a plume of smoke.

"Well, I've got a degree in education, but doubt I'll ever do much teaching. It's not really my thing."

"What is your thing then?"

"This," said Carl gesturing around him. "And yours?"

"Same," said Jake. "At least for now."

"What about music?" said Carl. "Like it?"

"Love it," said Jake.

"Me too," said Carl reaching for a guitar. "Play an instrument?"

"Not really," said Jake. "I can sing, though!"

"Great," said Jake. "Let's try a little duet then. Know this one?" he asked, launching into a folksy version of Stephen Stills "Love the One You're With."

"Yeah, sure," said Jake. "That's a great song."

And then they were singing together as Carl strummed his Martin guitar. When they got to the refrain, Jake took the harmony, and their voices blended surprisingly well together.

"Whoa," said Carl. "That was really cool! You've got a good voice."

"Thanks," said Jake. "So do you. We'll have to do more of this."

And so they did. For two weeks, they stuck together, exploring the islands of Formentera and Ibiza, falling in love with both places, and vowing to go back again someday. By the end of their brief sojourn together, Jake was running low on funds and decided to make his way to Switzerland to try and earn some cash. He and Carl said goodbye, expressing a vague hope that their paths might cross again someday, but neither one had any clue as to where or how that might happen.

***

Remarkably, they did meet again the following winter in a most unexpected fashion. Jake had found a job in the French-speaking village of Leysin in the Swiss Alps. It was December, and he was standing on a freezing block of concrete, rocking back and forth and stamping his feet to stay warm. Skiers were lining up to ascend the mountain, and Jake would check their lift ticket and load their skis into the front end of a gondola, then open the door and help them get inside. Then he'd shove off the carriage on its shaky journey toward the distant top of the mountain. One day, much to his amazement, Jake found Carl standing in the front of the line, all decked out in a blue and white ski outfit, his bearded face flecked with snow, holding a pair of skis in his right hand and ski poles in his left.

"Carl!" he said, "is that you?

"Oh ... my ... God ... Jake?"

"Can you believe this?" asked Jake, moving in to give Carl a hug. "What are the odds?"

"Pretty astronomical, I'd say," said Carl.

"Jesus, this is incredible!" said Jake. What brings you to Leysin?"

"Just wanted to do some skiing. Heard this was a cheap place to do it."

"Holy shit!" said Jake, glancing toward the corner of the slab where Jacques, his moody French supervisor, sat on a bench, giving them stink-eye. "Listen, we'll talk later. Let's meet at the café in town after the lift closes. There's a lot to discuss."

"You're not kidding," said Carl, shaking his head in disbelief as he climbed into the gondola. "See you later, *amigo*!"

Jake stood behind the carriage and pushed, stepping back to watch the silver cable car swinging upward toward the snowcapped peak, savoring the sensation that this was indeed a fateful encounter.

Chapter 15

IBIZA

The two friends set their plates aside inside Carl's van. The country chicken Carl had fried up with rice had been delicious, and they were each feeling full and lazy. Both were reluctant to leave the coolness of the van and step outside into the searing midday heat.

"How about a coffee?" asked Carl.

"Sure thing. Where is it?"

"Don't worry. I'll get it," said Carl. "You don't know your way around this van yet. Everything's got its own special place. Designed to save as much space as possible."

Jake gave Carl an admiring glance. He was organized to a fault. Organized in a way that Jake knew he would never be. He just didn't have that kind of internal commitment to order. Jake's life tended to be more chaotic and spontaneous, and he liked it that way, but he could admire the discipline Carl brought to his life. Carl was Mr. Practical. They were polar opposites in that regard, yet Jake felt there was a certain advantage for each of them in teaming up together. It had been an organic, mutually beneficial decision that each accepted as a necessary component of the "Living on Ibiza" dream they were currently trying to realize.

"So here's what we do," continued Carl stirring sugar into his Nescafé. "We simply start living our lives here the way we would if she weren't here. And that means nudity."

"Really?" said Jake. "Are you sure about that?"

"Well, of course I am, Jake. Nudity is a way of life here. Unless you happen to be an old peasant woman."

"Sure it is. On some of the beaches," agreed Jake, thinking of the clothing-optional beach at Salinas in particular. "But I don't see anyone walking around naked in town."

"No, of course you don't," said Carl. "That'd be stupid. You'd just get arrested in no time at all. But weren't you naked sometimes over at Jacqueline and Klaus's finca and them too?"

"Sometimes, yeah," admitted Jake.

"That's because they were at home," said Carl, "in their own finca that they were paying good money to rent. Just like we are now."

"Well, yeah," said Jake. "But they don't have an old peasant woman living with them."

"Exactly," said Carl. "And that's the way it's supposed to be. Nobody rents a place here expecting the landlord's mom to move in with them. This is a travesty, Jake, and we've got to take some action to change it."

"Hmmm," said Jake, still reluctant to accept the cold logic of Carl's argument.

"Don't you remember the discussion we had up in Leysin this past winter when you and I decided we'd try to come back here to live?" asked Carl.

"Sure," said Jake. "We both decided it must be some kind of sign that you and I met up again. I mean, what were the odds? And in Leysin of all places."

"Indeed," said Carl.

"And we reminded ourselves that we'd first met each other on our way here to Ibiza, and we both felt we wanted to return and spend more time here."

"Exactly," said Carl again in a way that was beginning to irritate Jake. "And implicit in that idea was the possibility that we'd find a place where we could live however we wanted to live. Otherwise, what's the point?

Hell, Jake, we're hippies, not anthropologists. We're not here to study the lifestyle of local peasants, are we?"

"A rhetorical question, I presume," said Jake.

"Hell, yes, it's a rhetorical question," said Carl. "You know what we gotta do, so let's go out and do it."

"Okay," said Jake. "I agree. But not all at once. I mean, let's not step outside of the truck naked. She might really get the wrong idea."

"All right," said Carl. "I'll grant you that. But soon, brother, real soon."

Something in Jake's persona was extremely resistant to the idea of exposing himself naked to Juanita. He was all too aware that the Catholic culture she'd grown up in allowed for no debate on the subject of public nudity. He imagined it would be a subject so beyond comprehension in her mind that the shock of being confronted by it might prove to be an experience she would never fully recover from. His friend Carl, however, was not burdened by any kind of sensitivity in this regard. Pragmatic as ever, he saw it simply as an effective tactic to bring matters to a definitive conclusion regarding their decision to stay in the finca or not. For Carl, Juanita was simply an obstacle to their plans who needed to be dealt with by the most effective means possible.

"Well," he said after they'd left the van and laid out their towels on the ground in front of the finca, "now is as good a time as ever."

Juanita had retreated indoors, at least temporarily, probably to escape the worst heat of the day. Neither Carl nor Jake had the least idea when she might come out again, presumably to return to her weeding or cook her dinner in the outdoor kitchen. Neither of them had any confidence she would ever return to her son's home in town to live with him again. Her basket still lay on the ground near where she'd been working earlier in the day, and the likelihood of her resuming her task again at any moment was a real possibility.

Carl stripped off his clothes, and Jake reluctantly followed suit. They each smeared suntan lotion on their skin and lay down on their towels to bake in the sun. They'd been lying there for some time with their eyes closed, and Jake was just drowsing off to sleep when he was suddenly awakened by a loud keening wail followed by a shrill incantation in an incomprehensible tongue. He raised himself up on his elbows and blinked a few times. Then shielding his eyes from the sun with one hand, he saw Juanita, her right arm wrapped around her face, babbling away in Catalan as she stumbled blindly back toward the entrance of the house.

"Well," said Carl calmly as the door slammed shut behind her. "I think we've definitely set something in motion here, don't you, Jake?"

"No doubt," said Jake nodding in agreement, "the question is, what?"

"We'll find out soon enough," said Carl. "In the meantime, whaddya say we drive into Santa Gertrudis and stop off at Bar Costa for a beer? Maybe we'll run into Jacqueline, and we can give her an update on the situation. Get her feedback. We can take your Simca, and I'll give you my expert analysis of your car's disorder."

"Sounds like a plan," said Jake, standing and wiping sweat from his body with a towel. "Let's do it."

Chapter 16

Sure enough, when they arrived at Bar Costa, Jacqueline was already seated at an outdoor table with her friend Cannelle beside her, shaded from the sun by the large burgundy awning covering the sidewalk in front of the café.

"*Hola*," said the men, smiling as they approached the table.

"*Hola*," said Jacqueline. "Would you like to join us?"

"Love to," said Jake.

"Yes, yes," agreed Carl. "Be most happy to."

"Where's Klaus?" queried Jake.

"Oh, you know Klaus," said Jacqueline. "Always tinkering with his mopeds. He should be joining us in a while, though."

Jake sat opposite Cannelle and immediately felt the force of her penetrating gaze. It was the same lascivious look she'd given him when they'd first met back at her finca. He suddenly felt even more exposed than he had earlier in the day when sunbathing nude in the old lady's presence.

"So how are you, Cannelle?" he asked to hide his embarrassment.

"I'm fine," she said. "So Jacqueline tells me you guys have finally found a finca to rent?"

"Well, maybe," interjected Carl, who then proceeded to describe the naked sunbathing episode.

"Ooh, la la," said Jacqueline shaking her head. "This is like some kind of soap opera, is it not?"

"Yeah, a really bad one," agreed Jake.

"Not at all," said Cannelle. "I think it's a good thing. Because now something has to happen. You're not just tromping water."

"Yes," agreed Jake. "We're not just treading water anymore, are we, Carl?"

"No way," said Carl. "You should have heard her scream when she first saw us *au naturel*. Either she'll be gone by tomorrow, or we will. Something's gotta give, for sure."

"I hate to say it," said Jacqueline, "but I think you guys have already lost the battle. I mean, look how you are having to live there. Always worrying about her. And after all, it is her place."

"Yes, but we're renting it," argued Jake.

"Not in her mind, you're not. Probably Tony was too cowardly to even tell her you were moving in. I'll bet she had no idea that you would be there at all."

"You could be right," agreed Jake reluctantly as the beers arrived. He was beginning to feel genuinely discouraged.

"But don't worry," said Cannelle, "If you have to move out, we can help you find another place. Isn't that right, Jacqueline?"

"Well, I helped you find this one. I can help you find another," said Jacqueline. "What else are friends for?"

"I'll drink to that," said Carl raising his beer.

"You guys have been so helpful," said Jake. "How can we ever repay you for your kindness?"

"On this island, Jake, everyone has to help each other," said Cannelle. "Especially foreigners like us. Carl has helped me fix my car when he was here last year, so now I'm happy if I can help you both. I'm sure there is some way that you'll be able to help me, Jake," she said, again with that smoldering look. "It's just a feeling that I have."

Jake felt a strange tingling in his groin as she spoke. He wondered briefly if she had cast some kind of spell on him. She certainly had a witchy quality that made that seem like a real possibility.

"Well, I do like kids," he said to his own surprise. "Perhaps I can babysit for you sometime if you need it."

"Yes, Jake," she agreed enthusiastically. "That's a really good idea. And the kids like you too. I could tell."

Babysit? Jake wondered to himself. *Where the hell did that come from?* He found himself submitting more and more to the undeniable sway this peculiar woman held over him. *Where the hell will all this end?* he wondered as he took another swig of beer.

Chapter 17

When Carl and Jake returned to the finca that evening, Juanita was gone. Her door was padlocked, and the place was utterly silent.

"Well, well," said Carl, "I guess we scared her off after all."

"I'm not so sure," said Jake. "I don't have a good feeling about this."

"Well, she's sure as hell not coming back here after dark," said Carl. "When the sun goes down, people like her just go to sleep. She must've walked to the village while we were gone and taken a bus back to stay at her son's house."

"You're probably right," said Jake. "In any case, it sure does feel different not having her around anymore. I feel like I can just really relax for the first time."

"Speaking of relaxing," said Carl, "whaddya say we play some music together? You roll a joint, and I'll go out to the van and get my guitar."

"A joint?" asked Jake. "That would require some hash, wouldn't it?"

"Oh, yeah," said Carl. "Well, I'll bring some of that too. But we'll have to find a source right here on the island real soon. My stash from Germany is just about gone."

"I doubt that will be a problem," said Jake.

Carl wanted to find a spot to build a bonfire in the front yard to sit around and play, but Jake didn't want to risk damaging any of Maria's carefully groomed plants.

"Let's wait until we're more settled in before we do that," he suggested. "That sounds like something you'd do when it's really our place, and I just don't have that confidence yet."

"Tell ya what," said Carl. "We'll give it one more night, and if she's still gone, then we'll consider it ours. We can't be wishy-washy about this any longer."

Jake agreed, and they ended up staying inside, building up a fire in the indoor fireplace and roasting chestnuts they'd bought in the village in Maria's big iron pan. Afterward, Carl pulled out his guitar and went through his repertoire of songs with Jake joyfully adding harmony. After singing their hearts out, the two friends went outside and stood together in front of the finca in the deep silence of the night. Swaying slightly in the cool evening air, they turned their heads to the penetrating power of another cloudless night, each star-sourced point of light stabbing into their stoned eyes with a welcome, painless intensity. Jake was still playing in his head the last song they'd sung together, feeling infused with the sad poignancy of the lyrics. It was a Leon Russell tune called "This Masquerade" from a George Benson album they'd both been listening to earlier in his van. It spoke to the loneliness which inevitably ensued when people failed to be authentic with each other and made Jake appreciate even more the solid friendship he felt had grown between him and Carl.

Chapter 18

The next morning they were awakened by the sound of a noisy engine approaching the house. Jake felt a gripping sensation in his gut as he unzipped his sleeping bag and arose from his mattress-less bed, quickly slipping on a pair of shorts and trying to rub the sleep from his eyes. When he stepped outside into the glaring sunlight, Carl was already standing outside his van, fastening the straps on a pair of old overalls, and glancing toward a cloud of dust accompanying the old pickup, which was barreling toward them on the dirt track leading to the house. Jake recognized the blondish fringe of hair on the otherwise bald head of their landlord Tony and quickly walked over to join Carl. Juanita, hunched over and diminutive, sat beside her son and scowled.

"Uh-oh," said Jake, "looks like Judgment Day is upon us." He and Carl exchanged glances and began walking toward the area in front of the house where the dirt track ended.

Tony turned off the engine and opened the door, looking hesitant for a moment before stepping out of the vehicle. Juanita stayed put, busily studying something in her lap.

"Hola," said Jake.

"Hola," said Tony with a forced smile. He took notice of Carl and extended his hand. "Hola," he said.

"Buenos Dias," said Carl.

"I uh, uh …" began Tony, suddenly stopping to mop his soaking brow with a large red handkerchief he pulled from his pocket.

"Si?" asked Carl. "Que pasa, Tony?"

Tony launched into a speech, scarcely making eye contact with either Carl or Jake. The essence of it being, as far as Jake could tell, that Tony had realized he'd made a tremendous mistake, that he never should have rented out his mother's finca because he never realized how unhappy she would be. Without mentioning the nudity episode, he made it clear that both Americanos needed to clear out, pronto.

"What about *el dinero?*" asked Carl, as if he'd been the one who'd paid the rent for the first month.

"*Si, si, el dinero … esta aqui,*" he said, reaching into a pocket and pulling out a wad of bills.

Jake looked at Carl with genuine surprise as he pocketed the cash. They'd been discussing this the night before. Carl had said that Tony would give Jake his money back, but Jake was skeptical. After all, Jake had argued, what do we do if he refuses? Go to the police? But Carl surprisingly, had in this instance, taken the less jaded view of humanity and assured Jake that the people here were basically decent and wouldn't try to rip him off. Jake had expected some sort of quid pro quo from Tony for their nudity shenanigan, the quo being: "You expose yourself in front of mi madre, you don't get your money back."

"So when do we have to leave?" he asked. *Quando tenemos que salir?*

"*Hoy,*" said Tony. Today. He was smiling weakly, but there was no joy in his eyes. He meant business.

"You mean right now?" asked Carl.

"*Si,*" said Tony.

The two friends looked at each other.

"Well, I guess it shouldn't take long," said Carl. "Everything I have is already in my van. Whatever you've got pretty much fits in a backpack. Let's get going. We'll drive into Santa Gertrudis and have breakfast there. Sound like a plan?"

"Sure does," said Jake. "At least we don't have to dink around wondering what's what anymore. Let the search for a new place begin!"

Twenty minutes later, they were each driving down the dirt track toward the village, Carl in his van and Jake in his sputtering Simca. As

Jake looked in his rearview mirror, he noticed Juanita finally getting out of her son Tony's pickup.

Chapter 19

FRANCE

Marie-Madeleine loved Jake, but she never tried to pressure him to stay with her in Paris. He'd been blunt with her about his desire to travel, and she could only smile and shake her head. It was not something she could imagine for herself. She craved stability in her life, and although grateful for the romantic and exciting interlude Jake's presence had provided, her ultimate desire was to settle down to the serious business of finding a more appropriate mate to share her life with.

Feeling nothing but gratitude for the solace she'd provided him during the lonely winter months, Jake jotted down a short poem in his journal the night before leaving her behind to set out on his road trip to Spain:

Bleary eyed, I stumble
Into my lover's nest
And stretch out on her narrow bed
Trying to feel the loneliness
That will smother her
When I'm gone.

The next day Jake was on the road stuck at Chartres just outside Paris with his thumb out, heading south. The sun was shining, the great cathedral was shimmering in the distance, and he was feeling ecstatic, his whole being awash with the thrill of being free and on the road. The idea of spending any more time in Paris failed to strike a single appealing chord in his soul. The same sense of restlessness that had driven him away from the States and back to Europe was still propelling him onward. Reaching in his pocket, he pulled out a final letter he'd received from Joan just before leaving Paris and reread it just to pass the time.

"Babe,

Now that your Paris chapter is coming to a close, I'm wondering if you've finally got this wanderlust out of your system? You did mention that you weren't sure what you were going to do next and held out some hope of returning to me … yes, ME! You'll recall, the one who loves you? You finished up what you started, right? You learned French like you wanted to. Now it's time to come home. I've gotta say your descriptions of the cold and damp there sounded so disheartening. Not that you would have been much warmer here in Johnson City, where we had three feet of snow at one point, but you would have had me to keep you warm! We could've cuddled up in bed together at night just like we used to, thrown a Jackson Brown album on the hi-fi and shared a doobie and a cup of hot cocoa and felt that special feeling, you know what I mean, that happens when you're in love? So come on home now, darlin'. It's time. You know what spring is like here. Everything is so beautiful now. Rebirth is happening everywhere you look, and that's how it's gonna be for us, too, sweet thing. I've got a yellow tulip just about to open its petals sitting on the bedroom windowsill overlooking Main Street. I think of that as you, Jake. My beautiful man. Just come home, please?"

Although it had only been four months since he and Joan had parted, it already seemed like a lifetime ago to Jake. Of course he'd never mentioned Marie-Madeleine to Joan. What would've been the point? He slipped the letter back in his pocket, knowing in his heart that their paths would probably never cross again. And yet his loneliness allowed the hope of an unlikely reunion to linger, despite the irresistible momentum of his own unquenchable wanderlust.

He'd been standing on the side of the road for two hours holding up a cardboard sign with the word *"Espagne"* scrawled on it when a trucker drove by, flipping his hand under his chin in a gesture of contempt for Jake's beard. *Son of a bitch,* thought Jake. *I'd like to make him stand in the same spot, hitching for a week!* Cars were whizzing by too fast, forcing Jake to keep walking until he reached a crossroad where vehicles had to slow down. He fantasized about an English camper full of hippies smoking pot, listening to The Incredible String Band, and joking all the way down to Bordeaux. Instead, a teenage boy, his face full of zits, unexpectedly stopped and picked him up, giving him a two-hour lift to downtown Tours, where he got out, stretched languorously, and shouldered his pack once again. Walking down the sidewalk, he stretched out his thumb lackadaisically, too tired to even bother looking behind him at the oncoming cars. The sun was starting to set, and the chances now of someone stopping for him were fading fast. He figured he'd probably need to find a youth hostel in town for the night, if there even was one. Before long, though, a honking sound startled him, and a sleek white Mercedes-Benz with a ruggedly handsome, mustachioed driver pulled up alongside him. Jake gestured for him to stop and popped his head in the open passenger-side window.

"You headed south?" he asked.

"You bet," said the man. "Where're you going?"

"Spain," said Jake.

"That's okay. Same direction as me. Hop in."

Jake hesitated briefly. What did this man really want? An unpleasant memory popped into his head of a man who'd picked him up once hitchhiking back in the States. It was a creepy experience with the man trying to stroke Jake's leg with one hand while driving the car with the other. But this guy didn't seem creepy at all. Jake quickly decided to go for it. He opened the rear door, threw in his pack, and slid into the front seat. As the car picked up speed, the driver, who introduced himself as Georges, revealed to Jake that he owned a farm forty kilometers away and that Jake could spend the night in his barn. Georges appeared so genuinely friendly and good-natured that Jake could think of no good reason to object to this plan.

"Sounds great," said Jake. "Thank you so much. I thought I might never get a ride."

"I don't usually stop for hitchhikers, but I suddenly just had an urge to give you a lift," said Georges smiling broadly and exposing a row of tobacco-stained teeth. "Are you cold?" he asked, turning the fan up on the heater.

"Well, yeah, I guess I am," said Jake sinking down into the firm leather seat. "That heat really does feel good."

Before he knew it, Jake had drifted off to sleep, waking only when the ride became suddenly bumpy. Very bumpy. Alarmed, he lurched forward in his seat and tried to get his bearings.

"What's happening?" he asked.

"Oh, we're almost there," said Georges kindly. "You fell asleep almost right away. We just got off the paved road. Now we're on a kind of dirt track that leads to my farm."

Jake looked around and was struck by a beautiful vision. The moon hadn't yet risen, but there were no clouds in the sky, and the entire countryside was lit up by a vast panoply of stars, revealing a broad but shallow valley with a stream running through it. Right in the center was a stone house with an adjacent barn, surrounded by fenced-in pastureland. The grazing area nearest the house was full of sheep whose whitish wool coats shimmered in the starlight. The contrast to the urban Paris landscape he'd just left behind couldn't have been starker.

"Wow," said Jake, entranced. "You really live in a beautiful place."

"Thank you," said Georges, looking genuinely pleased. "Now wait until you see my family. They are the most beautiful of all."

When the Mercedes pulled up in front of the farmhouse's front door, it opened abruptly, and a shapely woman with thick flowing chestnut hair stepped outside. She was wrapped in a black shawl and smiling broadly, followed by a young girl who barely came up to her waist. A large yellow dog bounded out as well, wagging its tail in pleasure at the sight of its master.

"*Bonsoir,*" said the woman, eyeing Jake with curiosity and then giving her husband a questioning look.

"This is Jake," said Georges. "I picked him up in Tours. He's going to be spending the night in the barn."

"*Ah oui?*" she said with typical Gallic aplomb. "*Bon.* Please come inside and warm up. Then we'll figure everything out."

That one night turned into a week as Jake found himself reluctant to leave the bosom of this remarkably friendly and loving family who'd welcomed him into their lives with open arms as if he'd been a long-lost friend. He'd barely left Paris and already felt as though his life had been given new meaning. They turned out to be goat and sheep cheese producers whose goal was to move to the island of Ibiza, a place Jake had never even heard of before, in order to live on the commune of a fellow Frenchman named Jacques Massacrier. He'd written a best-selling book about returning to nature, and Jake immersed himself in the book as well as the peaceful country life atmosphere, and by the time he was standing on the roadside again holding up his cardboard sign for Spain, he felt that he'd been shown another sign to guide him on his journey. He was going to go to Ibiza for sure.

Chapter 20

IBIZA

Jake and Carl found themselves back at Jacqueline and Klaus's place temporarily while checking out every lead they could find about available fincas for rent. All the while, Jake felt a powerful attraction coming from the direction of Cannelle's just a few kilometers down the road. One evening without telling anyone, he got into his Simca and headed off in her direction. The car, despite Carl's attentions, was becoming more and more derelict by the day. Its steering wheel was now held in place on the steering column by two bungee cords to make sure it didn't come off while driving, and the tapping sound was louder than ever. The sun was just starting to set as he came to the end of the dirt road and into the courtyard in front of Cannelle's finca. As soon as he turned off the ignition and got out of the car, the kitchen door burst open, and Johnnie and Atif came running out to greet him.

"Jake!" they cried, climbing up on him as if he were some kind of human playground contraption.

"Whoa," said Jake, "hold on, boys! You almost knocked me down!"

"We'll knock you down all right," said Atif, "and then we'll beat you up too!"

"You will, will you?" said Jake, dropping into a squat. "Well, we'll just have to see about that!"

An intense wrestling match ensued, accompanied by breathless giggling and screaming on the part of the two young boys.

"Stop it!" cried Johnnie at last. "You're hurting me!"

"Then how come you're laughing so hard?" asked Jake, continuing to tickle the boys' bellies and armpits. Unable to answer, the boys' giggling increased to the point where Jake feared they might be unable to breathe.

"All right," he said, standing up abruptly. "Enough is enough. Now, where's your mom? Is she home?"

As soon as he glanced up, there she was. Standing in the doorway, she leaned against the doorframe with her arms crossed in front of her, her lanky figure illumined by the soft light from an oil lamp behind her in the kitchen. Her face was in shadow, but Jake thought he could discern a smile on her lips.

"So you've come at last," she said as he began walking toward her.

"At last?" asked Jake.

"You know what I mean," she said as he walked up to embrace her. "Have a seat in the kitchen. I'll make us some tea."

Jake settled into a cane chair in the kitchen, sipping tea and eating some of Cannelle's banana bread while the kids got ready for bed. Once they had on their pajamas, they seemed even crazier than usual and kept racing into the kitchen to try and attack Jake with kamikaze fury—punching, slapping, and pinching him with the frenzy of crazed bees defending their hive. They were irritatingly quick about it, moving with the grace and speed of little athletes and retreating almost immediately back into the main room before anyone could catch them. Jake's senses were on full alert as the little imps proved to be surprisingly strong and their pinches exceedingly painful. He found himself both admiring and wary of the combined hellion power of the two little boys.

"Okay, you guys," he yelled at last. "That's enough! Now don't make me come in there!"

This threat made them dissolve once more into a fit of helpless giggling as if the idea of Jake being able to defeat them was too ludicrous to ponder.

"Go ahead," said Atif. "C'mon, we dare you! Just come in here, and we'll kick you in the nuts!

"Yeah," said Johnnie aping his older brother. "That's right. We're gonna kick you in the nuts!"

This prospect seemed to fill them with so much genuine glee that by the sound of their laughter, they were on the verge of involuntarily hurting themselves.

"Are you guys peeing in your pants right now?" asked Jake in awe of their intensity, wondering if he'd ever met such rascals before in his life.

"No ..." said the boys gasping for air. "We're not."

"Yes, they are," said Isabelle from somewhere inside their room. "They always pee in their pants when they laugh too hard."

Jake had almost forgotten about Isabelle. *Of course,* he thought, *she must also sleep in the main room with her brothers.*

"All right, boys, that's enough now!" yelled Cannelle. She was standing near the kitchen door, and Jake was struck by the unfeigned violence in her tone. *If that doesn't intimidate them, nothing will.* Before waiting to find out what effect her order had had on the boys, she stepped over the threshold and rushed into their room. Slapping sounds ensued, then loud wails and furious crying culminating in "I hate you, Mom!"

"Fine," said Cannelle unapologetically as she reentered the kitchen. "Hate me all you want. Just shut up now and go to bed. Isabelle, keep them quiet for me, will you please?" she said, as she slammed the door shut behind her.

Had Jake not been convinced that she truly loved her kids, he might have been alarmed by what could've been construed as child abuse. But the strange situation they were all in, he mused; the father in jail, the stress of monetary survival, the gypsy lifestyle they were accustomed to, and most of all, his conviction that Cannelle would never let anything bad ever happen to them caused Jake to withhold his judgment. After all, what did he know about raising kids himself? He felt an unexpected surge of admiration for Cannelle for refusing to feel sorry for herself in the midst of the contained chaos that was her life.

"*Voilà!*" she said, brushing her hands together in a gesture of dismissal. "It's time to smoke, don't you think?"

Jake had no objection, and as they were facing each other across the kitchen table and going through the familiar ritual of building a joint,

Cannelle assured Jake that there was nothing to worry about as far as the kids were concerned, that they always reacted this way when a new man came round, especially one that they liked, and that they would soon be sound asleep.

"And Isabelle?" asked Jake. "What about her?"

"Oh, she'll stay up reading for a while. She always does. Usually, I have to go in later on and pick up the book off her chest where she dropped it."

"And what is she reading these days?"

"Right now, *The Count of Monte Cristo.*"

"In French?"

"Of course in French. She still considers that to be her native tongue, you know."

"I think that's great," said Jake. "I'm envious. I wish my parents had been so concerned with me learning other languages when I was growing up."

"You're doing okay, though, aren't you? You have German and French and some Spanish … it's not bad for an American," she said with what Jake thought was just a hint of condescension.

"You're not … one of those French people who hates Americans, are you, Cannelle?"

"Hates Americans?" she said in genuine surprise. "Not at all, mon ami! I'm much more likely to hate the French if you want to know the truth. They're the ones I've had trouble with all my life."

"Sorry, I just thought …"

"You just thought that because Americans can famously be such assholes, you know, Vietnam, Nixon, and John Wayne…"

"John Wayne?"

"You know, that whole macho, superior thing that Americans have."

"Yeah, I guess," said Jake, wincing at the memory of American tourists he used to run into in Paris loudly demanding to know why people there didn't speak better English.

"Well, don't worry, I don't think you're like that at all."

"Really?" said Jake. "That's a relief because I really don't wanna be that ugly American guy."

"Don't worry," she said, smiling and stretching out a wiry arm in his direction. "You're not that guy at all."

Without loosening the grip of her hand on his arm, Cannelle handed him the joint, and he took a hit with his free hand inhaling deeply. As his head began to lighten up, all the tension he didn't even know had been there began dissipating, and he found that what had seemed all along to be an inevitability between them was now coalescing into reality. The pressure of her grip on his arm began increasing, and he raised his head to look at her face. Her green eyes, with their startling intensity, were filled with unbridled desire. There was no artifice in Cannelle. No attempt to cover or dissemble. What you saw was exactly what you got. Jake felt he was in the grip of a bluntly erotic force of nature, a woman of such elemental strength that to make love to her would be the equivalent of making love to a tree, or a rock, or a mountain. Jake had never felt this wanted before by anyone. Her need was so great that as she pulled him closer, slipping her hand behind his neck and parting her lips to kiss him, he felt no revulsion at the sight of the gap where her front lower teeth had been but rather saw it as proof of her commitment to the primal unvarnished life she led. Surrendering his tongue, he decided to let this fearless woman show him what she knew.

Chapter 21

Jake stopped by the post office the next day to check the lista de correos in Ibiza town, but there wasn't any mail. He still hadn't completely shaken off his attachment to Joan and half expected without any justification to find a letter from her there. Her letters, once so full of love and yearning, had dropped off sharply as the realization sank in that his path most likely did not lead back in her direction. He continued to write her, oblivious of her likely desire to forget him and move on with her life which he knew involved concrete plans for a career, marriage, and children, concepts which had become as alien to Jake as going to work in a suit every day.

It had taken Jake a surprisingly long time to absorb the reality of her absence from his life. The lingering sense that he'd left something indispensable behind created more than a few moments of self-doubt and intense loneliness. He fantasized that one day, perhaps after he'd redeemed himself as a published author, she'd regret her decision to move on from him and welcome him back into her life. This tenuous belief Jake held about himself as a writer-in-training, which required the accumulation of a vast array of new experiences, provided the grist he needed to keep launching himself into uncharted territory. The truth was, though, Jake didn't yet have a clue what it was that he should write about. He used an excuse that he'd read somewhere, from Henry Miller perhaps, of being too close to the events he was living through to actually be able to write about them. Distance from events, he conveniently concluded, was an essential component for a writer in order to have a more nuanced perspective. But that distance from events would have to wait. It played no part in the here and now existence he was leading on Ibiza. He was waiting for whatever it would take to make his heart catch fire and incinerate all his doubts. He was biding time while life itself, in the vacuum of his indecision, swept him along on its random currents, which might, for all he knew, end up leading nowhere. He found solace in a poem by the seventeenth-century Japanese poet Basho from his thin but classic volume, *The Narrow Road to the Deep North*, which he copied onto the first page of his journal:

"Determined to fall
A weather-exposed skeleton
I cannot help the sore wind
Which blows through my heart."

Chapter 22

SWITZERLAND

Jake's shift at the ski resort in Leysin was finally over, and he made his way hurriedly to the café in the village to meet up with Carl. He still found the unlikely coincidence of their reunion that day to be freakily serendipitous and couldn't wait to find out what his friend had been up to since they'd said goodbye all those months ago in Spain.

The café was a traditional wooden chalet fronted by a large concrete slab supporting red circular tables and plastic foldout chairs surrounded by the visually splendid panorama of the Alps. Their snowy expanse reflected the sun brilliantly, and the air was uncommonly crisp and clean. When it wasn't snowing and you weren't on the slopes, this outdoor cafe was the place to be.

Neither Jake nor Carl had ever seriously thought that they'd meet up again, so Carl's unexpected appearance had sent Jake's imagination into overdrive. He'd already discovered that certain seemingly random encounters like the one he'd had with Georges while hitchhiking outside Paris the previous spring could have far-reaching repercussions, and his intuition told him that this rendezvous with Carl would be equally consequential in his life.

By the time he arrived at the cafe, Carl was already seated at an outside table, leaning back in his chair, his gloved hands folded over his belly with his long legs stretched out before him. His skis and poles lay scattered on the ground, and his dark goggles twinkled with reflecting light as the dying sun's final rays numbed him with their fading warmth.

"Hey," said Jake standing over Carl, gently kicking his boot. Carl shook his head groggily and slowly straightened up in his chair.

"Look at you," continued Jake with mock solemnity, "scattering your stuff on the ground like that. The waiters here must hate you."

"Let me at least wake up," said Carl, yawning, "before you start ragging on me, will ya?"

"Just messing with you," said Jake extending a hand. "Actually, it appears that the waitstaff here is utterly ignoring you."

"It's true," said Carl turning to look at a pretty waitress with blonde pigtails who seemed to have her back turned pointedly away from him. "Maybe they'll come now that you've arrived."

Jake lifted his hand, and sure enough, the waitress turned, smiled, and made her way toward them.

"*S'il vous plaît?*" she asked.

"What'll it be, Carl, a Rivella?" asked Jake, referring to the popular Swiss soft drink mysteriously made from milk.

"You kidding? It's starting to get cold out here," he said, hugging himself. "Really cold. I'll have a coffee."

"Me too," said Jake. "*Deux cafés crème, s'il vous plaît. Et merci, Yolande,*" said Jake, who appeared to be well-acquainted with the waitress.

"*Tout de suite,*" said Yolande smiling.

"You do have a way with the mademoiselles. I gotta hand you that," said Carl.

"Just being friendly," said Jake grinning mischievously. "Now tell me again how you ended up here in Leysin?"

"It's like I said. Just wanted to do some skiing. Used to do a lot of it in winter growing up back in Minnesota. But basically, I'm just hanging out trying to see some more of Europe before I go back to Ibiza in the spring."

"So you really are going back there?" asked Jake.

"Hell, yes. Didn't you think I was?"

"Well, you know how things go, when you're traveling. One thing can lead to another, and then—"

"Whoa, *amigo*, there's one thing you gotta know about me. I may seem like I'm just drifting around without a clue, but I am a planner. I like to have a clear-cut idea of what's gonna happen next in my life. That's just the way I operate. And my plan is to spend a good deal of time in Ibiza. I don't know how long, exactly, but I think there's a lot to explore there, and I intend to take my time."

Jake was thrilled to hear this. He and Carl had talked about returning to the island after their initial exploration the previous spring, but neither had made a commitment. Now it appeared that they'd each, unbeknownst to the other, held onto that concept allowing it to nurture inside them. Jake liked the idea of having a friend to share an adventure with, and though he didn't really know Carl that well, he felt reasonably sure that they wouldn't drive each other nuts, which was a very important component of being on the road together.

"Sounds like a plan to me, too," said Jake marveling at the sight of the sun sliding down between two glorious mountain peaks.

"Great!" said Carl. "So then, howzabout letting me park my van over by your chalet for a while? I think I'd like to get to know this place a little better. Maybe advance my skiing skills? Bone up on my pitiful French?"

"Hmmm," said Jake. "I'll have to ask my roommates first. But I'm pretty sure it'll be okay."

Chapter 23

Jake had first heard of Leysin a few months earlier when he was doing the apple harvest in Valais, an extraordinarily beautiful Swiss canton where the source of the Rhône River lay, trickling down from a majestic alpine glacier. The river had carved out a narrow valley surrounded by resplendent snowcapped peaks on either side. The Rhône was still reasonably narrow there, and farmers had planted an abundance of fruit trees on either side of the river. There were plums, apricots, pears, and apples, as well as a variety of vegetables in need of workers to harvest them. As the country had become more and more urbanized and industrialized, the Swiss peasant had become a vanishing breed, so every year, a number of foreigners, mostly from southern Europe but also from as far away as South America, would gather in this fertile valley to spend nine-hour days picking fruit, beginning in early summer and ending in late fall as various seasonal crops became ripe.

Jake had been on a series of adventures since leaving Carl behind in Spain the spring before. Most notably, acting on a tip from a fellow traveler, he'd spent a month in the small Swiss village of Saanen attending talks by the Indian philosopher Jiddu Krishnamurti. Krishnamurti was a famous spiritual teacher, some would even say guru, although Jake recalled him admonishing the audience that gurus were springing up everywhere like mushrooms, and not to eat them, since in his view they were poisonous. Krishnamurti's worldview, Jake discovered, demanded a continual questioning of one's own conditioning in order to become a more genuine, truthful person. He also introduced the concept that thinking, while not the enemy, had its limitations. "In the space which thought creates around itself," he wrote, "there is no love." Meditation, he suggested, which had nothing to do with thought, should also be an important component of life. It was a state one could slip into where one could experience the state of simply being, without forming judgments or feeling judged.

The gathering of hundreds of seekers of truth in this small idyllic village made an indelible impression on Jake. With its rustic beauty and sense that something of spiritual value was taking place, Jake felt very much at home from the moment he set foot there. He felt as though he'd found someone who was speaking about the reality of existence in complete accord with his own intuitive grasp of truth, but in a way that he'd never been able to articulate before. After spending a few days in a borrowed tent at a local campsite, he heard about a farmer named Willy Hoffman, who allowed visitors to the conference to sleep in his barn on a heaped-up pile of hay, paying only a few francs a night for the privilege. Sleeping in that barn proved to be another pivotal event in Jake's life as he ended up meeting spiritual seekers from all over the world during his sojourn there. Like himself, they were all low on funds and in need of shelter while hanging out to hear the great man speak.

There were wealthy seekers too, of course, but they mostly stayed in nearby Gstaad, the famous resort town where there were fancy hotels and numerous luxurious chalets. Primarily German-speaking but with many French speakers as well, Saanen proved to be an ideal locale for Jake to put his linguistic skills to use. Willy was impressed and soon put Jake in charge of collecting "rent" every day from the campers in his barn, thus allowing the young vagabond to sleep in the barn for free.

Jake thoroughly enjoyed the old farmer's company. Willy was tough, wiry, and industrious but also a notorious drunkard. Crossing the road from the barn to his weathered chalet almost daily in the late afternoon after Willy's farm work was done, Jake would join the old man in his rustic bachelor pad for an intimate feast of homemade cheese perilously sliced from a huge wheel by the inebriated farmer with a razor-sharp blade. More often than not, Willy cut himself in the process, and drops of his bright crimson blood would spill onto the yellow cheese. Too drunk to care, the old man nattered on, thrilled to have someone to talk to, and Jake reveled in the delicious cheese and glass of wine that invariably accompanied it. They would switch back and forth between French and Willy's Swiss-German dialect, which with its singsong cadences, always struck Jake as far more relaxed and playful sounding than the stodgier German he'd learned at school. Willy puffed away on his pipe, which never left his mouth, and Jake wondered at the large purple lump that had formed on his lip. Could it be a cancerous growth? If it was, the old farmer never let on that he was in any way distressed about it.

It was in Willy's barn that Jake met up with the Irishman with whom he'd later share a chalet in Leysin. Sean Martin was handsome with chiseled dark features and ebony hair and might have been referred to as black Irish by people outside of Ireland. His startling blue eyes and a constant five-o'clock shadow lent him a slightly menacing look, even though, in reality, he was about as threatening as the Easter Bunny. Sean's personality had a Mark Twain quality in that he loved to philosophize in a playful, humorous fashion about deep subjects.

"I'm telling you, lads," he said one day as a group of J. K. buffs were all gathered at a table in front of the bakery in Saanen specializing in exotic pizza slices with toppings ranging from apricots to zucchini. "Back in Ireland, most people still believe that saints can control daily events. Ya wouldn't believe how many plaster saints me old grandmum has placed strategically around her house, especially on the windowsills, to prevent a burglar from gettin' inside."

"Well, does it work?" asked Jake.

"Keeps 'em from gettin' in sure but never stopped me from nickin' a bob or two from me grannie's purse."

"That's terrible," said Jake in mock incredulity.

"I'll tell ya what's terrible," continued Sean, always adroit at changing the subject whenever it suited his purposes. "Me grannie's cookin', that's what. She's the only person I know who can ruin a perfectly decent can of baked beans."

Sean could go on in this vein interminably, always gently poking fun at himself, his country, and humankind in general. Jake enjoyed his amusing banter and also understood that underneath the joking exterior was a serious person who truly was interested in the meaning of life. When Jake finally left to attend to the apple harvest, a day's hitch further south, he informed Sean of the possibility of finding work there picking fruit near the French-speaking town of Martigny should he too run low on funds.

In what turned out to be another fateful hitchhiking episode after the conference in Saanen had ended, Jake had the good fortune of being picked up by a woman just outside of Martigny who invited Jake to stay with her for a few days while he was looking for work picking fruit. Lulu, a sweet, optimistic young mademoiselle, worked for the local government tourist agency out of a booth in the town square, essentially helping foreigner workers and tourists alike to orient themselves in the Canton of Valais. She was round and voluptuous with short reddish hair, blue eyes, and an easy smile. Her freckles contrasted sharply with the otherwise creamy white texture of her skin.

"Are you sure me staying for a few days will be all right with your boyfriend?" asked Jake.

"Don't worry," said Lulu. "Pierre loves to have company. You'll see."

Chapter 24

Pierre and Lulu's house in Martigny, which ultimately became Jake's home during the entire length of the five-week apple harvest, sat back from the street by a picturesque covered wooden bridge spanning the Rhône. It was a large two-story white stone building with a red tile roof in a quiet neighborhood, so quiet in fact that the lapping of the river on its banks was audible at night. Pierre was a young apprentice electrician who came from a remote Alpine village high up on the side of a mountain. He'd been raised there by his grandmother, who'd encouraged him to revere nature, to ski, and to be kind toward his fellow human beings. He was short, freckled, and tightly muscled with the torso and legs of a man who'd grown up ascending and descending more or less vertical surfaces on a daily basis. He and Lulu were a harmonious pair, but there was something about their energy together that was more suggestive of siblings than of lovers. The day that Lulu brought Jake home with her, Pierre was in the kitchen preparing a pasta dish for dinner.

"*Salut!*" said Pierre, barely glancing up from his task.

"*Salut!*" said Jake. As they shook hands, Pierre gave Lulu a look as if to say, *What have you brought home with you this time?*

"This is Jake," she said. "He's American."

Pierre immediately put on a pair of glasses, placed both hands on his hips, and began inspecting Jake closely as if he were a living sculpture.

"So," he pronounced at last, "this is what an American looks like! I've seen them on TV and in the movies but never actually up close before."

"Do I pass the inspection?" asked Jake, not quite sure how to respond to this odd little man.

"*Non*," said Pierre emphatically, blowing out the word like a puff of smoke. He then proceeded to take off his glasses, lay them on the counter, and with a grim expression, gave Jake a final appraisal. When this scrutiny was at last concluded, he unexpectedly closed the gap between them, wrapped his arms around the taller Jake, and pulled him into a fierce embrace. Jake responded in kind, and the two of them were soon laughing and leaping around the room together like a pair of crazy kangaroos. Lulu, her arms folded across her chest, watched them with a knowing smile. "I told you in the car that he was crazy," she reminded Jake.

Pierre immediately halted the revelry, a hurt hangdog look creeping over his countenance. "I'm not crazy!" he said with nonetheless the hint of a smile. Stepping toward the stove, he abruptly turned his back on his guest, picked up a spoon, and began to stir the pasta.

"I already told Jake he could stay a few days," announced Lulu, setting the table, "while he looks for a job picking apples."

"*Ah bon*," said Pierre, giving Jake an indifferent glance. He then picked up a knife and began chopping up tomatoes, celery, and onions, deep in concentration as he prepared an aromatic sauce, saying nothing as Jake and Lulu chatted amiably at the nearby kitchen table. Finally, when the meal was at last ready, and a bottle of cheap table wine had been opened and decanted, he placed a bowl of pasta, some parmesan cheese, and a bowl of sauce on the table, sat down next to his girlfriend, and brushing his hands together in a gesture of finality announced "*Bon appétit!*"

"*Bon appétit!*" responded Jake and Lulu in unison.

Their invitation to spend a few days became more and more open-ended with each passing day. The more time the three of them spent together, the more they found they enjoyed each other's company. Jake understood that he 'represented' an American to them, and the fact that he spoke French allowed them to gain an unexpected insight into an alien but not completely dissimilar culture which they both found intriguing enough to forestall his eviction. Whenever Jake asked if it was time for him to leave and find another place to stay, they immediately shushed him as though he'd just handed them an insult.

Jake would not be the only stranger, though, to show up at Pierre and Lulu's door that fall. Although Jake himself, for purely selfish reasons, remained tight-lipped about his living arrangements, word somehow managed to spread among the young foreign contingent who arrived in the valley looking for work that a generous Swiss couple was welcoming guests to reside with them during the harvest. Almost on a daily basis, at least during the first week or so, Jake would arrive home after the grueling work of picking apples all day to find that a new young housemate or two had arrived. There was a German girl, a Chilean, a Spaniard, and a French couple, as well as random other guests who might just stay for a night or two. All were instructed by Lulu to spread their sleeping bags out on the floor of the living room at night and to generally make themselves at home. The only rules were that everyone had to buy their own food, keep the place neat, and clean up after themselves.

There was also the matter of the dog living upstairs with a rarely seen couple. Rumored to be drug dealers, they had a very protective husky, Pitou, whose ice-cold pale blue eyes kept watch at the top of the stairs, habitually planting himself in front of the door to the one and only bathroom. To use it, you first had to step over Pitou as he growled and eyed your crotch as though it were a T-bone steak. Not a few of the guests ended up walking to the public restrooms in town rather than have to confront this sinister canine. Jake had complained to his hosts about him, but they just shrugged and allowed that there was nothing they could do. Pierre reminded Jake that the upstairs tenants never complained about all the visitors downstairs, so it was probably better just to accept that they had a difficult pet. Remarkably though, Pitou never bothered Pierre. The young apprentice had an uncanny ability to defuse the dog's aggression. As the growling beast eyed him with a baleful gaze, Pierre would fearlessly reach down, enfolding him in a tight embrace, all the while telling him what a good boy he was, and *voilà*, Pitou would soon be licking him from chin to forehead. Jake was in awe of the courage and confidence it took to pull that off, and his respect for Pierre increased accordingly.

Downstairs the door was never locked. Jake would have preferred to have the whole place to himself with his newfound friends when he got home from work and on his days off, but he could hardly complain about his hosts' magnanimous behavior. Their generosity inspired him to confront his own selfish nature, and he began reaching out more to the newly arriving guests, being friendlier and focusing on the solidarity they all felt in sharing the grueling harvest experience. Climbing up and down a ladder for nine hours a day while taking care to fill a plastic bucket with large unblemished Golden Delicious apples under the withering gaze of a dour supervisor in sometimes bitterly cold weather was not for the faint of heart.

Pierre and Lulu, Jake decided, were perhaps the most openhearted people he'd ever met in his life, which was all the more remarkable in a country like Switzerland, whose citizens tended to be conservative, parochial, and very snobbish toward their non-Swiss residents. He would never forget the day when he was still camping out in the barn in Saanen, a friend had stopped by to visit Willy Hoffman. Upon seeing the young visitors camped out in the barn, he'd loudly announced in a voice steeped in contempt, "*Vous etes la poubelle de la Suisse!*" You are the trash of Switzerland!

Chapter 25

One evening to Jake's great surprise, his Irish friend Sean showed up at Pierre and Lulu's door. It was late, and everyone had already eaten and cleaned up. Most were gathered around Pierre's stereo listening to music and getting high. Pierre had a Deep Purple album that he loved, and "Woman from Tokyo" was blasting at full volume when Sean strolled into the living room together with an unknown companion. Pierre, always bringing back items he "found" at his job as an apprentice electrician, had somehow managed to appropriate a variety of powerful loudspeakers which he'd hung up and connected throughout the house, with wiring "acquired" from various job sites, and the rock and roll was deafening.

"Sean," yelled Jake, embracing his friend. "I can't believe it. You actually made it! I wasn't sure I'd ever see you again!"

"'Course I did," said Sean. "I had to, didn't I? Hardly had two francs left to rub together in me pocket. By the way, this is Peter. We're doing the grape harvest down the road a ways. Shite, that is a backbreaker, lemme tell ya. But what're ya gonna do? We're trying to save up enough to drive back to England, and from there maybe go to Ireland together. Peter's got a great old English Ford Anglia. Bought it for ten pounds off some wanker back in Brighton, and lemme tell ya, it runs just like an Irish filly! We call it Popeye, right Peter? It doesn't always run on all four cylinders, mind you, but it still gets us to where we wanna go. And Peter's a great one for driving, right Peter? Just put yer man behind the wheel and Bob's yer uncle! Say, Jake, wanna join us after the harvest?"

During Sean's little monologue, Peter, who was tall and wiry, with short blond hair, a deeply tanned face, and an enormous beaked nose over a pencil mustache, just stood there bobbing his head and smiling serenely in a beat-up leather bomber jacket clearly enjoying the partylike atmosphere in the room. He looked amused and relaxed, and Jake liked his easygoing manner.

"Dunno," Jake answered after a pause. "I may have a lead on a job as a waiter at a ski resort restaurant. They're looking for someone who speaks German and French, and they'd be willing to train me."

"Well, speaking of ski resorts, that's the other thing that's happened," said Sean. "Peter and I met this guy Jean-Paul who owns a chalet up in a place called Leysin. Is that where your restaurant is?"

"No, never heard of it."

"Well, Jean-Paul, you see, is a real fun guy. That is to say, he'd like to be anyway. And he thinks that we're real fun, right Peter? So he figures if he rents us his chalet this winter, he'll be able to come up sometimes on weekends and enjoy himself with his girlfriend, who otherwise might not want to go up there with him alone cuz she actually thinks he's pretty boring."

"Which he is," said Peter. "Really boring."

"Well, what's she doing with him then?"

"It's all about the bucks," said Sean. "Jean-Paul is rich! Or at least his dad is. He owns a mattress factory down here in the valley, and Jean-Paul helps him run it. He's just your ordinary Swiss business kind of guy, you know, kind of repressed and quiet and drinking a little bit too much vino. You ask him about mattresses, though, and you can't shut the lad up!"

"Oh God, mattresses," moaned Peter. "Don't ever bring up that subject if he's around, whatever you do."

"And you guys met him … how?" asked Jake.

"We wandered into this restaurant one night," continued Sean, "and there he was with a red nose staring into the void with his very bored-looking girlfriend seated beside him. The place was packed except for two empty seats at their table. Maybe people could see how boring he was and thought it might be contagious. I dunno. Fortunately for us, though, it turns out Jean-Paul speaks good English, so we ended up having a pretty good conversation."

"But what are you gonna do there in Leysin?" asked Jake.

"Well, that's just the thing, you see," continued Sean. "Jean-Paul knows the owner of the ski resort there, and he thinks he can get us jobs. Turns out there's a lot of tour groups that go over from England every winter, so they like to hire guys like us."

"Why don't we continue this conversation outdoors?" asked Jake, gesturing toward the door. "That way, we don't have to compete with Deep Purple."

Once outside, Sean pleaded with his friend as they stood beside the riverbank. "Just think about it, Jake. We could all live together in a really nice chalet while working at a ski resort, saving up money!"

"Wouldn't it be expensive, though, renting a chalet?"

"That's just it," said Sean. "Jean-Paul's willing to give us a good price. For some reason, he really likes us. I can't imagine why, can you? Anyway, it would be too expensive if it was just me and Peter. That's why we need you! If we split the rent three ways, it's entirely doable. You'll see! Plus, you speak French. You can be our translator!"

Jake considered this, weighing the pros and cons of sharing a house with these two men. He felt he knew Sean well enough from the time they'd spent together in Saanen. He was easygoing, fun, and full of entertaining stories. He'd just met Peter, but he seemed harmless enough, evincing easy laughter. He and Sean seemed to be great friends, so he had to be all right.

"Well," said Jake. "Renting a chalet together is kind of a big step, and we don't really know each other that well yet, do we?"

"Yet," said Sean. "That's why you've got to come on the road with us after the harvest. Driving around in Popeye together would be such a blast! We can make our way to the ferry at Dieppe, then stay with friends in London while we wait for the ski season over here to begin."

"To know us is to love us," said Peter with a deadpan expression. "And that includes Popeye."

Chapter 26

IBIZA

Soon after Jake and Carl got naked in front of the old peasant woman, Juanita, Jake was sitting by himself on the beach at Aguas Blancas, trying not to be too distracted by a nearby group of topless women. He was taking a break from searching for a new place to live and rereading a letter that had arrived that week via *poste restante* from Joan. The letter, ominously, bore no introduction.

"I won't bother asking how you are, Jake. I've tried that before and never really gotten a clear answer. Just these vague declarations about how wonderful freedom is and what a great big world it is 'out there' and how much your horizons are being expanded all the time now.

Meanwhile, I'm stuck back here in Johnson City, sprawled out on what used to be our bed, staying up way too late at night, drinking way too much coffee, preparing a term paper on Sartre's "Being and Nothingness," and getting fucking tired of wondering if your wanderlust will ever be spent and you'll decide to come back here … even as I write these words, the absurdity of that thought leaps out at me. It's clear to me now that you're not coming back to anything. 'Back' is no longer a point on your compass. I guess you're moving forward in your own mind. Where I don't know. And clearly, you don't either. At least, I'm pretty sure you think you're moving forward. But is a ship adrift at sea merely at the mercy of the elements moving forward? I don't think so. It's just staying afloat. Which is all, despite your attempts to romanticize it, your life is all about right now. Staying afloat. And I'm sorry to rain on your parade, Jake, but I think you can do better than that.

And here's the thing. Despite my reservations, I thought when you left for Paris that this journey would be good for you. For both of us, in fact. This yearning for adventure, for something different, for something new. I figured you'd go to Paris for a few months, soak in the atmosphere, take in the museums, and the *je ne sais quoi*, get a feel for the place and come back recharged with a new vision for your life that would end up energizing both of us and bring us even closer together. I imagined that my liberality in letting you go with my blessing would etch my love for you so deeply in your heart that you would carry me like a talisman around your neck, a reminder of who it was you were growing for … but oh, how foolish love can be!

Idiot that I was, I actually believed that you were thinking of me at all! Even when your letters were so dispassionately vague about us or our relationship. Typically they were filled with more excitement about the display window of the local patisserie you were patronizing than of our once and future romance. And yet I still held on to a seed of hope, proving that old cliché that absence does indeed make the heart grow fonder.

But that cliché has turned out to be no more relevant than the current state of our relationship. Which is why, dear Jake, it should come as no surprise that I have a new love in my life. One who absolutely adores me and has no plans for bolting off into the unknown on some dubious journey of self-discovery. Marvin is his name. (I know you'll find that amusing, but don't smirk too much. I believe the original meaning of Marvin is 'sea of wine' or something like that, and he is just so-o-o intoxicating, if you know what I mean!) The fact that he's Jewish doesn't hurt either. His people, after all, have been wandering long enough and are trying to settle down. And he's so solicitous of my feelings, and the fact that my heart is only just now starting to recover from the deep wound your abandonment of me has inflicted on my fragile, yes Jake— much more so than you ever realized—sensibility. So really, there's not much left to say, is there? Needless to say, you won't be receiving any more consoling letters from me addressed to whatever fucking poste restante address you happen to be monitoring at the moment. I can't even believe I used to try and console you for the loneliness you were suffering as a result of abandoning me! Marvin has really helped me see the light on that one! It's taken an accounting major (I see that smirk again, Jake, wipe it off your face!) to help me understand how ungrounded I was with you. I now understand the importance of having a five-year plan! And I'm not talking about the Chairman Mao thing either, Jake. I'm just saying you have to know what you're doing with your life! It makes all the difference in the world. Marvin says that if we set up a retirement plan now, we can actually be millionaires by the time we retire. Millionaires, Jake!

I feel as if the blinders have fallen away, and I'm seeing clearly now for the first time in my life. What we had wasn't real Jake. It was, dare I say it, nothing more than puppy love. It wasn't the love that a real man has for a real woman. I think Marvin's the first really mature man I've met. He's not a dreamer like you. He's someone who can actually accomplish something in life.

Try not to take this too hard, mon ami. The truth is I'm doing you a favor. We've reached the point of no return. You're free now, Jake. Free to fuck up your life as much as you want.

But seriously, I do wish you well. Maybe you'll get this all out of your system soon and start to have a meaningful life.

Joan

P.S. Don't bother writing back to this address. Marvin and I don't live here anymore."

Jake sighed, returning the letter to his shoulder bag. The inevitable distancing of time and separation had worn down his feelings for Joan into something more akin to nostalgia than to actual emotional engagement. In view of her evident disdain, he'd have to find a way now to dislodge her from his heart.

Taking a book from his bag, *The Razor's Edge* by Somerset Maugham, he opened it to the page he'd left off at and started reading. He was captivated by the hero of the novel, Larry Darrell, who, after a traumatic experience as a fighter pilot in World War I, decided to reject materialistic values and lead a Bohemian life of study, travel, and manual labor, eventually landing in India where he seemingly became enlightened. *When will I go to India?* Jake wondered. He had a strong feeling he would end up there eventually, but he wasn't in any rush. *Why would I want to be anywhere else,* he wondered, *besides this beautiful beach, enjoying the warm breeze off the Mediterranean while munching on some delicious figs?* Despite the uncertainty in his life, he was quite sure of one thing; it didn't get much better than this. He was so absorbed in this blissful sense of appreciation of the moment that he failed to notice the approach of a ruddy-looking stranger whose sun-bleached hair was pulled back into a ponytail. As soon as Jake became aware of him, though, he went on high alert. Especially when the man squatted next to the towel Jake had spread out on the sand. It wasn't a crowded beach. Why was this man so uncomfortably close?

"Hi," said the man, "whatcha reading?"

Jake grudgingly showed him the cover of his book.

"Oh, Maugham," he said. "Good choice. Did you ever read *Of Human Bondage?* That's really his masterpiece, ya know."

"Not yet," said Jake, leaning away from the man while keeping an eye on his shoulder bag containing his money and passport. He mentally made the calculation of how quickly he could reach out and grab it if necessary.

"I like to see what people are reading," said the man. "You never know. I might get turned onto something new and interesting."

"Uh-huh," mumbled Jake trying to get back to reading his book.

"I'm Ruben, by the way," said the man stretching out a hand. "Ruben Ross."

Jake cautiously reached out his hand in response. "Jake," he said.

"Been in Ibiza long, Jake?"

"Not that long, no."

"Plan to stay awhile, though, don't you?"

"Why do you say that?"

"Oh, I dunno," said Ruben, "just a hunch, I guess. I'm pretty good at reading people."

Are you now? thought Jake. But he said nothing, keeping his eyes on the book.

"You American?"

"Yes, I am," said Jake. "And you?"

"Same," said Ruben. "Grew up in Seattle. Howz about you?"

"New York," said Jake. "Upstate, though. Not the city."

"Oh, a country boy," said Ruben.

"Not exactly," said Jake. "More like the 'burbs. Lots of orchards and dairy farms though. Pretty nice place to grow up."

"I grew up on the streets," said Ruben. "Didn't really have much family, I'm afraid."

"Sorry to hear that," said Jake, not sure whether to believe him or not. After an awkward pause, he continued. "How long have you been here on Ibiza?"

"Well, let's see now," said Ruben pulling his knees up to his chest and gazing toward the sea. "Three years? Yeah, must be going on three years already. My, my," he said, cracking a smile, "time sure does fly when you're having fun, don't it?"

"I guess," said Jake, growing annoyed with himself for still engaging the man. "So you've been having fun?"

"Well, sure," said Ruben. "Aren't you? I mean, isn't that what people come here to do?"

Jake turned to really look at the man. He wore an old straw hat, and beneath it were two intensely blue eyes which shone with a feral intelligence. He had a scraggly blond mustache and a good week's growth of beard. Below his naked hairless torso, he wore a red thong bathing suit with a pronounced bulge. He seemed harmless enough, yet something about the man put Jake on edge.

"I have to ask," said Jake, "is this normal for you? Invading someone's space like this and getting in their face with personal questions?"

"What? Oh wow," said Ruben, his cheeks flushing darkly. "Jeezus, I'm sorry. Is that what you think I'm doing? Whoa! That is some accusation, brother. Look, I'm sorry if that's what you think. I really am. The truth is, I just thought you looked, I dunno, lonely?"

"Well, I'm not," said Jake testily. "I'm just trying to enjoy the beach and read my book."

"I got no argument with that," said Ruben apologetically. "I love doing that too. In fact, it's one of my favorite things to do. Really, I'm not kidding! By the way, can I ask you one more question? I promise it's not personal."

"Okay … what?"

"Thanks, um . . . Bill was it?"

"Jake," he blurted, instantly annoyed with himself for succumbing to the man's slyness and tenacity.

"Oh yeah, you told me that already. Jake, are you by any chance looking for a place to stay here on the island?"

"What makes you ask that?"

"Well, because … I'll be honest with you. I was watching you from over there," he said, waving his hand vaguely in the direction he'd come from. "And I thought, well, he looks like a nice guy."

"A nice, lonely guy?"

"Right, a nice, lonely guy. And so, I thought maybe you'd like to move in with me. Me and my girlfriend, that is."

"Move in with you?" asked Jake, stunned by the proposal. "Just like that?"

"Well, no, not just like that. Jesus, Jake," said Ruben with a friendly chuckle. "'Course not just like that. You must think I'm … well, I don't know what you must think. But, of course, I think you should see the place first. That goes without saying. That is if you are looking for a place to stay."

Jake had to appreciate the offer. How could this fellow—this Ruben Ross, if that was indeed his name—have possibly known that he was quite desperately looking for a place for him and Carl to stay. It truly was uncanny. He had no reason to trust this guy, but a part of him that understood that inexplicable forces did sometimes intervene and guide you in mysterious ways was intrigued by Ruben's completely unexpected and bizarrely convenient proposal. He decided to consider it without suspecting in the least how fateful this encounter would end up being in his life.

Chapter 27

Back at Jacqueline and Klaus's finca that evening for dinner, Jake was eager to tell his little group of friends about his encounter on the beach that day. He'd brought some fresh eggs and goat cheese home to make an omelet, glad to be able to repay the couple in some small way for their kindness, but Jacqueline wouldn't hear of him cooking.

"Let me deal with that," she said, whisking away the groceries, "and thank you for the food, Jake. But if there's one thing that I am sure of, it's that my omelet will be better than yours!"

"Can't disagree with that," conceded Jake, "but tell me what you know about this guy I met at the beach today. Says his name is Ruben Ross." Jake fully expected Jacqueline, who seemed to know everything about everyone, to have some information to share. Surprisingly, though, it was Carl who spoke up first.

"Ruben Ross, did you say? Blond guy with a mustache? American? Looks pretty weather-beaten?"

"That'd be the guy," said Jake. "Why? You know him?"

"Oh, everybody knows Ruben," said Carl.

"I don't," interjected Klaus, who was tinkering away at an old wire spool table next to a giant cactus plant in the courtyard.

"Oh, shut up, *chérie*," said Jacqueline affectionately. "You don't know anybody."

"It's true," said Klaus with an indifferent shrug. "I don't. I don't want to know anybody. Except for Jacqueline, that is."

"That's okay," quipped Jake as Jacqueline blew her boyfriend a kiss. "We still love you anyway, Klaus."

The German put his thin lips together in a pout and returned to the job at hand, namely cleaning out the carburetor from his most recent Vespa repair job with a gasoline-soaked rag. Looking down at his handiwork, he was soon smiling again, completely immersed in his task.

"Why do you ask?" said Carl. "About Ruben, I mean."

"I ran into him today on the beach at Aguas Blancas. Or rather, he singled me out on the beach."

"Singled you out? What for?"

"He just walked up to me, squatted down next to my towel, and started chitchatting. Eventually, he asked me if I wanted to move into a finca with him and his girlfriend."

"Really?" asked Jacqueline. "Is this true?"

"Yes," said Jake. "It's so bizarre, isn't it? Here we are looking desperately for a place to live, and some stranger walks up to me and says, 'Move in with us.' And apparently, it's a classic finca, too, remote and quiet. Could be just what we're looking for."

"Whoa, whoa, whoa," said Carl. "From what I know about Ruben Ross, he's a very peculiar guy. Never seems to have any money, always working some angle with his girlfriend. Always seems to be on the edge of…I dunno, but a real good talker by all accounts."

"How do you know Ruben?" asked Jake.

"He and I played music together a few times when I was here by myself last year. He told me he lived in a finca up by Santa Inés. Is that the one he mentioned?"

"Yeah, Santa Inés. He did say that. What's Santa Inés like?"

"It's north of here, maybe ten kilometers," said Jacqueline. "A very isolated place. The town is very small, even smaller than Santa Gertrudis. Maybe just a church and a bar or two. But it is beautiful. You should see the almond trees there when they blossom in winter!"

"Now we're talking," said Jake, eager to set aside his initial doubts about Ruben. "What do we know about this girlfriend of his?"

"She's pretty," said Carl. "Always kind of hovering in the background. Can't remember her name right now. They're always together, though. She wasn't with him at the beach?"

"Not that I could see," said Jake.

"Hmmm," said Carl. "I'll bet she was, and he told her to hang back while he chatted you up."

"Dunno," said Jake. "It's possible, I guess."

"I don't know her either," said Klaus, glancing up briefly from his carburetor.

"Of course not, mon chéri," said Jacqueline. "Remember, you don't know anybody! You know, I think I've heard of Ruben also. He plays electric guitar, does he not?"

"That's right," said Carl. "He used to have a few gigs at hotels here with a band he'd put together."

"Now I'm remembering," she said. "I think I heard him once at a bar in Ibiza town. Not very good, I think?"

"But very enthusiastic," countered Carl. "He really would like to be a musician. More than anything else in the world. Only trouble is he's self-taught like me and has a real hard time playing with other people. Always seems to be playing in his own time signature, if you know what I mean."

"How does he ever get other people to play with him then?" asked Jake.

"First of all, he's got a lot of charm," said Carl. "Seems to have an uncanny ability to bend people to his will. Then again, his bands don't usually last very long. But he does have occasional flashes of brilliance. I remember playing "Hotel California" with him, and he totally nailed the Joe Walsh guitar solo, but then when it came time for him to play rhythm again, he was just a tad behind the beat. Very frustrating to play with, I'm afraid. I feel kind of sorry for him, actually. You can't help rooting for the guy, but at the same time, you have to wonder if he's really got what it takes."

"Hmmm," said Jake, "sounds like a character, all right. A bit on the weird side, but let's take a look at his finca anyway. Whaddya say, Carl?"

"Well, we ain't got nothin' to lose," said Carl. "We do have to get our asses out of this place soon, don't we?"

"Right," said Klaus without glancing up from his repair job.

"Let's just see what happens," said Jacqueline diplomatically. "Yes, yes, by all means, have a look. Perhaps it will be perfect for you. How will you contact him again, Jake?"

"He said he'd be at Bar Costa around noon tomorrow. I guess we just meet him and go from there."

Chapter 28

Around noon turned out to be more like one o'clock by the time Ruben arrived at Bar Costa the following day. He jumped off the back of a local Ibicenco's pickup truck filled with sacks of onions as it slowed down in front of the bar. Stumbling toward Jake and Carl, he pulled up a chair at their table and dropped heavily into it.

"Buy me a beer," he demanded.

"Is that an order?" asked Jake taken aback by Ruben's surly demeanor. He decided to humor him, though, and called over a waiter.

"*Una cerveza por favor,*" he said pointing at Ruben.

"*Gracias,*" said Ruben. "I was standing in the sun for quite a while before that guy finally picked me up. I shoulda told you guys to meet me in Santa Inés."

"Yeah," said Jake. "That prob'ly woulda been smarter. But anyway, we're here now. You can drink your beer, and then we'll head out and see about this finca of yours."

Ruben glared at Jake. "Don't tell me what I can do, man," he said, his blue eyes cold beneath the brim of his straw hat. "If I wanna sit here and drink my beer for a while, then that's what I'm gonna do. Capeesh?"

Jake froze, momentarily taken aback by this unexpected outburst of aggression.

"Hey," said Ruben, forcing a smile, "Lighten up, will ya, man? I'm just fuckin' with ya."

"Oh-kay," said Jake, "I guess. By the way, this is my friend Carl, the one I told you about?"

"I figured," said Ruben squinting. "Do we know each other?"
"We played a gig together once in town. I think it was at Club Diablo. You played a mean solo on *Hotel California.*"

"Oh, yeah," said Ruben grinning. "That's right. That was cool. I do love that song. And Joe Walsh is the man. I remember you now. Howzit, brother?"

"It'll be better," said Carl, "when we find a place to live."

"You got one," said Ruben, "if you want it."

"Question for you," said Jake. "How do you manage to be in a band when you live so far out in the sticks?"

"Oh, I've got a vehicle," said Ruben. "A nice little Renault. Ran like a charm until just a few days ago."

"What happened?" asked Jake.

"Oh, the usual. A victim of the roads around here. I think the axle's in the shitter."

"Broke the axle?" said Carl. "Jesus. How fast were you driving?"

"Beats me," said Ruben. "Can't remember much at all about that night, as a matter of fact."

"So basically, you totaled your car," said Carl.

"Nah," said Ruben. "Nobody here ever really totals anything. I know a guy who can get me another axle. Has his own private junkyard, in fact. I just gotta get some cash together. Then I'll put it in myself. I've worked on cars before, man. Shouldn't be that big a deal."

"I don't know about that," said Carl. "That's—"

"Not our problem," interrupted Jake as the waiter arrived with the beer. "Our only problem right now is finding a place to live."

"Right," said Ruben, tipping the frosted bottle between his lips and draining it completely in a few large gulps. "Aaah," he said, wiping the froth from his mouth with the back of his hand, "that's better. Thanks for that. You guys ready to rumble?"

***

Despite being occupied, Ruben's finca had an abandoned look about it. Large and rectangular with flaking white paint, it was fronted by a courtyard of cracked and broken gray stones. Old wooden beams

113

overhead formed a kind of trellis on which weak desiccated grapevines had tried to gain a foothold and failed. An old baking oven, missing bricks, and an outdoor well with a dented tin bucket hanging from a frayed rope added to the forlorn ambience of the place. A few flakes of blue paint still clung to a wide roof beam that stretched above the wooden doorway. Large unpruned almond trees and cacti on either side of the house provided the finca with a picturesque frame, and its position, butted up against a high verdant hill, gave the whole scene a pleasingly rustic appearance.

Standing in the courtyard, the three men turned to look at the landscape below them. Stretching out far in the distance were almond, olive, carob, and fig trees surrounded by waist-high stone walls which the local farmers used to pen in their sheep and goats, whose distant bleating blended into the sage-scented breeze wafting through the courtyard.

"You hear it?" asked Ruben.

"Hear what?"

"The silence."

Both Carl and Jake nodded.

"Yeah," Jake finally said. "I hear it, and I love it."

"I'm telling you guys, this place is special," said Ruben, standing with his legs akimbo and hands planted on his hips like a lord assessing his domain. "C'mon," he said, after gazing for awhile. "It's time you guys met Mary Lou."

Ruben's girlfriend was seated at a bare wooden table in the kitchen, rolling a joint. She was unquestionably attractive with long flowing chestnut hair and puffy sensuous lips. A tight-fitting skimpy red dress showed off to advantage the shapely swell of her breasts and the walnut hue of her skin. She had an easy smile which she flashed at all three men as they entered the room. *This is a woman who enjoys the company of men,* thought Jake for no good reason. The men took seats at the table after Ruben introduced them and waited while she finished her task. Ruben fiddled with a small tape deck, and soon J. J. Cale was wailing about getting down to the ground with cocaine. Mary Lou lit the joint and passed it to Jake, who couldn't help but notice she had one lazy dark eye which tended to roam off in another direction while the other one looked right at you.

"How'd you guys end up on Ibiza?" asked Jake.

Ruben hinted at some problems with the law back in the States and claimed to have drifted into Ibiza via Barcelona, where he jumped off a tramp steamer three years earlier.

"What about you, Mary Lou?" asked Carl. "How'd you end up here?"

"Oh, I just came over here for my summer vacation after my sophomore year in college. Ruben and I met, fell in love, and I never went back," she said, winking slyly at her boyfriend.

"How long ago was that?" asked Jake.

"'Bout a year now, right, babe?"

"You said it, baby doll," said Ruben. "In fact, I'm pretty sure we've got our anniversary coming up. We'll have to think of something real special to do to celebrate, won't we?"

"Yeah," said Mary Lou, smirking, "like pay the rent!"

Everybody laughed. Mary Lou's charm helped deflate the tension in the room as the joint was smoked down to a nub. J. J. Cale had moved on to crooning about a Cajun moon.

"Let's take you guys for a tour, shall we?" said Ruben, nodding to Mary Lou to join them. "Once you check it out, you're not gonna wanna leave this place, I promise."

The finca proved to be simple and unadorned, with thick whitewashed walls and dark wooden ceiling beams. Large enough for Carl and Jake to each have their own small room, there were even beds with thin, uneven mattresses. As was typically the case, there was no bathroom, just a shovel and a roll of toilet paper to take out in the woods behind the house. It was primitive but also authentic and charming, with fresh cold water in the well and a pine-covered slope that rose gently to a tall bluff behind the house. The only sounds were birds calling to one another and the rustle of unseen critters in the trees.

After the tour, they all reassembled in the kitchen. Ruben proudly pulled out a neatly rolled joint, lit it, and proceeded to hold it for a very long time, taking one deep drag after another.

"Hey, Ruben," said Carl at last, "you ever gonna share that thing?"

Ruben took one more enormous toke, so powerful that his eyes filled up with tears before he passed it to his girlfriend. Mary Lou, in turn, took her time, holding it nearly as long as Ruben. By the time she passed it to Carl, there wasn't much left to smoke.

"You guys ever hear the expression, 'Don't Bogart that joint'?" asked Carl before taking a small toke and passing it on to Jake.

"One of my favorite songs," said Ruben ignoring the innuendo. "We should play it together sometime. Hey, man, did you bring your guitar?"

"No," said Carl. "I left it in my van."

"You and I should think about playing together sometime, man. With your van, we could probably get some gigs. Problem is until I get an axle for my car, I can't really make a play date."

"Lemme think about it," said Carl.

"You do that," said Ruben. "Meanwhile, what do you guys think about this place now that you've seen it? Everybody gets their own room. We can share the kitchen. Wanna toss in with us? We'd really like to have you as housemates, wouldn't we, babe?"

"Sure," she said, her eyes glistening from the hash. "Listen, you guys, if you think you're gonna find another place like this anywhere on this island, you're just kidding yourselves. This is the real deal. There just aren't that many places like this one left to rent. We know. It took us forever to find this place, didn't it, babe?"

"Took me, you mean," corrected Ruben. "You weren't even around yet!"

"I wasn't? Oh yeah, I guess you're right. But I heard all about how hard it was to find it!"

Ruben rolled his eyes and turned back to the visitors. "You can move in right away, you know. We can just prorate the rent."

"How much is it?" asked Jake.

Ruben named a figure, and Carl and Jake both looked surprised.

"That seems kind of high," said Carl. "You mean split four ways?"

"No," said Ruben, "that would be split between the two of you. You see, Mary Lou and I don't have money. Not enough, anyway."

"But that's the entire rent, right?" asked Jake.

"Right," said Ruben.

"So you guys would basically be living here for free, as our guests then?"

"Pretty much," said Ruben.

"Well, we wouldn't be their guests, would we, hon?" asked Mary Lou in a plaintive tone. "After all, without us, they'd never even have known about this place. That's gotta count for something."

"Good point," said Ruben. "Our staying here would be like a kind of finder's fee, I guess you could say. Of course, as soon as we get some money together, we'll pitch in as well, won't we, babe?"

"Oh yeah," said Mary Lou, her weird eye jiggling slightly. "Any day now, I'm sure. Ruben and I are pretty good at figuring out unusual ways to make money."

"That's good, I guess," said Jake, tugging on his friend's shirt. "Carl, can I speak to you outside for a moment?"

"Sure," said Carl.

"Sit tight," said Jake, "we'll be right back."

Standing outside in front of the finca, the two friends once again took in the sweeping panorama. "Well," asked Jake, "whaddya think?"

"It's actually about the same as we were paying Tony, isn't it?"

"I know," said Jake. "We could afford it. But that's not what worries me. It's those two. I can't help thinking we're getting ourselves involved with a couple of con artists."

"Oh, that's a given," said Carl. "They're a couple of characters, for sure. But I think they're basically harmless. I mean, what's the worst that can happen?"

"Nothing too bad, I guess. I'm not getting serial killer vibes or anything like that."

"So you're saying yes then?"

"Well, we do need to move out from Jacqueline's real soon, don't you think?"

"Yeah," said Carl. "I think so. Klaus especially wants us to go."

"Yeah, he really does," agreed Jake. "I wanna leave before we wear out our welcome. I say we go for it, at least for the time being. We'll just have to make sure they respect our space. In the meantime, we just keep looking. You know, keep our ears open. But at least this'll give us some breathing space until we find what we're really looking for."

"And what is it that you're really looking for?" asked Ruben, who'd stolen up behind them.

"Whoa," said Jake, "What the fuck? You scared me, man. You always sneak up on people like that?"

"You scare pretty easy then, don't you, son?" said Ruben. "Nah, I just wanted to make sure you guys didn't slip away without at least saying goodbye. Now, seriously, what is it that you're really looking for?"

Carl and Jake exchanged an embarrassed look.

"Seriously?" said Carl. "I think we'd like to find a place just for ourselves."

"You guys wouldn't be queer by any chance?" asked Ruben. "Cuz I mean, I'm cool with that, if you are."

"We're not," said Jake emphatically. "It's not like that. We're just good friends. And we trust each other. Right, Carl?"

"Wait, you're not queer?" said Carl feigning surprise. "Not even a little?"

The two men laughed. Even Ruben joined in.

"So what you're saying then is you don't trust me and Mary Lou," said Ruben. "Isn't that what this is all about?"

"Ruben," said Jake, turning to face the man squarely. "No offense, but of course we don't trust you. Why the hell should we? We barely even know you."

For a moment, Ruben just stood there, his mustache quivering, his mottled red skin growing darker. Jake had trouble reading him. Was he about to throw a fit and attack them? Finally, though, Ruben's shoulders relaxed, and he let out a deep sigh.

"'Course you don't," he said, shaking his head. "Hell, I wouldn't trust us neither if I was you. But hey, it's not so much about trust, is it? None of us is probably gonna even be spending that much time here. We've all got stuff we wanna do. Me and Mary Lou got some ideas about setting up some business on the beach, and you guys would really be helping us out a lot if you'd at least spend a month or two here with us while you're figuring out your next step. So let's just be real clear about this. We would like you to stay as long as you can, even if it's only for a month. That'll at least give me some time to get my shit together and figure out what my next step is gonna be."

"Don't you mean our next step?" asked Jake. "You and Mary Lou?"

"Look, Mary Lou may not always act like it, but she is a grown woman," said Ruben. "She gets to do whatever it is she wants to do. I don't control her, and she sure as hell don't control me."

"She seems okay, though," said Jake. "She is, right?"

"You gotta realize something," said Ruben, his expression suddenly somber, "and I'm telling you this in confidence, cuz you guys deserve to know the truth. Especially if you're gonna be throwing in with us here. Ever heard of datura?"

"Datura? What's that?" asked Jake.

"You know, loco weed? It's a plant that grows wild around here. It's quite plentiful, in fact. Has a beautiful trumpet-shaped flower? I'm sure you've seen some by the side of the road. Mary Lou read some book about it and decided it was the answer to everything! She's very impressionable that way. She always wants to try something new. So she's been gathering it and making tea out of it."

"Jeezus," said Carl. "What's it like? I mean, what's it do to you?"

"Well, that's just it," said Ruben. "It can make you pretty crazy. It's not so much hallucinogenic, like acid, which can be really amazing, ya know, in a good way. It's more like something that makes you delirious, like you really can't tell the difference between fantasy and reality anymore. I mean, you can truly go out of your fucking mind on this shit. I tried it once just to see what it was like, and I would not recommend it. I'm worried, to be honest, that Mary Lou's losin' it, and there's really not a thing I can do about it. She's harmless, but you can't really expect normal behavior. That's all I'm sayin'. I just wanted to give you guys a heads-up about that."

"Is that what happened to her eye?" asked Jake on a hunch. "I mean, did the datura do that, or did she already have it?"

"Well, that's a pretty goddamned personal question, isn't it? From a guy, who, as I recall, doesn't like personal questions?" said Ruben.

"Hey," said Jake. "You opened the door to this conversation. And anyway, I'm not judging her. I'm just curious, that's all."

"You're pretty perceptive, though," admitted Ruben. "It's actually since she started with the tea that her one eye started getting weird like that. And it's freaked her out too. I think it's a good thing cuz it scared her into stopping. She hasn't had any tea now in at least a month, and I'm hoping she's done for good. She's got to be, or else we're just not gonna be …

Ruben looked suddenly shaky, and Carl reached out an arm to steady him. "It's okay, man," he said.

"No, it's actually not okay," said Ruben brushing Carl's hand aside. "When I first met Mary Lou, she was really messed up, man. She wasn't really on summer vacation like she told you guys. She'd gotten involved in some kind of a sex scandal back home with some local male prep school where she lived; a kind of a gang bang scenario from what I could gather. I guess it was a really bad scene there. She was losing it, let me tell you, bursting into tears for no reason at all, that kind of thing, ya know? She kind of latched on to me like a lost child, and I didn't really know what to do with her, to be honest."

"Maybe just love her?" said Jake.

"Huh? Well, yeah, of course. How could you not?"

"It doesn't hurt that she's beautiful," said Carl.

"Well, there is that," said Ruben chuckling. "That is some compensation, I suppose."

"Maybe she needs some help," said Jake. "You know, therapy?"

"Aw, we don't believe in that crap," said Ruben. "I've had to see my share of shrinks in my life, and they're mostly full of shit. She'll be all right. Just gotta keep her off the loco weed. That's all. You guys aren't into anything like that, are you?"

"Hell no," said Carl. "We just smoke."

"Good," said Ruben. "At least you won't encourage her then. If you decide to stay here, that is."

"Thanks for being honest with us, Ruben," said Jake. "We appreciate it. So what do you think, Carl?"

Carl stood scratching his beard while studying the finca. He didn't say anything for a while, and both Jake and Ruben were waiting for him to speak, knowing that somehow his word would carry the most weight.

"Well," said Carl at last. "You're sure she's harmless?"

"Mary Lou wouldn't hurt a fly," said Ruben. "I can vouch for that."

"How about you?" asked Jake, arching an eyebrow.

"Well now, a fly for sure. But you guys got nothin' to worry about. Not from me at any rate."

"Okay then," said Carl. "As long as Jake agrees. But we do reserve the right to leave at any time. Especially if Mary Lou flips out or something."

"Cool," said Ruben. "That's great! Oh, there is one more thing, though."

"What's that?" asked Jake.

"I gotta have six months cash up-front from you guys. Plus a deposit fee."

"What?" said Jake.

"Hah, got you there, pal, didn't I? You should see the look on your face! Both your faces! C'mon, let's shake on it!"

Jake reluctantly stretched out his hand.

"And you too, Carl. C'mon, let's get this done!"

"Yeehaw," said Ruben gripping Carl's hand. "We're in business, amigos. Let's go back inside and celebrate some more just to seal the deal. I'm sure Mary Lou's already got another joint rolled and waiting."

Chapter 29

That evening Jake dropped Carl off at Jacqueline and Klaus's and headed over to see Cannelle. He and Carl had agreed to move up to Ruben and Mary Lou's finca in Santa Inés in the next few days, and Jake wanted to share the news with his new lover. He looked forward to seeing her again but had reservations about deepening their relationship. There were just too many mismatches to deal with— her age, her marriage to a man in prison, and her commitment to her kids, to name a few. Their lovemaking was intense and satisfying but without any sense of commitment, at least as far as Jake was concerned. His hope was for an uncomplicated relationship, but he felt a vague sense of unease about the whole situation given Cannelle's mercurial nature.

When he arrived at her finca, he noticed a red 2CV with French license plates parked near the house. The kids were playing outdoors and came running as soon as Jake stepped out of his car.

"Jake!" cried the boys, pummeling his thighs.

"Hey, you guys," said Jake trying to fend them off. "Who's the visitor?"

"Wouldn't you like to know!" said Atif in an aggressive tone.

"Well, yes, as a matter of fact, I would," said Jake.

"Why?" asked Johnnie.

"Well, I don't know," said Jake, beginning to feel exasperated, "C'mon, just tell me."

"Nobody you should meet," said the older boy clinging to Jake's leg.

"Really?" said Jake. "Why's that, Atif?"

"Cuz she's prettier than Mom!" said Johnnie with conviction.

"Yeah. A lot prettier!" agreed Atif.

"Well, that's okay," said Jake. "What's that got to do with anything?"

"We don't want you to like her," said Johnnie.

"Yeah," said Atif. "We want you to like Mom!"

"But I do like your mom," said Jake. "You guys know that. Now let's go on in and see who this pretty woman is, shall we?"

Just then, the kitchen door swung open, and two women stepped outside. The first was Cannelle, whose smile broadened considerably when she caught sight of Jake, and the second was a woman Jake had never seen before. It was getting late, and he couldn't quite make out her features in the encroaching dusk.

"*Salut*," he said as he approached.

"*Salut*," they responded.

After hugging Cannelle, he turned to her friend. "*Je suis* Jake," he said, stretching out his hand.

"She knows," said Cannelle switching back to English. "I've already told her about you. Jake, allow me to introduce my friend Mireille."

"*Enchanté*," said Mireille grasping Jake's hand. "I've heard a lot about you, Jake."

"Really?" said Jake, genuinely surprised. "I didn't realize there was that much to hear!"

"*Arrêt!*" said Cannelle. "Stop trying to be so humble. You are on quite an adventure, after all."

Jake found the expression on Cannelle's face, which he gauged as a mixture of lust and possessiveness, to be unsettling, especially in view of the sharp surge of involuntary desire he felt upon getting his first good look at Mireille. She was, without a doubt, an extraordinarily beautiful woman. Her shoulder-length dark blonde hair was thick and flowing around a perfectly heart-shaped face with a smooth uncreased forehead, thin arched eyebrows, chocolate-drop eyes, and sensuous ruby lips. Her chin had a slight cleft in it, and her skin was tanned and flawless. He was reminded of Catherine Deneuve but with a fuller, more voluptuous body. Her breasts, which were prominent, were partially visible beneath a gauzy green Moroccan top, and she wore sheer fluffy lime-colored pants like something out of *A Thousand and One Nights*.

She smiled at Jake revealing even white teeth. "I understand you speak French," she said in a mellifluous voice. "Not bad for an *Amerloque!*"

Jake took her usage of the derogatory term as a sign of playfulness and responded in kind.

"And your English is very good. Not bad for a *Française*. After all, many of your countrymen seem to not want to speak any language other than their own."

"Our countrymen seem to have that in common," she countered.

"Then you and I are exceptions to that rule, and that's a good thing," said Jake, suddenly conscious of the flirtatious tone the conversation had taken. "Look," he said, changing tack, "I don't mean to sound like a pompous ass. Let's just speak English as I know you both speak it better than I speak French … *d'accord?*"

"Sure," said Mireille. "My ex-husband is American, and that's the one thing he gave me that I didn't end up having to give back in the divorce. He was at least a very good teacher. I'll grant him that."

Her admission about the divorce was surprisingly welcome news to Jake, although he felt the need to hide any reaction, especially with Cannelle standing right there in front of him. He didn't feel she had any real claim on him, but she had confessed to him once that she got very jealous, and when he glanced her way again, her face held an inscrutably tense expression.

"How about a beer?" asked Cannelle making an effort to be sociable. "Out here in the courtyard?"

"*Ah oui!*" said Mireille. "I love to watch the changes in the sky when the sun is going down."

Cannelle turned and headed for the kitchen, leaving Jake alone with Mireille. Sitting beside each other in old, tattered, yellow beach chairs, Jake was imagining the sensation of an electric current running between them. He turned his head to look at her, but she met his gaze only for an instant, quickly turning her head back toward the sunset where the last light of the day was streaming blood-red from the horizon, bathing their faces in its dying light. *She must know how insanely gorgeous she is,* thought Jake, as a feeling of weakness in the face of her seductive beauty washed over him. This attraction, he realized, was something beyond his control, probably hardwired into his being. It was a peculiar injustice of nature, he mused, which granted this kind of physical perfection with its attendant power to only a very few.

"Sorry they're not cold," said Cannelle returning from the kitchen with the beers. "We'll just have to pretend we're Brits and enjoy them warm."

She sat down on the other side of Mireille, and the three of them clinked their bottles together.

"Here's to this incredible sunset," said Jake.

"Yes," said Mireille, "and to another beautiful fucking day in paradise."

"I'll drink to that," said Cannelle.

Mireille's comment felt ill-suited to Jake, who at that moment couldn't relate to its cynical thrust. "You know," he said, "I'm not even sure what that phrase means anymore. I think I'd rather drink to friends. No paradise could exist without them."

Mireille smiled and raised her bottle again. "Okay," she said. "Why not? I'll drink to that too. Here's to good friends!"

Cannelle raised her beer again also, this time saying nothing. Jake noticed she kept her lips together now when she smiled, so no missing teeth were visible.

"Jake makes a good point," said Cannelle looking out at the darkening horizon. "What does paradise even mean? People always speak about Ibiza like it's some kind of paradise, but it's not really. Sure it's beautiful and different from most places you can live, but you still have to face the same problems that you would have to face anywhere else; like how to make a living, how to feed your kids, how not to be lonely …"

This last was said without turning her head, but Jake felt sure it was directed at him.

"And it's not like all the people you meet here are so wonderful either," she continued. "There are a lot of *salauds* here. People who are not so nice. People who come here hoping to live this wonderful free hippy lifestyle but don't have the skill or the talent or the money to manage it. Some of them are real devils, too, I tell you. Trust me. I see them all the time at the hippy market in Es Canar. Many are foreigners. They pretend to want to help you but will steal from you the first chance they get. It is sad but true. There are drug addicts too. There's so much cocaine around here now, I can hardly believe it. You guys don't know Ibiza the way that I do. If you want to stay here, don't trust anyone until they have proven themselves to you. Otherwise, they may try to screw you in the end."

Jake had learned to expect the unexpected from Cannelle, but the timing of her diatribe annoyed him. *Why does she have to ruin this sunset with such a negative speech?* he wondered. Mireille had lit a cigarette and slowly blew out smoke while nodding her head in agreement.

"Thanks for the good advice, Cannelle," she said, undaunted by her cynicism. "You know this is one reason I value your friendship so much. You tell it like it is, and I believe you. It's why I want to fix up my place and stay at home as much as possible. I just want to lick my wounds and figure out what I will do next after the divorce. It's why I came here."

"I see," said Jake, "another lost woman."

"What?" asked Mireille.

"I said another lost woman. But please don't take offense. I mean it in the best possible way."

"I'm sorry," said Mireille beginning to bristle. "How can calling someone 'lost' possibly have any good meaning?"

"I didn't mean to insult you," said Jake. "As it turns out, 'lost' women, in the sense I'm describing, happen to be the kind I'm most attracted to. Maybe because I'm pretty lost myself."

"Are you saying I'm lost then?" asked Cannelle. "After all, you are attracted to me. We're fucking, by the way," she announced, turning to look at Mireille, who said nothing but lifted the beer to her lips and sipped.

"It's something that I think about every day," said Jake, determined not to let Cannelle's taunting distract him. "Why some people seem to know from a very young age what it is they want to do in life, whether it's becoming a doctor or an astronaut or whatever, while other people, myself included, seem unable or unwilling to make any kind of definitive commitment to the course their life should follow."

"I think that's pretty common," said Mireille. "Especially here on Ibiza."

"So you're not insulted then?" asked Jake sneaking another glance at her, "at being called a lost woman?"

"Well, that depends. You still haven't explained to me what the good, 'non-insulting' side is. I'm waiting to hear that."

"Well, we may have to redefine here what being lost really means," said Jake.

"Uh, uh, uh," said Mireille. "Now you are just trying to wiggle out of this. You can't do that, *mon ami*. It's too late for that!"

"Oh, but I can do whatever I want," insisted Jake. "It's one of the prerogatives of being lost. Whatever step you take in whatever direction, if it turns out to be misguided, can always be excused by the fact that you're lost. But that would be too convenient, and it's not what I'm really trying to say."

"Well, then," said Mireille, "what are you trying to say? C'mon, Jake, say it! We really want to know, don't we, Cannelle?"

"I suppose," said Cannelle in an indifferent tone. "Really, what the hell are you trying to say, Jake?"

"Okay, what I'm trying to say is that the negativity associated with the concept of being lost is rooted in the idea that you must hang on to a kind of false certainty that's been drilled into you for most of your life. From the time you're very young, you're just supposed to accept the direction for your life which other people have decided for you."

"Ooh, la la," said Mireille. "Now you're giving me a headache! What kind of crap is this? Are you trying on purpose to confuse us? Just make it simple. Can you please do that, *mon cher?*"

"You might want to just shut up for a moment then and listen," snapped Jake.

"Hey, you can't tell me to shut up!"

"I didn't mean it that way," said Jake, instantly regretting his comment. "Just let me explain without any interruption, please. I'm trying to think this through."

"Think this through? You mean you're just coming up with this now?"

"I think so," said Jake. "You must be inspiring me."

"Well," said Mireille, a glint of humor returning to her eyes, "that's good, I suppose. Go ahead then, *s'il te plaît*. Continue Jake."

Suddenly standing, Cannelle looked down at the two of them with a wry expression. "I'll be right back," she said. "But keep going, Jake. Maybe by the time I come back, you'll have it all sorted out."

Alone again with Mireille, Jake tried to gauge the tension between them. He seemed to have struck a nerve, and he knew that whatever he might say next would prove crucial in determining the course of their relationship going forward.

"I think what I'm trying to say," he continued in a more amenable tone, "is that the negativity associated with the idea of being lost is rooted in the notion that someone who is lost is necessarily suffering, right?"

"Okay," said Mireille.

"Okay?"

"I mean, yes, I follow you."

"Good," said Jake. "Then conversely, if you're no longer lost, then that must mean the end of suffering. You follow?"

"So far," she said.

"But as someone who is admittedly lost, I am here to tell you that I'm not suffering."

"No," she said, giggling in spite of herself. "I haven't known you very long, Jake, but I don't have that impression."

"Well," he continued, "maybe it's because I'm simply exercising my freedom to be lost. And discovering as much as I can about life in the process. Does that make any sense?"

"Being lost as an expression of freedom?" said Mireille. "Hmmm. Now there's an original thought. Or at least one I haven't heard before. But I think I can see where you're coming from. I've never thought about being lost as something positive before, to be honest. But exercising a kind of freedom? Why not? That certainly does put it in a more positive light. But are those just words, Jake? Or does it really make sense?"

"Well, it makes sense to me," said Jake. "I'm the living proof, in my own mind anyway. But you'll have to decide for yourself."

"I'm not sure," she said. "I'll have to think about it."

"Anyway, does it take some of the sting out of what I said before about you being a lost woman?" he asked.

"You mean, do I forgive you for saying that?" she asked.

"Could you?" he asked in an obsequious tone.

"You're not going to beg me now, are you?" she asked with a faux horrified expression.

"If that's what it takes," said Jake half-jokingly.

"You know that's not very attractive in a man," she said, teasing him. "I prefer a more assertive type."

"Well then, I'm assertively begging you to forgive me for saying you were lost," quipped Jake. "Which I've hopefully convinced you to reconsider the meaning of."

"Like I said," she continued, giving him a noncommittal glance, "I'll have to think about it."

It was clear to Jake now that she understood the power she held over men. How could she not? This insight did nothing, though, to prevent his heart from pounding a little bit faster in his chest as he found himself clinging to the hope that this discussion may have somehow created an opening between them.

"Well," he said, sighing, "at least you're thinking about it. That gives me hope."

"Hope for what?" asked Cannelle, suddenly re-emerging from the darkness with a newly rolled joint she held up for inspection.

"Hope for all lost people everywhere," said Jake.

"Ooh, la la," said Cannelle, lighting the joint. "Are we still talking about being lost?"

Chapter 30

The three of them sat in silence for a while, getting more stoned and enjoying the harmonious sounds of nocturnal insects coming alive in the dusk. "You know why I came here to Ibiza?" asked Jake after a while, staring at the still glowing spot where the sun had been.

"Because you were lost?" asked Mireille in a mocking tone.

"The first time I came to Europe," he continued, ignoring the jibe, "I was on a student exchange program in Austria. I couldn't believe my luck. I was nineteen years old and finally able to get away from where I'd grown up in upstate New York. One day I was riding on the streetcar in Graz, the town where I was studying, practicing my German vocabulary by reading the ads inside the car, and I saw this one from some life insurance company. It said quite literally, "Work until you're 65. And then enjoy life!" I was flabbergasted. That struck me as one of the most grotesque ideas I'd ever heard of. The presumption of the phrase really rattled me. Put your nose to the grindstone whether you want to or not until you're old and tired, and then, at last, allow yourself the freedom not to do it anymore at a point in your life if you're even still alive when you probably don't have the energy or the imagination to do anything else. I found that concept absolutely appalling. My whole being rose up against the idea, and I resolved to never be that person."

"And that's why you're here on Ibiza?" asked Mireille sounding puzzled.

"In a sense, yes," said Jake. "It helps explain why I'm not sitting in an office somewhere or punching a time card every day waiting to expire."

"Makes sense to me," said Cannelle. "It's why I had to leave France. I was married, had a daughter, and a steady boring job in an office. My whole life was planned out for me. Every day was on a tight schedule that could never be deviated from. I found myself hating my life. It was all very secure, but I felt totally suffocated by it."

"My point exactly!" said Jake. "That's what so-called security does, or should I say, the illusion of security? Because you never really know what's going to happen to you in life, do you? How can you? All your plans could just crumble to dust in an instant. And then what do you do?"

"Then you're lost!" said Mireille.

"Exactly," said Jake. "Unless you have real security. And that can only exist within yourself."

"Is this really you talking, Jake? Or is it Krishnamurti?" asked Cannelle, recalling recent discussions they'd had about the philosopher.

"Well, in a sense, it is him," he admitted. "What I learned from him, which resonated so deeply, was that you have to have a sense of being grounded inside yourself, no matter what circumstance you are in, in order to be happy. And if that sense is there, then your outer circumstances don't matter nearly as much."

"Well, I can relate," said Mireille, taking another drag on the joint. "All of my outer security has just gone to shit!"

"I'm sure you can," said Jake, reaching out to squeeze her hand briefly. She allowed it to stay there, which both surprised and encouraged him.

"But tell me," said Mireille, finally sliding her hand out from under his. "How is one supposed to achieve that sense of being grounded within? Did anyone tell you how to do that?"

"Well, J. K. would say through meditation."

"So you are a meditator then?"

"Not so much," he confessed. "I mean, occasionally I do, but I'm generally too undisciplined to just sit and meditate. But meditation is really nothing more than becoming aware of your own thoughts, whether or not you're sitting in formal meditation. J. K. points out that when we become aware of our own conditioning, we can be free because we understand which thoughts are really our own and which ones come from somewhere else—be it teachers, priests, parents, or whoever. If we can let go of those thoughts that aren't genuinely our own, which may be driving our behavior, then we're free to just be ourselves. Or at least discover who we really are. Does that make any sense?"

"I think I get what you mean," said Cannelle rejoining the conversation. "But do you think it's really that easy? Our conditioning goes very deep, don't you think? Most of the time, we probably don't even realize it's there."

"Agreed," said Jake. "Probably the only time we can be sure we're not the product of conditioning is when we have no thoughts at all."

"That sounds like . . . how do you say . . . a pretty tall order," quipped Mireille.

"Indeed," said Jake. "It's kind of embarrassing to talk about because it can sound like such dribble. And yet here I am, going on and on about it. Forgive me, please. I wouldn't blame you for thinking I'm completely full of shit."

"There is nothing to forgive," said Mireille, her dimpled face lighting up in a smile. "I think I know what you mean. Orange Tom calls it No-Mind."

"Orange Tom?" asked Jake. "Who's that?"

"You should come to Orange Tom's finca sometime and find out," said Cannelle. "He's a neighbor. Not too far from here. Haven't you seen the people wearing orange clothes with the wooden beads around their necks?"

"Hmmm, not really," said Jake. "Not yet."

"Oh, you will," said Cannelle. "They have an Indian guru named Bhagwan. You've heard of him, right? The guy who talks about sex all the time?"

"He does?" asked Jake.

"He says you have to get rid of sexual repression in order to reach enlightenment or something like that," said Cannelle.

"How come I never heard of this guy?" said Jake. "Sounds pretty interesting."

"Well, you'll see plenty of his followers around. Especially if you come to the hippy market. They're all over the place there."

"Oh, do take me, won't you, Cannelle?" said Mireille. "Please? The next time you go … Thursday, is it?"

"Me too!" said Jake. "I want to see what you do there. You've told me so much about it. And maybe meet some of these Bhagwan people too. They do sound intriguing. I might get some ideas about how to make money here too, which would be great!"

"*D'accord!*" said Cannelle. "Agreed. Just meet me here, both of you, early Thursday morning. You can help me load up my little truck and then follow behind me. It'll be fun to have some company. We'll bring some food and some wine and make a party of it. And Jake, you can help me watch the kids!"

Just then, Isabelle appeared at the door to the finca wearing a white knee-length nightgown. "Boys," she yelled. "Come inside now. It's time for bed!"

"*Merci*, Isabelle," said Cannelle turning to look at her daughter and smiling unselfconsciously again. "Johnnie! Atif!" she yelled into the darkness. "You heard your sister. You guys get into the house immediately! Or else you know what!"

There was giggling in the dark followed by the patter of running feet, and Cannelle's two sons suddenly burst into the courtyard, huffing and puffing. "Did you see us, Mom?" asked Johnnie as they pulled up in front of the chairs.

"Yeah, Mom, did you?" asked Atif.

"No, I didn't see you. Was I supposed to?"

"NO!" chimed in both boys at once.

"We were hiding," said Johnnie, grinning with excitement.

"See, it worked!" said Atif, still panting.

"Well, it sure did," said Cannelle pulling both her sons into her chest. "Now give me a kiss, and then go inside and let Isabelle put you to bed, okay?"

The boys dutifully kissed their mother, then glanced at both Jake and Mireille, simultaneously sticking their tongues out before racing inside the house, where further giggling and yelling ensued.

"Those boys," said Mireille. "I love them."

"Me too," said Cannelle.

"Do you have any kids, Mireille?" asked Jake.

"No, not yet," she said. "And to be honest, I'm not so sure that's really on my list of things to do."

"Don't do it," said Cannelle.

"What?" said Jake. "Really, Cannelle? I'm surprised to hear that advice from you."

"I love my kids," she said. "And I would die for them. But it's so hard sometimes. You really can't imagine."

Both Mireille and Jake sat in silence for a moment, considering her pronouncement. "You're right," said Jake at last. "I can't imagine. How could I? But I find your commitment to them to be pretty impressive. You're clearly a very good mom."

"Thanks," she said, "but do I really have a choice? You can't have kids and then just abandon them, can you? Would you do that?"

"No," said Mireille adamantly. "I would never do that. But I might try not to have them in the first place."

"You mean no sex?" asked Jake.

"I didn't say that," said Mireille giving him a sultry smile, the force of which hit Jake like a sledgehammer.

"Well, that's good to hear," he said.

"What's that?" asked Cannelle. "What's good to hear?"

"That Mireille hasn't given up on sex…yet?" said Jake.

"Why? Do you think you have a chance with her?" asked Cannelle.

"Hello," said Mireille. "I'm sitting right here!"

Jake lapsed into silence, rattled by Cannelle's bluntness.

"I'll take that as a yes then," said Cannelle rising abruptly from her chair and slipping into the shadows.

"Jeesh," said Jake. "That was … awkward."

"Yes, it was," said Mireille, who suddenly appeared confused about what to do with her hands. "You know, Jake, I just met you, and I like you, but Cannelle is a very good friend of mine."

"Understood," said Jake.

"Well, aren't you two … I don't know … um …?"

"We are having sex, yes. Well, twice, to be exact. I like her a lot too. But I wouldn't call her my girlfriend if that's what you mean. It's not like that between us."

"I see," said Mireille, fumbling in her bag for a cigarette. She passed one to Jake, who normally didn't smoke but was reluctant to refuse her offering. They sat smoking in silence for a while until Cannelle reappeared and sat down again, presenting them with yet another joint.

"*Voilà*," said Cannelle. "Just what the moment calls for, I believe. Now, what would Krishnamurti say about this, I wonder?"

"You mean about the joint?" asked Jake.

"Well, yes, let's begin with that."

"He'd say, 'Don't do it.'"

"And why is that?"

"Well, because he doesn't think that one should alter one's consciousness in an unnatural way," said Jake.

"Unnatural? Would you call this unnatural, Mireille?"

"*Moi? Non, pas du tout!*" said Mireille. "Not at all. This is completely natural. It comes from an herb, after all. And herbs are from nature, are they not?"

"*Bon*," said Cannelle. "Then Mireille and I will just have to share it between us."

"But what about me?" asked Jake.

"I don't know," said Cannelle looking peeved. "What about you? First, you are getting stoned with us, and then you are telling us that it's bad to smoke a joint. Which is it, Jake?"

"I said that Krishnamurti presumably would say that it's bad."

"Well," said Cannelle, "don't you always agree with him?"

"Not necessarily," said Jake.

"*Merde*," said Cannelle angrily. "When have you ever not agreed with him? Sometimes I think you are full of shit, Jake."

"I probably am," admitted Jake. "But if you share it with me, I promise to at least tell you an interesting story."

"Oh ho, so that's how it is," said Mireille puckering her lips in a disapproving pout. "You're basically trying to bargain with us in order to get some 'unnatural' product into your body. How does that sound to you, Cannelle?"

"I can deal with bargaining," said Cannelle. "I do it all the time. How else can you survive in this world? But how do we know that your story will really be that interesting? Shall we just take your word for it?   And what happens if we decide it's not? What will be the punishment then?"

"Punishment?" said Jake, "Do you really want to punish me, Cannelle?"

"We'll see," she said, glaring at him with her best *"don't fuck with me"* expression.

"It sounds to me," interrupted Mireille, "that Jake is worried that his story is not really going to be so interesting. Don't you think so, Cannelle?"

"Bah oui, bien sûr," said Cannelle exhaling smoke. "I think you may be right. And he doesn't like the idea of being punished either. You can see that it's freaking him out!"

Suddenly both women were laughing. "Don't freak out, Jake, please?" implored Mireille, handing him the joint. "We wouldn't want that!"

"Who's freaking out?" he protested, grinning.

"Okay, we're just teasing you," said Cannelle. "Now, please, let's hear your story. It must be pretty good, or you wouldn't be taking such a big risk to tell it."

"Brace yourselves," said Jake, "because again, it's about Krishnamurti."

"Ooh la la, big surprise," said Mireille.

"Do we really want to hear this?" asked Cannelle.

"But this time, it's a different Krishnamurti," continued Jake. "I promise it's not what you think. While I was in Saanen, I found out there's another Indian guy, U. G. Krishnamurti, who likes to go to Switzerland every summer as well, the same time that J. K. is there, giving talks."

"So they both have the same last name?" asked Cannelle.

"Yes, they do, and they're both Indian, and they're both philosophers. How do you like that?"

The two women exchanged amused glances.

"Go on then," said Cannelle.

"Wait. Why does this U. G. guy follow the other guy around?" asked Mireille.

"Because he's not as famous, I suppose, and it gives him a ready-made audience," said Jake. "J. K.'s written lots of books. He even has his own school in England. There's this whole big organization built up around him. When he comes to Saanen every summer, it's a really big deal, and there are hundreds if not thousands of people waiting there to see him and hear him speak. But poor U. G. has nothing. He lives by his wits. And he was shrewd enough to figure out that when J. K.'s followers would hear there's this other Krishnamurti staying nearby in Gstaad, who's giving talks there on days when J. K. isn't speaking, at least some of them would be curious enough to want to go and hear him. And, of course, he was right. I was no different from the rest. So naturally, I had to go!"

"Well, that's no surprise," said Mireille holding out the joint for Jake. "You are a Krishnamurti freak, after all!"

"I guess I am," said Jake shrugging as he carefully plucked the joint from her fingers. Inhaling deeply, he leaned back and stared into the cloudless night with its emerging stars overhead. The cooler evening air filled with the aromatic scent of night-blooming primrose helped create an even more relaxed and communicative ambience. "So anyway," he continued, "I hiked to Gstaad together with a friend who knew where U. G.'s chalet was, and we sat on this very nicely manicured lawn and waited for the great man to emerge. It got pretty crowded after a while. I'd say thirty or forty people were there, and everyone was anxious to hear what this so-called guru had to say. He finally did come out, accompanied by an older Dutch woman. I think it must've been her chalet he was staying at."

"What did he look like? This U. G.," asked Mireille.

"Quite nondescript looking, actually. South Asian but with intensely dark brooding eyes. He sat down in an ordinary lawn chair looking out at us, and if I had to describe his expression, I'd have to say he looked extremely bored."

"What an odd guru!" said Mireille.

"Yes," said Jake, "very. But I think that's part of his allure. He just sat there in silence, observing us for quite some time, although his gaze sometimes shifted to the sky or to a tree or anywhere but the audience, and people were starting to get fidgety. I was actually getting ready to leave myself when he finally spoke up. 'Why are you all here?' he demanded. Someone from the audience yelled out, 'To hear your wisdom!'

'Wisdom?' he said, chortling, 'I'm afraid you've come to the wrong place then. There is no difference between the sounds coming out of my mouth and the barking of a dog.' He then repeated himself to make sure that what he said had sunk in. The implication, of course, was that the same was true of anything we had to say as well. There were a few titters of laughter and a rather uncomfortable silence, but from that point on, it evolved into a question-and-answer session. All the questions had to do with spirituality: 'What is the meaning of life?' 'Why should we meditate?' 'How can we access our higher Self?' 'Is there such a thing as an after-life?' You know, all the usual impossible-to-answer questions."

"Well, and how did he answer them?" asked Cannelle.

"Yeah, come on, Jake," said Mireille with an impish grin, "the suspense is killing us!"

"Well, his answer to all of them, in a nutshell, was 'Why are you wasting your time?'"

"What did you think about him, though?" asked Mireille. "Did you like him?"

"Hmmm," said Jake. "Hard to say. Did I like him? To me, he was a completely nihilistic character who'd utterly given up hope of finding any answer to the mystery of existence. What was fascinating, though, was that he had nonetheless managed to attain this aura of being a guru. I wouldn't say I liked him because what was there to like? His aloneness seemed impenetrable, and there was a kind of smugness about his 'attainment' which created an unbridgeable distance between him and the audience. On the other hand, he'd won my grudging respect by being what I felt was consistently honest. Here was a person who was basically saying, 'Look, I've been to see all the gurus myself, and I've looked long and hard at these questions you're asking, and there basically are no valid answers. Furthermore, you're a fool if you think there are or if you think someone other than yourself could aid you in investigating these matters.' I found myself admiring his tenacity and conviction about the lack of any meaning in life, or at least the lack of any foolproof way to discover it, and felt he came from a place of hard-fought integrity, the likes of which I'd never encountered before. After all, people were constantly questioning his conclusions, and he never backed down. Anyway, he offered a quite unexpected counterbalance to J.

Krishnamurti, who discussed things like freedom and love and awareness, all of which U. G. would have scoffed at as delusions."

"So which did you prefer?" asked Cannelle. "Never mind. I think I already know the answer."

"Well, you're right if you think that my preference was for J. K., probably because of my optimistic nature. Still, I couldn't help but appreciate the cynicism U. G. brought to the table, largely because I'd met so many people on so-called 'spiritual paths' in Saanen and elsewhere who seemed eager to embrace any kind of nonsense whatsoever, without the least kind of critical judgment. To my mind, he was a kind of flashing warning light reminding us not to be a sucker when it came to spirituality, and I just found it so remarkable that these two diametrically opposed men with the same cultural origin and even the same last name should show up together at the same remote Swiss locale."

"It is pretty remarkable when you think about it," said Mireille.

"Are you saying Jake's story is good?" asked Cannelle.

"Well, it's certainly not bad," said Mireille. "Probably good enough to avoid punishment. At least for now. What about you, Cannelle? What do you think?"

"Good enough for another joint, I'd say. I'll be right back."

As soon as she'd left, Jake turned again toward Mireille. "Now, what are you looking at?" she asked, smirking slightly.

"You," he said, abandoning any attempt at subtlety. "I can't help it. You are just so beautiful, you know."

"Yes, I know. And do you know how I know? It's because men like you are always telling me that."

"I wonder what that must be like for you?"

"It is flattering," she admitted. "But I think it also triggers a kind of insecurity, to be honest. Like what if it's not really true? Because trust me, there are times when I don't think it's true at all. So what if you're just saying that because you want something from me?"

"*D'accord*," said Jake. "Okay, I get it. I won't say it again. I promise."

"For some reason, though," she continued, "I feel like you are someone who really means it. But it doesn't always make life easier, you know."

"I can imagine," said Jake.

"Can you?" she asked. "Well, maybe you can. I don't know. It's something I hate talking about because no one believes me anyway."

"I believe you," he said. "Really, I do. But for the moment, I'm just enjoying the admittedly selfish pleasure of observing your beauty, and I make no apologies for that. But I'll look away now. I don't want to make you uncomfortable."

"Thank you," she said. "I appreciate that."

Sitting together in silence, observing the starlit sky, they were finally at ease with each other by the time Cannelle returned. While they were sharing the latest joint, Jake told them both of his and Carl's decision to move in with Ruben and Mary Lou in Santa Inés.

"I think that's great," said Cannelle when he'd finished. "That's not so far away. We'll still get to see you, and you'll have your own place. And if those guys give you any trouble, you just let me know. Nobody gets to mess with my friends."

"Ooh, la la," said Mireille. "Did you hear that, Jake? She's not kidding. It's a good thing to have Cannelle on your side. That is for sure."

No doubt, thought Jake. *But what about the opposite,* he wondered. *What if you were to somehow become her foe?* He winced inwardly at the thought, knowing now with certainty that sooner or later, Mireille would prove to be an insurmountable challenge to his friendship with Cannelle.

Chapter 31

The truth was Jake could not get Mireille off his mind. She had given Jake directions to her finca, and he boldly took this as an invitation to drop by and see her a few days after meeting her at Cannelle's. Of course, there was no way to forewarn anyone that you were coming for a visit. No one had a phone. You just showed up somewhere, and if you were lucky, the person you hoped to visit was home and in a welcoming mood. If not, you apologized for the intrusion and left, or else you scribbled a note, slipped it under the door, and hoped for better luck next time.

The Simca had by now lost its muffler, a victim of the severely rutted and rocky dirt roads on the island. Jake had taken to calling it "the Tank," and the roar of its motor could be heard far in advance of his arrival. As he parked his car on the road below her house, he felt certain Mireille must know he was there. He'd felt no small amount of anxiety about visiting this woman whose beauty had captivated him from the moment they'd first met. He was anticipating some awkwardness with her, perhaps even outright rejection, especially in view of her closeness with Cannelle, but he was being driven by an instinct that was too strong to deny. His only agenda was to obey the powerful yearning he felt to try and connect with her in some way, without being able to predict what form this impromptu encounter might take. He could have waited for another chance meeting at Cannelle's or somewhere else on the island, but the pull of desire was already too strong, demanding an immediate response.

Mireille's finca, a rectangular building with sand-colored stone walls, blended seamlessly into the landscape. A fig tree in front of the house held plump purple fruit looking juicy but neglected, causing Jake's mouth to water as he strode up the path to her house. Before knocking, he reached out and plucked one of the ripe fruit and bit into it, marveling at the exotic burst of flavor on his tongue. It was a pointed reminder that he had indeed traveled very far from upstate New York, where apples, pears, berries, and watermelons were pretty much the extent of fresh fruit he'd been acquainted with. He was still savoring the pink and white seedy flesh of the fig when the arched wooden door swung open, and Mireille stood before him. Her red and white flowered dress reaching midway down her thighs with thin straps at the shoulders and a plunging neckline nearly took Jake's breath away. Her dark eyes were twinkling, and she looked genuinely pleased to see him.

"*Salut*, Mireille," he said, looking intently into her eyes.

She held his gaze in silence for a long moment before stretching her right arm toward him, her fingers closed in a fist.

"*Tu en veux?*" she asked, opening her hand, palm up. "You want?"

Jake looked down and had an instant flash of recognition. He'd seen this back in college. Nestled in her palm was a small orange pill.

"Orange Sunshine?" he asked, raising his eyes to meet her luminous gaze.

She nodded. Jake could see from the intense energy she was exuding that she was probably already coming on to it. The realization that he'd unknowingly interrupted an acid trip sent a shudder of excitement through his body. He'd taken LSD before and knew that there was no comparable experience. It took you on an unparalleled, unpredictable adventure from which there was no turning back. Once ingested, there was no other choice but to surrender to the experience. Any effort to resist what was happening was futile and could even trigger a "bad" trip. On the other hand, remaining open to the experience and being a willing passenger on the journey could also be mind-altering, ecstatic, and even life-changing. Insights into deeper levels of reality, normally beyond reach, would suddenly appear obvious and accessible. Bullshit perceptions about life that you might have allowed yourself to believe were real would dissolve and cease to be a limitation. It was a kind of truth serum, and as long as you embraced the revelations, there was nothing to fear.

He was suddenly overwhelmed by an immense sense of gratitude, cognizant of the fact that Mireille did not have to open her door to him at all. She could have stood behind it and waited until he went away if she hadn't wanted to see him. Jake understood that the opportunity to share an experience like this was not something you offered to just anyone. It had to be someone you felt a basic sense of trust with— someone you felt would be a worthy fellow traveler into whatever unfamiliar dimensions the drug might lead you into. Whatever he might have imagined that this meeting between them would be, this turn of events far exceeded his expectations. She was inviting him to be her co-traveler on what might end up being the wildest, most unforeseeable ride imaginable. After a brief moment of hesitation, he reached out, picked the pill off her palm, and placed it on his tongue.

"*Voilà,*" he said.

"Cool," she said, her eyes twinkling as she invited him in and closed the door behind them. Once inside, they momentarily stood across from one another, regarding each other with curiosity. A hug would ordinarily have been in order, but the space between them suddenly seemed too highly charged for any kind of physical contact.

"I thought I was going to be alone today, but … you …" she said, smiling sweetly.

"Yes," said Jake, unsure of how to respond. "Me. Did you want to be alone, though?"

"I expected to be, yes. But anything can change at any time. You showing up like this … I mean, I could hear your car from far away— seemed like a kind of sign to me. So I just decided to let you in."

"You could just as easily have seen it as a sign to lock your door!"

"I could have, yes. But I didn't. I'm not sure why, really. Anyway, signs don't always announce to you what kind they are. I guess we'll find out, though."

"Yes," said Jake. "For sure … I …"

"You what?" asked Mireille, still smiling.

"Honestly, I don't know what to say, Mireille. I'm just happy… so happy to be here with you. That's the truth."

"I'm glad," she said. "Really, I am! Can I offer you something to drink? Some tea, perhaps?"

"Sure," said Jake. "Tea would be excellent."

"What kind?"

"Whatever you're having would be fine."

He looked around the large room they were in, trying to get his bearings. It seemed comfortable enough. A window was carved out of the thick stone wall in the back. Sunlight streamed through onto a counter with a built-in metal sink and a propane gas stove next to a tiny fridge. A worn-looking, waist-high pine table with two plain wooden chairs stood in front of that. A few feet away, an old couch with faded green fabric faced the door, creating a kind of living area. The stone floor in front of the couch was covered by a knotted beige throw rug, and watercolor paintings depicting Ibicencan landscapes lined the walls. It was simple and homey and had a cozy feel about it. A half open door on the side of the kitchen led to a room with a low bed covered in bright yellow fabric, and next to that was another room with a closed wooden door.

"What's in there?" asked Jake, pointing to the closed door.

Mireille hesitated for a moment. "That's my sister's room," she said.

"Oh," said Jake, taken aback. "I didn't even know you had a sister."

"*Ah, oui* … Julienne," said Mireille almost wistfully as she busied herself with the tea. "She's a few years older than me but still quite beautiful."

Still, thought Jake. *Why still?* It seemed an odd thing to say.

"I believe it," said Jake. "How could she not be? She is your sister, after all."

Mireille smiled at the compliment, giving Jake a meaningful look as she approached with two mugs of steaming hot tea. She nodded toward the couch, and Jake took one of the mugs from her and sat down, leaning back against the cushion. Mireille did the same on the other side, crossing one of her shapely tanned legs on top of the other. Light was streaming in through a window by the front door, and both Jake and Mireille looked toward it as they blew gently on their tea.

"I am worried about her, though," said Mireille abruptly.

"Oh?" said Jake. "Are you? Why?"

Mireille said nothing for a moment, stirring her tea and staring out the window. Her eyes became teary, and Jake sensed how the drug was intensifying whatever it was she was feeling.

"Because," she said at last, "Julienne is a junkie."

Jake just stared at her. He didn't know what to say. He was shocked but also not totally surprised. This was Ibiza, after all.

"Really?" he said at last.

"Yes," she said. "I'm afraid so."

Rather incongruously, she smiled at him just in the instant that Jake felt the acid beginning to take hold. The allure of her smile in that moment was so powerful that he felt as though a physical wave of energy was passing from her upturned lips toward him, forcing him deeper into the cushions of the couch and creating a shiver of bliss as his awareness of how deeply blessed he was to be a witness to the exquisite beauty radiating from her countenance took hold. Despite the gravity of her admission about her sister, he couldn't help smiling back at her. Part of him thought that she must be joking. But then, he wondered, why would anyone joke about that?

"Where is she now?" he asked.

"In there," she said, nodding toward the door.

"What?" asked Jake, genuinely taken aback. "You mean she's in there now?"

"*Mais oui*," said Mireille sounding strangely detached. "Don't worry, though. I don't think she will be coming out any time soon. Sometimes I never see her for days."

"Oh," said Jake, pausing to consider this. "Well then, I won't."

"Won't what?" asked Mireille.

"Worry about it."

"That's good," said Mireille. "Then neither will I."

They eyed each other, sighing simultaneously, which quite unexpectedly elicited a rumble of laughter between them. Jake felt oddly reassured by her seeming indifference to her sister's plight. Not perceiving Mireille as heartless, he had to believe that her attitude was the result of deeper knowledge of the situation and would ultimately prove to be sensible. He looked over at Julienne's door, his senses acute, but picked up only silence. He felt himself shrugging internally and decided to trust Mireille's judgment on the matter. After all, he reminded himself, he'd never even met Julienne before.

"You're sure she's all right then?"

"Yes," said Mireille without hesitation. "I am."

Jake began sipping his tea, suddenly aware of how dry his mouth had become. "Do you have any music we can listen to?" he asked as if the silence emanating from Julienne's room had suddenly become oppressive.

"Ah, *oui*. Good idea, Jake!" said Mireille enthusiastically, setting down her tea and rising gracefully from the couch. She headed toward a portable boombox on the kitchen table. "What would you like to hear, *mon cher?*"

"Well," said Jake. "Do you have anything good?"

"As a matter of fact, I don't," said Mireille flashing a playful grin as she looked through some cassettes. "I prefer really bad music."

Jake grinned back, acknowledging her sarcasm, noticing that her energy level had picked up considerably. "Sorry," he said. "That truly was a dumb question."

"Not to worry," said Mireille fiddling with the cassette player. A moment later, Bob Marley's "Exodus" filled the room.

"Oh great," said Jake, "I love that song!"

"Me too!" said Mireille dancing her way back to the couch. "I'd better sit down, though," she said, easing herself into the cushions and closing her eyes, her face radiating happiness. Shortly thereafter, she began taking deep breaths through her nose, then bending forward to exhale slowly. Reaching down to grab her ankles, she allowed her hands to run slowly up her bare legs over her knees to where her dress began mid-thigh, then continued over the fabric itself to her breasts, finally extending her arms above her head and waving her hands in the air as her upper body swayed to the irrepressible reggae beat. She was clearly in some immensely pleasurable realm, and Jake regarded her with fascination. She was so close, and he so wanted to reach out and touch her, but some intuitive sense of restraint held him back. It wasn't time yet, he realized. Maybe later, when she wasn't so internally focused, he decided. To touch her now would be a kind of intrusion. He rose instead just as the acid began washing over him like a tidal wave. Standing up in front of the couch in his bare feet with his eyes closed, he felt his entire body becoming infused with light. An all-encompassing ecstatic energy was beginning to envelop him, the power of which, paradoxically, was making him increasingly still. Every cell in his body was tingling now with an acute sense of ease and physical grace. He was suddenly as light as a helium balloon and quite certain he could float away if he chose to. At the same time, he felt curiously grounded, secure in the knowledge that he, Jake, was uniquely essential to the planet. No, not just the planet but the entire Cosmos. He was simply being, in the purest sense of the word, and that was absolutely all that mattered. There really wasn't anything else that needed to be done. This was an overwhelming, staggering recognition, and any sense of regret he'd ever had about not being fulfilled in this life was instantly erased. There was only this moment and within this moment was everything. The past was irrelevant, and the future didn't exist. Everything essential was right now. Only the interruption of a familiar voice behind him caused Jake to forsake this timeless, blissful space.

"Jake. Are you all right?"

He was so deeply inside himself that it registered only peripherally at first like Bob Marley's music in the background. A moment later, Mireille stood in front of him, looking up into his face with concerned soulful eyes.

"Jake, look at you. You're crying!"

In response, he reached up and touched his cheek, surprised to feel the wetness there.

"*Ah oui, mon cher*, there are tears running down your face." She reached up then and touched his face with one hand, allowing a fingertip to gently brush away the moisture on his cheek.

"It's so … incredible," said Jake quivering with energy.

"I know," she said, reassuring him. "Believe me, Jake, I know."

He looked down at her upturned face and could see without a doubt that she completely understood what he was going through. Their eyes locked, and all at once, they were completely in this thing, this trip, together—this quintessentially ineffable be-all and end-all of existence—feeling it, Jake sensed, in exactly the same way, which only increased the amplitude of their shared bliss. In that moment, any societally contrived barriers dissolved between them, and they began playfully embracing each other with the innocence and purity of children. Mireille leaned in against his chest, closed her eyes, and pressed her face sideways against him. They stood that way for a long moment, and then she slid her arms around his waist and pulled herself in even closer. Jake locked his arms around her, and they stood there, embracing one another and swaying gently to the sound of "I Shot the Sheriff."

Jake marveled at the intensity of feeling in Marley's voice as his fingers threaded their way up inside Mireille's magnificent growth of dark blonde hair. He spread his fingers and cupped the bone of her skull, all the while feeling its remarkable pliancy and fragility. "Your skull," he said, "is throbbing with energy."

"And your heart is beating really fast too," she replied.

They locked eyes again, seeing each other as if for the first time, as their playful observations brought them back into their bodies once more, returning them from some inexpressibly distant realm.

"Look at you!" she cried, placing her hands on Jake's chest and pushing off, propelling herself a few steps backward. She began inspecting him with intense curiosity, as if he were a figure on display in some luminous diorama. "You're wearing Cannelle's stuff," she exclaimed.

Jake looked down at himself. He was indeed wearing an outfit that Cannelle had gifted him, a one-piece beige cotton overall with big wooden buttons at the shoulders, the kind that she sold in the hippy market. It had quickly become his favorite article of apparel, loose and light, with plenty of room to move. It was sleeveless, and Jake's strong, tanned arms hung loosely at his sides, unsure of what to do next.

"Yes, you're right," said Jake sharing her sense of revelation. "I am. It's great, though. I love it."

"Yes, me too," agreed Mireille. "I wonder, though, what Cannelle would think?"

"What Cannelle would think about what?" asked Jake.

"About, you know, this!"

"This?" asked Jake, regarding her with eyes full of adoration. "Do you really care?"

"No," she admitted, "I really don't." And they laughed again as they fell into each other's arms. Jake soon found himself shuddering uncontrollably, teetering on the verge of implosion from the intensity of excitement and pleasure he was experiencing while holding this beautiful and unexpectedly compliant woman in his arms.

"Jake," said Mireille with concern in her voice, "you're shaking!"

"I-I know," he said. "I-I'm s-sorry. I ... c-can't help it."

"Breathe with me," she said, pulling him in closer. "C'mon. I'll help you."

Jake soon found himself adjusting his breathing to mirror her own. Within moments they were in sync with one another, taking in deep gulps of air and releasing them slowly. His heart, which had been beating wildly, began to slow down. He found himself loving this woman, this extraordinary woman, loving her with all his heart, which was beating now in rhythm with her own. As they embraced he felt sure that he'd never felt so much love for anyone before in his life. The immediacy and intensity of this feeling felt like more than he could bear.

"Mireille," he whispered. "I love you."

"I know," she said, squeezing him harder. "I can feel it."

Despite the intensity of her response, Jake felt a momentary sense of dismay. He'd caught himself having an expectation of her—an expectation that she would echo his own sentiment—that she would say, "I love you too, Jake." It was ridiculous, he knew, and the illusory egocentric nature of that wish became instantly clear under the illuminating power of the acid, which seemed particularly adept at stripping away all false layers of Self. The question *How does my desire for her to love me have anything to do with love?* hung in the air, as well as *who* was asking her to love him, anyway? And although he said nothing, the look in her eyes revealed to Jake that she was wondering the same thing herself. It was as though the acid would not allow any kind of clichéd romantic notion to exist between them. The abrupt disruption of any sense of ego displaced disappointment with a soaring sense of gleeful liberation. Clearly there was nothing to do but continue their embrace, feeling the heightened energy rushing through their bodies, letting out small moans of indeterminate pleasure, bearing witness to the dissolution of whatever barriers remained between them. In an instant they'd become inseparable, and each had surrendered to their lack of separation without quite knowing how it even happened. The kissing, when it started, took Jake by surprise, but suddenly, their tongues began sliding in and out of each other's mouths with the exploratory verve of sensory organs that had only just discovered their purpose in life, thrusting down each other's throats to the point where they risked choking on their ardor.

"Whoa …" said Jake pushing her away slightly.

"What?" asked Mireille, her eyes ablaze with passion. "What's the matter, Jake?"

"Come," he said, grabbing her hand.

"Where are we going?" she asked.

"Over there," he said, pointing toward the bedroom.

"No," she said in a sultry but insistent tone. "I want to stay here."

"Okay," said Jake knowing it would be impossible now for either of them to do anything the other didn't want. "But you know that I want you?"

"Oh yes," she said in a husky voice. "Believe me, Jake, I want you too."

"Really?" he asked as he reached out to run his fingers through her hair again. *It's such a curious thing,* he thought, as her words echoed in his brain. *Being wanted.* He'd wanted someone before, no question about that, but he'd never thought about being wanted himself. He allowed the impression to settle in, deciding there was no sensation more pleasurable in life than two people simultaneously wanting each other. It was a perfect storm of sensual bliss, magnified almost beyond endurance by the powerful drug they were on.

Playing with her shoulder strap, he slipped his finger underneath it, pulling it slowly downward, curious to see her reaction. His intentions were clear now, and she'd expressed hers as well, but some part of him— the part which remained incredulous that this was happening at all— doubted the possibility of going any further. It was Mireille who finally put an end to his indecision. Looking at him with tender, loving eyes, she reached up and pulled down the straps from her shoulders, allowing her dress to fall to the belt around her waist, releasing her exquisite breasts, her dark nipples taut with desire. While Jake was absorbing the magnificence of this stunning unveiling, her hands were already fussing with the belt until it finally released, dropping, along with her dress to the floor.

"I … like … that," said Jake, his voice straining with desire.

"Like what, mon cher?"

"That you're not wearing any underwear."

"I almost never do," she said matter-of-factly, looking down at herself. She, too, seemed momentarily stunned by what she was viewing. She stood a little apart from Jake now, and he sensed that she wanted him to look at her—to see her and appreciate her for the first time in her natural state. The acid had erased whatever inhibition might have prevented her from exhibiting herself in such a guileless fashion. Her confident stance expressed the full awareness she possessed now of the extent of her own remarkable beauty. There was no question she was completely inhabiting it, maybe for the first time ever, thought Jake. Her vulnerability on display was flooding Jake with a sense of awe and gratitude. In another flash of acid insight, it occurred to him that this expression of naked vulnerability lay at the very heart of what love was all about.

As Jake had suspected from the first moment he'd set eyes on her, Mireille's body was almost impossibly sensuous. It met all his criteria for feminine loveliness: the full, firm breasts, the slightly rounded belly, the graceful curve of the hips, the dark golden thatch of hair between her legs, and the strong, shapely thighs and calves. Everything about her exuded formidable confidence and strength. Her deeply tanned skin was the glowing topper to this impressive tableau of amorous delight.

"Well, Jake," she said, her voice uncharacteristically hoarse, "did you get your fill of me yet?"

"Oh, no, no!" said Jake, pulsing with vitality. "I haven't even begun to fill you yet."

They both had to laugh at this awkward slip of the tongue. They were each so committed now to following the energy of the moment that it seemed entirely apt. She reached up then and placed her hand on his chest, covering his pounding heart.

"Jake," she whispered. "You know we have to go here first."

He smiled at her, enthralled by her gesture. He understood this was about more than just the sensual pleasure they were momentarily immersed in. It was about the deepest kind of exposure—the willingness to reveal oneself so completely to another person that nothing more lay hidden in the shadows.

"Yes," said Jake at last. "And I don't think there are any words for that."

"No," said Mireille reaching up now to cup his face gently in her hands. "You're right. There aren't."

She let her hands slide slowly downwards from his face, continuing down the sides of his neck and onto his shoulders. When they reached the wooden buttons on the shoulder straps of his overalls, she stopped and slowly moved her thumbs over their smooth surfaces, tracing little circles around them. Using the straps for leverage, she pulled Jake's face down to her own and kissed him once more on the lips, lingering there while allowing the flood of erotic energy between them to flow unimpeded. Then standing on her tiptoes and biting her lower lip with the effort, she slid the straps down his arms without breaking eye contact until both his hands were free. His entire chest and belly exposed now, Jake stood there expectantly, tingling with excitement, not quite sure what to do next but trusting his instinct to let her be in charge.

And she was. Mireille's movements, smooth and fluid, were emanating from a source deep within herself which Jake intuitively felt connected to. She slipped her fingers inside his overalls and began pulling them slowly downward. When she reached the clump of dark hair at his crotch, the clothing got snagged, and she reached in with one hand, pulling out his swelling penis, handling it with the tenderness and care one would give to a baby, squeezing it gently, all the while murmuring in French into its one and only eye. She went down on her knees, and with one hand pulled his clothes down into a pile on the floor while holding onto his manhood with the other. Jake stepped gingerly out of his overalls, placing a hand on her shoulder to maintain his balance as Mireille turned her attention back to his engorged cock. She had just begun filling her mouth with it when a curious noise reached both of their ears. It was the unmistakable sound of a latch jiggling and a door with rusty hinges swinging slowly open. They simultaneously turned their heads, their bodies frozen *in flagrante delicto* as a tall thin woman with deathly pale skin and dull brown hair flowing down to her shoulders, appeared just outside of the previously closed door, rubbing her eyes and shaking her head. She was dressed only in a pair of brief red panties, the elastic of which had seen better days. Her exposed small breasts looked depleted and sad.

"Qu'est-ce qui se passe?" she asked, squinting in their direction. The light streaming in through the windows was obviously distressing her, and she disappeared back into her room, returning momentarily with a gaudy pair of red sunglasses perched on the bridge of her nose.

Mireille had disengaged her mouth from Jake's cock but was still pressing her face against it, as if squashing it into Jake's belly might somehow camouflage what they were doing. It took both of them a few moments to process what had just occurred. The new reality had dramatically altered the euphoric space of their acid high, imposing an abrupt end to their blissful experiment. Jake found himself glaring at Julienne, his sense of disappointment so massive he could do nothing but stand there panting in disbelief. He looked down at the ruined spectacle of what had just moments before been a wondrous vision of erotic glory and viewed Mireille's frozen figure with a terrible longing. Still on her knees, she looked up at Jake with doleful brown eyes as she released his shrinking sex and scrambled up to face their intruder.

"Julienne, what are you doing?" she asked sternly as she reached down to gather up her clothes.

"What am *I* doing?" asked her sister in a frail voice. "What does it look like I'm doing? I'm coming out of my room ..." Her voice trailed off then, and a frightened look crept over her face.

"I can see that," said Mireille pulling her dress down over her shoulders. "But why now?"

"Well, I just thought ... I don't know ... I just felt that ..." She paused here and pointed a scrawny hand toward Jake, who, like Mireille, was pulling on his clothing. "Who is that?" she asked in an accusatory tone.

"This," said Mireille, pulling his head down to plant a full-lipped kiss on his mouth, "is Jake." She pulled away from him slightly but lingered there a moment, looking into his eyes as if trying to recapture the feeling that had so irrevocably escaped them both, before turning again toward her sister.

"Well," said Mireille. "What's going on? Are you okay?"

"I'm … not sure," said Julienne throwing her hands up toward her face, sliding her fingers underneath the sunglasses, and pressing them into her eyes. "I-I don't think so, Mireille." And suddenly, she was crying and wailing and stumbling toward her sister.

"There, there," said Mireille folding her into her arms. "It's okay, *ma soeur.* It's all gonna be okay."

"Do you think so?" asked Julienne, slobbering onto her dress. "I need some more stuff, Mireille. I really do!"

"Come," she said. "Come over here to the sofa with me. I'll take care of you now," said Mireille, embracing her and drawing her toward the couch.

"I'm sorry, Jake," she said with an imploring look. "But can you go now… please?"

Jake just stood, still fumbling with one of the wooden buttons at his shoulder, his whole body still tingling with heightened energy. It was an excruciating request. The idea of separating himself from Mireille was almost too painful to contemplate. He'd fallen in love with her just like that. That was the truth. Yet somehow, he sensed that the closeness, even more so the entwinement they'd experienced together, despite the enormous imprint it had left on their hearts, was gone forever, like sparks into a night sky. Mireille was already gone. Altready too deeply enmeshed with her junkie sister to be able to come back to the space where they'd been soaring only moments before. Had it all been just an acid dream? Feeling devastated and with enormous reluctance, Jake began edging toward the door, his heart ready to burst, as Julienne sobbed and wailed into her sister's breast, which had only moments before been swollen with desire for him.

As he swung the door open and faced the fig tree once again, now in shadow from the declining rays of the afternoon sun, he found himself taking deep gulps of fresh air as though the room inside the finca had somehow been deprived of oxygen. Without allowing himself any time to think, he continued moving toward the corner of the building, breathing deeply, until rounding the corner, he spied a stone wall a short distance away, which shortly became his perch and refuge. As he sat there on a flat hard stone facing west with the bright yellow sun dropping lower in the darkening blue sky, he found consolation in the way that the stones and weeds and carob and lemon and fig trees as well as an endless succession of small green lizards, all appeared to be throbbing with life, exuding the same constant vital force which had been streaming out of Mireille's eyes during their magical encounter what already seemed like eons ago. Jake knew there was a word for this, and the word was "love," but he doubted that any word could ever provide a fully satisfactory explanation for what had just occurred inside the finca between himself and Mireille. The love he felt now as he viewed the landscape around him was far more impersonal, emanating only a weak residue of the intensely intimate connection he'd felt with Mireille. But even out here in the vastness of nature, the impact of her words, "We have to go here first," as she placed her hand against his chest, continued to resonate. That was to be her great gift to him, the acid wisdom she'd managed to impart. Turning his head from time to time to look back at the finca cloaked in silence, Jake saw it now as merely a decorative prop, just another inert part of the landscape. The quietude surrounding him, with the exception of the occasional bird call, was complete. It had been a surreal, magical, irreplicable day, and the genie of acid had granted him a wish which, incomplete as it was, would leave its mark forever.

***

Like an addict lost in an opium dream of love, Jake felt compelled to return the next day. He couldn't help himself. The entire experience had been so replete with unfulfilled promise that as his Simca roared up on the road beneath her finca once again brazenly announcing his arrival, his heart was pounding with intractable hope.

Seeing her 2CV parked alongside the house, Jake strode unhesitatingly toward the building, not even stopping to pluck a ripe fig, and began rapping on the door. He paused and waited, but there was no response, despite his certainty that someone was in there perched behind the door. He could sense it. They're both in there, he thought, probably huddled together on the couch, holding their breath, not daring to move. He rapped some more, this time louder, but still, there was nothing. "Mireille," he yelled. *"Est-ce que vous etes la?"* He used the plural form, knowing that she had to be there with her desperately needy sibling, which was, in fact, exactly how he felt … desperately needy. It was as though he'd been given the keys to a magical kingdom only to find that the lock had been changed. He just stood there, sending out a silent dare for them to make a sound, accidentally betraying their presence and confirming his worst fear; that what had happened the day before with Mireille had simply meant far less to her than it had to him. In fact, it may have meant nothing at all.

But they were sly and still, and no sound reached his ears. He walked around the edge of the house again and made his way back to the wall. But this time, the stones and the plants and the lizards did not speak to him the way they had done the day before. They were not throbbing with love or anything else. Only the daunting heat of the day. The vision of the drug had disappeared as soon as it had left his system, leaving only a homeopathic trace behind. Jake felt, for the first time since his forced stopover in Nevers, where his car had broken down on his way to Ibiza, a woeful sense of inadequacy and loss as his entire being ached for what had proven to be an unattainable mirage—an impossibly beautiful woman who ultimately had no interest in an itinerant hippy, at least not for more than the duration of an acid trip. His thoughts drifted inevitably back to Joan. Would she have locked her door to him after an experience such as that? Probably not, he mused. In fact, they'd had a not unsimilar experience. The pull of Joan, though, had by now grown weak, almost to the point of irrelevance. Jake realized that she represented the chimera of a life he might have chosen based on the illusion of safety, stability, and social acceptance. But she was no longer part of his journey. It was clear now to Jake that his addiction was to the journey itself with its constant promise of new experience, unexpected friendships, and the endless quest for love. There was no turning back. Caught up in the excitement of riding this unchartable wave of his own singular fate, he found this path beyond his power to resist.

Chapter 32

SWITZERLAND

A few days after Carl had arrived in Leysin, Jake decided to do some skiing after his shift on gondola duty was over. All employees were allowed to use the lift facilities for free whenever they were off the job, and Jake felt almost obligated to take advantage of this perk. His work there was such drudgery—cold and boring and subject to his dyspeptic boss's temper tantrums, and the temptation to blow off steam after work with a downhill run was just too appealing to resist. It had been a while since his one and only skiing venture several years earlier when he was still a student in Austria. He'd spent a week in a ski lodge up in the Alps, taking lessons and skiing every day, and he thought he'd gotten pretty good at it. But that was his one and only venture on the slopes, and his plan now of taking the gondola up to the top of the mountain where the best skiers started from and skiing all the way back down again, might have been deemed ill-advised. Nonetheless, he reminded himself that he'd done it before, and after scrounging around in the chalet basement and finding an old pair of skis with boots and poles which the owner Jean-Paul had said he could borrow, he'd brought them with him to work and set them aside to use as soon as his shift was over. At the end of the day, after finally arriving at the top of the slope just as the sun was beginning to slide down between the snowy peaks in the west, a disquieting sense of trepidation began to set in as he slid his old borrowed boots into the battered skis and knelt down to attach the old-fashioned releases.

His trip up on the gondola was the last one of the day. There was no other way to get back down now except on his own power, and the ski patrol was already beginning to check on people to make sure they were on their way down. Jake looked nervously at the moguled slope, to the very distant end of the run where tiny figures were stamping their skis in the snow and heading for the exits. He stood there for a while in a state of semi-paralysis perched on an icy ledge, struggling to keep his skis parallel when he inadvertently started sliding down the slope. Forced to take action, he jammed his poles into the icy crust of snow, and yelling "Banzai!" at the top of his lungs, pushed himself off, and was soon barreling down the mountainside at an increasingly perilous rate of speed. Despite his best efforts to brake naturally by following a zigzag course the way he'd been taught, he soon found himself veering out of control. It was all he could do not to collide with other skiers as he struggled to stay upright during his breakneck run. Despite a few close calls, he miraculously managed to navigate the course unscathed to the very end. Almost, that is. Just as he was beginning to congratulate himself on his unlikely achievement, disaster struck. Unable to slow his momentum enough at the bottom of the slope, the tips of both his skis rammed into a large plowed heap of snow just yards from the exit. The right ski release—old and rusty—remained locked in place, and so did the boot, causing a searing pain in Jake's right ankle as his leg continued its forward motion. Collapsing into the snow, Jake grappled furiously with the defective release, finally managing to free his boot and hobble toward the exit.

Limping back to the chalet, grimacing in pain, frightened and clueless as to the extent of his injury, he had to ask himself if his ski resort job, which he'd only been employed at for a few weeks, might already have come to a disastrous end. Upon seeing his condition, both his roommates at the chalet, Peter and Sean, insisted he seat himself in a chair in front of his open bedroom window. They made sure that his foot, carefully positioned inside a roomy snow boot, was sufficiently elevated and resting on a convenient snowbank that had piled up just beyond the windowsill.

"You've got to keep it cold and elevated," insisted Sean. "That way, you'll keep the swelling down at least until tomorrow morning when you can go and see the doctor."

"There's no way I'm keeping my leg outside this window all night long," replied Jake. "I'm already freezing to death as it is."

"Just for a while, mate," said Peter reassuringly. "Then you can keep it propped up on a pillow while you try to sleep. No worries, we'll help you get set up for the night. Here, better take a few of these aspirin too."

"You guys are great," said Jake. "Thanks for taking care of me. I'll try and go in to work first thing in the morning, though, just so they know I'm not faking it. Anyway, maybe it'll be better by then."

"Sure, mate," said Peter. "And monkeys'll fly out of me arse. My guess is you broke something. Maybe nothing major, but probably enough to keep you off your feet for a while. Serves you right for using that ancient crappy equipment. I think it belonged to Jean-Paul's grandfather! What were you thinking, mate?"

"I was thinking this is the only way I'll be able to ski here since I can't afford any new stuff. Obviously, a major miscalculation."

"I'll say," said Sean. "Don't freak out yet, though. I think some kind of medical insurance comes with the job. You should be all right."

The next morning, his ankle throbbing more than ever, Jake hobbled slowly down the snow-packed road using a ski-pole for support toward his workplace—a roofed-over slab of icy concrete at the base of the mountain. His ornery boss Jacques saw him coming and glared contemptuously down at him. A heavy drinker who bragged about beating his wife, Jacques was consistently surly. He had a chip on his shoulder about being a Frenchman in Switzerland, where he was convinced people looked down on him, which they probably did.

"What the hell happened to you?"

"I had a skiing accident after work last night."

"Well, *putain bordel de la merde!* That was really smart, idiot! Don't even bother coming up here now, asshole. Go and see Rene. He'll tell you what to do next."

Rene was the big boss. He was tall and fit-looking, with a bald, deeply tanned head, and Jake liked him immensely. Unlike Jacques, he was very down-to-earth and respectful. He never got excited about small stuff, and his piercing blue eyes were always twinkling as if he were constantly amusing himself with some private joke. Rene interviewed him briefly and, without any further ado, wrote down the address of the local doctor who was very experienced in these kind of injuries. He assured Jake that his medical costs would be covered and that, should he be unable to work, he would still be able to collect his paycheck during the period of his convalescence.

"Jesus, Rene," said Jake. "I had no idea we had these kind of benefits. I'm so grateful."

"It's the Swiss way," said Rene with typical aplomb. "But I do expect to see you back on the job as soon as that ankle is healed."

Greatly relieved by this unexpected assurance, Jake made his way to the nearby doctor's office. There he was x-rayed and diagnosed with a severely sprained ankle, fitted with a plaster cast, given a pair of light aluminum crutches, some anti-inflammatories, and told that he'd probably need six weeks of recovery time. "You'll have to come and see me again next week," said the doctor. "And every two weeks after that."

All of this was fine with Jake, especially the revelation that he'd still be getting a paycheck. Feeling in a celebratory mood, and with most of his friends still at work, Jake hobbled his way to the village café to enjoy his first day of enforced vacation with a steaming cup of café au lait. No sooner had he arrived at the café, huffing with exertion, than he spied Carl already seated in the sun.

"Hey," he said, limping toward his friend. "I thought you'd gone to Verbier for a few days for some more advanced skiing."

"I decided to come back early. It was great there, but too expensive. It's not as challenging here but definitely more affordable. What the hell happened to you?"

"Turns out the 'not as challenging' slopes here in Leysin were too advanced for me! Fucked up my ankle pretty bad. Slammed into a snow heap, and one of the shitty skis I was using didn't release the way it was supposed to. Doctor says I'll be out for about six weeks. So here I am! Buy me a coffee?"

"Well, I guess I do owe you," said Carl, who was able to park his van at the chalet. "And guess what?" he said, waving his hand. "Your favorite pretty waitress is here. Yolande, s'il vous plaît!"

"Very smooth, Carl," said Jake. "You're learning,"

"*Ooh la la, qu'est-ce qui est arrivé?*" asked Yolande, her voice full of concern as she approached the table and Jake's chalky white cast came into view. He explained briefly, and Yolande looked appropriately concerned. "Does this mean you'll be spending more time in our café?" she asked.

"Ah, *oui*. I'm sure it does," Jake assured her.

"Ah, *bon*," she said, her pixie face smiling. "I look forward to seeing more of you then, Jake. May I sign your cast?"

"*Mais oui!* Go ahead."

"Let's see," said Yolande pulling a felt-tipped pen from her pocket, "what shall I write?"

"Up to you," said Jake.

"How about, 'What goes up, must come down?'"

"Or vice versa," said Jake smiling.

"Jesus Christ, can you ever not flirt with a waitress?" asked Carl in mock annoyance after she'd gone back to get their drinks.

"I wasn't flirting," insisted Jake. "Honest! She was flirting with me!"

"Yeah, right," said Carl. "Anyway, I'm just jealous. It's probably been too long since I've had a girlfriend."

Jake nodded in agreement, and the two friends sat in silence for a few more minutes in the chill air, enjoying the sensation of intense Alpine sunlight beating down on their upturned faces. The pleasurable heat, together with the cool, crisp air of the high-altitude town, the magnificent scenery, and the palpable sense of being physically removed from the troubles of the world, combined to produce a feeling of deep contentment. Jake considered what his friend had just said about him. It seemed that women did like him, so why was it that he still hadn't managed to find someone to settle down with? Perhaps the very phrase "Settle down" was the crux of the issue, he mused. His desire to continue his exploration of the world was simply too strong to deny. Women were certainly a part of that, but freedom of movement was also key. He felt as though from the moment he'd first set foot in Europe, a kind of slingshot force of fate had been propelling him forward into adventures which he could neither predict nor entirely fathom, and that was exactly where he wanted to be—smack dab in the middle of the mystery and uncertainty of it all.

"Listen, Jake," said Carl after Yolande had returned with their coffees. "I've been thinking."

"I'm listening," said Jake, licking at the foam from his café au lait.

"In light of this new development with your ankle, why don't we take my van and drive down to Ibiza together to do some more exploring, you know, really check it out and make sure it's somewhere we both wanna spend more time."

"That does sound tempting," said Jake. "Only trouble is I've gotta be here for a doctor's appointment next week. Otherwise, they cut off all my benefits."

"Hmmm," said Carl. "Next week is pretty soon. And after that?"

"Well, after that, it's every two weeks."

"And you don't have to check in with your boss during that time or anything like that?"

"I don't think so. Nobody's mentioned that."

"Well then, it's perfect!" said Carl.

"Whaddya mean?" asked Jake.

"I'll just stay here until your doctor's appointment next week. Then we can leave right after that, and you can be back here in time for your follow-up appointment fourteen days later!"

"You think?" asked Jake.

"Well, why the hell not?" asked Carl. "We should be able to make it to Barcelona in twelve hours or so. Then another twelve on the ferry. That still gives us about a week on Ibiza before you have to go back."

"And you? What will you do?"

"Once I get to Ibiza, I want to settle in for a while," said Carl. "I'll leave my van parked in Barcelona at first so we can rent a car while we're on the island. That way, we can really explore. Then I'll just stay there after you leave."

"Hmmm," said Jake as the idea began taking hold in his imagination. "Actually, Carl, I would love to go back. But what about me wearing a cast?"

"What about it?" asked Carl. "At least you won't be moping around here getting bored. And I can help you if you need any help."

"Oh, I'm never bored," Jake assured him. "I just bought *Moby Dick* in French. That should keep me busy for a while. But I like your idea. It really does feel like Ibiza might be the next step in my journey. I've felt that way ever since I first heard about it hitchhiking down from Paris last spring."

"Only one way to find out," said Carl. "So it's a go then?"

"I think so," said Jake. "But I'd like to think it over for a while. Can I let you know tomorrow for sure?"

"I'm on a pretty tight schedule," quipped Carl, "but I don't see why not."

Chapter 33

Jake understood that leaving Leysin and going on an unauthorized jaunt to Ibiza was not part of the accident recovery plan, at least not according to strict Swiss protocol, so he got his roommates to swear to secrecy about his whereabouts before he took off with Carl. The trip started out uneventfully enough, with the exception of Jake—despite the cast on his leg—having to get out and push the van several hundred yards to a gas station after the first few hours of driving. Carl, always the skinflint, had gambled on driving with the gas gauge on empty despite Jake's pleading at every town to "Fill it up now, pulease!" Carl was convinced the gas would be a little bit cheaper if they could just make it one town further. At this point in their relationship, Jake had already come to terms with Carl's thriftiness, admiring his ability to stretch limited resources to the max through a kind of self-sufficiency and discipline that didn't come naturally to Jake. Rather than complain about his penny-pinching, though, Jake resolved to just go along with it. Carl was nothing if not a survivor, and Jake sensed that his friend's survival skills were something which he himself, if he were able to emulate them, would benefit from immensely.

By the time they reached the South of France with blue skies and mild Mediterranean weather, any doubts which Jake may have been harboring about leaving cold wintry Leysin behind had vanished. Jake had his comfy bucket seat pushed back, his bum leg stretched out in front of him, and was digging the scenery and Carl's extensive musical cassette collection as they tooled along the highway. It wasn't long before they stopped to pick up a lone hitchhiker, an Armenian-American girl named Shushan who was studying in France and also on her way to Barcelona. She was chubby but attractive with long dark hair and the slightly exotic middle eastern look of her ancestry. Carl took an immediate shine to her, and both she and Jake had to endure his awkward attempts at flirtation as they rolled on toward the Spanish border.

"Hey," said Carl. "Is that a violin you're carrying?"

"Yep," said Shushan, who had arranged herself on a small stool just behind the two front seats so she could look out through the large front windshield of the van.

"So," he said. "You like to fiddle around?"

"Um, I guess," said Shushan, looking puzzled.

"Me too," said Carl. "Maybe we can fiddle around together sometime."

"Why? Do you play too?" she asked.

"Sure," said Carl. "I play. I love to play."

"Hey, there's some other instruments in the back there you can look at," said Jake after a few seconds of awkward silence. "Maybe you play them too?"

"No, I'm afraid I only play the violin," she said.

This girl appears to be genuinely innocent, thought Jake. Carl's innuendo had been painfully obvious, yet she had managed to either not notice or not care. Jake wondered how an attractive girl, seemingly so naive, had managed to thumb rides around France all by herself without running into trouble.

"Tell me, Shushan," he said, turning in his seat to face her. "Do you hitchhike a lot?"

"Actually, no," she said, giggling nervously. "This is my first time, really. It's been really cool so far. Everybody's been nice like you guys."

"How many rides have you had so far?"

"Quite a few coming down from Paris."

"That's good. Really good," said Jake. "You gotta be careful, though."

"Oh, I know that," she said. "I'm not stupid."

"Of course not," said Jake. "Sorry. I wasn't implying that you were." Had he misjudged the girl, he wondered. Maybe she had some kind of hidden strength or even a weapon which had yet to be revealed.

"I'm really good at seeing inside people," she said as though reading Jake's mind. "I can tell even before I get in someone's car what kind of person they are. I get that from my grandmother."

"Your grandmother?" asked Carl. "What kind of person was she?"

"Kind of a witch, I suppose," she said. "I mean, that would probably be the easiest way to describe her. She's from the old country, you know, Armenia, and she has the sixth sense. She can read palms and tea leaves and tarot cards and stuff like that. She can even tell from the shape of a person's head what their personality is like."

"No kidding?" said Jake. "And you feel like you've inherited some of her abilities?"

"Oh, most definitely," said Shushan revealing a slight Valley girl twang. "That's why I never worry about hitchhiking by myself."

"That's pretty cool," said Jake doubtfully. "So what did your sixth sense tell you when you stepped into our van?"

"Oh, I don't need to step in to know. I could tell as soon as we spoke through the window that you guys were all right. Maybe a little bit goofy, but all right."

"Goofy?" asked Jake.

"Yeah, especially Carl," she said, nodding in his direction. "I could tell that he's actually a sweet guy, but that whole sexual innuendo thing he's got going on, you know, about 'fiddling around'? I mean, how goofy is that? You really need to work on your pickup lines, Carl."

Carl said nothing as a crimson flush rose upward from his neck.

"Carl comes from the Groucho Marx School of Romance," explained Jake.

"Hah, I guess that explains it then," said Shushan grinning. "But you might wanna think about a different approach to the ladies."

"You hear that, Carl?" said Jake. "You are so busted, man. The needle on your babe-o-meter just dropped about ten points."

"At least," agreed Shushan.

Carl began to squirm in his seat. He kept his eyes on the road and steered, but his cheeks were flaming red. Jake, pretending to be insensitive to his friend's plight, began addressing Shushan in a stage whisper, "The thing about Carl, you see, is that he's—"

"All right, you guys, all right," said Carl at last. "So I tend to be a little too obvious at times. I get it. But here's the thing. With me, what you see is what you get, okay? I don't try to pretend to be anything I'm not. That's a good thing, right? I may not be the smoothest talker," he said, glaring at Jake, "but I do get my needs met, know what I mean?"

"Jeesh," said Shushan, "it's cool, Carl, really it is. If I thought you were some kind of weirdo pervert, and I would've known if you were, believe me, I never would've gotten into your van. You're just kind of, um, corny, that's all. I suppose some girls find it rather endearing."

"Endearing?" said Carl intrigued. "Really?"

"Yeah, really?" asked Jake.

"Oh, c'mon, Jake. You two are friends, right? Pretty good friends by the looks of it. Now quit making fun of Carl. He's really a good guy at heart. I can tell by the shape of his head."

"Really?" said Jake.

"Yeah, really?" said Carl.

"Sure," said Shushan. "I told you. I just know this stuff!"

"What about me, then?" asked Jake.

"You're a good guy too," she said.

"Because of the shape of my head?"

"Well, no. Turns out the shape of your head is rather inconclusive. It's more just, I dunno, your smile, your eyes…"

"Oh boy, here we go," said Carl.

"Go on," said Jake grinning.

"Oh, stop, please," said Shushan. "I can see where this is going. Your ego doesn't need any more stroking, Jake."

"Oh, but it does," he insisted. "I think I've been suffering from ego stroke deprivation lately."

"Oh, Christ," said Carl, shaking his head. "And what are the symptoms of that, pray tell?"

"Well, it's interesting that you should ask, Carl, because I've been meaning to tell you about it, but I was worried you'd make fun of me," said Jake.

"Oh, wouldn't that be a pleasure," said Carl.

"You see what I mean?" said Jake appealing to their passenger. "Anyway, Shushan, when I look at myself in the mirror now, which happens, well, I have to admit at least several times a day—"

"At least," said Carl.

"Please let me finish," said Jake feigning exasperation. "Anyway, Shushan, as I was saying, while I look in the mirror and tell myself as is my wont how great I am, I've been getting the distinct feeling that my reflection is being, how shall I put it, insincere?"

"Insincere?" asked Shushan, sounding puzzled.

"Yes, what I mean is, you know how when you're speaking, and your reflection is speaking right back at you simultaneously?"

"There's a scientific explanation for that," said Carl.

"Anyway, I'm quite sure that even though I'm telling myself how great I am, my reflection is not on the same page. I get the sense that it's mocking me!"

"Jeesh," said Carl, swerving to avoid some debris in the road, "must be just soul-crushing!"

"Oh, it is," continued Jake, "you have no idea. It turns out, Shushan, that my ego may be more fragile than anyone supposes. It may indeed need some strokes," he complained.

"Aww, there, there," said Shushan reaching out to stroke the thick thatch of hair on Jake's head.

"You see …" sputtered Carl, "you see … that's just what I'm talking about. Now you've gone and won her over with your nonsense."

"It's a gift, Carl," said Jake scrunching down in his seat so that his head was more within range of Shushan's fingers. "Get used to it."

"You know, you guys," said the girl continuing to massage Jake's scalp, "you two do make a pretty amusing pair, I must say. You remind me a little bit of Abbot and Costello. Did you say you're going to live together on Ibiza?"

"Maybe," said Carl. "It remains to be seen, though."

"Well, I think," said Shushan, tilting her head and half closing her eyes, "actually not just me but my grandmother as well … anyway, we both think it would be a great idea. You two are good for each other."

The two friends exchanged glances, raising their eyebrows. "Enough with the talking," said Jake, who'd decided he'd heard enough about what Shushan's grandmother had to say. "Let's put on some music."

"Eagles?" asked Carl.

"Sounds good to me," said Jake.

"Ooh, I love the Eagles!" said Shushan. "Gosh, I'm so glad you guys stopped to pick me up. We're gonna rock our way into Spain!"

****

At the Spanish border, some customs officials walked out in front of the van and signaled for Carl to pull over to the side of the road. Two hippies in an overly large Mercedes van with U.S. license plates was a pretty obvious red flag. Despite this unhoped-for delay, Jake's heart was brimming with excitement at the prospect of crossing over the border into Spain again. Being on the road was such a high. As he was parking the van, Carl turned to speak to Shushan.

"Listen," he said. "I want you to start playing your violin now!"

"Why?"

"Just do it," he said. "I'll explain later. I'm gonna come back there and play some guitar with you. Jake, you stay up front here. We're gonna employ some classic distraction technique."

"Are you worried about them finding something?" she asked. "Oh, never mind. Forget I said that. I don't wanna know."

"Let's just say there's a lot of reasons they could hassle us. My registration's expired for one thing. Let's just be cool and put on a charm offensive."

After a long interval where no one paid them any attention at all, an official finally sauntered over to their vehicle. Carl and Shushan were busy improvising "Amazing Grace" together in the back of the van while Jake sat in the passenger seat, his plaster-encased leg stretched out in front of him. Their documents in his hand, Jake leaned out the open window as a man approached the van.

"*Pasaportes, por favor,*" said the heavily mustached official. After receiving them from Jake, he glanced down at the three American passports and jerked his head toward the back of the van. "*Que pasa detras?* What's going on back there?" he asked.

"*Son músicos, señor*," said Jake, shrugging his shoulders. Almost immediately, he regretted his words. Everyone, nowadays, equates musicians with drugs, he chided himself.

"Please, *señor*, step outside of the vehicle," said the Spaniard politely in Spanish.

"Okay," said Jake beginning to grow nervous. He realized he had no idea what kind of contraband Carl might be carrying in his van. It hadn't occurred to him to grill Carl on the subject. The official glanced at Jake's cast as he hobbled a few steps and then asked him to please open the back door. Jake unlatched the side door and swung it backward, revealing Carl and Shushan seated together just in front of the Hieronymus Bosch triptych of the *Garden of Earthly Delights.* Jake's gaze fell on a naked white figure in the painting who was apparently getting a thorny rose stem shoved up his ass. *What could be delightful about that,* he wondered.

"*Buenos días,*" said the man as he stepped up into the van. "Do you have anything to declare?"

"No, sir, we don't," said Carl. He translated, and Shushan just shook her head. The man gazed silently around the van for a moment. "What are you doing in Spain?" he asked.

"We're just tourists," said Shushan after Carl translated. "*Turistas?*" she said, smiling at the official while flashing her perfect teeth. The official then turned to focus his attention on her.

"You play this?" he asked, indicating her violin.

"Yes, yes, sir, she does," said Carl before she could speak.

"Play something, *por favor,*" said the man, spreading his legs out shoulder-width and folding his arms on his chest.

"We could play 'Amazing Grace,'" piped in Carl.

"I wasn't talking to you," said the man in an authoritative tone. "Just her."

"Oh-kay," said Shushan, nervously placing the instrument under her chin. She carefully placed the bow on top of the strings just as two other customs officers appeared at the side of the van. They began speaking animatedly amongst themselves before stepping up into the crowded space.

"My friends say they'd like to hear that guy play the guitar," said the first officer.

Carl translated.

"No violin?" asked Shushan, clearly confused now.

"No," said the officer. "My friends say no violin. They want you to dance with them while he is playing the guitar."

Carl translated again.

"D-dance with them?" said Shushan. "I don't understa—"

"Just do it!" whispered Carl. "It'll be okay. Don't worry." He then immediately launched into a powerful flamenco-style rhythm, his fingers flying up and down the frets of his guitar. "*Arriba, arriba!*" he yelled, smiling and faking excitement.

Shushan placed her violin carefully back in its case and stood up to face the uniformed men, who were beginning to sway to the beat while regarding her expectantly. She turned her head to glance at Carl, her eyes brimming with tears. "I'm not going to dance with them, Carl," she whispered. "I can't." Within seconds of saying this, however, after apparently receiving some kind of inner prodding, she closed her eyes and began tossing her head back and forth as if in a trance, her long hair swinging from side to side, a luminous expression creeping into her face. "I'm just dancing for myself," she announced in a low voice as the van began to quake from her exertions, "not with them!"

"Bravo," said one of the officials standing very close to her and clapping, seemingly unable to take his eyes off her bouncing breasts. Now all three of the border guards were smiling and clapping. Jake, who stood frozen outside the van, witnessed the scene with increasing anxiety. *What the hell's going on?* he wondered. *Could they all be drunk?* The official standing closest to Shushan began dancing with her, gyrating his hips and cheering her on. "*Olé, olé!*" he shouted.

"Tell me," said his partner in English, slurring his words slightly, "where is it that you sleep in here?"

Shushan opened her eyes briefly as if trying to determine if she'd heard the man correctly. Before her eyes stood a squat leering man with a few days' growth of beard and a thick mustache. There was a gun on his belt, and he was standing way too close. His gyrating hips almost thrust into her own. The nauseating smell of alcohol mixed with garlic was wafting toward her on his breath. The two other officials had gathered behind her now, and one of them was gesturing for her to join him on a cushioned bench in the back of the van. Carl, who'd been keeping a vigilant eye on things, kept playing and smiling as if everything was hunky-dory. Suddenly though, he added his voice to the guitar and began singing in a high-pitched gypsy style, improvising some very instructive lyrics:

"Don't freak out my Shusha Just close your eyes and dance

Don't make eye contact whatever you do Just give them all a chance

To pretend that they are naughty boys But we won't let them hurt you!

And Jake please you just stay

Outside the van and keep on watching!

Oh yes, these guys are naughty boys

But soon they will grow tired

Yes soon they will grow tired."

He repeated these lyrics or something very like them several times. Shushan kept dancing while the men continued to sway and leer at her. The van filled up with the ripe aroma of sweat and garlic and some indefinable male scent until suddenly, as if on cue, Carl's right hand came crashing down on the strings, creating a final resounding chord which hung heavily in the air like the last note of the famous Beatle's song, "A Day in the Life."

Still smiling, Carl looked into the men's faces just a few feet away and yelled "*Finito*" in as loud and authoritative a voice as he could muster. Remarkably, the men all started clapping, even calling for an encore, but Shushan stood her ground. "No," she said, smiling bravely. "No encore. *Finito*." She'd made the transition from a kind of fearless trance to barely controlled rage, and there was fire coming out of her eyes now.

"*Bueno*," they said, tipping their hats as if sensing the possibility of a dangerous eruption. "*Gracias, señorita*," they all said as something akin to respect crept into their facial expressions. And then, almost as abruptly as they'd entered the van, they departed. Hitching up their belts and adjusting their guns, they hopped onto the ground outside, slapping each other on the back and laughing but almost immediately straightening up and resuming their professional rigid posture as two of them walked back toward the booth they'd come out of. The original interrogator held back and, turning to face Jake, handed him back the passports.

"Welcome to Spain," he said in Spanish with a final glance in Shushan's direction. "Go over there to get your passports stamped. And have a nice day!"

"Jesus," said Jake, after the man was beyond earshot. "I was freaking out there! I mean, what if—"

"Yeah," interrupted Carl. "I know. What if? But nothing really bad happened, did it?"

"Thanks to you," said Shushan going over to hug Carl. "You did some really fast thinking there."

"I just gave them what they wanted," said Carl. "A little bit of fun. I think they were probably just bored, that's all."

"Well," said Jake. "I'd say Shushan did some fast thinking too. She gave them some fun as well. Actually, you were both amazing! Neither one of you freaked out or panicked, and you managed not to piss them off, either. That was quite a balancing act. Who knows what would've happened if you'd made 'em mad? You kind of just acted like everything was groovy even though it definitely was not."

"I have my grandma to thank for that," said Shushan, her eyes glowing with emotion. "She was right there with me. In fact, I could feel her the whole time. She was telling me not to worry, and to close my eyes and dance, just dance!"

"You know somethin', darlin'," said Carl, turning his palms up in a gesture of surrender. "Somehow, I believe you."

Chapter 34

IBIZA

Unable to convince Shushan to join up with them while they explored Ibiza, they reluctantly dropped her off at Las Ramblas in Barcelona and headed to the ferry terminal. Carl drove around until he found a spot which he deemed safe for long-term parking, and the two friends waited to board the ferry for the nighttime journey. Once on board, they settled into chairs on the top deck, and Jake wound up with plenty of room to stretch out his injured leg, while happily enjoying his newfound freedom from having to work on the frozen concrete slab in Leysin under Jacques's withering gaze. The two friends were relaxing, looking up at the star-strewn sky, and savoring the smooth progress of the boat as it glided through the opaque water when a tall blond lanky fellow sat down beside them. He introduced himself as Cliff, said he was from Cape Town, and launched right into a lengthy conversation, apparently anxious to vanquish the boredom of the hours-long journey. He ended up taking a shine to the two young Americans and invited them to stay in a spare room in the back of a nightclub he managed on the island.

"You guys can use it as your home base while you're out there exploring," he said.

"That is an incredibly generous offer," said Jake. "You must've known we had no idea where we'd stay once we got on the island."

"We were just going to wander around until we found a cheap place to crash," added Carl.

"It's nothing fancy," said Cliff, "but you're welcome to stay for a few days anyway. You'll have to arrange your own transportation, though."

Cliff's club called Aphrodite was one of the new discos which had sprung up on the island. It lay just outside of the Ciudad de Ibiza on a promontory overlooking the port and was being readied to open in May, just in time for the start of the tourist season. When they got there, both Jake and Carl were duly impressed by the lavishness of the club's exterior. It had a Parthenon look about it with faux marble columns and stone steps leading up to a terrace featuring a shallow pool with well-fed multicolored koi. Clubs like this were evidence of how much the island had transformed itself from an off-the-beaten-track artist's retreat with relatively few visitors into Party Central of Europe. Cliff's boss, Felipe, had invested a lot of money in new equipment for the club, and Cliff was anxious to test out the enormous, obscenely expensive speakers that had just arrived from Germany. The night after they arrived, after passing around a joint, Cliff put an album on the turntable, and they began listening to the eardrum-crushing sound of "Do What You Wanna Do" by a Bahamian group called T-Connection.

Jake couldn't believe his ears. He'd never heard that kind of sound before. The searing bassline and conga-led percussion seemed to invade every cell of his body with its boogie-inducing energy. The state-of-the-art audio components kept the sound distortion-free, even at volume levels which could fairly be described as pain-inducing. This new sound, combined with the hash, the starry night sky, the cooling breeze, and the palm-covered terrace, filled Jake with a palpable sense of euphoria. He stood swaying with eyes closed, his upper body moving to the music while his cast-covered leg kept him anchored to the ground like a bird tethered to its roost. Soon Carl was swaying beside him while checking out a shapely blonde in a tight blue dress who was dancing by herself on the opposite side of the dance floor.

"What are you looking at?" asked Jake.

"Can't you tell?" he asked.

It was a woman Cliff had pointed out earlier. "That's Brigitte," he said. "She's the club owner Felipe's girlfriend." She was one of the many Germans they'd met on the island. The fact was that Northern Europe, with its famously hard-working people, had become very prosperous since the bad old days after World War II. The economic miracle was in full swing, and the population there had money to burn as well as an insatiable longing to escape the notoriously unpleasant northern climate. The daily two or three-hour flights back and forth from major northern European cities to sunny Ibiza, where the booze and cigarettes and hotel rooms were cheap, were reliably full even in winter.

"I'd be careful if I were you," said Jake. "Felipe might get jealous."

"No harm in just looking," said Carl, shrugging off the warning as Brigitte shook her hips and breasts with increasing abandon.

Carl and Jake ended up meeting Felipe and Brigitte a few days later when Cliff insisted on taking them out to visit their abode in the countryside near San Carlos.

"If you guys want to see the true possibilities of what a finca can be, then you've got to check it out," said Cliff. This turned out to be no exaggeration. Felipe's finca consisted of several large rectangular interconnected stone buildings with flat white roofs tastefully arranged around a kidney-shaped swimming pool, framed by brown terracotta tiles with numerous strategically planted palm trees providing welcome shade. The stone walls were sand-colored, providing an eye-pleasing contrast with the blinding white of the rooftops. Arches had been cut into the stone walls, and tinted glass windows installed, ensuring that the inside of the finca would be well-illuminated during the day, without the wilting heat of direct sunlight. All around the property were terraced stone walls with grazing sheep and goats and various harvestable trees, including olive, fig, and lemon.

Cliff yelled *"Hold"* as the three men entered the living room, slipping off their sandals at the door. A distant voice responded, and Cliff jerked his head toward the rear of the house, indicating that Carl and Jake should follow. Jake was enjoying the coolness of the tile floor on his bare feet and the views of meticulously framed abstract art on the walls as they passed through the house on their way to Felipe's bedroom. There, propped up against a bank of white pillows at the head of a king-sized wood-framed waterbed, lay Felipe and his girlfriend. Brigitte had pulled a sheet up above her breasts, while Felipe casually displayed his slender naked torso, the sheet barely covering him from his sex downward. His left hand held a cigarette, and the room reeked of post-coital energy.

"Cliff," said Felipe with a sly grin. "To what do I owe the pleasure?"

"Just wanted to bring some friends by to see your place. Hope you don't mind?"

"And who might these friends be?" he asked, slipping on a pair of black-framed designer glasses.

"Americans," said Cliff. "They're here looking around for a place to stay during the summer, and maybe beyond."

"Oh," said Felipe, "the ones you told me about? Who are staying up at the club?"

"Right," said Cliff. "Felipe, allow me to introduce you to my new friends, Jake and Carl."

The two friends stepped up and extended their hands which Felipe shook amicably. "What happened to your leg?" he asked Jake.

Jake explained briefly about the skiing accident and how he was on a break from his job in Switzerland. He was struck by Felipe's willingness to expose himself in such a casual way to complete strangers. He seemed to be utterly unselfconscious about being naked in bed with his girlfriend in front of people he'd never even met before. From his relaxed position on the bed, he appeared to be taking them in with the air of a man whose curiosity and lack of inhibition were equally boundless.

"By the way," said Felipe, "this is my companion, Brigitte." Still holding the sheet to her chest, she reached out her other arm and shook hands with the men.

"*Hola,*" she said.

"You're just in time," said Felipe, grinning. "We were about to smoke a joint." And with that, he leapt out of bed and sauntered toward a shelf on the opposite wall of the bedroom. His uncircumcised penis, still moist and semi-turgid from sex, swung heavily between his legs, prompting Brigitte to ask if he didn't want to put on his robe.

"What for, *mi amor?*" he asked. "It's my house, isn't it? And, anyway, I'm sure they've seen a man's cock before."

Jake caught Carl's eye. "What the hell?" he mouthed silently.

"Felipe," said Cliff, unfazed by his friend's behavior, "as long as we're here, I wondered if you and I might talk privately for a few minutes?"

"About what?" asked Felipe without turning around.

"Well, I'd rather not say," said Cliff. "It's rather important, though."

Felipe turned around then and sauntered back toward the bed. He was holding a joint in one hand, and with the other, he scooped up a blue silk Chinese robe which lay crumpled on top of the sheets. Placing the spliff between his lips, he slipped on the robe, tied the belt into a knot, and passed the joint to Cliff.

"If you say it's important," said Felipe, "then I can't really say no, can I? But first, let's all have a toke together. Then you and I can go outside and sit by the pool and have a little *tête-à-tête.*"

The joint got passed around until it was no more than the tiniest roach. Felipe then put his arm around Cliff's shoulder and ushered him out of the room, abandoning Brigitte to Carl and Jake. At some point, she'd slipped on a skimpy pink robe which managed to accentuate her sexuality even more than when she was naked under the sheet. She arranged herself provocatively on top of the bed with her ankles crossed and the robe riding well up on her muscular thighs, regarding the two friends with suspicion. The easygoing mood in the room seemed to have evaporated with Felipe's departure.

"So where are you guys from?" she asked in heavily accented English.

"The U.S.," said Carl. "But you knew that already."

Her face held a blank expression. "I did?"

"Yeah," said Carl. "Cliff just introduced us as Americans. A few minutes ago. Remember?"

Looking annoyed, she lifted a well-manicured hand and waved him off in a gesture of dismissal.

"That's what I was thinking anyway," she said.

"That we were Americans?" asked Carl. "Why's that?"

"Something about your energy," she said, pulling her robe tighter around her breasts. "It's so . . . I don't know, you Americans are always like that."

"Like what?" pressed Carl.

"I don't know. Careless, I think you say."

"Careless?" asked Jake. "You mean carefree?"

"Yes. That's right. Carefree."

"You say that like it's a bad thing," said Carl.

"I don't know. Maybe it is. Sometimes I think that Americans have it too easy, you know, and well, it pisses me off."

"Pisses you off? Why?" asked Jake.

"I'll tell you why," she said, starting to get agitated. "It's like nothing bad has ever happened to you."

"What's that supposed to mean?" asked Jake.

"Not like what has happened in my country."

"Are you speaking of the war?" asked Jake.

"Of course," she said. "What did you think?"

"But it's not something that you experienced personally, is it?" asked Jake wondering where she was going with this.

"That's not my point," she said, her blue eyes flashing with annoyance. "Everything with you Americans is about, 'Look at us, we are the good guys.' It's like you never do something wrong before. But we Germans have our past always in our faces. Everyone knows about what we did. Things you cannot forgive. We cannot hide from that. Sometimes we pretend like we don't know nothing about it. But we do."

Jake was surprised to see a look of genuine anger on her face. Who was her anger directed at, he wondered. Was it at them? Or herself? At Germany? Or just everyone in general? He was genuinely shocked to be the target of such an unexpected diatribe. It made him wonder, unfairly perhaps, whether the recent bout of lovemaking between her and Felipe was somehow responsible for this outburst of belligerence.

"Well," said Jake, "if it makes you feel any better, Brigitte, we don't feel like we're such good guys anymore. Not since Vietnam, anyway. Turns out Americans can do really bad things too!"

"That's right," said Carl. "People like Sergeant Calley killing all those women and children. You've heard of him, right? We lost our innocence in that war for sure."

"Were you there?" she asked.

"No," said Jake. "Turns out neither one of us was too anxious to go into the military."

"Maybe that's why you seem so carefree then," she said, a smile returning to her face. "This is how Americans are, the ones who don't go to war."

Carl raised an eyebrow, trying to gauge her level of sarcasm.

"Brigitte," said Carl, "isn't that why we're all here now? On Ibiza, I mean? No matter where we're from? Because we want to be carefree?"

"I suppose," she said, swinging her legs over the side of the bed, appearing to lose all interest in the conversation they'd been having. Standing up, she sauntered toward the sliding glass door which led out onto the terrace. She stretched her arms above her head so that her palms pressed against the glass and for a moment her body, framed against the light streaming into the room took on a translucent quality creating a shimmering outline of her slim waist, shapely legs, and curvaceous hips and buttocks. Her presence radiated an undeniably erotic force, and Jake might have remained there frozen in a lustful trance had he not caught a glimpse beyond the glass door of Cliff and Felipe seated next to each other on lounge chairs next to the pool. He saw Cliff reach into his leather shoulder bag and pull out little clear plastic satchels filled with a powdery white substance. He shifted his glance to Carl, who, transfixed by Brigitte's mesmerizing form, appeared not to notice what was happening. Gently placing a hand on his shoulder, Jake turned his friend toward the bedroom door. "C'mon," he whispered. "Time to go."

As they walked through the finca, Jake filled Carl in on what he'd seen outside by the pool. "I don't know about you," he said, "but if that's what I think it is, this is not something I want to have anything to do with."

"Me neither," agreed Carl. "Somehow, I'm not surprised, though."

"Well, maybe this is how they've gotten the money together to get their disco started," said Jake. "It must be costing them a fortune."

"Yeah, could be … although I've heard that Felipe comes from a very wealthy family. I suspect he's more into it for the cachet than the money. Being known as the cool guy with drugs sure can't hurt when you're in the entertainment business."

Jake nodded. "And Cliff?" he said, "where does he fit in?"

"I think Cliff just needs the money," said Carl. "He's a long way from home without a work permit, so what can he do? I think Felipe keeps him around because he knows how desperate he is and that he can't afford to turn down any kind of work that gets thrown his way. Plus, he's good at his job."

"Sounds pretty cynical," said Jake.

"Well, there's a friendship there, too," said Carl. "But Felipe is definitely the one calling the shots."

Once outside the house, Jake and Carl cautiously made their way toward the pool, purposely slapping their feet hard on the tiles to make sure the two men knew they were coming. Cliff hurriedly closed the flap on his shoulder bag as the two men approached.

"Okay to join you?" asked Jake.

"Sure," said Felipe flashing a broad grin. "Cliff and I were just finishing our discussion, anyway. I'm sorry that I can't invite you guys to stay longer, but I really have some business to take care of now."

"That's okay," said Jake noticing a dusting of white on the man's mustache. "We just really enjoyed seeing your place. It's incredible."

"Yeah," said Carl. "We really do appreciate you letting us come out to have a look. Gives us an idea of what's possible here on Ibiza."

"You think this is possible for you guys?" asked Felipe, giving them a patronizing look.

"In our dreams," said Carl.

"In your dreams is right. It takes a lot of connections, and a lot of money, you know. What kind of money do you guys have? I mean to rent a finca?"

Carl named a figure.

"Hah!" snorted Felipe, bursting into laughter. "Good luck with that. You couldn't rent my bedroom closet for that amount."

"Well, we're not really looking for anything luxurious," said Carl.

"It's okay," said Felipe. "I get it. I really do. You guys are a couple of hippies with no money trying to hang out on Ibiza. It's nothing unusual. I see guys like you every day down on the beach at Aguas Blancas when I go for my daily swim. Or in the cafés in town. You seem like nice guys, and I admire you for trying. But this," he said with a panoramic sweep of his arms, "is, how do you Americans say, 'a whole other ball game.'"

The two friends just stood there feeling chastened and unsure how to respond to Felipe's blatantly arrogant, dismissive remarks. Jake thought back to Felipe's behavior in the bedroom. This was a man who thought he could do anything, he reminded himself. The confidence he projected, though, was impressive. Or was it just the bombast of a cocaine-addled brain? Whatever the case, Jake felt pretty sure that just beneath the surface of Felipe's welcoming exterior, where his true feelings lay, was real disdain for someone like himself or Carl, who didn't value the kind of material success which he'd achieved in the world. Despite his hippy trappings, Felipe's roots were aristocratic, and he was inured to power and wealth. *Those are the two things he respects most,* thought Jake, *and we have neither. He's right about one thing, though,* he mused. *This is not our scene at all.* The lure of decadence was as old as mankind itself, and Jake couldn't deny that the pervasive air of luxury and self-indulgence held some appeal. But he hadn't lost contact with that part of himself that really didn't need any of this to be happy. It seemed too complicated and, ultimately, burdening on the soul.

Just before being led away by Cliff, who was driving them back to Aphrodite, Jake glanced toward the glass door of the bedroom, hoping to catch a final glimpse of Brigitte, but her seductive figure had disappeared from view.

Chapter 35

After spending six days on the island with Carl, Jake prepared to return alone to Leysin for his next doctor's appointment. Despite his limited mobility and the itchiness of his leg inside the cast, he'd had about as good a time as he could've hoped for. The winter Mediterranean weather had been deliciously sunny and warm, and Jake had exulted in riding around in their rented 2CV, its top peeled back, his shirt off, soaking up all the sun he could before heading back to the breathtakingly beautiful but cold and snowy Alps of Switzerland. After this, his second visit to the island—its beauty, climate, and laid-back lifestyle had won him over completely. He'd seen enough to convince him that Ibiza was indeed a place where he'd like to try and live, at least for a while. He put returning there at the top of his wish list of things to do once the ski season ended and he had more money in his pocket.

Standing in line at the station in Barcelona as the bus pulled up which would take him back to Switzerland, Jake noticed a petite round-faced woman, with deep-set ebony eyes and a light dusting of freckles across her wide cheekbones who turned her head to smile at him as she mounted the steps to the bus. *Was she just checking me out?* wondered Jake, returning her smile. She had dark ringlets of curly hair and ample breasts beneath a brightly colored peasant blouse. Jake felt an immediate attraction and wondered if there would still be an empty seat beside her by the time he'd boarded the bus. Much to his delight, he saw that she'd been saving him a spot, having placed her hand on the seat beside her, which she promptly removed as he drew near. Hoisting his bag up onto the rack above the seat, he eased into the space beside her.

"*Hola*," he said.

"*Hola*," said the woman.

"Do you speak English?" he asked.

"Yes, some."

"Are you going to Lausanne too?"

"No," she said. "Only as far as Grenoble."

"Well," said Jake. "That's still quite a ways. Do you mind if we talk a little?"

"Not at all," said the woman as she reached into her handbag to pull out some figs. "Would you like one?" she asked.

"Yes, thanks," said Jake. "I love figs. You know I never ate one until I came to Spain."

"Really?" she said in amazement. "You never ate figs before?"

"Nope," said Jake. "They don't grow where I'm from."

"You are from where?" she asked, giving him a curious glance.

"The U.S.," said Jake. "New York, basically. Oh, I'm sorry. We forgot to introduce ourselves. I'm Jake," he said, extending his hand.

"I'm Luz," she said, grasping his fingers. Jake was immediately struck by how small and soft her hand was. There was something sublimely vulnerable and delicate about it, and he gave it a brief gentle squeeze.

"Luz? That means light, right?"

"That's right," she said. "Do you know Spanish?"

"A little," said Jake. "Are you from here?"

"No," she said, frowning slightly. "I'm not. I'm from Santiago. In Chile."

"Is that right?" said Jake. "It must be quite beautiful there. I've seen pictures with the Andes in the background."

"Oh yes. It is. Very beautiful. But ..." Her voice trailed off, and she turned to look out the window. Jake could see that she was biting her lip.

"I'm sorry," said Jake. "Are you all right?"

"Yes," she said, making an effort not to show her emotions. "I'm all right." She turned her head again to face him, and Jake noticed that her dark eyes had suddenly gotten moist, but she was smiling. Following a hunch, Jake decided to ask her a personal question.

"Has it been tough there for you since Pinochet?"

"How did you know?" she asked, eyeing him with suspicion.

"Well," said Jake. "I've read about what's going on there in the newspaper. I think he's not a good man."

"No, he's not," she agreed. "But it's not something I like to talk about."

"I understand," said Jake. "Let's talk about something else then." It would soon be dark, and he did not want to spend the long night on the bus sitting next to her in silence. The undeniable attraction between them still felt so palpable. The prospect of her just turning away and going to sleep seemed like a miserable option.

"Well then," she said, "tell me what happened to your leg?"

Jake told her about his job at the ski resort in Leysin and the accident resulting in his trip to Ibiza.

"That's so funny," she said, giggling.

"Why's that?" asked Jake.

"I'm not really sure," she said, eyeing him with amusement. "It's just so ... I dunno. I just like that you decided to come to Ibiza with your broken foot, and nobody knows about it. It takes a certain kind of person to do that."

"Yeah, a certain kind of crazy person, maybe," conceded Jake.

"But that's okay," she said, smiling. "I think it's good to be crazy sometimes."

"You do?"

"Yes, I admire someone who just does what he wants. It seems like such a ... luxury?"

"Hmm, I guess I see what you mean," said Jake. "But tell me about Luz," he continued, genuinely curious. Despite her initial reluctance to talk about it, she allowed herself to be gently coaxed into revealing what life was like in Santiago under the regime of a cruel and brutal dictator. She revealed that she was a scientist and had a job in a laboratory. She spoke of the pervasive fear that someone was listening in on her phone, the rumored disappearances of friends and colleagues, and the general overwhelming state of paranoia and depression into which she and everyone she knew had fallen. Jake listened sympathetically with curiosity and compassion, knowing instinctively that her tale was not one she shared often or willingly with others. He sensed that she enjoyed unburdening herself, something which the unusual circumstance of riding in a bus at night far away from home with a sympathetic fellow traveler made not just possible but oddly necessary. Aware that his own problems were trivial by comparison, he might have remained reticent had she not encouraged him to tell her all about his trip to Europe starting from his arrival in Paris the year before. She interrupted frequently, asking lots of questions, and Jake sensed that she found his tale in equal parts intriguing and incomprehensible.

"You know," she said. "I don't know anyone like you, Jake. Your life seems like a kind of fairytale to me. You don't seem to be struggling like so many do. At least not with the same kind of things. Your adventures are very interesting, but I don't see the point."

"The point?" asked Jake.

"Yes. I guess I don't understand what it is that you want."

"I don't want anything, Luz, except to exercise my freedom to experience life the way that I choose to."

"But isn't that what everyone wants?"

"I'm not sure, Luz. I can't speak for everyone. But I don't think it's something that most people think about that much."

"I mean, sure, I would love to do that too," said Luz. "But how can I when Pinochet is telling me what I can and cannot do?"

"But isn't that why you came here to Europe?" asked Jake. "To have more freedom?"

"Yes, of course, it is. But only for a short time. I have to go home again soon."

"Why?"

"Not everyone can leave everything behind them like you did, Jake. For most people, it's just not possible. I cannot leave my mother, for example. She might die without me."

"I'm not saying that everyone should live the way I do, Luz."

"Don't misunderstand me, Jake. I don't want to judge you. Not at all. Many of the things that you've done, like traveling to Paris and living there and learning French, are things that I would like to try myself. Maybe I'm just jealous."

Jake picked up her hand and held it in his own. "Luz, I can't really imagine what your life in Chile is like but from what you've told me, you must be incredibly brave to go back there even though you could apply for asylum in Spain as many Chileans are doing right now. I even met a few on Ibiza. I don't know if I could ever be as brave as you, Luz, and I admire you greatly for that."

By the time they'd finished this exchange, they'd already crossed the border in the Pyrenees into France and were cruising east on the highway under a starlit sky. There was no moon, and except for a few passengers with their reading lights on, the interior of the bus was dark and silent. The low thrumming noise of the motor made it very difficult to carry on a conversation without raising one's voice and running the risk of waking the mostly sleeping passengers. The two travelers found themselves huddling closer together so that they could speak in low tones to one another and still be heard. As the hours passed, Jake felt that a genuine bond was forming between them. Having bared their souls to one another, the prospect of parting company only a few hours hence seemed like a depressingly cruel conclusion to their unexpected tryst.

"Aren't you cold?" asked Luz, fumbling in her bag for a woolen serape and draping it across both of their laps. Jake reached across underneath the serape and gently pulled her closer. She eagerly complied, curling up into his chest and tilting her face upward to look at him. They were so close now, and the shining chocolate depths of her eyes seemed to Jake to be brimming with love. The earlier sadness he'd seen there was gone. Her tongue darted out, moistening her lips, and disappeared again as Jake slowly lowered his face, until closing their eyes, they joined together in a long impassioned kiss. Jake was delighted to discover that she wanted it at least as much as he did. The ardor with which she set her tongue loose in his mouth, while her delicate hands reached up from beneath the serape and began to explore his thick long hair, set his body on fire. He cradled her head in his hands, his fingers thrust deep within her own silky curls. He could feel the blood pumping upward from her heart into her head, rapid and excited, and he felt he had his fingers on the pulse of life itself. It was all he could do not to pull her onto his lap, so hungry was he for her life-affirming energy.

"Jake," she said, panting slightly and pulling her face away just enough to look him in the eye. "I wish we had more time together. I really do. I want to spend the whole night in your arms, kissing you and holding you. But Grenoble is coming soon …"

"I know," said Jake, gently brushing the hair from her eyes. "I feel the same way, believe me. It's such a powerful feeling between us, though, isn't it?"

Luz nodded her head, her eyes glistening with pleasure.

"It doesn't feel right, Luz," Jake continued. "Having to leave you so soon. This kind of feeling just doesn't happen every day."

"No," she said, sighing deeply. "It really doesn't … feel right, I mean."

"Are you sure you can't continue on with me? Spend some time in our chalet in Switzerland? I still don't have to work for a few more weeks. We'd have lots of time together."

They sat huddled together for some moments, cuddling under the serape before she finally responded. "That's a very nice offer, Jake. I appreciate it, I really do, but no, I can't, even though it's very tempting. But maybe, if you want to come and visit me in Santiago, it could be possible. I have a nice place with plenty of space. You can see the mountains from where I live. Just like in Switzerland, I think."

Jake fell silent as he considered this completely unexpected proposal. He was utterly enraptured by the remarkable sense of intimacy and familiarity that had developed so quickly between them. She'd unbuttoned the top of his shirt and was twirling his chest hairs as if he were a lover she'd long been intimate with. The words he spoke next came not from his head but from somewhere much deeper inside him, underneath where her fingers played on his chest.

"Luz," he said at last. "Why not? It's possible, I guess. I'll have money saved at the end of the ski season. Money I was planning to spend in Ibiza. But nothing's set in stone. Like you said, I can do whatever I like. I could come to Santiago, Luz."

"You could?" asked Luz, her dark eyes glistening. "Really, Jake?"

"Yes," said Jake. "Really."

"That would be wonderful," she said.

The rest of the trip, until the bus arrived in Grenoble, passed in a dreamlike state, their happiness together offering a fleeting refuge from the harsh discipline of ordinary time. At some point, unable to restrain themselves any longer, each reached down and carefully unbuttoned and then lowered the zipper on the other's pants one click at a time lest the distinctive sound alerted their fellow passengers to their erotic intent. Jake allowed his fingers to slowly but inexorably creep underneath the elastic of her panties and into the tangled bush of hair above her pubic bone, slipping over the springy pearl of her clit until his middle finger slid between the moist lips of her vagina. Luz bit her lip, suppressing a moan as she struggled not to betray their passion, her thighs squeezing together so tightly that his finger locked in place while she ever so slowly rubbed her groin against it, trembling with the effort. Jake found himself arching up against her own small hand, which was struggling with his underwear in her fumbling effort to extract his swollen shaft. Luz began pleasuring Jake, tentatively at first, but with increasing fervor as her strokes became more and more coupled with the rise of her own mounting lust. Careful as they were, holding themselves in check— although just barely—their erotic play remained undetected beyond the bounds of her colorful serape as the inexorable crescendo of their passion forced them to gag one another with probing tongues, preventing them from betraying their bliss to their fellow slumbering passengers, huddling obliviously beneath the cloak of their midnight dreams.

At three in the morning, they were finally forced to take their leave of one another, still tingling with the excitement of the unexpected joy and future promise they'd discovered in each other's arms. The bus depot in Grenoble presented an icy panorama, its vast array of artificial lighting illuminating a surreal stage for their final impassioned embrace on the frozen ground while the driver finished unloading Luz's luggage from the baggage compartment on the side of the bus. With her address jotted down on a slip of paper in his pocket, Jake remounted the steps to continue his journey alone, pausing for a moment on the top step for a final yearning look at Luz as he felt his heart swell with the fervent hope that everything he longed for in life was attainable, if he just kept succumbing to his own heart's desire.

Chapter 36

SWITZERLAND

Although the doctor had recommended six weeks of recuperation, the management of the ski resort was having none of it. Perhaps word had leaked out after all about his unsanctioned trip to Ibiza. Both his roommates, Peter and Sean, were relentless talkers and might have easily spilled the beans despite Jake having elicited promises from each of them to not tell a soul. In any case, having finally had his cast removed after a month, he found himself back on the concrete slab bouncing from one frozen foot to the other, trying to keep his toes from getting frostbite. Jacques, who Jake suspected was pickled in alcohol most of the time, kept a jaded eye on him as he gathered tickets and skis and pushed crowded gondolas off the slab and into space with only a thin metallic thread preventing their quivering silvery forms from crashing downward into a snowy abyss. The season was only halfway finished, and he knew he had no right to complain, but a nagging impatience was gnawing away in his gut, making the slow pace of the remaining dark winter months feel especially onerous.

Meanwhile, his heart had decided. There was only one destination now. He and Luz had been corresponding, and his entire being resonated with the prospect of romancing her in her native land. He sent her poems and letters telling her in no uncertain terms how he was burning with excitement at the thought of the heartfelt adventure which lay before them both in her hometown of Santiago. Even after Luz dropped the bombshell that she'd been seeing a guy named Pablo, who might or might not be her boyfriend, Jake ignored the innuendo and refused to give up hope.

"I think that our relationship, Luz," he wrote to her, "will either be passionate or not at all. And I'm betting on passionate, which really excites me. Perhaps it is bad to theorize about our relationship, but does it not exist right now entirely in our imagination anyway? You've become so important to me, Luz, in a way that I can't even really begin to explain. I think about you all the time. I look at travel brochures for Chile and try to imagine what your life must be like there. That's why it's very important for me to try to imagine how significant a role I'm playing in your own thoughts. Probably you aren't sure anymore how you feel about me since many weeks have passed now since our brief encounter. But it's a certainty that if we don't get together in the near future, and I mean very soon, the chance of us getting together ever will fade away, and who knows what precious aspect of life we will have missed out on? What I'm trying to tell you, Luz, is that I'm willing to take the gamble, and come to you, without being able to predict any outcome. I hope you can appreciate my seriousness about this. The important thing is that we each be true to our own hearts. I'm convinced that is the only way to be happy. I'm counting on your heart being as open to me as mine is to you. There are so many things we must discuss together, Luz, things that are very frustrating to try and talk about from such a distance. So let's just say I'm coming to Santiago to continue an intimate discussion I had with a certain very charming and intriguing and beautiful woman between Barcelona, Spain, and Grenoble, France."

The letters between them, which took a week to arrive, were as frequent as could be expected. Jake had been pressuring Luz to make her decision soon, before the end of the season, at which time the rent on their chalet would be up, and Jake would finally have to leave Leysin. He'd even done his research at the sole travel agency in the village and sent her the flight details he expected to follow. A week after that, the following letter arrived in the mail:

"I read your letters, Jake. They are beautiful. You say very beautiful things to me. You have plenty of tenderness and love. You say you love me and write warm poems for me. I wish I could be there with you and forget all that is affecting me now and be able to try something with you, become a great illusion, and live a dream.

Reality is different. I'm here with plenty of doubts I won't be able to solve in a long time. Here in my reality now, I find myself in that situation where I cannot offer you anything. There is no security in me. It would not be honest in the moment if I would ask you to come, besides all the things I would like to show you and share with you here in my sentimental part. I feel blind and deaf and terribly sad for having forced you to decide your trip without ever imagining that it could happen to me.

Do not come.

I do not change one character of all I wrote since my first letter because I was sincere with you as I am now. All I said I felt deeply. I do not know what damned thing made me to arrive to that situation just now when everything could be better for us.

I do not understand what is going on with me. You certainly understand less than I do. I beg your pardon for having grown on you that illusion about me, for having done to you all those problems.

I saw you were wearing a moneybag on your chest. I send you this made by Aymara Indians from Ishiga, a very small town in the north cordillera of Chile at three thousand meters above sea level. Its name is Wayuna, and it takes two months of work. They cut the wool from the alpaca, spin it thin, color it, and wattle it in a loom.

It is a bag with plenty of life and love from me, and with it, I want to go to you and remain on your chest as a remembrance."

Jake read the letter many times, and he reread it at 3 a.m. as he looked through the open window of his chalet bedroom. The shock of the freezing air felt appropriately chilling and unbearable. The sky was a dark blanket peppered with holes, allowing a twinkling glimpse of light to shine through. Three black cats appeared out of nowhere, crouching in the snow, creating an eerie cacophony of sound as their backs arched into threatening poses. Jake made a quick lunge forward, and they scattered like vanishing spirits of the dead. Shivering now, he reached for the window and pulled it down, locking it into place. What was that all about? he asked himself, holding the Wayuna to his chest. How did we allow things to get so intense between us? Was it ever even real at all? What kind of madness was that? he wondered. He imagined Luz with her small and delicate hands holding this piece of cloth before placing it in the envelope. *Did she kiss it first?* he wondered. A sudden wave of overwhelming sadness swept over him, and he felt a sob escape from his chest. He lifted up his wrist to his mouth and held it there like a dog with a bone in its muzzle. Pressing his eyes shut, he felt the tears streaming down from his cheeks onto his arm. He wanted her to love him, he realized. He needed her to love him. He had felt on the bus that she could love him. Who was going to love him now? And who would he love in return? Not Joan, he thought. It was far too late for that. Jake felt as though he'd been confronted with a crucial insight into his own being. Nothing mattered more than love. Not for him. Not money, not status, not security; all paled in comparison to this enormous gaping need within himself. He thought of his mother, who'd died when he was still a young boy, eleven years old, after suffering miserably from cancer for years. He knew that she was a special person because she knew how to love; deeply and sincerely. Although his memories had faded over time, the one unshakable impression of her that remained was her radiant smile, and the love emanating from her dark brown eyes not just when she looked at him but at anyone she came into contact with. She was one of those rare souls capable of loving unconditionally from a private spiritual font of inspiration that she never lost touch with, even in the midst of unbearable pain and suffering and sorrow. How Jake would have loved to seek out her advice now in this lonely moment of doubt and confusion about the one thing he knew that she understood better than most; how to live your life with love, no matter what the circumstances. With the illusion of Luz and Chile finally revealed for the pie-in-the-sky that it no doubt always had been, Jake's attention reverted to Ibiza, his original destination and source of inspiration. He knew that in a few hours, he would get up and pack his few possessions into his beat up Boy Scout knapsack, say goodbye to his roommates, then stand on the side of the road and hitchhike back to Paris, where he would stay with some old friends while searching for a used car he could buy with his savings and drive down to Ibiza. Maybe love awaited him there. He hoped with all his heart that it did.

Chapter 37

IBIZA

Shortly after Carl and Jake moved out of Ruben's place in Santa Inés, having finally found a finca of their own, Carl introduced Jake to Gisela, a German woman Carl had been friendly with for some time. Just how friendly they'd been, Jake didn't really know, as Carl tended to be discreet about such matters. Gisela was musically gifted, which appealed to Carl, and she and her husband Dieter liked to throw parties at their lovely home in San Carlos, a town whose main attraction was its proximity to the secluded white sand beach known as Aguas Blancas. While exploring the island with Jake in his van one day, with no particular plan in mind, Carl announced it was high time the two of them made a visit together to San Carlos to see if his friends there might be at home.

It was midafternoon by the time they arrived, the hottest time of day, and the blue shutters on the windows were closed. At first glance, the house appeared to be locked up and deserted. Carl, in his usual deliberate fashion, pulled right up to the gate and shut off the diesel engine, which rattled to a halt.

"You think somebody's home?" asked Jake.

"I suspect so," said Carl. "Looks like Dieter's Mercedes is in the garage. Door's half closed, but I think I saw it in there."

"What did you say he does again?" asked Jake.

"Well, that's kind of a good question," said Carl. "He's a businessman, I guess. He owns a boutique in Ibiza, which is where Gisela works. But that seems to be more of a sideshow. It gives Gisela something to do and keeps her happy. She's quite the fashionista, after all."

"Hmmm," mused Jake, "not sure I've ever run into a fashionista before."

"His real business is in West Berlin," continued Carl. "But nobody seems to know exactly what it is he does there. I've asked Gisela about it, and even she doesn't know for sure. Sometimes he's gone from Ibiza for extended periods leaving her behind with their daughter, Chloe."

"Jeezus, that must be hard on them."

"Well," said Carl giving his friend a sardonic look, "I wouldn't feel too sorry for Gisela. She never seems to mind when he's gone. In fact, I think she prefers it that way. They *are* married, but well, I guess you'll see for yourself. "

Carl reached behind his seat and picked up a guitar, then he opened his door, and Jake followed suit. No sooner had they both slammed their heavy doors shut than a dog began barking inside the house. Its barking grew in intensity as Carl opened the front gate.

"This way," said Carl, following along the freshly whitewashed outer wall of the finca, curving around to a small terrace in the back. A white circular table with a glass top surrounded by matching metal chairs stood in front of two broad louvered doors open wide with long blue curtains flapping inward in the gentle breeze. In front of the curtains, a medium-sized dog of indeterminate breed stood quivering with excitement. He was black and white with the jaws of a schnauzer. His growls turned to yips of delight when he recognized Carl, who bent down to receive an eager bath of sloppy kisses on his bearded face.

"Moische! So good to see you again, my friend," said Carl squatting now and allowing the dog to place both paws on his shoulders while he continued to slather away. "Come on now," he said, finally pushing the dog back to the ground, "go and see your new friend, Jake!" The dog sniffed cautiously around Jake at first, barking a few times before allowing his outstretched hand to gingerly stroke his head.

"Moische?" asked Jake, peering into the creature's dark eyes. "What kind of a name is that? Are you some kind of a Jewish dog? Is that it? Doesn't Moische mean Moses in German?"

"As a matter of fact, it does," said a mellifluous voice from somewhere beyond the dog's furiously wagging tail. "How did you know that? Do you speak German?"

"*Jawohl!*" said Jake straightening up and continuing to scratch the dog's neck as he stretched his paws upward onto Jake's belly. "As a matter of fact, I do."

"Moische, get down!" commanded the woman. "Is that any way to treat a guest?" She had bent forward to scold him and was herself now getting the full facial lavage from her pet. "I'm sorry," she said. "He's really impossible you know. If he likes you, he won't leave you alone, and it appears that he does like you . . . uh, I'm sorry, I forgot your name."

"That's because we haven't been introduced," said Jake continuing in German. "I'm Jake, and it's very nice to meet you."

"That's right. You see, I *did* forget your name. Carl's already told me plenty about you."

"Good stuff, I hope," said Jake, who stood with both hands on his hips, taking in this striking woman with all his senses, already enthralled by the scent of some exotic flowery perfume swirling all around her.

"Well ..." she said, waggling her hand in a gesture of uncertainty. Jake saw the playfulness in her eyes and felt immediately attracted to her mischievous demeanor. He also couldn't help but notice how beautiful she was. Her lustrous auburn hair, parted in the center and flowing down off her shoulders, fell to the middle of her back, and her skin was tanned and glowing with health. An aquiline nose, high cheekbones, full cherry-red lips, and a strong cleft chin complemented sparkling blue eyes carefully outlined in mascara. She wore an ankle-length white caftan with red and gold embroidery and handcrafted leather sandals exposing shapely well-manicured toes. An ivory cigarette holder dangled from her right hand with a smoldering cigarette attached.

"You must be Gisela," said Jake. "I've heard a lot about you too from Carl."

"Well then," she said, eyeing Jake with interest, "I trust you also heard good things."

"Oh, nothing too bad," said Jake.

"Oh yeah?" she said, eyeing Carl. "What did he say then? I'm really curious."

"Well," said Jake switching back to English, unable to tear his gaze away from her, "mostly that you're very musical and have a wonderful voice!"

"Wonderful voice? You said that, Carl?"

"Might have done," admitted Carl. "I've told you before, Gisela, you remind me of Joan Baez, remember?"

"Well, that would be pretty great," admitted Gisela smiling. "What girl wouldn't like that? So why don't you guys come inside and join us? Some music should be happening shortly."

Jake and Carl exchanged glances. This was exactly what they'd hoped for. It gave Carl a chance to join in with his guitar, which he was becoming increasingly serious about, and Jake was finding more and more joy in singing, especially adding harmony to Carl's melody lines. An easy musical rapport had grown up between the two friends, and they reveled in any opportunity to join in the pervasive and frequently spontaneous musical events on the island.

Gisela's living room, much to Jake's delight, was decorated with actual furniture—not the makeshift orange crate and random cushion improvisations which so often passed for chairs and couches at friends' fincas on the island. A low-slung leather sofa and several expensive-looking Danish-design chairs ringed the room with a light blue Persian rug in the center and throw cushions of various sizes and colors strewn about. On one of the cushions, a skinny man with long stringy hair, a sparse beard, and a careworn face sat with crossed legs, tuning a guitar. He looked up and nodded at the newcomers, smiling slightly without interrupting his tuning. He had a particularly intense look about him as though he'd seen his share of suffering in life. Behind him, a man with an angelic face and curly blond hair with a blue silk scarf wrapped around his neck sat at the end of the couch, casually strumming his guitar. Both men seemed lost in their own private worlds.

"Everyone," announced Gisela gesturing toward the newcomers, "this is Carl and Jake. And these guys are Ernst and Jodi. They're visiting from Switzerland. Can I get you guys something to drink?" she asked, turning to the new guests.

"Some water'd be nice," said Jake.

"That's it?" she asked, again with that sly twinkle in her blue eyes. "You wouldn't like a beer? It's okay, really. You don't have to be shy."

"Is it cold?" asked Jake hopefully.

"Of course!" said Gisela. "We have a real fridge, you know." She said this with pride in her voice, and it occurred to Jake that he didn't know anyone on the island whose home was even hooked up to the grid, so the idea of having a modern kitchen was a novelty indeed.

Jake followed her into the kitchen, where a young girl with a deep tan and silky blonde hair to her waist was seated at the kitchen table doing what appeared to be her homework. She stared blankly at Jake and quickly bowed her head again to focus on her task.

"Chloe," said Gisela peering into the fridge, "say hi to Jake. He's a friend of Carl."

"Oh, hi," said the girl perking up immediately. "Are you American too?"

"As a matter of fact, I am," said Jake. "Is that okay with you?"

"Of course!" she said in a clipped British accent. "I love Americans. They're fun!"

"You mean Josie is fun," corrected Gisela, pulling out two frosty bottles of San Miguel from the well-stocked fridge. "That's her best friend from the British school she attends here," she explained to Jake. "Not all Americans are fun though, darling."

"They're not?" asked the girl, bewildered. "Well, I think they are. And, of course, Josie is fun," she pronounced, "otherwise, she wouldn't be my friend! But I like Carl too. He's kind of fun, isn't he?"

Jake had to laugh. "You're right, Chloe. He is kind of fun."

"You know, in a peculiar kind of way."

"I think I know exactly what you mean," agreed Jake. "Peculiar, eh? My, that's a big word for such a young girl."

"I'm not that young," she protested. "I'm almost eleven!"

"Oh then, I do stand corrected," said Jake. "I didn't realize you were that old."

"You're not making fun of me, are you?" she asked.

"Whoa, what?" said Jake. "Making fun of you? How would that even be possible? You're so …"

"So what?"

"Exactly. So what. That's what I was going to say. I'm so glad we can agree on that."

"That's not what I … oh, *you*," said the girl, crinkling up her eyes.

"What then, my dear?" said Jake. "C'mon now, spit it out!"

"I'll spit it out on you!" she proclaimed, suddenly pushing her chair back and moving rapidly around the table until she was standing directly in front of Jake, her head barely reaching his chest. Standing on her tiptoes, she arched her head backward, made a throat-clearing sound, and pointed her foaming lips upward.

"Chloe!" warned her mother.

"All right then," said Jake crossing his arms on his chest and tilting his head back with a stoic expression. "I'm ready. Go ahead, then. I can take it!"

This unexpected challenge created a gurgle of laughter rising up from the young girl's belly, increasing more and more until quite abruptly, saliva started dribbling from her mouth, quickly flowing to the tip of her chin. Looking around frantically for something to wipe her face with, she made a desperate lunge forward, grabbing the front of Jake's coverall, and pressed her slimy chin against it.

"*Ach, du Schweinchen* (Oh, you little pig)," said her mother.

"It's his fault, Mummy," she insisted, punching Jake in the gut with her fist.

"Oof," said Jake, staggering around the room like a punch-drunk fighter until he crashed into the table and collapsed to the floor, his long hair splayed around his head.

"Now see what you've done!" said Gisela in mock horror.

"Oh, Mummy, he's just faking it. You'll see."

But Jake remained motionless on the floor.

"Jake!" said the girl kicking him gently with her bare foot. "Wake up! You can stop pretending now. It's not funny, you know."

Jake's head just rolled to the side. He moaned as saliva began trickling out of his gaping mouth onto the red tile floor.

"Mummy, tell him to stop," said the girl, concern beginning to creep into her voice.

"Oh Ja-ake," said Gisela bending down to roll a cold bottle of beer across his cheek, eliciting a low groan. After another pass, this time across his forehead, Jake's eyes snapped open. "Huh? Where am I?" he asked, blinking furiously, his gaze finally alighting on Chloe. "Oh, it's you, is it?" he said, leaping to his feet. Releasing a low growl, he advanced toward her, his arms stretched out in zombie fashion.

Chloe shrieked in terror and took off, racing through the living room with Moische following close behind, stopping only when they reached the safety of the terrace. Jake dropped his arms and turned to look at Gisela, winking mischievously.

"Well," she said with an amused grin. "It looks like you've made a new friend."

Ernst and Jodi were stoic witnesses to Chloe's flight, no doubt having witnessed her histrionic tendencies on previous occasions. Carl, however, addressed his friend with real concern.

"What'd you do now?" he asked, glaring at his friend as he looked up from tuning his guitar.

"Dunno, Carl. Sometimes when people first get to know me, they just freak out, I guess."

"I think these two have met a match," said Gisela.

"Met *their* match," corrected Carl. "Hmmm, well, I guess they are both a couple of natural-born fools ..."

"I'm not a fool!" corrected Chloe storming back into the living room.

"Fooler-arounders is what I meant to say," corrected Carl.

"Did not!" said Chloe, who'd crossed the room and now stood next to Jake, her arms crossed on her chest.

"Sure he did," said Jake, who casually dropped his arm around her shoulder. "I'll bet you fool around all the time. I know I do. I think that's what Carl meant to say."

"What does it mean exactly, 'fool around?'" she asked.

"You know, have fun!" said Jake. "Isn't that what you like to do?"

"Sure," she said, leaning into Jake. "Who doesn't?"

"Well," said Jake, half whispering in her ear, "some people don't, believe it or not. I'll bet you've met some people like that before, especially back in Germany," he said, winking at Gisela.

"I don't go to Germany much anymore," said the girl.

"Because it's not as much fun?" asked Jake.

"Actually, yes!"

"I rest my case," said Jake.

"That's not really true," said Gisela firing up another Marlboro. "You always love it when we go back to Berlin."

"That's true, Mummy. But to be honest, I'd rather stay here," she said, continuing to gently pound her fist into Jake's solar plexus.

"Who wouldn't?" asked Ernst, who was beginning to play some blues riffs on his guitar. "This is the mellowest place of all."

"Where exactly are you from, Ernst?" asked Jake.

"I'm from Basel," he said. "Do you know it?"

"I've been there," said Jake recalling a weekend break he'd taken from work at the ski resort. "That city goes crazy at Karneval. The drinking, the costumes, the revelry—I love it!"

"My favorite time to be there," said Ernst, his craggy face finally smiling. "It's the one time of year when the Swiss really let down their hair."

Jake noticed that the angel-faced Jodi, who reminded him of Harpo Marx, had finished rolling a joint and was holding it up for Gisela's inspection. She nodded, announcing to her daughter that it was time to get back in the kitchen and finish up her homework. To Jake's surprise, Chloe acquiesced without objection, saying 'Yes, Mummy,' before disappearing back into the kitchen.

"Wow," said Jake. "No argument there!"

"She knows I don't allow her in here when we're smoking," said Gisela.

"Marijuana, you mean."

"It's hash," corrected Jodi.

"Yes, exactly," said Gisela. "She knows it's something that adults do. Just like drinking."

Just then, the sound of someone stumbling in the kitchen diverted Jake's attention. A tall man with a protruding belly suddenly appeared in the doorway wearing bell-bottom jeans and a blue Moroccan shirt stretched tightly over his distended gut.

"What's this about drinking?" he asked.

"Wouldn't you like to know?" asked Gisela, eyeing him coolly.

"Well, well," said the man in German. "Who have we here?"

"Dieter, this is Carl's friend, Jake."

"Oh shit, another American?" he asked, using the pejorative term *Ami*.

"*Ja, ich bin ein Ami!*" Jake assured him.

"You speak German?" asked Dieter, taken aback.

"*Jawohl,*" said Jake. A brief conversation regarding their lives on the island ensued. Dieter summarized his own activities with the vague term *Geschaefte machen* or doing business without providing many details. Dark puffy bags beneath his eyes betrayed his exhaustion, and Jake ascertained that he'd just woken up from an apparently ineffective nap. A little wobbly on his feet, he strode into the living room, grabbing a red Fender electric guitar which was leaning against the wall. Plugging it into an amp, he turned up the volume and proceeded to pound the strings while fanning the instrument back and forth, producing a screeching crescendo of ear-splitting noise. Jake winced, wondering if his Hendrix-style warm-up might lead to something more enjoyable, but it sadly turned out to be the whole show. Upon completing his performance, Dieter stood there for a moment swaying in place, his puffy eyes closed, lost in some inner revery, before stretching his arm out to Ernst, who grabbed the guitar just as Dieter slumped onto the couch. Sliding down on the cushion, he allowed his thin legs to stretch out on the carpet in front of him while both hands held onto his belly, which stretched out his shirt like a large inflated beach ball.

"Go on, Carl," he pleaded, yawning. "Play something."

"Sure thing," said Carl. "What about that song we were working on last time?" he suggested, smiling at Gisela. "That Joni Mitchell tune, remember?"

"You mean the one off the *Blue* album?" she asked, unfazed by Dieter's theatrics.

"Yeah, that one," said Carl, strumming the introductory chords.

Jake picked up a pair of bongo drums and began softly pounding out a rhythm as Carl called out the chord changes so that Ernst and Jodi could join in as well. Gisela closed her eyes and leaned back against a leather Moroccan cushion, her lovely head swaying back and forth to the beat. After a few more rounds of chords, her soulful voice began filling the room, lamenting the lonely road she was traveling on.

Carl wasn't kidding, thought Jake as a shiver ran down his spine. What a voice! He looked around the room, feeling an odd sensation of familiarity. *Am I having a déjà vu experience?* he wondered. It wasn't a concept he ordinarily gave much credence to, but Gisela's long ornate dress put him in mind of some courtly raiment from the Middle Ages, and he couldn't shake the impression of revisiting a troubadour scenario from some lifetime long ago. It was a powerful sensation and convincing enough to persuade him that this impromptu gathering might prove to be pivotal in his life. He found himself wondering if some kind of old bond was being re-established, which might prove to be of momentous importance.

Yes, thought Jake, as he listened to her singing Joni's lyrics about searching for the key to set her free, her mellifluous voice filling his heart with a curious blend of elation and anticipation. *Aren't we all, indeed?*

Chapter 38

Sometime after midnight, wending their way back to their recently rented finca in the van, Carl and Jake found themselves in a particularly expansive mood. The sky was clear and full of pinpricks of light, magnified in intensity by their hashish high from the impromptu party at Gisela's. Jake loved riding shotgun in Carl's van with its huge front windshield, allowing for a panoramic view of the terrain. It was especially pleasant late at night when traffic was minimal, stoking the illusion they were travelers on a deserted highway like some lonely heroes from an imaginary song Leonard Cohen might have written.

Listening to a tape of their favorite music on the stereo and cruising along carefree, they could enjoy the starlit terraced fields and palm tree-dotted landscape whizzing by, with an occasional glimpse of the opaque Mediterranean Sea in the distance. Carl slid in a Steely Dan cassette, and "Deacon Blues" began booming from the speakers crooning about the expanding man, providing the perfect accompaniment to their dreamlike state of mind.

For some time, they cruised along together without exchanging a word, grooving to the sound and the lyrics until Carl finally spoke.

"You and Gisela seemed to really hit it off."

"You noticed?" said Jake.

"Who didn't?" said Carl. "Except maybe Dieter. He was too out of it to notice much of anything."

"Yeah, I get the feeling he's like that a lot," said Jake.

"That's cuz he mixes all kinds of shit together. Booze, pills, maybe a little coke, and hash. It's hard to maintain like that."

"I noticed," said Jake.

"I used to have a thing for Gisela too, y'know," said Carl.

"Too?" said Jake.

"Oh c'mon now, don't pretend, *amigo*. There was some real energy there between you guys."

"Okay," said Jake. "I won't deny it. But what about your thing? I vaguely remember you mentioning that. What happened there?"

"Nothing, really. Just looks and glances. Hugs that went on a little too long. I tried to kiss her once, but she pushed me away. Said she didn't feel that way."

"That's good," said Jake.

"Why's that good?" asked Carl.

"Cuz she said she just didn't feel that way. It's not like she said, 'Stop, I can't do that. I'm married.' That means there's a possibility she might feel that way under different circumstances."

"Like with you?" asked Carl turning to give his friend a sardonic grin.

"Yeah," said Jake grinning back. "Why not?"

"Why not indeed," said Carl. "It would kind of make sense. You speak German. And you're both romantics."

"She's romantic?"

"How else would you interpret that look on her face when she's singing Joni Mitchell?"

"You're right about that," said Jake. "There's no hiding romance when it's in your blood."

"Exactly," said Carl. "Just watch out for Dieter. He's a strange one."

"I could tell," said Jake, pulling the recliner lever. His seat went nearly flat, and he drifted back into the music, contemplating Steely Dan's poetic portrayal of ramblers and gamblers, crazy schemes and dreams, throwing kisses and saying goodbye as the midnight island highway rumbled along beneath them.

Chapter 39

Ever since their introduction, Jake had found himself scheming to meet Gisela again, whether on the white sands of the beach at Aguas Blancas or in Ibiza town, where she worked a few days a week in her husband's boutique. He was reluctant to visit her at home in San Carlos, being fearful that Dieter might become suspicious of his intentions and manage to somehow put the kibosh on their budding relationship. He knew that it made no sense, but the feeling of *déjà vu* and inevitability he'd had when they first met remained profoundly real for him. She was married, but in Jake's mind, her relationship with Dieter was like a building on the brink of collapse. It was just a matter of time before the rotting foundation fell in upon itself.

Hoping to meet her in town, Jake drove the Tank in early and parked near the central plaza. The sun was baking the Vara de Rey with relentless intensity that morning as Jake sat at a table under the awning of the Café del Teatro, a café like any other, except that perhaps by virtue of its name, it attracted a more Bohemian crowd. He had just finished emptying coins and wrinkled 100 peseta notes from his pockets onto the table in front of him when a surly-looking waiter approached.

"Una cerveza, por favor," muttered Jake, sending the man scurrying back toward the kitchen. Jake could no longer deny it. He was running out of cash, and his old strategy of leaving the island to earn money in Switzerland no longer seemed like a feasible plan. He wanted to be able

to stay where Gisela was—right there on Ibiza. He just hadn't yet figured out a way to make that happen.

It wasn't his habit to drink beer so early in the day, but today there seemed no reason not to. Maybe a little alcohol would loosen up that rational part of his brain, which until now had been incapable of coming up with a solution to his problem. He needed inspiration no matter where it came from. He knew if he didn't find a job very soon, he'd be completely broke, and legal work seemed out of reach. Spain didn't just casually hand out work permits for Americans.

"Hey, *amigo, que pasa?*"

Jake recognized the gravelly voice without even looking up. It was Ruben, his former housemate from Santa Inés. After Jake and Carl had moved out, Ruben and Mary Lou had soon followed suit, unable to pay the rent there on their own. Having never managed to repair the axle on their broken-down Renault, the couple ended up stuck at the beach in Salinas, doing whatever it took to survive. In the meantime, despite Ruben's edginess and Mary Lou's eccentric behavior, the three of them had managed to become friends. Jake enjoyed hanging out on Salinas Beach, which was not far from the finca that he and Carl were currently renting. While Carl stayed home and practiced for the hotel gigs he was starting to get with a band he'd joined up with, Jake would take the Tank and drive to Salinas to enjoy the serenity and beauty of the nudist beach there while he wrote in his journal and tried to figure out what the next step of his adventure would be. The three of them would often commiserate about ways to stay afloat on the island. Ruben had tried playing guitar in a café on the beach for tips until the owner grew tired of his erratic playing style and surly remarks to customers. But Ruben and Mary Lou weren't easily discouraged. They always had a contingency plan. There was the plan to sell tiny, almost nonexistent string bikinis on the beach, the plan to sell sliced-up cantaloupes and watermelons on the beach, and the plan to sell mini-massages on the beach. As far as Jake could ascertain, all aspects of their plan revolved around being on the beach. They were full of ideas that might result in a brief period of provisional work until the Guardia Civil would step in demanding to see work permits. And the *guardia* in their shiny black tri-cornered hats with lethal-looking machine guns slung over their shoulders could be very intimidating. It was a wonder to Jake that the couple were still allowed to sell on the beach at all, although he suspected that Mary Lou's shapely figure on display in her string bikini may have played a role in the guardias' tolerant attitude. Jake had noticed more than once that they seemed to train their binoculars on her voluptuous figure far longer than seemed necessary.

The waiter soon appeared, setting Jake's beer down in front of him. Ruben immediately reached out, grabbed the bottle, and took the first swig. He smacked his lips and wiped them with the back of his hand before handing it back to Jake.

"Go ahead, brother," he said, emitting a murderous belch. "My beer is your beer."

"Very funny," said Jake lifting the bottle up to his cheek and savoring the icy coolness. "I suppose you're here to tell me about some new idea you have about something you guys wanna try and sell on the beach?"

"Jake, whassamatter? You got some kinda better idea? My guess is you drinking beer at 10 a.m. means you don't. Unless, of course, you're celebrating something like that letter you've been talking about with a check from Paris? No? Didn't think so. And, anyway, pal, this time it's nothing to do with the beach."

"It's not?" said Jake squinting up at the man. Ruben's long blond hair, the texture of straw, was tied back in a ponytail, and his deeply tanned, freckled skin looked prematurely wrinkled and old. One earlobe held a golden loop, and his penetrating blue eyes were hidden behind the silver mirror lens of his shades. Despite his reservations, Jake couldn't help but feel a grudging respect for the man. Ruben came from the rough and tumble world of life on the streets of Seattle. Or at least that's what he claimed. He had survival skills, and Jake admired that. He always imagined himself to be deficient in that department, perhaps because he'd mostly had his nose buried in a book while friends of his had learned practical things like carpentry or mechanics.

"You're giving up on the beach?" asked Jake, his curiosity piqued. "I thought that's what you and Mary Lou lived for. The easy life of the beachcomber."

"I gotta admit, *compadre*," said Ruben exhaling smoke from a hand-rolled cigarette, "this living from hand-to-mouth is starting to get kind of old. We've been together for a long time now, and whadda we have to show for it? I mean don't get me wrong. We love the beach life here. It's cool and all that, but we wanna try something different."

"Like what?"

Ruben removed his shades and leaned into Jake conspiratorially, his blue eyes flickering with excitement.

"Well, me and Mary Lou've been talking about trying something over on Mallorca, you know, where nobody knows us," he said, winking. "Something a little bit different where you can make lotsa money real fast. Easy work too."

Jake wasn't sure if he liked that wink. It felt like someone pulling down a shade to cover up some sordid deed. He drained the bottle, belched, and placed both elbows on the table, leaning into Ruben. "Listen," he said, "I'm not sure where you're going with this, but I'm guessing it's the kinda thing you can get into trouble for. How much trouble are we talking here?"

"No trouble at all, Jake. Not if we do it right."

"Do what right?"

Ruben dropped his voice even lower. "Mary Lou told me she's ready to give it up," he said.

"Give what up?"

"You know," he said as his lips and eyes formed a leering mask. "Are you talking about—"

"Pussy," Ruben interrupted. "I'm talking about peddling some goddamn pussy."

"Wait … you and Mary Lou?" asked Jake incredulously. "Your own girlfriend?"

"That's right," said Ruben, grinning steadily.

"Jesus," said Jake. "You're not kidding, are you?"

"Nope," said Ruben. "Serious as a heart attack."

"Why do I get the feeling you think this has something to do with me?" asked Jake.

"Well," said Ruben, leaning in. "It's not just me and Mary Lou, see. There's this other girl, Nancy . . . from London."

"Nancy?" said Jake, scrunching up his face in thought. "That name sounds familiar. Do I know her?"

"Yes," said Ruben, "you do. You met her at the beach selling melons with Mary Lou."

Jake recalled now. She was a plump vivacious strawberry-blond with red rosy cheeks and a big ass. They'd spent a few hours on the beach together just hanging out and chatting. He remembered she said "blimey" a lot. He used to think only pirates said "blimey."

"Okay," said Jake. "So Nancy wants to sell her body too. What's that got to do with me?"

"Don't you get it?" asked Ruben. "I'm gonna have my hands full with Mary Lou. I'm not gonna have time to look after Nancy too."

Jake slumped back in his chair, feeling stunned. He held the still cool bottle to his forehead rolling it back and forth.

"So let me get this straight . . . you're saying you want me to be Nancy's ... what? Her pimp?"

Ruben smiled. He appeared to be enjoying himself. "I like to think of it as being more of a promoter," he said, winking again. "Once we get to Mallorca, you can help her get set up in a hotel, maybe chat her up to some of the oil workers who hang out in the bars there, you know, from Algeria and Libya and the Middle East. Follow her at a distance. You know, just keep an eye on her, be there for her if and when she needs you...."

Jake tried to imagine himself, decidedly not a fighter, with hair hanging down to his shoulders and a face that exuded the toughness of a marshmallow, confronting hard-drinking oil field workers who considered brawling a sport and women nothing more than dispensable objects. The incongruity of it made him shake his head and laugh out loud.

"What does 'be there for her' mean?" he asked.

"You know, just so she knows she's not out there by herself. So she knows somebody cares."

"Why can't you do it?"

"Mary Lou wouldn't like it," said Ruben.

This all sounded more than a little crazy to Jake, but the heat and the beer had given him just enough of a buzz to allow him to relax with the absurdity of it. He took a deep breath and sighed, looking out at the sun-drenched plaza where busy Ibicencos were scurrying back and forth earning their livelihood, unconcerned with work permits or harassment from the Guardia Civil. Ibiza was starting to boom, and they were loving it. He adjusted a threadbare strap on his overalls and gave Ruben a weary look.

"What's in it for me?"

"That's the spirit," said Ruben, "I knew you'd come around! Thirty percent of whatever she brings in."

What a bizarre idea, thought Jake. *But ... could it work?* Could it give him more time to pursue Gisela? Could he really actually be someone's pimp? What a horrible word. *Okay, promoter.* Was Nancy really going to be okay with it?

"And you've discussed this with Nancy?"

"*Absolutamente*, pal," said Ruben. "As a matter of fact, when I mentioned to her that *you* might wanna get involved, she got all excited. No, really, she did! She likes you, Jake. She'd really like to have you on her side."

"Sounds like you were pretty sure you could recruit me."

"Look, we've been talking for a while now about how hard it is to make any real money here, haven't we? This is a good opportunity, Jake. For us and for the girls. It's a win-win, in fact! And the girls wanna do it! It's not like we'd be twisting their arms."

Jake lifted his bottle up to the sun and turned it upside down, catching the few remaining drops on his outstretched tongue.

"I dunno, Ruben. Sounds pretty loco if you wanna know the truth."

"Listen, Jake," he said, his voice rising in intensity. "This isn't just about the girls or the money. This is about you and me doing stuff together! *Los dos compadres!* We're gonna hang out together over there, and I'm gonna teach you stuff. Stuff you never knew before, like how to play pool for money and how to cheat at poker ... you're always saying you like to learn new stuff, right? It ain't no big deal, bro. I've done this before. Back in Seattle. I'll show you the ropes, okay? We're gonna have a kick-ass time...I promise! And then we're gonna come back here with our pockets full of *dinero!*"

Ruben stood up and looking down at Jake, stretched out his hand. "Shake on it, *amigo*?" he asked.

Jake hesitated. "I'm not saying yes," he said, reluctantly extending his hand. "I'll think about it though."

Ruben smiled, the triumphant look in his eyes sending an involuntary shiver down Jake's spine.

"Come out to the beach this afternoon then," said Ruben, "just to feel things out with Mary Lou. You need to see she's into this too. It's not just my idea. But don't bring it up until I do, okay?"

"Why's that?" asked Jake.

"I got my reasons," said Ruben, vaguely. "You'll see. Just come, okay, *compadre?*"

Chapter 40

Ruben and Mary Lou's beach pad was a strange place to live—a kind of brick and plaster bungalow attached to a power generator which supplied electricity to the little shops and restaurants strewn along the beach. A termite-ridden telephone pole stuck out of the flat roof with wires leading off in several directions. Every once in a while, the motor would kick in and loudly clatter and hum like a misfiring engine for a quarter of an hour and then shut off again. The place had originally been built as a supply shed, but the two beachcombers had convinced the owners to rent it out very cheaply and turned it into their version of a cozy little nest just big enough for a few battered pieces of furniture and a propane powered hot plate to cook on. The owner of a nearby café serving mainly omelets and fried sardines allowed them to use their bathroom.

Jake showed up in the early afternoon, and the three of them were lounging around inside the bungalow, avoiding the sun and sipping cold beer, which Ruben had brought back from the local tienda and stored inside a bucket filled with ice. Jake was stretched out on a makeshift sofa a few feet away from where his friends lay entwined on the bed. The walls were decorated with colorful Indian prints of Hindu deities like Ganesha and Krishna, which you could buy for a song at the hippy market in Es Canar. Eric Clapton crooned softly on their small battery-powered tape deck in the corner, and the flowery scent of Mary Lou's favorite patchouli incense permeated the room. Jake took a deep drag on a joint filled with the typical mix of hashish and tobacco and looked out the room's only window, a square opening inlaid with rusty metal bars.

"Jesus, Ruben," he said, struggling to hold the smoke in his lungs, "doesn't this barred window ever freak you out? You know, remind you of when you were in jail?"

Jake wasn't shy about drawing Ruben out about his criminal past. He romanticized the man's bad boy image and fantasized that the darker episodes in his life must necessarily have imparted a kind of hard-won wisdom unattainable to someone like himself who'd grown up in a safe suburban world. Ruben leaned up on his elbows, exposing a set of rock-hard abs, which he was clearly very proud of. Settling his shoulders back into the peeling whitewash of the wall behind the bed, he offered Jake an enigmatic smile.

"Sometimes," he said, stretching out a hand to grab the joint Jake proffered. "But it's not like I have nightmares about it."

"Liar," said Mary Lou poking him in the ribs.

"Ow," said Ruben looking annoyed. "Don't do that, Mary Lou. Anyway, you'd have nightmares too if you'd had to pass a kidney stone lying on the floor of your cell, and it took a couple days to do it, and the guards wouldn't take you to the infirmary cuz they were motherfucking sadists," he said pausing long enough to take a big toke. "Do you have any idea what that kind of pain is like?" he asked, holding the smoke in his lungs. "They say," he continued with Mary Lou chiming in, "it's the closest thing there is to what a woman goes through at childbirth."

"Very funny!" said Ruben glaring at his mate as he blew out a cloud of smoke.

"Well, it's not like I haven't heard this story before," said Mary Lou, fixing him with her one good eye.

"So what happened?" asked Jake. "Did you end up finally passing it?"

"Eventually, yeah. Goddamned thing wasn't any bigger than a booger, neither. But Jesus did that hurt."

"I know you were in for drugs," said Jake. "But how'd you get caught? You never did tell me."

"Same as they catch anybody. Just plain bad luck. Didn't I already tell you all this?"

"C'mon, humor me, man. You know you're my favorite outlaw."

"Mine too," said Mary Lou reaching her hand up to pat his chest.

"I was just in the wrong place at the wrong time," said Ruben, clearly enjoying the attention. "Simple as that. I was driving through New Mexico on my way back to Seattle from Texas. The cops set up a roadblock for somebody else. But there I was with so much weed in my trunk you didn't need to be a goddamned sniffer dog to smell it. Ended up going down for interstate trafficking."

"A federal offense," said Mary Lou matter-of-factly.

"Sure as shit," said Ruben. "Hired me a good lawyer, though, and was out in only eighteen months. Don't plan on ever going back again neither. C'mon, I already told you this, didn't I?"

Ruben pretended to be annoyed, but Jake knew he loved telling and retelling tales of his renegade existence.

"So besides the kidney stone," Jake prodded, "did anything really bad ever happen to you inside?"

Ruben's eyes had narrowed into slits as he took another ferocious toke.

"You mean did I ever get gang-banged in the shower? Stuff like that?" he asked.

Jake hesitated. "I guess."

Ruben grimaced slightly, pushed himself further up against the wall, and reached for Mary Lou's hip as he blew out a dense cloud of pearly gray smoke. "You been readin' too much pulp fiction, pardner," he said, turning his head toward the window. A troubled look came into his eyes, though, as he gazed past the bars to the immaculate sandy beach beyond. The sun was dropping like a melting scoop of mango gelato into the sea, and the day was beginning to cool down a little. They all agreed it was time to go outside and get some fresh air. By now, the beer, the hash, and the incense were all combining to lift Jake's mood. He was feeling happy in a way that had nothing to do with having nice things, or a good job, or faith in God, or a loving family. He had none of those things. He was happy in a way that only comes from getting ripped: from having the pleasure centers of the brain plugged in and lit up like a Christmas tree. He felt high and lucid and free and eager to lend his uncharted life some fresh momentum.

"Where's Nancy at these days?" he asked, suddenly anxious to find out if Ruben's plan was for real as they all three emerged into the fading sunlight. He remembered Ruben admonishing him not to bring it up, but his reticence had begun to make Jake suspicious of his claim that Mary Lou was totally on board with the project. Ruben just stood there saying nothing, glaring at Jake with his hands thrust deep into the pockets of his shorts. Finally, Mary Lou spoke.

"Nancy?" she asked, sounding surprised. "She's … around. Why do you ask?"

"She came up earlier today in a conversation Ruben and I were having in town. That's all."

"I see," said Mary Lou evasively. "I've actually been wanting to talk to her. Shall we go and find her then?"

"Sure," said Jake. "You mean go back into town?"

"Why not?" asked Mary Lou, her lazy eyelid fluttering like a wounded moth. "That is if you wanna go."

Jake looked at the two of them and grinned. He was always up for a trip into town at night, especially the old town with its hustle and bustle and cobblestoned rise to the lookout on top of the city with spectacular views of the sea. "Why not?" he said. He felt somewhat duplicitous, sensing that both he and Mary Lou were trying to feel each other out about the as yet unspoken new endeavor without being too direct about it. "Nancy's always fun to hang out with," he continued. "C'mon, we can ride in the Tank."

Chapter 41

Mary Lou sat beside Jake in the front seat of the Tank with Ruben curled up in the back. Jake had to crawl over the gear shift and into the driver's seat through the passenger door, avoiding the bungee cords that now held the steering wheel in place. He drove slowly on the way into town, hoping not to attract the attention of any guardias despite the conspicuous roar of the engine. No one had the energy to compete with that noise, so there was little conversation driving into town. They had just arrived and were cruising along the waterfront looking for parking when a tall figure in a glossy tri-cornered black hat with a machine gun slung over his shoulder suddenly rose up in the headlights, his white-gloved hands waving them over to the side of the road. Jake glanced anxiously in the rearview mirror where his eyes met Ruben's, which were unexpectedly twinkling with merriment as though this were just part of the evening's entertainment.

"It's gonna be all right, *amigo*," he said, leaning forward. "Just be cool, man. No worries."

Jake took a deep breath and sighed, aware of a sudden churning in his guts.

"Everyone got their papers?" he asked as the Tank lurched to a halt.

"I think so," said Mary Lou digging in her purse. "How 'bout you, hon?"

"Always," said Ruben patting his chest where a leather pouch hung loosely round his neck. There was no more time for discussion. Jake quickly shut off the noisy engine as the guardia, a handsome young man with the inevitable moustache, swaggered toward the vehicle. Ignoring the passengers, he walked slowly around the car, his black boots throwing up little puffs of dust. For a moment, Jake, who'd grown used to wearing nothing but sandals, felt sorry for the man, imagining how his feet must suffer in the baking heat of the day. The hopeful thought flashed through his mind that now that it was evening and cooler, the guardia must necessarily be in a better mood.

Jake felt Ruben's hot breath in his ear. "Just be your normal charming self, Jake," he whispered, "and everything will be just fine."

The taciturn guardia had finished circling the car, which was bathed in light from a streetlamp, and stood in front of the shiny orange hood, staring down at the space where a license plate should have been. He pointed at the space, peering into Jake's face through the windshield, his chin thrust upward in a questioning posture.

"Smile, Jake," whispered Ruben.

Jake nodded his head and, without dropping his gaze, reached underneath the seat and pulled out the license plate. The bolts holding it onto the front of the car had rusted off, making reattachment impossible. Jake held it up in front of his chest, upside down at first, but then quickly righted it, making him appear like a criminal posing for a mug shot. He jabbed at the front of the plate with his finger, shrugging his shoulders and grinning like a fool. Everyone held their breath. The possibility that Jake's frivolity might be just the provocation the guardia needed to take out his frustrations on some hapless hippies after a long hot day in a sweltering pair of boots hung ominously in the air. In the end, though, apparently amused by Jake's goofy pantomime, he grinned and shook his head, for some reason having decided to cut them all some slack. Turning and walking away without a backward glance, he laced his gloved hands together behind his back and continued sauntering into town.

"Oh, my God!" yelled Jake after restarting the engine. He pounded on the steering wheel so hard the bungee cords started humming. "I don't even wanna think of how that could've turned out."

"You did good, amigo," said Ruben. "Fortunately for us, I doubt that guardia was really interested in doing any work tonight."

"Yeah," agreed Mary Lou flashing one of her enchanting smiles. "Somehow, I get the feeling that guy was already slinking off to wait out the end of his shift playing backgammon in a cafe when he heard the roar of your car, Jake."

Jake started cursing the Tank but stopped short, feeling suddenly spooked. What if the car possessed some kind of anthropomorphic awareness? Might it react to a curse by breaking down even more? He gripped the steering wheel gently with his left hand and patted the dusty dashboard with his right, taking pains not to piss off his troublesome jalopy.

Chapter 42

T he city of Ibiza at night was always gorgeous to behold. An ancient walled town built on a hill, it started out at sea level, working its way up by a series of winding cobbled alleyways to sixteenth-century bulwarks on top of the remains of Moorish walls, which had mostly been restored to their original majestic condition. Whitewashed houses along with bars and shops and restaurants lined the way, competing for the most alluring view of the dark sea at night. Illuminated by spotlights, the oldest part of the town, D'Alt Vila, with its medieval fortifications, was a stunning sight to behold.

The trio found themselves drawn to the heights overlooking the harbor and worked their way steadily upward. The narrow streets were bustling with tourists and locals alike eager to enjoy the prevailing carnival atmosphere. Crowded restaurants and bars with their savory tempting plates of mouthwatering tapas were roaring with laughter and chatter. Pop music blared from powerful sound systems creating a dance club ambience on the cobblestoned streets, and gawkers crowded the outdoor cafés leering at passersby. Strolling past a boutique, Mary Lou stopped to look at some dresses, and Ruben quickly pulled Jake aside.

"Listen," he said, keeping his voice low, "about that thing we discussed this morning. I appreciate you not saying anything at the beach this afternoon. I haven't worked out all the details yet with Mary Lou."

"Christ," said Jake. "You made it sound like a done deal."

"It is, Jake … it is," insisted Ruben. "It's just that Mary Lou's being a bit, I dunno, hesitant, that's all."

"Hesitant?" asked Jake. "What's that supposed to mean? You mean she doesn't wanna do it?"

"No, that's not what I mean. I just need to work on her a little more."

Jake raised both hands to his face and squeezed his fingertips into the flesh beneath his eyeballs, pulling downward. He could feel the blood pounding in his temples. He suddenly felt weary and doubtful and verging on despair.

"Ruben," he said, "this is so fucked up. I would never agree to this if I didn't think Mary Lou was into it."

"I know, man, I know," he said. "Don't worry! She's into it. She really is. She just has to know that we're really gonna be there for her."

"How do we prove that?"

"Leave it to me, will ya man? We just need to find Nancy, and then we'll all sit down and work this thing out together, okay? It's gonna be a piece of cake, you'll see."

Sure enough, they soon found Nancy sitting on the terrace of an outdoor café in the Placa Desamparadors high up in the old quarter. She had a carafe of vino tinto in front of her and was smoking Fortunas and scribbling postcards. Mary Lou was the first one to spot her.

"Nancy!" she yelled. "*Hola, chica!*"

Jake could see that Nancy was half in the bag when she looked up from her writing. Her gaze was bleary, and her fair skin looked mottled and puffy. Her shoulder-length ash-blonde hair was parted in the middle with an unattractive oily sheen. Peering up over a pair of tortoiseshell glasses, her blue eyes were sunk into dark-rimmed sockets.

"Oh, hall-oo," she cooed, gathering up her postcards into a pile. "I was just thinking about you guys."

"Mentioning us in your postcards, were you?" asked Mary Lou as they all sat down at her table.

"Just scribbling a few words to Mum and Dad in London. You know, let them know their lovely daughter's still alive and kicking! Blimey! C'mon, sit down. Let's all have a drink, shall we?"

"Uh, Nancy, you remember Jake, don't you?" asked Ruben.

"Of course," she said, moistening her lips with her tongue and giving Jake a lascivious wink.

Jake smiled, remembering how he'd been lying stoned and mostly naked at Salinas beach the day they'd met. Peering out through a cheap pair of shades at the blue-green waves, he'd been eavesdropping on some tacky euro-pop from a nearby boom box as Nancy and Mary Lou made the rounds with a tray full of luscious green melon slices. His trim, tanned body had been glistening with coconut oil, laid out on display like a prime filet of beef. He remembered leaning up on his elbows to watch the heavy globes of Nancy's thonged ass jiggling up and down as she picked her way through the tourists laid out haphazardly along the beach. Later that day, Nancy'd approached him with her last unsold slice of melon, and they'd sat chatting together on the beach for a while as the sun sank slowly beneath the horizon. She'd been friendly and sincere, and Jake had liked her enormously.

Before Jake had gotten a chance to speak, the waiter arrived, and they all ordered beer and fried sardines with French fries, the cheapest meal on the menu.

"Tell me, Nancy," said Jake after the waiter had left, "what have you been up to lately?"

"Not much, I'm afraid. Trying to keep my bloody body and soul together. It hasn't been easy of late."

"Can't you find a job?" he asked. "After all, you Brits are at least allowed to work here, right?"

"Yeah, sure. I mean legally, yes, I could. But so could a thousand other Brits. And they're the ones who've taken all the jobs. All the good ones, that is."

The way she said it clued Jake in that Nancy hadn't been trying all that hard to find gainful employment. From what Ruben and Mary Lou had already told him about her, he suspected she wasn't all that interested in working. Nobody Jake knew was.

"So what did you do in London?" he asked. "Before you came here."

She looked down at her plate, twirling her fork in a puddle of grease.

"I was what I guess you'd call a go-go dancer. Worked the club circuit. Was damned good at it too, I dare say."

"But that's great!" said Jake. "Can't you do that here? Discos are sprouting up all over the place."

"Well, Jake, in case you haven't noticed, I did put on a bit of weight. It's so kind of you, by the way, not to notice. Don't look quite the same in my go-go outfit anymore. Hah! And the competition is stiff, believe me. That's why I'm stuck here, to be honest. Flew down on a whim with a long-since flown the coop boyfriend and haven't done anything since but eat my way into a bigger dress size like some bloody calf being fattened for slaughter."

"Hey," interrupted Ruben, who'd been shifting nervously in his seat. "Let's talk about something else, shall we? How about a toast … to us!" He extended his beer over the center of the table, and they all reached out to toast each other.

"Cheers," said Nancy, belching after draining her glass. "I guess it could be worse. At least I've still got friends."

"You bet you do," said Ruben. "Right, Mary Lou?"

"Right," she said, smiling. They all drank and engaged in aimless chitchat for a while, mopping up the grease on their plates with thick chunks of hearty white bread, amusing themselves with remarks about the passing tourists, and enjoying the nighttime ambience with its welcome coolness and the gradual emergence of a panoply of stars.

"Well then," said Ruben at last. "As long as we're all here together, we might as well talk business."

"Now that is a bloody good idea, Ruben, bloody good," said Nancy, whose cheeks were glowing now like shiny red apples. "Because to tell you the truth, I am desperate to make some *mun-eh*!"

"I hear ya," said Jake. "Aren't we all, though?"

"That's what I'm talking about!" said Ruben growing excited. "Let's quit beating around the bush then, ladies. It's time to either shit or get off the pot, know what I mean?" His eyes darted back and forth between the two women daring them to challenge him.

"Look," said Mary Lou, "we all know what you're getting at, Ruben. It's what we've been talking about for weeks now. And, you're right, we do need to finally make a decision about, you know … that!"

She turned to Jake, her one droopy eyelid slightly aquiver. "I assume you're in on this as well?"

"I am," said Jake nodding his head, "but only if you and Nancy really are willing partners."

"Good," she said, flashing her smile. "That's what we wanted to hear, right, Nancy?"

Nancy tilted back her head and howled—a real loose belly laugh.

Settling back in her chair, she took a deep drag on her cigarette. "Ah, Jaysus Christ himself," she said in a mocking Irish lilt. "Jake," she said, turning to face him. "Can you and I take a little stroll together? Just the two of us? Please?"

Ruben and Mary Lou looked taken aback at first but finally just shrugged as Jake and Nancy excused themselves and made their way arm in arm toward a higher elevation. Leaning against a stone wall for support high above the town, the two of them gazed down at the bustling scene below. They could see Ruben and Mary Lou hunched over their beers, apparently deep in conversation.

"Well now, Jake," said Nancy, huffing and puffing from the climb, "I just wanted the two of us to get away from the two of them, at least for a moment, to make sure we're both on the same page and all."

"Nancy … first tell me. Are you about to throw up, or is that just air in your cheeks?"

"Blimey, Jake. It's only me tryin' to catch my breath! I may be drunk, but I'm not that drunk. Just relax. I'm not gonna puke on ya, mate."

"That's a relief," said Jake chuckling. The two of them stood in silence for a moment, leaning against one another, shoulder to shoulder, feeling each other out.

"I think," said Nancy, giggling nervously, "that I can't believe I'm asking you to do this. Be my pimp, I mean. Because that's one thing I'm definitely not sending any postcards home about."

"I prefer the word promoter," said Jake. "Pimp sounds, I dunno, too ominous. God, if my parents knew half the shit I'm up to these days …"

"What would your mum think about this?" prodded Nancy.

"My mum? Well, my real mum's dead. Has been since I was eleven. I suppose the real concern, if I had one, would be what my dad would think."

"You mean you don't care anymore?"

"Not really," said Jake, taking a hit on her cigarette. "Ever since my mom died, he's been drifting further and further away, not just from me but from everybody. I think something died inside him too, and he doesn't even realize it. Or maybe he does. Hard to say. It's not like he would ever talk about it. He's one of these kind of guys who gets up and goes to work every day at a soulless job in an office that I'm pretty sure he hates, although even that's hard to say for sure. I think he's lost his way, and he just doesn't know it. Or maybe he does. That's even sadder to think about."

"Oh, Jake, look at you! So serious all of a sudden."

"You're the one who brought it up," said Jake.

"Brought what up? Parents?"

"Yeah," said Jake. "Whether we like it or not, they exist, don't they? Secretly influencing our lives from a distance. Or not, as the case may be."

"But how is he influencing yours, Jake? You don't seem that sad or unhappy."

"Thanks, Nance. I don't think it's my nature to be unhappy. But I do think about him from time to time. This sad, pale man with neat short Brylcreemed hair, wearing a suit with a briefcase in his hand, trudging through life like a robot, oozing heaviness, full of mostly negative judgments about everything and everybody. Is that how your dad is?"

"My dad? Good lord, no," said Nancy. "I mean, thank heavens he's not like that. Mine is actually quite a bit of fun. Loves going down the pub and telling stories from the old days. And he and my mum go out dancing quite a bit as well. Your dad sounds like, well, quite the crashing bore, if you don't mind my saying so."

"It's all right," said Jake. "He is what he is. I'm not trying to put him down. I just don't want to be like him, that's all."

"Well, don't worry, Jake," said Nancy, putting her hand inside his. "From what you've described just now, you're nothing like him at all. Nothing to worry about there, mate. You're warm, and fun, and caring. I could tell that from the first day we met. That's why," she said, turning to look into his eyes, "I want to have you nearby if we're going to do this business with Ruben and Mary Lou. I need someone who'll just be there for me. Someone I can trust. And I trust you enough, Jake, more than I trust Ruben, that's for sure."

"Why do you say that?" asked Jake.

"Well, you know," she said, "it's a bit hard to put yer finger on, isn't it? But he seems like someone who's capable of anything, you know what I mean? And that scares me a bit."

"I've been thinking that about myself lately, seeing as how I'm up for this," said Jake snickering.

"That's not what I mean, Jake. I'm pretty sure there are certain lines you would never cross. I'm not so sure I can say the same about Ruben."

"I can't believe I'm saying it out loud," said Jake, "but I think I know what you mean. So why are we doing this again?"

Nancy didn't answer directly but rummaged in her purse for another cigarette, lit up, and blew smoke out through both nostrils. "We're doing it, Jake," she said, "because we're gonna do it right, you and me, and it's gonna be great, and we're gonna make money, and we don't have to do it the way Ruben and Mary Lou want us to. They can do what they want. We don't have to play their game."

"You," said Jake, "are remarkably lucid for someone who's clearly intoxicated."

"You like that, do you?" she said, reaching up to pinch his cheek.

"Ow," said Jake. "That hurts."

"Poor baby," she said, slapping him lightly. "That's when I'm smartest, Jake. After I've knocked back a few. I've always been that way. I'm fucking brilliant when I'm loaded. You'll see, Jake. You might see a lot more of me like this if we end up over on Mallorca together. So, is it cool then? Do we have a deal?"

"So this is what you want to do then, for real? I need to hear you say it, Nancy."

"Jake, I have to do this. I am shit out of dinero, and I'm not afraid, Jake. Really I'm not. Not if we do this right. And trust me, we will!"

But maybe you should be afraid, thought Jake, as they stretched out their hands and shook on it. *Maybe we should both be afraid.*

After that meeting in town, it was only a question of ironing out the details. Ruben said he knew of a hotel in Palma. He said it would be the perfect place to work from. He claimed it was right in the middle of the district where the oil field workers liked to stay. That Ruben would be privy to such information was something Jake had just decided to accept on faith. It was also agreed that Nancy, who'd been moving around from one friend's place to the next, would stay with Ruben and Mary Lou at their little casita on the beach until it was time for them to leave. Jake was expecting a long delinquent euro check to arrive any day from Paris from a friend whose apartment he'd painted there, so they all agreed to wait a few more days so he wouldn't start out broke in Palma. Jake failed to mention that should the check arrive, he might not go to Palma at all.

Chapter 43

After driving his three cohorts back to Salinas Beach later that night, Jake was anxious to go home himself and declined an invitation to stay and smoke a final joint. He knew how that went. The final joint was never final, and then there was always a beer to be drunk after that, and he could easily end up passed out there on the hard, bumpy floor or on the beach, waking up with a sore back and a stiff neck at dawn, and feeling more and more like his already chaotic life was spiraling even more out of control. He was feeling unsettled, unsure of himself, and in need of isolation. Some inner voice was trying to grab his attention, to shake him out of the spiritual torpor he'd fallen into, but he wasn't ready to listen. Not yet. He had a nagging suspicion he was probably making a mistake with Ruben. He just wasn't sure how big or costly the mistake would be. But a realistic alternative had so far failed to materialize.

Halfway between the towns of Ibiza and the northern port of San Antonio, an inconspicuous *tienda* on the highway marked the turnoff to Jake and Carl's latest finca. It was a good three miles into the countryside, on a winding dirt road that grew increasingly impassable, twisting its way past other rundown fincas with belligerent dogs chained to stakes in the front yards. By the time Jake reached their place known colloquially as *L'amagatall* (the "Hideout") at the end of a mile-long driveway, the Tank was creeping along in low gear from one deep rut to the next, avoiding large rocks and trying not to do any new and possibly fatal damage to the car. It was definitely not a destination for the casual visitor, and the two friends decided they liked it that way. They cherished their little hideaway and had settled in for what they hoped would be a long stay. They each felt relieved to truly have their own place now without any interfering landlord or mooching housemates.

L'amagatall sat on a large untended parcel of land with scattered patches of lemon, fig, olive, and carob trees comprising the front yard and behind it a forested hill of scraggly aromatic cedars. On a clear day, you could just catch a glimpse of the sea off in the distance from the front of the finca—a splash of deep hazy blue on the horizon. Occasionally, they heard muffled gunshots from local hunters chasing wild pigs. But for the most part, there was silence all around, except for birds, the rustle of wind through the trees, and the occasional overhead groan of a plane.

Jake didn't expect anyone to be there when he got home that night. Carl was playing hotel gigs now, and he sometimes didn't get back before dawn or else stayed away for days at a time, hanging out with his bandmates in their homes. But as Jake drove up to the finca—the low-geared roar of the motor announcing his arrival—he was delighted to see Carl sitting out front with his German girlfriend Renata, the two of them faintly illuminated by the starlit sky.

After turning off the engine, Jake sat still in his car for a moment listening to a bluesy guitar riff spilling out into the profound silence of the night. This was what he needed now more than anything; the healing presence of music and genuine friends. He wasn't about to back out of his commitment to go to Mallorca—not yet anyway—but he found himself relishing the time he still had left to contemplate his situation and decide if what he'd just signed up to do with his life really made any sense at all.

"*Hola, amigo,*" said Carl. "*Que tal?*"

"*Bien,*" said Jake with a broad grin.

Something about Carl made him happy. Perhaps it was his kindness and the fact that he truly loved what he did and never wasted time trying to do anything else. His recent decision to devote himself to music lent him an admirable simplicity which Jake found inspiring to be around. With Carl, there were no hidden agendas. It was clear he'd found a way to be happy and desired the same for his friends, however they might achieve it. He'd become a beacon of stability in a landscape of personalities too often marked by desperation and confusion.

"So where have you been, Jake?" asked Renata in her heavily accented English.

"In town," Jake answered. "With Ruben and Mary Lou. And another gal named Nancy. I don't think you know her."

Renata was a slim blonde with perfect Aryan features, someone who, in the Third Reich, would have been proudly put on display as an outstanding example of *Rassenreinheit*, the pure northern race. But she was about as far from being a Nazi as anyone ever could be. She was sweet, spontaneous, and eager for pleasure, yet still maintained the strong work ethic of her Teutonic roots. She'd begun a small clothing business and, with the help of local seamstresses, was cranking out a series of Batik dresses, one of which clung sensuously to her now. She sat beside Carl with her legs crossed, looking tired but relaxed with a glass of red wine in her hand.

"Did you have a good time?" she asked.

"Yeah. I guess so. Well, I mean, I'm kind of wasted, to be honest."

And he was. He suddenly felt utterly exhausted, as if he hadn't slept for days.

"I can see that," said Carl examining him briefly as he looked up from his playing.

"Yeah, I guess I'll go inside and catch some zees," said Jake.

"No, wait," said Carl. "You just got here. C'mon, hang out with us for a little while at least. It's not like you've gotta get up early for work in the morning, right?"

"Not likely," said Jake.

"Here," said Renata. "C'mon and roll something for us, Jake. You always make the best joints."

Despite her busy schedule, Renata was one of the biggest potheads around. She presented a strong counterargument to the prevailing view that hashish made you lazy and unambitious. Jake never knew her not to be stoned, and yet her days were filled with a whirlwind of events, appointments, and responsibilities. She was always off on her small

Honda motorbike, taking care of errands. She seemed to have attained a perfect balance between mellowness and striving.

Jake pulled up a wobbly canvas chair and positioned himself next to Renata in front of a wooden cable spool tipped on its side, which served as a rustic outdoor table. Everything he needed was already laid out in front of him; rolling papers, matchbooks, cigarettes, and hash. There was even a Swiss army knife with its small pair of scissors extended for trimming off the excess paper. Jake felt blessed. It was turning out to be one of those perfect Ibiza moments, uniting them in a bond of natural beauty and music interspersed with the nocturnal sounds of nature. Jake finished building the joint, clipped off the little twist of paper at the end, stuck the joint in his mouth, and lit up, inhaling deeply. Passing the joint to Renata, he leaned back and looked skyward, shuddering involuntarily as the impressive grandeur of the vast star-strewn sky hit home with full force, erasing whatever tension remained from the long strange day he'd spent with his wayward friends.

"Look," said Carl halting his playing. "A falling star! Everyone make a wish."

The intensely beautiful nighttime panorama enveloped him with its magnetic force, drawing him upward out of his body into the vortex of an immense and unfathomable universe. He felt an upsurge of emotion and an urge to share his enchantment with his friends, but a lump in his throat prevented him from speaking. All he could do was shake his head in wonder and blink back the tears in his eyes.

Glancing at his friends, he noticed that Renata was sitting upright in her chair with her eyes closed, the joint hanging loosely from her fingers, an expression of perfect contentment on her face. Carl had rolled back in his chair, both forearms resting on his guitar, and was staring up at the sky, his mouth agape in wonderment. He must have sensed Jake looking at him.

"Well," he asked. "Did you make your wish?"

"Yeah," said Jake rising slowly from his chair to go inside. "I wish this moment would never end."

Zipped inside his sleeping bag on his rough bed inside the finca with the thick stone walls creating a muffled silence, but for the occasional mouse scurrying across a ceiling beam, Jake's heart ached with loneliness.

He found himself imagining Gisela curled up beside him, allowing him to stroke her hair while they whispered plans for their future together. His vision of the two of them finding love together, a love that would last, had never left him. He didn't know how or even where their future together might come to pass. The number of obstacles to be overcome to achieve such an unlikely outcome seemed insurmountable. But even as he prepared to leave on his improbable adventure, he never doubted that ultimately, regardless of what happened in Mallorca, he'd come back here to try and win Gisela's love and devotion.

Chapter 44

Jake's oppressive sense of loneliness from the night before, which he'd been unable to shake off, got a welcome reprieve as he came within sight of the Café del Teatro the following morning.

"Jake, over here!"

His heart leapt at the sound of that clear, melodious voice, and he instantly put his planned trip to the post office on hold.

"Gisela!" he said, "How wonderful to see you. How are you?"

She studied him through an expensive pair of designer sunglasses, her glossy auburn hair curling down to her graceful shoulders, a chic island-style dress with a floral pattern clinging tightly to her body. Her right hand held a smoldering Marlboro in a maroon holder as Jake bent down to kiss her on the lips.

"Fine," she said, smiling. "And you?"

"Okay, I guess."

"Are you really?" she asked. "You seem tired. You have some dark circles underneath your eyes."

His hands flew up to his face to rub them away, and he immediately regretted not shaving. He hated not looking his best for her.

"Yeah, well, I guess I haven't been sleeping too well."

"Oh? Why not?"

"Well," he began tentatively, his mind searching for some lie he might tell her in order to put off her judgment of him for what he was about to do. But then, on a whim, he decided to risk sharing with her the outline of his brazen plan, determined to just be himself and trust that the mysteriously compelling bond he'd felt with her since they'd first met was reciprocal. It was a bold move, and he knew it. Nonetheless, he steeled himself and told her about Ruben and Mary Lou and Nancy and Mallorca, watching her closely as he spoke, feeling as if his entire future now depended on how she might respond.

"You really are crazy, you know that, Jake?" she said when he'd wrapped up his tale.

"You think?"

"Yes, I do think," she said, shaking her head. "Just how far did you figure you would get with this idea?"

"How far?" he asked, feeling flustered.

"Yes, how far?"

"Look, Gisela, this is not about getting someplace. This is about survival."

"It's not survival, Jake. It's insanity. You can find something else to do if you only want to survive. Would you like me to buy you a coffee, by the way?"

Jake smiled, touched by her sudden kindness.

"Uh … sure …I guess … if you don't mind?"

"Of course I don't mind," she said, signaling for a waiter. "It's not like I don't know how broke you are. But is this really the best plan you can come up with?"

Perversely, Jake found her nagging gratifying. Wasn't it proof after all that she cared? In an attempt to justify himself, he began recounting a litany of his failed efforts to raise some cash since coming to live on Ibiza.

"Jacqueline tried to help me earn some money," said Jake.

"How?" asked Gisela.

"Her plan was to get me started in the clothing business making coveralls. Kind of like the ones I'm wearing now. She convinced me I only needed to spend a few hundred dollars which was all I could afford, and I could get a dozen of them made just for starters."

"And how did that work out?" asked Gisela.

"Well, the idea was that once I sold those, I would reinvest the money and just keep going. She knew this woman, Maria, out in the countryside near her place in Santa Gertrudis, who was inexpensive and a very good seamstress. She made a pattern, gave it to Maria to sew from, and suddenly I was in the clothing business and boosting the local economy, to boot."

"So did you manage to sell them?" asked Gisela.

"Unfortunately not," said Jake. "Turns out the cloth we used was too flimsy. It was very affordable but ended up tearing too easily. That's because I didn't have enough money to buy stronger material. Anyway, after a few weeks of bringing them to the hippy market at Es Canar, I realized it was a bust. I'd only managed to sell a few pairs in the end."

"A few pairs?" asked Gisela. "That's all?"

"Afraid so," he said, grimacing. She took a moment to light up another Marlboro as she mulled over Jake's sad tale of woe.

"But the ones you have on don't look so flimsy," said Gisela reaching out to pull on his shoulder strap.

"Yeah," he said, allowing her to pull him in a little closer. "That's because they're not mine! They're from Cannelle."

"Well, hers are certainly very good. I don't think I've seen you wearing anything else, have I?"

"Only because, sadly, you haven't seen that much of me," he countered.

"Oh, I see. So it's just coincidence that I've only ever seen you with overalls on?"

"Yep. Sure as the sun shines. Actually, my wardrobe is rather extensive. All the latest Paris fashions, *ma chérie*, which by the way, I brought with me from Paris. Why don't you come over to our finca sometime, and I'll give you the grand tour of my closet."

"You have a closet?"

"Ha ha, very funny! But of course, I do! If you consider a long wooden pole hanging horizontally from the ceiling with a few clothes hangers on it a closet. Still, there are a few nice garments. I like to call it my spring collection. You really ought to come by and see it."

"That is a tempting offer," she said, grinning. "I still haven't been to see this new finca you and Carl have been talking so much about. So what else have you done?"

"Done?"

"Yes, done. You know, to make money. Isn't that what we're talking about?"

"Well, I did flirt briefly with a culinary career."

"Culinary? What does that mean?"

"You know, cuisine, cooking, that sort of thing."

"You? A cook?"

"Why do I have the feeling that no matter what I say, you're going to mock me?"

"Well," she said, chortling, "I think you could probably do anything you wanted to, Jake. I just don't know if you've found anything you want to do yet. So tell me about the cooking."

"You're sure you want to hear it?"

"Yes, I'm sure."

"Because I could just skip it. It's really not that big a deal."

"No, Jake. I really want to hear it," she said, her eyes twinkling. And there it was again. That ineffable spark between them. However unlikely their connection—the sophisticated European fashionista and the indigent American hippy—some enigmatic force kept bringing them together as mysterious as the aura of the island itself.

"I like you, Jake," she added in a spontaneous declaration of affection. "Don't you know that?"

"That makes me so happy," he said, his voice choking with emotion. He reached across and placed his hand on top of hers, holding it there, wondering how long she'd allow such a public display of affection.

"So," she said, "the food story. Go on. What were you cooking anyway?"

"Do you know that guy everybody calls Orange Tom?" he asked.

"No, why?"

"Well, he lives over near Cannelle, and I got to be friends with him."

"What does his name mean?"

"Well, his real name's just Tom, I guess. Tom Smith, for all I know. He's an American guy. I think from Iowa or someplace in the Midwest. But he traveled to India and got involved with this guru named Rajneesh and, ever since then, everything he wears is orange."

"Ooh," said Gisela, "I'm jealous. I would love to go to India."

"Me too!" said Jake squeezing her hand. "Maybe we can go there together someday …"

"Who knows?" said Gisela. "Maybe we will." With those unexpected words, Jake felt a sudden surge of hope as though some unspoken pact between them had been agreed upon. It wasn't the first time they'd spoken of this. It was a topic that kept coming up again and again, a destination they'd each been dreaming of long before they'd met one another.

"So what does Orange Tom have to do with cooking?" she queried.

"Well, there's a whole group of people that are also into Rajneesh that live either with or around Orange Tom. For some reason, a lot of them are South Americans. They're wild people, very uninhibited. Always singing and dancing, doing strange meditations, very open with nudity and sex …"

"Ooh, I'll bet you like that …"

"I have to admit, there is a certain fascination there … at the same time, though, I do feel a bit uncomfortable around them."

"Why?"

"Well, I guess it's because I'm not really one of them. I could be if I wanted to, I suppose, but joining a group like that doesn't really appeal to me. Maybe if I went to India and met Rajneesh, I'd feel differently. I do find him to be very wise whenever I hear him speak on a cassette or read one of his books. But if you're not in their group, they have a way of making you feel excluded, even though they can also be quite friendly and open. It's like they have this special knowledge or wisdom or something, and you don't. If you're not wearing the mala, that is."

"The mala?"

"Yes, it's a beaded necklace with a picture of Rajneesh they all wear around their necks."

"Is that what they call it? I have seen a few people wearing those, come to think of it."

"They sometimes remind me of an experience I had when I was a student hitchhiking around Europe. I visited this group of Jesus freaks up in Copenhagen in a place called Christiania. At some point, they all started praying for me, don't ask me why."

"Maybe they knew you would decide to be a pimp someday?"

"Hah! That must be it!" said Jake chuckling. "But I think they just did that whenever anybody new arrived. They were set up right outside this notorious discotheque called Electric Ladyland. You know, like the Jimi Hendrix album? Whenever people would stumble out of the disco late at night, usually stoned or tripping on acid, they would gather them in and do their best to save them. I ended up there because I needed a place to crash for the night. I'd just hitchhiked in from Hamburg and didn't know anyone in Copenhagen, and of course, as usual, I was pretty broke."

"Well, I have to say," interrupted Gisela. "Being broke never stopped you from getting around, Jake."

"True enough," said Jake smiling. "Anyway, whenever they prayed together, they just looked so serene and blissful. I have to say I envied that about them."

"Did you feel like you were missing out on something?"

"Yeah, I guess that's probably it. But it was more like they were able to access something that I couldn't. I think, more than anything, it made me feel kind of sorry for myself, sad to say. How can they have that kind of bliss and not me? How can they have that kind of faith, and I can't? What am I missing? There was this one woman in particular."

"Of course," said Gisela.

"A Jesus freak from Texas," continued Jake. "Carol was her name. I'll never forget her. I'm telling you, she was the genuine article. You know, the real deal. I've never experienced such a feeling of peace and joy and contentment resonating from anyone in my life. I was utterly smitten! There's a part of me that was really tempted to stay there and just worship Jesus with her for the rest of my life."

"I'm guessing she was gorgeous too?" said Gisela.

"Well, yeah," said Jake chuckling in spite of himself. "But then I had to ask myself, would you still want to do that if she wasn't there? If she wasn't part of it? The truth was I had fallen head over heels in love with her. Just like that. Right there on the spot. It wasn't until the next morning after I crawled out of my sleeping bag, and she was already on her knees with her hands folded in prayer and her beautiful face turned toward heaven, that I realized my mistake. She could never love anyone the way she loved Jesus."

"Too bad for you, eh?"

"Yeah, it was, kind of. Because that is what I wanted, believe it or not. For her to love me just like she loved Jesus. Or maybe even more. It sounds ridiculous now when I say it out loud. And let me tell you. When you're talking about the genuine article, and I'm sure that's what she was, that ain't never gonna happen!"

"What is this 'genuine article'? What does that mean?"

"What does that mean? I guess it means someone who feels they are doing totally 100 percent what it is they're supposed to be doing in life where all doubts are erased. You know, the real thing. Not being a phony."

"Hmm," said Gisela. "I think I understand. Is that what you're doing, Jake, being a phony?"

It was an innocent query. There was no charge in the way she asked it, but he felt a sudden tightening in his chest. He took a moment to ponder her question.

"No," he said finally. "I don't think so. I'm being as real as I can be at this point in my life. I'm just not consumed with passion the way she was. At least not that kind of passion. I would love to be, believe me. But I don't think that's anything you can try to achieve."

"Why not?"

"Because it has more to do with grace than anything else. You either have it, or you don't. Carol was in grace, and I was just in awe of that. She had somehow managed to banish all doubts from her mind, and I've never been able to do that."

"Well, you have to admit," continued Gisela after a moment's reflection, "asking a woman like her to love you more than she loves Jesus *is* asking quite a lot."

"You think?" asked Jake, grinning. "That's my whole problem in life, Gisela. I ask too much in love, I guess."

As he said this, he peered into Gisela's twinkling blue eyes, trying to interpret her expression. It was hard to fathom. He felt as if he was witnessing an enigmatic calculation going on inside her head.

"Help me out here Jake, please," she said, beginning to sound impatient. "What does any of this have to do with Orange Tom?"

"Well, it's kind of the same with Orange Tom and his friends," he continued, "you get the feeling they're all spiritually blessed, or at least they think they are. I sensed that when I saw them all sitting around meditating together, or I should say jumping around."

"Jumping around?"

"Yeah. They have these, how shall I say, very unusual meditation techniques. There's lots of jumping and howling and yelling and … very active stuff. But in the end, everyone gets quiet and becomes very still. That was my favorite part."

"You mean you've done it? With them?"

"Yeah … a few times. Just to see what it was like. It was inside Orange Tom's finca. There's a soundtrack that goes along with it. A very loud soundtrack that's mostly percussion. You're supposed to be blindfolded when you do it, but I ended up peeking."

"Peeking?"

"Yeah, I couldn't help it. A lot of them were naked and…"

"Meditating … naked?"

"I told you, it's a very unusual technique."

"Oh, I get it. You dirty dog you."

"Okay, I deserve that. But let me tell you something, Gisela. It turns out there's nothing very sexy about sweaty breasts and asses and penises flapping up and down while everyone's blindfolded and screaming like howler monkeys. It's hardly what you'd call erotic."

"No, it certainly doesn't sound that way to me either. But then, why should it be? Anyway, I'm not sure that would be something that I would enjoy doing. And by the way, will we ever find out about the cooking part?"

"Oh yeah. That. Turns out that one way the Orange Tom people support themselves is by cooking up big pots of brown rice and throwing in a bunch of raisins and cinnamon, rolling it up into little balls, wrapping it in fig leaves, and selling it at the hippy market. I figured, since I was there anyway trying to sell my overalls, maybe I could have a little rice ball action on the side."

"And did you?"

"Yup. I did. And I think I can safely say with some degree of certainty that I'm the first one at the hippy market to ever stand around yelling, 'Get your rice balls and overalls here!' And of course, sometimes, just for fun, I'd shorten it to just 'Balls and Overalls!'"

"You!" she said, dimples flashing. "But didn't Orange Tom's people mind you using their recipe? After all, you were competing with them, right?"

"They acted like they didn't care. And I really don't think they did. According to this one foxy Brazilian chick I talked to, my energy was off. I think what she meant was that if you weren't a busting-out-all-over babe coming on like her with a skimpy little bikini on, your rice ball sales would suffer. And she was right! By the end of the day, most of the rice balls I made ended up being dinner for me and my friends."

"Poor Jake."

"Yeah, poor Jake is right."

"Anything else?"

"What do you mean?"

"I mean, is there anything else you did to try and earn some money here?"

"Yeah, one more thing. So far, that is. I was a typist for a while."

"A typist?"

"Yup. I brought this portable typewriter with me down from France, kind of to remind me what my true vocation here was meant to be."

"Which is?"

"Writing, of course. I've always wanted to be a writer. Didn't I tell you that?"

"I don't think so, Jake. But you're always talking about books you love. I think that's wonderful."

"Well, to make a long story short," continued Jake basking in her acknowledgement, "I met a French translator named Pascale on the beach at Salinas."

"Do I know her?"

"I doubt it. She's a short, squat, rather unattractive woman with kinky red hair and freckles. Does that ring any bells?"

"I don't think so. No."

"Anyway, she's a good translator but a lousy typist. She finds out I speak decent French and decides she wants me to type up her handwritten notes for her, which she then mails back to her boss in Paris."

"Sounds like a pretty good deal."

"Yeah, that's what I thought too at first. I was pretty excited about it, even though …"

"Even though what?"

"Even though I felt like a complete failure; y'know, sitting there in her lovely finca at my typewriter but instead of working on my own stuff, I was typing up this woman's translations about literary criticism and not even of books that I was interested in. But hey, I didn't need a work permit to do it. And it paid pretty well."

"So, what happened?"

"What happened? I got fired is what happened."

"Fired?"

"Yeah. Turns out Pascale was interested in more than just my typing skills. Ultimately, I refused to have sex with her and that was the end of that."

"I guess she didn't know about your high principles when she hired you?"

"Very funny," said Jake, squeezing her hand. "The truth was she turned me off. She was very stuck up for one thing. Looked down her nose at everybody the way the French sometimes do, and on top of that, she would put on these sexy little outfits whenever I came over. Sexy on anybody else, that is. Everything was way too tight, and believe me, tight is not always a good thing. She just did not have the body for it. And too much makeup too. Purple mascara, fake eyelashes, way too much rouge on her cheeks. She could've been right out of a Toulouse-Lautrec painting! It was just too loaded. She made me feel like I was obligated. I just don't function that way."

"That's good to know," said Gisela, smiling as she lit up a fresh Marlboro. "You know what your trouble is really, Jake, don't you?"

"Uh oh," said Jake, "am I gonna wanna hear this?"

"I think you should," she said. "After all, you're often talking about how important it is to know yourself."

"Okay then," said Jake. "Hit me with it!"

She took a long drag on her cigarette holder, allowing the exhaled smoke to linger in the air for a moment before answering. "You're lazy, Jake, and you just don't want to work."

"Wow, do you mean that?"

"Yes, I do. Because it's true."

Jake paused to reflect on her words. He knew he should probably feel offended or disappointed or at least wary of where she was going with this, but somehow he didn't. The word "lazy" conjured up an early childhood memory of himself lying on a living room rug, twisting his hair and sucking his thumb as daylight streamed through the window, illuminating tiny dust motes dancing in the air. Jake had been mesmerized watching them, and that vision of beauty had remained with him ever since. That was what laziness was to him. "Okay," said Jake, "let's assume that's true. Just for the sake of argument. And just what do you propose to do about it?" The absurdity of his query caught her off guard, and she laughingly shook her head.

"*Ach, du bist ein Arschloch,*" she said shaking her head.

"I am not an asshole," insisted Jake.

"Oh yes, you are," said Gisela. "But at least you're an amusing one."

"As opposed to just a plain asshole?"

"Yes, definitely. I actually rather like the amusing kind. Just plain assholes can be so dull. And I have enough of them in my life."

"You don't mean Dieter by any chance?" ventured Jake.

"Ach, I don't want to talk about him right now. Let's get back to you and your laziness. What about that job in Switzerland you were telling me about?"

"You mean picking fruit?"

"Yes, why can't you do that?"

"Because it's only May, and the harvest doesn't really start there until the fall. I mean, I could probably go back there and get some kind of work picking carrots or something, but I'd rather not. It's backbreaking work."

"And you don't have enough money left to last until the apple harvest in the fall?"

Jake fell silent. Looking down, he studied his hands, feeling suddenly embarrassed. Gisela was right. He was an asshole. He really didn't have anyone to blame but himself for his dilemma. He was young, educated, and healthy. Mere survival shouldn't even be an issue. The truth was he'd dug himself into this hole, and now he'd have to dig himself out again.

"What the hell are you doing here, Jake?"

Had it not been for the thick German accent and the gravelly voice, he might have imagined he was thinking out loud. Jake looked up to find Gisela's husband, Dieter, hovering above them, his surprisingly delicate hands planted on the table, his breath already reeking of alcohol.

"Dieter!" said Jake taken aback.

Grabbing a chair, Dieter turned it around backward and plopped down next to his wife, taking care to adjust his protruding gut. Gisela immediately removed her cigarette from its holder, tamped it out in an ashtray, and returned keys and other items to her purse, readying herself for departure. She let out a little sigh, and her attentiveness to Jake dropped off precipitously. Dieter, straddling his chair, laid his black, bearded chin on the back of one arm and began drumming the table with his fingers.

"Am I interrupting something?" he asked, giving Jake a suspicious glance.

"We were just talking," said Jake, "about work."

"Work?" asked Dieter. "Isn't that supposed to be a dirty word around here? This is Ibiza, after all. Since when do you work, Jake?"

"Dieter," said Gisela. "Be nice. Jake and I were just enjoying a cup of coffee together."

It had occurred to Jake that Dieter must live in constant fear of his beautiful wife abandoning him. And with good reason. His drug and alcohol abuse was legendary, leading to frequent horrendous verbal brawls between them, several of which Jake had witnessed firsthand. Gisela's lack of enchantment with her husband was common knowledge, and if they'd lived full-time in Berlin, they'd almost certainly have long since divorced. But like Jake and so many others, Gisela had fallen under the spell of the island and hadn't figured out a way for herself and her daughter Chloe to be there without the financial support that Dieter provided. Jake decided to let Dieter in on his pimping plan, just to elicit his reaction. With his alleged underworld connections, Dieter held a fascination for Jake that was similar to Ruben's. Although the two men's backgrounds were very different, each man had figured out a way to survive in an adverse world, and Jake admired that.

"You?" said Dieter, snorting in disbelief. "A pimp? I don't think so. Not unless you want to see that handsome face of yours get messed up very badly."

"Why do you say that?"

"Because," he said, leaning in toward Jake, "that's what pimps do. They like to fight. And even if they don't like it, they had better be prepared for it. How else do you think you're going to keep a whore in line? And the unruly customers too?"

"So then," said Jake, "you don't think I have what it takes?"

"You're kidding, right?" he said, snickering derisively. "Of course not. You're too soft. It's a tough business, and you're hardly what I'd call a tough guy. Why don't you stick to selling hippy shit to tourists?"

"Ouch," said Jake, although he suspected that Dieter was right. He still clung to the idea, though, that the venture he was about to enter into with Nancy fell into a different, less dangerous category than what Dieter was imagining. Ruben and Mary Lou were a different matter, but Jake imagined himself disengaging from them once they got to Mallorca, should things get too crazy between them. He was putting his faith in Nancy, who he didn't see as a whore at all, any more than he saw himself as a pimp. He felt a synergy between them had been established that just might allow them to avoid any really bad situations and escape any violent consequences. At least, that's the story he told himself. Nonetheless, Jake couldn't easily dismiss Dieter's opinion. His whole persona had been shaped as a Jew in post-war Berlin in the midst of a culture which had called for the extermination of his entire race. Consequently, he never really felt accepted in German society and had decided early on, rather than try to adapt, that he would do his best to exploit it for all it was worth. He had an unerring instinct for knowing when to hold 'em and fold 'em, to use the poker analogy. His one great skill in life turned out to be survival. He counted pimps, gamblers, drug dealers, and racketeers among his friends and acquaintances back in Germany, but also liked to hang out with members of the Woodstock generation, spouting peace and love. His travel back and forth between the divided city of Berlin and Ibiza was a curiously apt lifestyle for someone with a soul as conflicted as his. Having learned all this from Gisela, Jake was deeply wary of Dieter but also intrigued by his unusual story. In any case, he'd made a conscious decision not to alienate himself from Gisela's husband. It was simply too risky as far as his quixotic campaign to win over his wife was concerned.

"Just suppose," said Jake leaning in, "the woman I was pimping for was a friend."

"What do you mean, a friend?"

"I mean, let's say she wasn't really a whore at all but just someone who'd decided it would be a good way for her to earn some money."

"What kind of shit are you talking, Jake?"

"I'll admit it sounds strange, Dieter, but don't you think it could work? There would be no question of beating her up because she *wants* to do it, see? And we plan on being very careful about the kind of customers we choose."

"Do you believe this shit?" he asked, turning to his wife. "Is this guy gaga or what?"

"Yes," she admitted for the second time that morning. "I think he very well could be."

When Jake glanced up, he noticed that her eyes held an inscrutable expression. He sensed that she was finding the whole discussion increasingly tiresome.

"Gisela," said Jake, desperate to change the subject. "Before I depart on this mad adventure, what do you say we all go back to your place and play some music together?"

"I think that's a great idea," she said before Dieter could object. "I just need to pick up Chloe at school first. Can you give me a lift, Jake? I think Dieter will need the car here in town."

"Of course," he said, "if you don't mind riding in the Tank."

"Oh, I don't mind. Dieter, perhaps you'd like to meet us later? You could join in with your new guitar."

Jake groaned inwardly. Dieter's tone-deaf, couldn't-carry-a-tune-to-save-his-life guitar style was truly torture for Jake. But he considered the insult to his eardrums a small price to pay in order to spend more time with Gisela.

"Why not stay here with me, Schnookie?" asked Dieter, suddenly adopting a plaintive tone. "We could work together for a while in the boutique and then have dinner here in town."

"I don't think so," she said abruptly. "You know I have to pick up Chloe, and besides, I have some shopping to do. You can join us later for dinner back at the house."

Dieter glared at Jake before turning to his wife.

"Okay, Gisela," he said, "you win. But don't let this Ami here take advantage. We've got enough moochers at the house now as it is."

Jake remained silent, choosing not to rise to the bait. He knew enough to quit while he was ahead. And besides, what Dieter said was true. Jake would take advantage of any opportunity to spend more time with Gisela.

Chapter 45

In the Tank together on their way to pick up Chloe from school, Gisela and Jake barely exchanged a word. Neither had the energy to compete with the noise from the engine. Gisela shoved her seat back, stretched out her legs, and blew smoke out the open window, allowing one of her delicate bejeweled hands to dangle outside the door. She had her head turned away from Jake and was looking out at the arid landscape, lost in thought.

Jake focused on the driving, his left arm hanging out the window, his fingers tapping out the rhythm to the Beatle's "Help!" on the side of the car. He'd decided not to dwell on his plan for Mallorca. He knew he'd have to deal with it sooner rather than later but didn't want to let it interfere with the precious time he was spending now with Gisela. And besides, being in her presence made it impossible to focus on anything but her. Despite the improbability of it happening, a sense of inevitability was beginning to form in his mind about their relationship, and he was finding it less and less easy to spend time away from her. As for Dieter, Jake had no illusions. Dieter's ego required him to be seen with a beautiful and charming woman, and Gisela fit that bill to a T. Jake felt certain Dieter loved her the same way he loved his shiny new Mercedes stored away in a garage in Berlin. Her need for Dieter's wealth and protection, especially for Chloe's sake, made sense to Jake, but he was convinced he'd discovered in Gisela the same desire to be truly loved that he felt himself, and this conviction fueled his hope for their future together. He sensed her heart was crying out for recognition, and he felt the same cry resounding in his own heart as well.

Chloe and her best friend Josie were squatting on the ground outside the gate of the white picket fence surrounding the Mary Baker English Academy playing an animated game of jacks when Gisela and Jake pulled up in the Tank. The two ten-year-olds looked like twins: blonde, blue-eyed, and identically coiffed with straight bangs in the front and shoulder-length hair hanging down at the sides.

"Jake!" squealed Chloe, jumping up as the Tank released its final sputter. "What are *you* doing here?"

Gisela had already gotten out and was walking toward them, and Jake was just squeezing his way out of the passenger door when Chloe and Josie came running, dust flying, each flinging herself into one of Gisela's outstretched arms.

"Mummy, you're late!" chided Chloe.

"Sorry," she replied in German. "I met Jake in town, and we ended up having a long conversation."

Once outside the Tank, Jake instantly became fair game for Chloe to leap into his arms as well. "Jake," she cried. "How fun! Are you going to come and spend the night at our house?"

"I don't know," he said, giving her a quick squeeze. "That's up to your mom, I suppose. I'm just the chauffeur here, I'm afraid."

"Oh, Mummy, Mummy, please can Jake come and spend the night at our house and Josie too? Please, oh, please, Mummy, please!"

Gisela stood with her hands on her hips, pretending to weigh the decision. "Is it okay with Josie's mom?"

"We can stop by her house and ask her," said Chloe. "Oh, can't we, please?"

"That's up to Jake," said Gisela.

"Oh, Jake," said Chloe, hanging onto his neck with one arm. "Please, please, please, please, can we stop by Josie's? Oh, and Mummy, you still haven't said … what about Jake?"

"Well," said Gisela, pursing her lips, "I guess if he agrees to stop by and ask about Josie, he might as well spend the night as well."

"Jake," said Chloe pulling his head down to her own eye level, "you'd better say yes!"

"I'm sorry," said Jake sounding remorseful, "but I have to go and see a man about a dog,"

"A dog?"

"You heard me."

"What dog is that?" asked Josie, who'd come running over.

"Oh, just an old guard dog," said Jake.

"A guard dog?" asked Chloe suspiciously. "What do you need a guard dog for?"

"What for? Why, to protect myself from little kids who might attack me I suppose."

Both girls looked confused, but not for very long.

"Ooh, you!" said Chloe. "We're not little kids, but we'll attack you all right, won't we, Josie? C'mon, let's get him!"

She grabbed one of Jake's legs while Josie grabbed the other and the battle was engaged. A minute later, as he lay on his back in the dust with two giggling girls bouncing on his torso, Gisela announced it was time for them to go.

"C'mon," she said, "before you two tear poor Jake to pieces!"

"Poor Jake?" said Chloe. "He's not poor at all!"

"Oh yes," said Gisela shaking her head. "I'm afraid he really is."

****

A surprise awaited them at the house in San Carlos. Two friends were already seated in the living room.

"Well, well," said Gisela, "what have we here then?"

"Carl!" cried Jake. "Renata! What are you two doing here?"

"We uh, let ourselves in," said Carl, looking sheepish. "It was unlocked, and we didn't think you'd mind, Gisela. It was just too damned hot to wait outside in the van. Anyway, Jake, we had a feeling when you slunk off this morning that you might end up here," said Carl, turning to address his friend. "So the two of us decided to take the day off and come here for a visit. It's been a while. I thought Dieter might want another music lesson, too."

"You mean a Pink Floyd lesson, don't you?" asked Gisela.

"Same difference. Hey, give the guy some credit. He really does try hard. He can't help it if he's not really…"

"Talented?" asked Jake.

"Well," said Carl, always hesitant to pass judgment, "I suppose that would be one assessment…"

"You mean 'true assessment,' don't you?" asked Gisela, smirking. She was clearly not disposed to defend her husband's musical talent.

"He's terrible," interjected Chloe. "Oh, please don't make him play, Carl. We don't like it, do we, Josie?"

"No," agreed Josie looking like she was sucking on a lemon, "we don't." She then began singing "Wish You Were Here" in a stridently off-key voice. Chloe's voice, equally obnoxious, soon joined in.

"All right, you two, that's enough," said Gisela trying not to smile.

"But that *is* what it sounds like, Mummy," insisted Chloe.

"We'd rather listen to Abba, wouldn't we, Chloe?" asked Josie.

"Oh yes, let's do," said Chloe. "We can work out a new dance routine to 'Dancing Queen'! Dieter says if we're good enough, he'll introduce us to one of his friends in Berlin who might want to produce us."

"What does that mean?" asked Josie.

"You know, make a video, put us on German TV…"

"That would be s-o-o-o cool," said Josie. "C'mon, let's go turn on the stereo."

"Children, *bitte,*" said Gisela, "don't you want to go to the beach first?"

"Why? Is everybody going?" asked Chloe.

"Why not?" asked Jake, turning to wink at Carl. "I'll bet the beach is gorgeous now."

"Oh, yes then, Mummy, please, please, please! We want to go too!"

Gisela gave Jake a pleading look.

"On the other hand," he said, "perhaps I'll stay here with Gisela."

"Then we're staying too!" said Chloe stamping her foot.

"Chloe, c'mon! You mean you'd make us go to the beach all by ourselves?" asked Carl.

"Yeah," said Renata. "That's not very nice. We're not even sure how to get there, are we, Carl? We were hoping you two could hop in the van and show us the way."

"You mean we could all go in Carl's van?" asked Chloe excitedly.

"Sure," said Carl. "You could even ride up front with me if you want to."

"Wait," said Josie, "you mean you've never even been to the beach here before?"

"I don't think so," said Carl. "Well, maybe once. But I really can't remember the way."

"We'll show you then, won't we, Chloe?" said Josie. "We can practice 'Dancing Queen' later after we come back from a swim."

"I'm only going if Carl brings his guitar with him down to the beach," said Chloe.

"I will if you'll watch it for me when we're in the water," said Carl.

"I'll play it for you when you're in the water," said Chloe, whose mom had been teaching her how to play.

"Deal," said Carl winking at Jake.

"C'mon," said Chloe, "last one in her bathing suit's a rotten egg!"

Chapter 46

"Well," said Gisela, returning from the kitchen with two ice-cold bottles of beer, "don't you look happy."

"Do I?"

"Yes," she said emphatically. "You really do!" Jake leaned on a cushion in the living room with his legs splayed out in front of him, and Gisela lay on the carpet an arm's length away.

"How is it you say?" she continued. "Like the cat who ate the canary?"

"Oh," he said. "Then I must look very satisfied indeed."

"So what's going on with you?" she asked.

"I don't know," he said. "I'm just happy to be here … with you."

"*Schön,*" she said. "That's nice." She smiled, and her dimples flashed, and her blue eyes twinkled, and he felt utterly lost in the moment with her, unable to believe his good fortune in having found such an exotic treasure, even if she wasn't with him. Yet.

"I think this is the first time we've ever been alone together," she said, "except riding in your noisy car."

"I know."

"There's always so many people around."

"That too," said Jake.

"I get so tired of it sometimes."

"You do?" asked Jake.

"Yes. Of course. Sometimes I'd just like to get away from everything. You know, just run away and do something completely different."

"Isn't Ibiza completely different?"

"For you, it is, sure. But I've been in this scene much longer than you, and it's starting to get old."

"I can see how you might feel that way," said Jake, "but humor me, please, just for a moment. What specifically feels old about it? Do you mean Dieter?" *There,* thought Jake, *I've broached the subject.* "How is that for you anyway?" he continued, leaning back on his cushion and knocking back a healthy slug of beer.

"How is it with Dieter?" she asked almost nonchalantly. "Oh well, that's getting kind of old too." She peered at Jake through a haze of smoke, her blue eyes looking sad and vulnerable.

"Do you have anything to smoke?" he asked. "A joint's probably apropos right now before we delve any further into that particular subject."

"Good idea," she said, getting up and disappearing into her bedroom. She soon returned with a small box made of ivory-colored soapstone intricately carved with swirling images of roses.

"You'll find everything you need in there," she said. "The finest Afghani. Dieter brought it back from Berlin."

Jake opened the box and inspected the contents, inhaling the familiar pungent aroma. He began constructing a joint, relaxing into the ritual of it, conscious that the distraction it created made his next question seem perhaps more casual than it was intended.

"Do you think you'll ever leave him?" he asked, focusing on the task at hand. He was giving her a chance now to tell him to fuck off. Or not.

She took a long drag from the Marlboro in her ivory holder. "I don't know," she said wistfully, her words accompanied by a white cloud of smoke. "I mean that, Jake. I just don't know."

"It must be hard," he said, trying not to sound too engaged. "I mean, he sure isn't going to let go of you, is he?"

"No, I don't think that Dieter would ever do that," she said, studying her finely manicured hands. "Why would he? I'm a good wife, after all. I take care of so many things for him," she said with a shrug, "but still, I'm not sure there's a lot he could do if I really wanted to leave."

"I imagine you can be a pretty determined person once you've made up your mind about something," said Jake, eyeing her carefully.

"Yes," she said. "And don't forget that I'm a Taurus. We can be very stubborn when necessary."

"Yes," said Jake. "There's that. And then there's Chloe, too."

"Yes," she agreed. "There's Chloe too. But you do know, Jake, that Chloe is not Dieter's daughter, don't you?"

"Yeah, she told me that," said Jake.

"In fact, you want to hear the biggest joke of all?"

Jake nodded.

"Chloe's father is … get ready for it … a cop in Berlin!"

"A cop? No!" said Jake, burning off the loose paper and taking a deep drag on the newly formed joint. "Are you kidding me?"

"No," she said, "unfortunately not. But try to imagine. I was a teenager living in a tiny apartment with my sister and mother. When we met, he drove a Porsche and had his own apartment. That meant I could move in with him. That was enough of a reason back then to get married."

"Back then? You're talking what, ten years ago?"

"Eleven."

"You make it sound like it was a lifetime ago."

"It really does seem that way. Could you have imagined ten years ago living the life you're living today?"

"Let's see," he said. "I would have just started high school. And I was still in the Boy Scouts! My hair was short, and I think my biggest concern was not getting beat up in the boys' room at school. And, of course, I was a virgin too. I hadn't even had a real girlfriend yet. I'm sure I'd never even heard of Ibiza back then. In fact, I'd never been anywhere, really."

"And you'd certainly never smoked one of these," she said, passing him the joint.

"That's for sure," agreed Jake.

"You should have seen me, Jake. I had a big puffy hairdo, and my belly was as big as a house."

"Well," he said, laughing. "I guess it really was a lifetime ago, then. Did you drop out of high school? Or whatever the German equivalent is?"

"I'm not proud of it, but yes, I did. I really didn't have much choice once Chloe came along."

"Didn't you have to work?"

257

"You mean when I was pregnant?" she asked. "No. Max promised to take care of me."

"Max? You mean the cop?"

"Yeah. Max the cop. And he did … at first. As long as there was hot food on the table and cold beer in the fridge and the house was tidy when he came home from his shift, he was a happy man. A happy boring man."

"You really do go from one extreme to the other, don't you?"

"You can say that again," she said.

"You really do go from one extreme to the other, don't you?"

Despite the idiocy of it, they both had to laugh. Exacerbated by the harshness of the smoke from the hash, the laughter triggered a wrenching bronchial spasm bringing tears to their eyes.

"You really are an asshole, Jake," she said between gasps of laughter. "You know that, don't you?"

"How can I forget? That's the second time you've mentioned it today," he reminded her. "Or maybe the third?" By now, the Afghani had gone to his head and spread into every fiber of his being. He felt as though he was hovering slightly above the cushions on the floor and that there was no longer a clear boundary between his body and the space around him. "Woof, woof," he said for no good reason.

"Woof yourself," she said. "Do you always bark like a dog when you're high?"

"Honey, I am a dog when I'm high!"

"Ooh," she responded in a low growl. "I'm a big fan of dogs, you know." As if on cue, Moische came bounding into the room right after those words left her lips. "Moische!" cried Gisela, "Moische, *komm her!*"

The dog's relentless enthusiasm made it impossible for Jake to resent his presence for more than a moment or two despite its feckless timing. The dog raced around the room as if he'd just been released from shackles, interrupting his frenzy only to leap on either Gisela or Jake and lick their faces with the intensity of a love-starved convict just emerging from a long stretch of solitary confinement.

"Oh, yuck," said Jake, trying to cover his face with his hands but failing to prevent Moische's frantic wet tongue from penetrating between his fingers. "Oh my God. Yuck, yuck, yuck! Where did this maniac come from anyway?"

"Down, Moische!" commanded Gisela, grabbing his collar and pulling him off Jake. "You know he's the neighbor's dog, right?"

"No," said Jake, befuddled. "How does that work?"

"Well, he's usually tied up over there. And ignored. Or worse. So whenever he can escape and come and hang out with us here, he's, of course, very happy … aren't you, boy?"

"The poor guy," said Jake, wiping the dog's saliva off his face with the back of his hand. "He looks like he's about to have a heart attack. Look how fast his tail is wagging."

"He's just happy to see us, that's all. Aren't you, Moische?"

The dog responded by giving her face another flurry of rapid licks and then rolled onto his back, exposing his belly and manhood with irrepressible ardor.

"You are one intense doggie, aren't you?" said Jake, stretching out his hand to scratch Moische's belly. The dog responded by reaching up with his paws to try and grab Jake's arm.

"Guess what, Jake, I think he likes you," said Gisela.

"Is that what that means?"

"You must have a good touch," she said, giving Jake an appreciative glance. "And a good heart, too. You can't fool a dog, you know."

"Well, actually, you can," said Jake.

"What do you mean?"

"Well, what about Hitler?"

"Hitler?" said Gisela warily. "What about him?"

"He was a dog lover. Presumably, they loved him too."

"Of course they did," said Gisela wryly. "Otherwise, he would have had them exterminated!"

"No doubt," said Jake, already chiding himself for bringing up Hitler. "My apologies for mentioning der Führer."

"Well, the fact that he liked dogs makes him a little bit more human, don't you think?"

"Hitler? Human? Nah," said Jake.

Gisela looked down for a moment studying her nails. "It was Dieter who named him, you know."

"Named who," asked Jake. "Moische?"

"Yes."

"Are you trying to change the subject?" asked Jake.

"Why? Did you want to keep talking about Hitler?"

"No, I really didn't," said Jake, grinning ruefully. "By all means, let's talk about Moische—the neighbor's dog who's not really the neighbor's dog."

"That's right, but … well … Dieter says that one day when we leave Ibiza, he's going to take him away with us back to Berlin. He's very fond of dogs, you know."

"Like you know who?"

This time they both had to laugh.

"But doesn't Moische have another name? One the neighbors gave him?"

"Yes, but we don't like to call him that. It's so mean. The neighbors call him Tonto, which of course, means 'stupid' in Spanish." The dog's ears began twitching nervously at the sound of his original unfortunate moniker.

"Oh, that is cruel," said Jake, rubbing his face in the dog's furry chest. "Geez, what an insult. But you're not really stupid at all, are you, boy?"

"I agree," she said. "That's why when he's with us, he's Moische."

"Moische it is then. Which happens to be Jewish, right?"

"Right. I think I told you that when we first met. It means Moses, you know."

Jake nodded. "You know," he said, "I'm curious about Dieter being Jewish. He must be one of the few Jews running around in Germany nowadays."

"Oh," she said, "there are some. But sadly, not that many."

"What about you?" he asked. "It never occurred to me before, but I guess you could be Jewish, too?"

"That's funny," she said, avoiding the question. "I thought that *you* might be."

"Why?"

"Well, look at you. You have dark features. You're from New York. Aren't there lots of Jews in New York?"

"Yes," he said, "as a matter of fact, there are. But I'm not one of them. At least, I don't think so."

"You don't think so? Well," she said, "so you don't really know?"

"I was brought up as a Methodist," Jake explained. "But my mother was a kind of semi-orphan. She never knew who her father was. I suppose she could have been half Jewish."

"I can relate," said Gisela. "My grandfather was a rich Jewish art dealer who drove around Berlin in a Rolls-Royce. He married a Protestant, and she gave birth to my mother."

"Which makes your mother half a Jew."

"Correct."

"And what about your grandfather?" he asked. "The guy with the Rolls-Royce. Whatever happened to him?"

"What you might expect," she replied in a somber tone. "It's a very sad story, I'm afraid. I really don't like to even think about it."

"Don't then," said Jake reaching out to stroke her hand.

"I want you to know, though, Jake," she said, releasing a deep sigh. "He lost everything, of course. Or rather, the Nazis took away everything he had. He did manage to escape to France but was too romantic for his own good. His love for my grandmother finally sealed his fate. He missed her so badly that he decided to write her a letter which turned out to be a fatal mistake. In those days, every apartment building in Berlin had a Hausmeister who went through everybody's mail. If anything suspicious turned up, they handed it over to the Gestapo. It seems they'd been expecting my grandfather to write, and once he did, that led them right to where he was living in France. So they picked him up, and shipped him off to Auschwitz. He didn't survive, I'm sorry to say."

"Wow," said Jake, thunderstruck. "I'm truly sorry to hear that."

"Well," she said, "it affected my grandmother and mother much more than me, of course. I never even met the man. It really affected my mom, though ..."

"How?"

"You'll understand if you ever get to meet her."

"I'd like that," said Jake.

"I wouldn't be surprised if you do. She likes to come down here for a holiday. I have to warn you, though, she can be a very difficult person."

"I'm not surprised," said Jake, "with that kind of history to deal with."

He relaxed back on his cushion then, pondering this promising new revelation that Gisela could actually imagine him meeting her mother.

"Tell me," he said, stretching his arm across the space between them and allowing his fingertips to lazily tickle the back of her hand, "how did you and Dieter first meet?"

Before she had a chance to respond, Moische lifted his head, cocked both ears, and listened in an attitude of intense concentration. For a moment, Jake feared that Dieter had returned home for dinner earlier than expected, destroying this golden opportunity to have Gisela explain whatever bond there was between her and her husband. It was a bond he needed to understand, if for no other reason than to justify how it might ultimately be broken. The dog's alert turned out to be a false alarm. After releasing just a few weak woofs, Moische relaxed once again into his voluptuous belly-rubbing posture. As if inspired by his example, Gisela suddenly turned her hand over, exposing her naked palm to Jake's fingertips, sending an erotically charged shiver through his entire body.

"Dieter was a very sick man when we first met," she said, briefly releasing her hand from his touch to reload her cigarette holder with a fresh Marlboro. She lit up, inhaling deeply, and continued with her story.

"He was actually a friend of my sister back then. He used to manage rock bands. That's how he got to know my sister Petra, who I guess you could say was a groupie. He was also addicted to heroin at that time, and he'd gotten a case of hepatitis from using dirty needles. His skin was almost completely yellow the first time I set eyes on him. Lots of curly black hair and just skin and bones. You should have seen him, Jake. You never would have recognized him."

"Geez," said Jake, "it's hard to imagine Dieter being that helpless or that thin."

"Anyway, Petra asked me if I wouldn't mind bringing him some chicken soup. Apparently, he'd stopped eating altogether, and his friends were really quite worried about him. And of course, because he was a junkie, he didn't want to go to a doctor and have to answer any questions.

He was just wasting away in an apartment he was sharing with some friends."

"And he was still on heroin?" asked Jake.

"Well, he was coming down off the heroin when I met him. In a way, he had the disease to thank for getting him off the stuff. He was just too weak to deal with all the hassles involved in being an addict."

"God, it's amazing he didn't die."

"It is," she agreed. "But he's a tough one. Even so, he probably would have died if I hadn't been there for him."

"Been there for him? So what did you do besides bring him some soup? And what about Max, by the way?"

"Oh, yes, Max. He and I were already finished. Turns out he had no real interest in being a father, and I had no interest in playing the obedient wife, especially to someone I wasn't in love with. The marriage only lasted about a year, and then I took Chloe and moved in with my sister, who by then had gotten her own apartment. She was a few years older and quite the party girl, believe me. Anyway, it wasn't long before we both were party girls! Don't forget I was only eighteen, and I wasn't about to settle down and be a housewife again. That's just not my style at all."

"I never imagined it was," said Jake, gently squeezing her fingers. "Tell me, what exactly did 'party girls' do in Berlin in those days?"

"The same thing we do today," she said, eyeing him with amusement. "Go out to clubs, listen to music, dance, drink, take drugs, have fun."

"And sex?" asked Jake.

"And sex," she said, squeezing his hand for the first time. "Of course. Don't forget, I was already *not* a virgin, unlike yourself."

"So anyway," said Jake, pressing ahead, "you discovered Dieter who lay sick and dying, and you nursed him back to health?"

"That's right. After a few weeks, he was starting to feel better, and I was getting really tired of living with my sister, so—"

"Let me guess. He asked you to move in, and you did."

"*Jawohl.* You see, he'd gotten very attached to me Jake. I think in his mind, I'm the one who saved his life. And I probably did. I'm the only one who ever cared about him enough to make sure that he didn't go back on heroin."

"But I still don't get why you cared about him so much."

Gisela paused for a moment to think. "Because he cared about me, I guess would be the answer. He was the first one, really. The first man to treat me with respect. And he could be really charming once he cleaned up his act. And funny too. He made me laugh. The way you do!"

Jake paused a moment considering the compliment. "And I suppose he helped you with your daughter as well."

"Well, he's paying for her to go to school here in Ibiza. That's quite a big deal, believe me."

"And he never went back on heroin?"

"No," said Gisela. "He never did."

"That might explain why he drinks so much."

"Well, if you have to pick your poison, it's still better to be an alcoholic than to be shooting up heroin. At least you don't have to worry about getting busted or dirty needles."

"I guess," said Jake, "although it seems like there must be other options that don't involve liver disease."

"You think that doesn't hurt your liver?" she asked, pointing to the final remnant of the joint he was smoking.

"I don't know," he said. "But do I have to think about that just now?"

"Spoken like a true pothead," she said, stretching her fingers up to caress his forearm. "Or should I say *hash*head? Moische, what do you think," she asked. "Is Jake just an addict in denial or what?" The dog responded by licking his chops, posing as a sympathetic listener.

"Well, you'll never see me drunk the way that Dieter gets drunk, that's for sure." said Jake self-righteously. "I don't like it. Getting sloppy just isn't my style."

"Oh no?" she said, her long hair falling over her eyes so that when she looked up at him, he had to guess her expression. "What about sloppy kisses then?"

"Well," he said, scooting the dog away with one arm and glancing toward the doorway, "now that's something else entirely." Jake bent his head toward hers then, and she shook the hair out of her face, exposing eagerly parted lips. Grasping one another's forearm, they each fell off their cushions and pulled themselves together across the carpet until their lips finally met in a passionate collision, while fending off a frantically struggling Moische desperately trying to thwart their embrace by forcing his snout in between them.

"Moische, *NO!*" yelled Jake, reluctantly breaking off the kiss. The dog's determined attempt to get in on the action made it quite impossible to muster the necessary anger to put him in his place. He was simply too much of a clown, and their attempts to enforce any discipline on him kept breaking down in laughter.

Gisela finally managed a guttural command. "Moische, *mach Platz!*"

The German scolding did the trick. He reluctantly backed off and plopped down on the floor, hiding his snout between his stretched-out forelegs while eyeing the amorous couple intensely with barely disguised lust, his tail slapping out an irregular beat on the carpet.

"Well," said Jake, still chuckling, "There's no question about the power of the German language to tame the wild beast."

"He knows what it means," said Gisela. "He's heard it before, believe me. He's a good dog, but very … hmm, I can't think of the word …"

"Rambunctious?"

"Yes. I think that sounds right."

"What about me?" asked Jake. "Was I being too rambunctious?"

"You?" she asked, lifting up her right palm against an invisible barrier between them, inviting Jake to hold his against it. "Not at all, Jake. If anything, I think that you could take a lesson from Moische."

Jake shook his head in mock disapproval. "That's got to be a first," he said, pressing his palm against her own. "I don't think that any woman has ever asked me to perform like a dog before."

"Oh, I'm not asking you to perform like Moische," she said, playing with his fingers. "I'm talking about his passion."

Raising his eyes to look deeply into her own, Jake felt something warm and wonderful opening up in his chest. Up until this moment, Gisela had remained a romantic fantasy. He'd always assumed that seducing her would prove to be a monumental, if not impossible, task. Yet here she was against all expectations, inviting him to love her. He felt the conviction crystalizing within him that he hadn't been fooling himself after all. Gisela was indeed the next fateful step on his journey.

Chapter 47

Despite the increasing ardor between them, nothing was consummated that day. There was too much going on for that to happen. Apart from Moische's jealous presence, there was, of course, the impending arrival of Carl and Renata with the girls back from the beach, not to mention the looming possibility of Dieter returning that evening for dinner. They had kissed, and that had been delicious, but as far as finding release for the growing ache in their loins, they had both agreed to settle for a rain check. The prospect of being discovered *in flagrante* was unnerving to be sure, especially to Jake, despite Gisela's attempts to downplay whatever threat her husband might pose should their tryst be discovered. Her protestations struck Jake as naive. The truth was no one really knew how Dieter might react.

"I doubt if he would try and hurt you," she reassured him in the kitchen, searching in the silverware drawer as they began preparing a sumptuous meal of spaghetti and meatballs together.

"You *doubt* that he would hurt me?" asked Jake. "Is that supposed to make me feel good? I'm sorry, but that's hardly reassuring."

"Anyway, he doesn't actually hurt people, you know. I mean, look at him. He's just a big pussycat, really."

"It's not him so much I'm worried about," said Jake. "It's the people he does business with."

"Well, it's true some of them aren't so nice. Especially the ones in Berlin. Believe me, I've met them, and they're not the kind of people you want to have pissed off at you."

"What are you saying, Gisela? That by loving you, I could end up dead?"

"Are you saying that you love me?"

"I'm saying that I definitely could!"

"Relax, I'm kidding!" she assured him, taking out a colander. "Nothing's going to happen to you Jake, I promise! Usually, he just pretends like nothing's happening."

"Usually?" said Jake. "You mean …"

"What I mean is yes if that's what you're asking. It has happened before, Jake. Not a lot, but occasionally. I'm a very picky person you know."

"Oh yeah? Then how did you end up with Dieter in the first place?" This was a low blow, and Jake knew it. He immediately chastised himself, fearing he may have crossed a line.

"I already explained that to you," she replied tartly.

"Not really," persisted Jake. "You explained to me that you felt sorry for him and that you pretty much saved his life. But that doesn't explain how you ended up getting married!"

"He adored me, Jake!" she said, exasperation creeping into her voice. "That's how. He showered me with presents. He made me feel like I was someone special. I didn't have a lot of that in my life before I met Dieter."

"That's hard to believe," said Jake.

"It might sound pathetic now, but I didn't know who I was back then. I was basically a scared kid. I'm a different person now."

"But you never loved him?"

"Oh, Jake," she said, reaching for his hand across the kitchen counter. "Why do you have to make things more difficult than they are? Can't we just keep this simple between us?"

"But I need to know," he insisted, "do you love him or not?"

She sighed. "If it means so much to you, then no," she said at last. "To be honest, though, I'm not really sure what that even means. But …."

"But what?"

"But," she said, her eyes moist, "it's still something I believe in."

"I'm with you there," said Jake, moving in to embrace her while Moische eyed them lustily from the floor.

Chapter 48

It wasn't easy to find a telephone in Ibiza. There was one in Anita's Bar in the village of San Carlos, but almost no one had one in their home. So there was no way of knowing why Dieter failed to show up that evening for dinner. Everyone had come back from the beach and already eaten dinner before anyone started to worry. But after all the dishes had been washed and put away and Moische returned to his alternate life as Tonto in the neighbor's yard, Jake began to wonder where he was. Gisela seemed more relaxed about it. After all, it wouldn't have been the first time for Dieter to spend the night away from his wife without any prior explanation. His absences, according to her, were usually linked to excessive drinking or drugs and were a frequent source of rancor between them.

The girls had retired to Chloe's bedroom to practice their Abba routine, and Carl and Renata, as well as Gisela and Jake, were lounging around the living room listening to "Creepin'," Stevie Wonder's hypnotic ballad about what an amazing phenomenon love can be. Carl and Jake fell instantly in love with the seductive beauty of the song. Jake was writing down the lyrics, and Carl was figuring out the chords so they could add it to their repertoire while Renata and Gisela lit scented candles, drank mint tea, and chattered away in German. The cheerful, muted tones of Abba seeped through Chloe's bedroom door adding to the tender snapshot of domestic bliss.

After a while, a car door slammed shut in the driveway, and Tonto started barking next door. Dieter's heavy, uneven gait could be heard outside on the pavement, and everyone looked toward the door, anticipating a dramatic entrance. Everyone, but Jake, that is. He was looking at Gisela, curious to see how she would deal with the return of her errant husband. She lifted her cigarette holder to her lips, sucking down hard as he entered the room.

"Well?" she said, exhaling a pearly gray cloud of smoke.

"Wuzz goin' on?" he asked.

Jake studied the man as he stood weaving in the doorway, barely able to stand. His eyes were unnaturally shiny and opaque, and it occurred to Jake that he'd probably been doing more than just drinking. Behind him stood another figure, barely visible in the shadows.

"I thought you were coming home for dinner," chided Gisela.

"We already had dinner in town," he said, slurring his words. "Anyway, I ran into someone. Someone you'll be glad to see … I think."

As Dieter stepped inside the room, his guest came into full view in the doorway. Jake was immediately struck by the magnetic presence of the man, who was tall and slender with a sensitive face and hair like Jimi Hendrix. He was clean-shaven but with the dark shadow of a beard typical of Latin men. The nostrils of his aquiline nose flared over prominent lips and his dark eyes glittered with curiosity. He had a powerful aura, but not in any threatening way. As he came into the room, Gisela let out a gasp of recognition.

"Michel!" she cried, her apathetic tone of a moment before vanishing in an instant. Rising rapidly from her cushion, she stepped forward to embrace him.

"Gisela!" he said, pulling her into his chest. After a lengthy hug, they separated long enough to gaze into one another's eyes before resuming their embrace.

"It's been a while," said Michel, finally pulling away.

"Yes," she said, "it has indeed."

"I told you," said Dieter, leaning up against a wall and grinning from ear to ear, clearly pleased with himself for having brought his wife such a lovely surprise. Once again, Jake's opinion of Dieter was being tested. He might be tough in the world he did business in, but here at home with his wife, he'd converted to a marshmallow and an extraordinarily generous one at that. *What kind of man*, wondered Jake, *with a jealous nature to begin with, would persist in creating circumstances where his wife would come into contact with attractive and desirable men?* Jake found this obvious paradox in Dieter's nature intriguing. Or did it have more to do with Gisela's extraordinary ability to bend men to her will?

"Michel!" cried Chloe, running into the room and leaping into the visitor's arms. Michel allowed her to hug him but failed to reciprocate with any real enthusiasm. Nor did Chloe persist in her efforts. The man had a certain gravitas, Jake noted, which even Chloe deemed worthy of respect. Michel looked around the room then with a concentrated gaze, almost squinting as Gisela began introducing him to everyone.

"I ran into him in town," said Dieter. "He just got back from Barcelona. I told him he could spend the night."

"But Mummy," interrupted Chloe, looking anxiously in Jake's direction. "I thought you said that Jake was going to spend the night."

"He is, sweetheart. I mean, he can if he wants to. There's plenty of room here in the living room for anyone who wants to stay."

Gisela nodded at Jake with a mischievous grin. Clearly, she was in her element as the matron of the house.

"How do you guys know each other?" asked Jake, unable to suppress his curiosity any longer.

"We met on the beach at Aguas Blancas a few years ago," said Gisela, smiling at her friend. "You were working on a painting, remember?"

"Probably," said Michel smiling. Then he shrugged his shoulders as if to say, *What else would I have been doing?*

"Michel's an artist," said Chloe, trying to insinuate herself under the newcomer's arm. "He does wonderful paintings, doesn't he, Mummy?"

"Yes," agreed Gisela, "he does. Now excuse me for a moment while I go and get some more wine."

Dieter, meanwhile, had slid down the wall and sat slumped on the floor, his spindly legs stretched out in front of him, his head bobbing on his chest. Jake realized with astonishment that he'd already fallen asleep! Carl was playing a blues progression on his guitar while Renata looked on, and Chloe and Josie had apparently decided that Jake would best serve their purposes as a human pillow, each flopping down unceremoniously on top of him.

Michel, with the contained grace of a panther at rest, easily dominated the gathering, although he hardly spoke. Ultimately, he let his art speak for him. By the time Gisela had returned with the wine, a drawing pad with his artwork had been circulating around the room. She asked to see it and began flipping randomly through the drawings and watercolors. After a while, she stopped, and Jake noticed that her eyes were devouring a particular image.

"This is really amazing, Michel," she said at last. "I mean, you're amazing! This is unbelievably good!"

The two girls quickly abandoned Jake, squeezing in behind Gisela to get a better look. Jake felt a sudden surge of jealousy rising in his chest.

"That *is* good," said Josie.

"You see, I told you he was an artist," said Chloe, trying to take as much credit as she could for his achievement. Jake forced himself to wait patiently to see what all the fuss was about, all the while closely observing Gisela's every interaction with the artist. When the pad was finally passed his way, he looked with great anticipation. He'd half expected to see a depiction of Gisela in some revealing pose. But the image, in fact, had nothing to do with her at all, and the powerful impact it had on him only served to validate her response. The fact was he'd never seen anything quite like it.

"My God," muttered Jake, "This really *is* special."

He was looking at a very detailed watercolor depiction of a jungle scene full of exotic plants and animals. The heart of the piece seemed to be a waterfall placed squarely in the middle of the page. It had a streaming vaporous quality to it with a freshness and vibrancy that put the viewer right in the middle of a verdant slash of riotous flamboyant nature. But there was something else about the piece, something that Jake couldn't quite put his finger on, that made him feel strangely uneasy. The more he looked at the waterfall, which at first glance seemed so refreshing you could almost smell the ozone around it, the more he realized that all was not as it seemed. Underneath the silvery curtain of crystal clear water, something not so pure was lurking. All of a sudden, it leapt out at him, the way that a hologram can suddenly reveal its hidden image when held at the proper angle. A kind of face was hiding behind the curtain of water as if the anima of the jungle offered up its visage ingeniously disguised as an ordinary waterfall. The cascade, when viewed just right, held a mysteriously disturbing expression, revealing pain tinged with unbearable sadness and longing. At first glance, it seemed innocent enough, thought Jake, but the longer one stared at it, the more it took on a sinister, threatening aspect, as though a sentient being were trapped inside the image, longing to escape what was undoubtedly an unwanted and unrelenting captivity. The mastery behind the painting was immediately evident to Jake. Only an artist with extraordinary skill could have so seamlessly and subtly blended such an antagonistic image into what was, at first glance, an idyllic jungle landscape. The hidden forces of darkness it evoked spoke to him with frightening clarity, and he looked at Michel with unabashed respect and admiration.

It was not uncommon on Ibiza to meet people with artistic aspirations. Most of the people Jake knew were of that variety, himself included. But a true artist was rare, and he felt impacted by the scope of the Brazilian's talent and evident devotion to his art. Jake found himself feeling simultaneously elated and disappointed. Elated because he knew in that instant, when his eyes took in the artistry of Michel's work, that the man could never be a real threat to his pursuit of Gisela, for his true passion in life lay obviously elsewhere. The disappointment lay deeper within himself. Michel's evident deep devotion to his true purpose in life—that of being an artist—couldn't help but remind Jake of his own failure in that regard. He had neither the necessary belief in himself nor the tunnel vision needed to keep his eyes on the prize of creation no matter what distractions might arise. Jake's own sporadic attempts to write had thus far brought him nothing but disillusionment. He had yet to find the faith in himself to truly pursue such a lonely calling.

The party that night ended in a predictable fashion. Shortly after the girls were sent to bed, the first joint began to circulate. After a while, Dieter finally arose and made a wobbly departure assuring one and all he'd be back shortly, but he never returned from the bedroom he shared with Gisela in the back of the house. Rather than feel emboldened by Dieter's absence as his snores drifted into the living room, Jake settled into some cushions on the floor and sank into exhaustion. His moment with Gisela had passed. It wasn't gone forever, but the momentum which had been building up all day had been deflated by Michel's unexpected arrival. At least for now, the continuation of his lonely existence seemed assured.

274

Chapter 49

When Jake awoke the next morning, Michel was asleep on the couch, still dressed in all his clothes, his back turned to the world, presumably harvesting rich new images from his unconscious mind to utilize in his artwork. Gisela was nowhere to be seen, but Jake assumed she was lying in bed with her husband. He left a note for her on the kitchen table:

"Dear Gisela,

Thanks for your wonderful hospitality and for introducing me to Michel. You sure do have some fascinating men in your life! It's time for me to go into town and take care of some unfinished business. I can hardly wait to find out what life has in store for me next. I'll be back again soon, I hope.

Jake"

His pen had hung in the air for a moment before he signed his name, prepared to add the word "love," but in the end, he opted for discretion. Dieter after all, might see it and become alarmed, and Jake wanted to nurture at least for a while longer the truce between them. As he sat outside in the Tank, listening to the rumble of its faltering engine, Jake couldn't help but wonder what Gisela might be thinking as she heard him drive away. Would she feel even the slightest pang of regret at not having said goodbye, especially knowing what lay in store for him, or was her mind still full of images from Michel's notebook the night before? Jake reminded himself again that Michel's real passion was for his art. He wasn't someone who would ever invest much energy in the kind of love which Jake envisioned growing between himself and Gisela. His mind continued imagining romantic scenarios of himself together with her during the drive into Ibiza, where he parked the Tank on a side street near the post office. He kept putting off thinking of his impending departure for Mallorca with Ruben, Mary Lou, and Nancy. There was still the possibility that his check from Paris had arrived, which could be a game-changer, and he waltzed into the building in a hopeful mood. If the check was there, perhaps he wouldn't go to Mallorca after all. It wasn't that much, but it might last him long enough until some other option came along, something less drastic than what he was about to do. But as it turned out, the check had still not arrived. In fact, there was no mail for him at all.

It was clear now that reality was forcing Jake's hand. Ruben's offer had coincided precisely with the moment of his deepest destitution. Fate, he told himself, had led him to this point, and he should just embrace it and ignore all lingering doubts. And why not? Ruben had described it as a bonding experience and thought they could actually have fun. So why not just relax a little and trust the man? He was the one, after all, with the know-how in this scenario, allegedly at least. But Jake couldn't shake his feeling of uneasiness. He even imagined, weirdly enough, that he felt a warm spot on the back of his head as if someone were watching him. He turned around slowly, half-expecting to find Ruben staring at him, but there was no familiar face. Just an anonymous crowd of tourists and strangers.

Jake left the post office and made his way to the Café del Teatro. He found a seat at an empty table, the same one where he'd emptied out his pockets just a few days earlier. He ordered a café con leche, adding two packets of sugar, savoring the sweet, creamy richness of it. His enjoyment was curtailed by the nagging suspicion that whatever small amount of control he still had left in his life was about to slip away. Maybe forever.

"Hello, pardner."

Jake nearly leapt from his seat. Ruben had managed to sneak up on him once again.

"*Hola*," said Jake, affecting a breezy tone. "I figured you'd show up here."

"Show up?" said Ruben, whose forehead was beaded in sweat. "Yeah, I guess that's a good way to put it. On the other hand, I kind of figured you'd show up here too."

"You okay?" asked Jake.

"Sure," said Ruben, "sure I'm okay. Why'd you ask?"

"Just wondering," said Jake. "You seem a little on edge."

"That's 'cause I'm an edgy kind of guy," said Ruben, polishing his sunglasses on the front of his T-shirt. He looked really good for a change, Jake had to admit. He was clean-shaven, with his hair tied back in a neat ponytail. He wore a clean white V-neck T-shirt with tan safari shorts and sandals. A thin leather cord with a gold Egyptian ankh hung loosely round his neck, and his muscular legs looked taut and ready to spring into action.

Jake held up a hand to shield his eyes from the sun and grinned. "My, don't we look purty?"

"I don't know about 'we,'" he said, "but I know for a fact I've been turning heads left and right since I got up this morning."

"You think so?" said Jake, laughing in spite of himself. "Sit down and take a load off."

"Don't mind if I do, pardner," he said, pulling up a chair.

"What's with this pardner shit? Who're you? Slim fuckin' Pickens?"

"No, I'm Ruben fuckin' Ross, and you and I are gonna be partners now, right?"

"I guess so, yeah," said Jake.

"Whatcha mean, I guess so?" asked Ruben. "I just saw you in the post office, Jake."

"So what?" said Jake, noting that his premonition had been correct. Someone *had* been watching him.

"I followed you from there and noticed you didn't go to the bank to cash that check you've been waiting for all this time from Paris."

"Jeezus Christ," said Jake laughing. "You really are one sneaky son of a bitch."

"Yep."

"And you don't care who knows it, do you?"

"Nope."

Jake shook his head. The man was truly incorrigible. The fact that he would tail him like a private dick instead of just confronting him about whether or not he'd received the check spoke volumes about the man, making Jake wonder even more about their upcoming alliance. Would he ever be able to really trust this guy?

"Did you order that?" asked Jake as the waiter arrived, setting down a chilled bottle of beer.

"Yep. Just before I snuck up on ya."

"Well then, *salud*," said Jake.

"*Salud*," said Ruben, draining half the bottle in one gulp, his Adam's apple bobbing.

"Blimey!" called a familiar voice. "Just the two men I was looking for!" Nancy came into view then, sporting a pink straw hat and a white peasant's blouse with a matching pink miniskirt reaching the middle of her ample tanned thighs. A bulging straw bag hung over her right shoulder. "I just had to do some last-minute shopping," she said, standing behind Jake and casually rubbing his shoulders. "We are leaving tonight, right?"

"Tonight?" asked Jake taken aback. "Why so soon?"

"Soon?" said Ruben. "It ain't soon, pardner. It ain't soon at all. In fact, it's getting pretty damned late, I'd say."

"What about you, Jake?" asked Nancy. "You're still on board, I hope."

"I'm good, Nancy," said Jake reaching up to grab her hand. "You and me, we're gonna be a team, right?"

"Right you are," she said, sounding chipper. "Are you guys feeling nervous about it?"

"Nervous?" snorted Ruben. "What makes you say that? This whole thing's gonna be a piece of cake. You wait and see."

"You keep saying that," said Jake.

"Well, I'm glad to hear it," said Nancy, unflappably cheerful. "And what about Mary Lou? Where is she, by the way?"

"At the beach," said Ruben. "Closing things up. Getting ready to go."

"I can't believe this is really happening," said Jake, giving Nancy a worried glance.

"Hey, don't look so down in the mouth," said Ruben. "I told you … we're gonna have fun, remember?"

"Yeah, I remember," said Jake.

"Hey," he cajoled. "I'm counting on you, pardner. We couldn't do this without you, y'know."

"We?" asked Jake.

"He's right, Jake," said Nancy jumping in. "We do all need to support each other, don't we? We are friends, after all."

Jake had to smile. What kind of universe was it, he wondered, where this is what friends did together?

"Jake," said Ruben, "you gotta know something, *amigo*. You're my main man, brother."

"I dunno, Ruben …"

"Of course you know, Jake," insisted Ruben. "This is the only chance we've got right now. Not just for me, but for you too … and, of course, the girls too! Right, Nancy? We just need to do this thing right, that's all, and that's what you got me for. Just trust me, amigo."

Scrunching up his lips in a kind of half smile, Jake nodded. Despite their attempts to convince him otherwise, Jake couldn't shake the feeling that what was about to happen on Mallorca was not what any of them were anticipating. He took a deep breath and slowly let the air escape from his lungs. *Tranquillo, amigo,* he told himself. Just be *tranquillo.*

Chapter 50

After the meeting with Ruben and Nancy, Jake drove back to the finca to pick up some provisions and say goodbye to Carl, who he prayed would be there to drive him to the airport. Otherwise, it was going to be a long walk to the highway, and then he'd have to hitchhike from there. As he roared up noisily to the finca, creeping along the rough rock-strewn driveway, he saw Carl seated alone near the doorway holding his guitar, his long brown hair swirling down around his shoulders.

"So, you're really gonna go through with this?" he asked as they sat out in front of the finca together.

"Looks that way."

"That's it? That's all you've got to say about it?"

"Why?" asked Jake, "you don't approve?"

"It's not that I don't approve. It just seems kind of wacko, that's all."

"Maybe I am wacko."

"No," said Carl, setting down his guitar. "I don't think so, Jake. Ruben, maybe. Mary Lou, very likely. But you're a different story. You know what I think?"

"Uh-uh."

"I think you're looking at this as part of some grand romantic adventure, which is kinda how you see your life...."

"Could be," said Jake nodding. "But it's not just me, is it, Carl? Isn't that how you see your life too? I mean, c'mon, we're on Ibiza!"

"Look around you, Jake," he said, making a sweeping gesture with his arm. "This place screams romance. No one can deny that. And that appeals to me for sure. But I know what I want now, Jake. I wanna play music. That's it. I'm focused on that now. You, on the other hand, seem to just be letting the chaos unfurl that started in your life the moment you left the States and hit the road."

"You say that like it's a bad thing," said Jake, smirking.

"Seriously, Jake, I think there's a part of you that sees this episode with Ruben as a necessary chapter in the 'Kerouac-ian' novel of your life that you're inventing as you go along."

"Kerouac-ian?" said Jake, grinning. "I kinda like the sound of that."

"You may like it now," he continued, "but let's see how much you like it when the shit hits the fan with Ruben in that seedy situation you're getting yourself into over in Palma."

"You've gotta have seeds to grow, Carl," said Jake.

"Very funny. But do you think this is some kind of joke?" asked Carl. "Listen, you're gonna grow all right. But into what kind of a twisted tree?"

"C'mon, Carl. I thought you had more faith in me than that!"

"Look," he said, sighing. "I do, in fact. I just don't have a good feeling about any of … this."

"I can always leave, ya know. If things get too out of hand. But I gotta admit, I'm kinda curious. Could we actually pull this off?"

"Yeah, right," said Carl, clearly exasperated, just as an enormous black raven emerged from the woods above the driveway. It floated above them for a moment before veering downward and landing on the top branch of a nearby tree. Jake followed it with his gaze, its unexpected appearance sending a shiver down his spine. "Well, you're gonna do your own thing," continued Carl, "and seeing as how you would never do something like this on your own …. That's the attraction, isn't it? He's Neal Cassady to your *Jake* Kerouac. I can see how you'd like that … except …"

"Except what?"

"Except I'm not so sure you're gonna be believable in your role in this tale. Ruben as a pimp? Yeah, I can see that. And Mary Lou doing tricks? Possibly. And maybe Nancy, too. But you? Nuh-ah. You're a little incongruous in this particular scenario, my friend."

"Ah," said Jake lighting up a joint, "but that's what could make it interesting, don't ya think? If I was just like Ruben, it would be all too predictable."

"Oh, it's pretty predictable, all right."

"Ya think?"

"Yeah, I do," said Carl. "But I'm not gonna say how I think it's gonna turn out. That would spoil the suspense."

They both paused again as a jet flew high overhead, squeezing out a long white trail behind it in the blue sky as it bore weary revelers back to London, Stockholm, or Berlin.

"It *is* suspenseful," Jake admitted, releasing a cloud of smoke from his lungs. "I'd feel different, of course, if the girls weren't okay with it. But I'll tell you what, Carl. I can hardly wait to see how it all turns out."

Jake looked up to find his friend staring at him with real concern in his eyes.

"All kidding aside, pal, I'm worried about you."

Jake felt a jolt of uneasiness pass through him. He'd never heard Carl speak this way before.

"Carl," said Jake, taking another hit on the joint, "to be honest, I'm a little worried myself. But it just can't be helped."

"What's that supposed to mean?"

"It means that this whole thing has gained a certain momentum that I just can't stop now, Carl. It's hard to explain, but I think I really need to go through with it despite the risks involved. Even if I don't make any money, it's gonna test my limits. Know what I mean? In a weird sort of way, it's gonna show me who I am."

"Like you don't know that already?"

"I don't think we ever totally know who we are, Carl. I've never been around people like this before. And certainly not in a situation like this. It'll be, well, revealing to see how I respond."

"So you see it as a kind of test?"

"You could say that," said Jake.

"And is this test pass-fail? Or graded on a curve?"

"Good one!" said Jake. "Pass-fail, I guess. If I come out more or less unscathed with some money in my pocket without getting hurt or arrested, then I pass."

"What about you hurting someone, Jake? That's what worries me about you going over there. You might have to!"

"I won't," said Jake with conviction. "I don't even think I could. I see myself more as Nancy's friend and companion than anything else. I think that's how she sees me too. And I'm pretty sure she knows how to handle herself with men."

"You'd better hope so," said Carl. "What about Mary Lou?"

"Not so sure about her," said Jake. "But she's not my problem. She's got Ruben, remember?"

"God bless her," said Carl. "That's all I can say."

"Yeah," said Jake. "I know what you mean."

"What I find interesting," said Carl, twisting a peg on his guitar neck, "is that you're not even talking that much about money. Isn't that what this whole operation's supposed to be about?"

"Absolutely," said Jake. "It is. But I have such little grasp of the money aspect of this business that my mind can't even go there. I expect Ruben and I will figure it out as we go along. He's supposed to be the one who knows all about that side of things."

Carl began improvising a riff on his guitar:

'He doesn't know what it's all about even though he's an Eagle scout...'

"Sound about right, Jake?"

"Hmm, yeah. But that was a long time ago."

"I gotta say," said Carl, chuckling, "I don't think being an Eagle Scout was in any way predictive of the life you've been leading lately."

"No," admitted Jake. "I guess it wasn't. But ya know, I still do pretty much follow the Boy Scout oath."

"Oh yeah? Which is?"

"I can still rattle it off, believe it or not," said Jake. "Let's see now... A scout is trustworthy, loyal, helpful, friendly, courteous, kind, obedient, cheerful, thrifty, brave, clean, and reverent."

"Wow," said Carl. "I'm impressed. Can't believe you still know that by heart!"

"I know," said Jake, chuckling. "It is pretty hard to believe. But I guess by the time you get to be an Eagle, it's really drilled into you."

"But wait a minute now … obedient … and reverent?"

"They're in there, yeah."

"Now that's funny," said Carl.

"I did say *pretty much* follow," said Jake.

"Yeah, I noticed you left yourself some wiggle room."

"Hey, ten out of twelve ain't bad. But you're right, Carl. An Eagle Scout volunteering to hang out with a wannabe pimp and whores … what the hell happened to me?"

"You tell me, man." Their eyes met, and their mutual grins soon dissolved into gut-crunching laughter. The absurdity of Jake's situation, amplified by the hash, simply left no other option. As the laughter finally died down between them, Carl strummed a few chords on his guitar, unwinding yet another blues progression.

"Tell me something, Jake," he said. "Who was it you were trying to impress?"

"Whaddya mean?"

"When you decided to become an Eagle Scout. Who were you doing that for?"

"Myself, I guess."

"Bullshit," said Carl. "Kids at that age are always trying to impress somebody."

"Okay," said Jake. "If I had to guess, I'd say my dad. He was my idol back then."

"Back then? Isn't he still alive?"

"Yeah," said Jake, "technically speaking, I guess. But he kinda died a long time ago. Around the same time my mom did."

"Whaddya mean, kinda died?"

"His heart, I mean," said Jake. "I think his heart died."

"Which was right around the time you joined the Boy Scouts, right?"

"You are correct, Doctor Brothers."

"But you kept trying to impress him, right?"

"Probably more than ever. But trying to impress somebody who's given up on life gets pretty old after a while."

"What do you mean, given up on life?"

"You know, just plays it safe, kinda falls back into a very predictable, sad routine, just waiting for retirement … and ultimately death."

"You know what I think?" said Carl.

"No, but I'm pretty sure you're gonna tell me."

"I think you're still trying to impress your old man, Jake, but in a different way."

"You think so?"

"Sure. It's like you're saying, 'Look at me now, Dad, I'm alive! I may have my balls out on the chopping block, I may crash and burn, but at least I'm alive. I'm not just this sad guy waiting around to die, like you. I'm out here living life!'"

"Gosh, Carl," said Jake feigning shock. "I had no idea you were so impressed with me."

"Not so fast," said Carl, shaking his head, "I'm looking at a whole other possibility here, bud."

"One where you're not so impressed with me?"

"Dig this. Obviously, when you want to impress, you can do it, right? The whole Eagle Scout episode proved that. But forget what I said before. Maybe the real crux of the matter is that you don't have anybody to impress anymore."

"What?"

"I'm saying," he said, swiping the joint from Jake's fingers, "you've got to figure out who it is you want to impress, that's all. You wanna impress Ruben, you go right ahead. Be my guest."

"Maybe I wanna impress myself," said Jake.

"Oh yeah? And this is how you do it?"

"Maybe. You can impress yourself in all sorts of different ways, ya know."

"Oh, that's precious," said Carl. "You must be really stoned."

"No, Carl. I mean it. Haven't you ever heard of rites of passage?"

"Uh-huh," said Carl. "Like those kids from the Amazon who whack on a bee's nest with a stick and let the swarm attack them? Just to prove how brave and impervious to pain they are like real men?"

"Exactly," said Jake, "that's what this is about for me. I haven't quite figured it all out yet, but it is for sure some kind of rite of passage. One that I've kind of stumbled into."

"But what's the point?"

"It's about survival, Carl. Just like it is for those kids in the jungle. To prove that I can ride the wave of life anywhere it takes me and still end up all right in the end."

"By 'end up all right,' you mean not end up dead inside like your old man?"

"Well, that is for sure how I don't want to end up."

"Sounds like a worthy goal," admitted Carl, "even if I'm not quite sure about your plan to accomplish it. But if it's any consolation, I do have faith that you're gonna get through this thing intact."

"For real?" asked Jake. "Really, Carl? That means a lot. But then, why'd you give me that whole rash of shit just now?"

"Just playing my part in your rite of passage."

"Thanks," said Jake. "I guess."

"You're welcome," said Carl. "There is one other thing, though, that bothers me, pal."

"What?"

"Never expect a guy like Ruben to help keep your heart alive."

"You know," said Jake. "I think you underestimate him. You may not approve of him or like him very much, but at least he's not dead. The one thing I genuinely respect about the man is that he is a risk-taker. That's what you do when you're alive, right? You take risks."

"Yeah, but to what purpose?" asked Carl.

"Apart from money, you mean?" asked Jake. "Don't forget, Carl, that Nancy asked me to be there too. In her mind, I'm the anti-Ruben. The one person who might be able to keep his worst impulses in check."

"Good luck with that," said Carl. "So that makes you the savior in this scenario?"

"Of course not. That's not what I'm saying at all."

"Just don't go and get Ruben riled up," warned Carl, taking another hit on the joint. "I think I'd rather be stung by a swarm of bees. If he gets his stinger in you, you may never recover, man."

"You know something about Ruben I don't?" asked Jake.

"I know he hurts women," said Carl.

"What are you talking about?"

"Remember when we were all living together up in Santa Inés, and we came home one night, and Mary Lou was sitting at the kitchen table with her face all swollen and her lip bleeding, and she limped when she got up to go into the bedroom. Remember that?"

"Yeah," said Jake. "She said she'd taken a spill off the back of a friend's moped coming back from town. I remember."

"Bullshit!" said Carl. "What friend? I never saw her go anywhere without Ruben."

"Well, he's never hurt her in front of me," said Jake. "He knows I wouldn't go for that."

"Course not. It's a clandestine game they play with each other."

"Some game," said Jake shaking his head. "Anyway, I appreciate your concern, Carl. I really do. And I'll definitely be careful."

"So you're still gonna do it?"

Jake reached over and grabbed his friend's knee. "Yeah, Carl," he said, looking him in the eye. "I am fucking gonna do it."

"I figured as much," he said, sighing. "C'mon. Let's get you to the airport then. There's some horny motherfucking oil field workers over in Palma who don't know what's about to hit 'em!"

A short way beyond the end of the long driveway, a small white stucco building squatted next to the road. It served as a police ammo dump, had a heavily bolted and locked wooden door, and was guarded by a vicious black schnauzer the size of a small pony. The beast never failed to work itself into a frenzy whenever anyone drove by. Both Jake and Carl had tried befriending the animal, even bringing it snacks to eat, but it proved to be a futile endeavor. The dog's rage was unappeasable. Carl drove up and halted the van just beyond reach of the cur, who was straining against his thick chain and steel-studded collar at the edge of the road, barking furiously. Its ragged black lips were stretched tight, exposing a jagged set of yellow teeth flecked with white foam.

"Will you look at that?" said Carl, shaking his head. "No matter how many times he sees us go by, he still goes nuts every time."

"Yeah," said Jake. "It's kinda like he just can't help himself."

"Sounds like someone else I know," said Carl, as he put the van in gear and continued toward the airport.

Chapter 51

That evening after the short flight from Ibiza to Palma de Mallorca, the motley crew checked into the hotel Ruben had recommended. It was low rent, but not too low rent. It had a restaurant and bar in the lobby with tables outside on the sidewalk. The furnishings looked like they'd seen better days, but the crowd was noisy and lively, especially at the bar, which was hosting an assortment of oil-field workers, if Ruben was to be believed. They all four agreed they were too tired after their busy day of preparation and would start "work" the next day. Jake couldn't help but notice though, as he and Nancy got into the lift to go up to their rooms that Ruben and Mary Lou were locked in a heated discussion at the bar. A moment later, the lift doors rattled shut and the antique elevator, rumbling and shaking, delivered them up to their adjacent rooms on the third floor.

"We'll figure everything out in the morning over a nice pot of tea, right Jake?" said Nancy, wrapping her arms around him and pressing her face in his chest. "Okay?" she asked, tilting her face upward. "You'll have to forgive me, but I'm really knackered. I'm afraid I've been on a bit of a bender of late. I know you Americans like to say 'time is money' and all that, but I'll really be much more prepared to go at this full tilt in the morning, you'll see. You look a bit knackered yourself, Jake. Probably better we both get some sleep. See you in the morning, okay love?"

"Sounds good," said Jake, feeling relieved. In fact, he *was* tired. More, he thought, from the stress of not really knowing what to expect than anything else. "I'll see you at breakfast then."

***

The next morning in the lobby, they found Mary Lou slumped in a chair at a table in the back.

"Hat and sunglasses on … indoors?" said Nancy, by way of greeting. "That's never a good sign. Did you and Ruben have a fight?"

Mary Lou looked down and began fiddling with a napkin. "Can you tell?" she asked.

"Blimey, darlin', what's the matter?" asked Nancy, pulling up another chair. "You look like shite."

"Well, that's how I feel too," she said.

"Mary Lou," said Jake in a gentle tone, "can you tell us what happened?"

"H-he was supposed to *be* there for me," she said, her voice beginning to break. "B-but …" A fat tear began rolling slowly down her cheek beneath her roving eye.

Jake reached out and squeezed her hand. "Go on," he said.

"I don't know if you really want to hear this," she said, sniffling. "And I don't think Ruben would want you to either."

Nancy quickly reached inside her purse and pulled out some tissues. "Here, take these, love," she said.

"Thanks," said Mary Lou, wiping away what was draining now from her nose onto her puffy upper lip.

"Forget about what Ruben wants," said Jake. "Just tell us what's going on."

"All right," she said, gathering herself. "I guess you'd hear about it anyway, sooner or later. And frankly, I'd just as soon you heard my version of events before you talk to Ruben. You see, last night, he and I, well …we decided …"

She stopped again, too choked up to speak. "Sorry, I'm not very good at this," she said, sniffling. "You see, Ruben and I decided to do a little business already."

"Go on," said Jake.

"So anyway, last night, after you guys went to bed—"

"But I thought we all agreed we were too tired last night!" said Nancy.

"I know. And I was, too. But Ruben was restless. He didn't want us to waste a night … kept going on about how much money we were paying for the hotel, so we decided to 'test the waters', as he said. We sat down at a table near the bar to have a drink, and that's when Ruben noticed this Spanish guy giving me the eye."

"Giving you the eye?" asked Jake.

"You know, giving me flirty looks whenever he thought that Ruben wouldn't notice."

"So what happened?" asked Jake. "I mean, what'd Ruben do?"

"He wanted me to flirt with the guy, find out what he wanted and whether he had a room here in the hotel or not."

"So, did you?"

"Did I what?"

"Flirt with the guy?"

"Yeah, after Ruben left. He didn't stick around long. He acted like we weren't even together. He said he'd hang around out of sight and then follow us up to the guy's room if he had one and wait outside. Then he'd stand outside the door and listen to make sure nothing funny was going on."

"And what would he do if he thought there was?" asked Nancy.

"Start pounding on the door, I guess. I don't know. Yell or scream or do something."

"So did this guy have a room here?" asked Nancy.

"Yeah, turns out he did," said Mary Lou.

"So then what?" asked Jake.

"I made him an offer just like Ruben said I should."

"And this guy, what was he like?"

She sighed again. "Well, he was kind of slick looking, like he had money. I think that's what got Ruben so excited. Anyway, this guy had on one of those white linen suits with a blue silk tie, y'know, very expensive looking. He was well-groomed, too, with one of those little black pencil moustaches. He looked, kinda like, I don't know, a Mexican divorce lawyer—the kind you see down in Tijuana."

"That conjures up an image," said Jake.

"Right? So anyway, all I had to do after Ruben left was look over and smile at the guy. He picked up his drink right away and made a beeline for my table."

"Go on," said Jake.

"I said my name was Lola. He said his name was Pedro, which was probably about as real as Lola. Then we chitchatted for a while, and I let him buy me a drink. His English wasn't that good, and neither's my Spanish, so there wasn't much conversation. But I gathered he was a businessman staying by himself here at the hotel."

"So not even an oil field guy," said Nancy.

"No, no way," said Mary Lou. "After a while, I mentioned a price and told him I'd go back to his room with him if he could pay."

"Just like that?" asked Jake.

"Whaddaya mean, just like that? It was part of the conversation, Jake."

"And?"

"And what?"

"Did you tell him what he could get for that amount?"

"Not really," she said, sighing again. "But it was understood. At least I thought it was."

"And he agreed?"

"Yeah. He seemed to be fine with it. More than fine, actually."

"Did you guys leave together?"

"Hell, no. He just gave me his room number, leaned in, said '*vinte minutos*,' and left. I should've known when he rubbed his greasy little mustache up against my ear and flicked his tongue inside that he'd turn out to be a creep," she said, shuddering.

"Jesus Christ," said Nancy, digging in her purse for a cigarette. "That sounds horrible. Here, have one of these, Mary Lou. It'll calm you down."

"Thanks, Nance," she said, leaning in for a light.

"Well," said Jake. "I guess we're about to get to the good ... or should I say, the bad part of the story."

"It's not funny, Jake," she said, glaring at him. "Please don't take this lightly."

"Sorry. I didn't mean it that way. Go on, Mary Lou, please."

"When I got to the room, Pedro was waiting. He'd left the door unlocked, and I just let myself in. He was standing by the bed in a bathrobe with a big smile on his face looking like the cat who'd just ate the canary. He said he wanted to watch me get undressed—"

"Wait a minute," interrupted Jake. "Had you met up with Ruben before this? I mean, before you went to the guy's room?"

"Sure," she said. "He was in the stairwell just like he said. He told me to be sure and get the money before anything happened and that he'd be outside standing guard in the hallway."

"So did you?" asked Jake. "Get the money, I mean."

Mary Lou lifted a chipped red fingernail to her mouth and started chewing. "Not exactly," she said. "I mean, I don't know ... I got flustered, I guess. I was going to ask for it, I mean after I got undressed. But then ..."

"Yeah?"

"Well, I'd just turned around for a moment to hang up my clothes on this hook on the door, and when I turned back around, there he was, right in front of me, and he'd taken off his bathrobe, and he was ... he was ... so *big!* Anyway, I got all flustered and, well, I just forgot to ask for the money... it's like my brain froze or something."

"Uh-oh," said Nancy. "I'm so sorry, honey."

"He started rubbing up against me then," she said, still chewing on a nail, "trying to push himself inside."

"Jeezus," said Nancy.

"I started pushing him away," said Mary Lou. "That's when he grabbed a handful of hair and pulled my head back, so I was practically looking up at the ceiling. And then he tried to kiss me. It was ... nauseating. I thought I was gonna throw up!"

"Didn't you think of yelling?" asked Jake. "You know, to get Ruben's attention."

"I guess I thought I could still handle it," she said. "Don't ask me why. I mean, you know how guys get! I've been around plenty of horny guys before. Like I said, I thought I knew how to handle him. I guess I thought he was just being playful in his own disgusting way. I didn't think it would, you know..." She hesitated, removed her fingernail from her mouth, and used it to scratch the palm of her hand. "Anyway, he ... he managed to pull me back to the bed and pushed me down on my stomach ... really hard. It knocked the wind out of me for a few seconds. Then before I really knew what was happening, he got behind me . . . and ... and he ..."

"Oh God," said Jake, turning away.

"You have no idea," she said, releasing a sob. "He really hurt me, Jake."

"Wait a minute," said Nancy. "You mean you didn't try to get Ruben's attention? I would've been screaming my bloody head off by now, I can promise you that!"

"I couldn't," said Mary Lou burying her face in her hands. "He ... he kept pushing my head down into the mattress. I thought he was going to smother me. It was all I could do just to breathe."

Nancy grabbed Mary Lou's hand. "What a bastard!"

"What did he do ... afterward?" asked Jake.

"I'm not really sure, to be honest. I think I may have passed out for a little while. The next thing I know, he's just standing there leering down at me, and he's got his suit back on. I remember he was straightening his tie looking down at me like I was a real piece of garbage. He tossed me the key and told me I could spend the rest of the night there, that the room was paid for, that he'd had a good time and was leaving. Then he reached down and grabbed me. I'd covered myself with a sheet by then. He . . . he grabbed my ass through the sheet really hard and squeezed and ... and laughed and said how much he liked my *culo* ... Christ! I'll never forget that voice as long as I live. It was as if a viper could talk. It made me just want to crawl under the bed and disappear."

"I think I would've killed him," said Nancy icily.

"I was so scared," said Mary Lou, studying her hands. "There was something ... I don't know, really wicked about this guy . . . this Pedro or whatever his name really was. All I could do was ... was ... hope that Ruben would ..."

"That Ruben would *what?*"

In his typically surreptitious manner, Ruben had managed to sneak up on their table. He had a western-style red and white bandanna wrapped around his forehead holding his unkempt hair in place. His sallow complexion and bloodshot eyes gave him a decidedly unsavory appearance. His wrinkled clothes from the night before, his beery breath, and the odor of ripeness exuding from his armpits created a striking aura of dissoluteness. "… would thank you for doing your job? Well, I do. I always do. You know that! And I did last night, too, remember? Look, you did what you were s'posed to do. It didn't go quite the way it was supposed to, which, by the way, is par for the course, but you did get paid, right? Thank God Pedro left the money on the dresser cuz otherwise …"

"Otherwise what?" asked Nancy, glaring at Ruben with undisguised contempt. "What do you have to say for yourself?"

"Nothing to you, bitc—" he started, then caught himself. "Look, Nancy. This is a private matter between Mary Lou and me. We'll discuss this between ourselves if you don't mind. Ain't that right, babe?"

Mary Lou said nothing, but nodded while biting her lip.

"Listen, babe. I told you this last night. What we do together stays between us. They're not gonna understand how we are. We've been over this a thousand times. They're our friends, sure, and friends are great, but nobody really gets us, baby. You know that. And nobody loves you the way I do! You and I've got something real special goin' on," he said, leaning in to kiss her on the forehead. "You did awesome last night. No, look at me. You really did."

"Jake," said Nancy, getting up to leave, "I think that maybe we should go now. I'm sure that Ruben and Mary Lou have things they need to talk about."

Jake, flustered and confused, felt unsure how to respond to this unexpected turn of events. Weren't they supposed to all be in this together, he wondered. But studying Mary Lou, Jake couldn't help but notice that her expression had brightened considerably after Ruben showed up. She was still downcast, but there was a hopefulness in her expression that took Jake by surprise. He would have expected righteous indignation on her part at the very least. Perhaps even murderous rage. But whatever wrathful state she'd been building up to had apparently been quelled, at least momentarily by her partner's abrupt appearance in the flesh.

"Mary Lou," said Jake, "are you sure you'll be all right? I mean—"

"I think Nancy's right, Jake," she interrupted, her dark eyes flashing a warning. "Ruben and I do need to talk."

"Are you okay, though?" he asked. "I mean do you need a doctor?

"No," she said. "Nothing like that. I'll be okay."

"But . . . "

"But what, Jake?" asked Ruben, whose smile had disappeared, replaced by a more sinister expression.

"Ruben, I've gotta ask you something," said Jake, whirling on his friend, "Where the hell were you last night when she needed you?"

"Around," he said tight-lipped. "That's all you gotta know. Okay Jake? I was around. And this is between me and Mary Lou. Nobody else."

Jake looked his presumptive partner in the eyes. But the malevolent expression there warned him away. "Okay," he said. "Whatever."

Jake stood up then and moved next to Nancy.

"Are you sure you're all right, Mary Lou?" pressed Nancy, ignoring Ruben's menacing posture.

"I'll be okay," she said, "but thanks, Nancy. And thank you too, Jake."

"For what?" he asked, confused.

"For being my friend?" she said, attempting a smile.

"Hey," interrupted Ruben, grabbing Nancy's arm and eyeing her cigarette. "You got one of those for me?"

"Sure," said Nancy, shaking off his arm, and shaking out a cigarette. "Should I leave you the whole pack then?"

"Nah," said Ruben, "this'll do just fine."

"C'mon," said Jake, placing an arm on Nancy's shoulder and turning her toward the lift. "Let's go."

"Hey, Jake," growled Ruben.

"What?"

"Catch you later."

"Yeah. Maybe."

"Oh no, Jake," he said. "I'll catch you for sure."

Chapter 52

Aside of Ruben was revealing itself, which was impossible for Jake to ignore. The stakes were simply too high. Ruben's cruelty and inattentiveness threatened to disrupt their whole enterprise before they'd even gotten started. There had been glimpses before, but Jake had mostly chosen to disregard them. Now he had no choice but to deal with the man's increasingly reckless and belligerent behavior. Retreating to Nancy's hotel room, the two of them huddled on the bed, trying to decide what to do next.

"He is such a fucking asshole," began Nancy.

"I have to agree," said Jake. "Especially when he drinks. But what are we going to do about it is the question."

"Well, I, for one, want nothing more to do with the guy," she continued. "I'm quite sure about that."

"Easy for you to say," said Jake. "He and I are sharing a room."

"Well, you can always move in here," said Nancy giving Jake a lascivious wink.

"Yeah, right," said Jake, "except that this is your work pad, remember?"

"Blimey, you're right about that. How soon one forgets!" she said, her humor returning. "Speaking of which, there's this Danish seaman I was chatting up at breakfast who I think may become my very first client. What do you think of that?"

"Not the Pedro type, I hope?"

"Not a chance. I know how to suss 'em out, Jake, believe me. This guy's about as threatening as a pussycat. I don't wanna put down Mary Lou, but I really do think her judgment might be impaired. I would've been on to that guy as soon as he stuck his forked tongue in my ear."

"I'm so relieved to hear that," said Jake. "That's why I feel I can trust you, Nance! You have good judgment, unlike either one of those two. Ruben and Mary Lou can go it on their own from now on, as far as I'm concerned. I really can't handle being around them anymore. Not in a situation like this. You know it's never gonna end well."

"Well, we should've seen it coming. I mean we did, really. We just didn't want to admit it," said Nancy. "You never seriously thought this would work out with them, did you, love?"

"I've always had my doubts," said Jake. "But I've always been an optimist, and somehow they did get the momentum rolling, didn't they? Gotta give 'em credit for that."

"Yeah, sure, will do. And I wish them the best, I really do. I mean, they're their own worst enemy to begin with…anyway, I'm glad we can both agree that we're done with them now."

"Except for the fact, as I mentioned before, that I'm sharing a room with Ruben. Right next door."

"Don't worry, love. I'll bet you a pound of my tummy fat he'll spend next to no time in that room. He'll either be in the bar, the pool hall down the street, or else in her room the whole time until this whole thing blows up in their faces, which I'm sorry to have to predict, it almost certainly will."

"That is a sad prognosis," said Jake.

"I'm sorry, but you see how they are together. This situation is a lot of pressure for them both, and apparently, they don't do well under pressure. Now close your eyes while I slip into something sexy. I've gotta get to work. Or else peek if you like. I really don't mind," she said, caressing Jake's cheek with the back of her hand.

Jake stood up and walked to the window overlooking a bustling street. "When you're dressed, let's go out together," he said. "I wanna get a glimpse of this Danish sailor of yours."

Her sailor, as predicted, turned out to be a harmless-looking guy who had a few friends who wanted to get to know her as well, so Nancy was kept busy for most of that first day, and all went as planned. Jake shadowed her when she left her room, keeping an eye on her from a distance and then following discreetly when she returned to the hotel. None of the men she brought back looked particularly threatening, which was a huge relief to Jake. Almost as huge a relief was Ruben's absence each time he returned to their shared room. Wherever he was, Jake didn't miss him. Nor did he miss the disruptive chaos which invariably swirled around him. He just wanted to be able to listen undisturbed for any cries of alarm coming through the thin wall separating his room from Nancy's. There were cries all right, but mostly blissful-sounding ones. *Could Nancy actually be enjoying the sex*, Jake wondered? He convinced himself she was, probably so he could feel less guilty about the kind of work they were both engaged in.

That evening they met up in the hallway after Jake heard her bid her latest client farewell. "Take this for now," she said, pressing a small wad of bills into Jake's hand. "Consider it spending money. We'll figure out the rest later. I'm on my way to a bar now at the yacht harbor that one of the Danes told me about. Just wanna have a drink and some dinner. Nothing professional, though. You wanna join me?"

"No thanks, Nance. I think I'll stay in and read a book if you don't mind. I'm kind of knackered. Ruben seems to have abandoned the room, so hopefully, I can have some alone time."

"Got it," said Nancy. "Sounds like a great idea. What's that old saying? When the cat's away, the mouse will curl up and read a book? Now that's a new twist!"

"Yeah, I guess it is," said Jake. "Anyway, have fun, and knock on my door when you get back. We can go over the day's events and figure out what to do tomorrow."

"Not much suspense about that, I'm afraid," she said, moving in to give Jake a hug. "But yeah, I will see you later on. Hopefully, you-know-who won't be back by then."

***

But Ruben did come stumbling back to the room that evening, hours after Nancy had gone, collapsing face down on his narrow bed.

"Oh fuck," he mumbled.

"Oh fuck what?" asked Jake, putting down the novel he was reading. It was Malcolm Lowry's *Under the Volcano,* which was blowing Jake's mind with the beauty of its prose.

"Ohfuckohfuckohfuck," he continued, his voice muffled by the pillow which was pressed into his face.

"Something happen with Mary Lou?" asked Jake warily.

"I dunno … maybe," said Ruben.

"Whaddya mean, maybe?"

Ruben rolled over on his side, facing Jake, and let out a deep sigh, closing his eyes as if trying to gather his thoughts. His headband, wrapped around his long scraggly blond hair, was stained with sweat, and his face was covered with stubble. Reaching in his shirt pocket, he pulled out a crumpled pack of Dorados and a BIC lighter, shook out a cigarette, placed it between his teeth, and lit up, exhaling a stream of gray smoke toward the slowly twirling ceiling fan.

"Well," said Jake, "I'm waiting."

"Just a sec, okay," said Ruben, pushing himself up off the bed and wobbling toward the tiny refrigerator in the corner of the room. He extracted a bottle of San Miguel beer, knocked the cap expertly against the bedpost, and held the foaming liquid up to his lips until he'd gulped down the entire contents of the bottle. "Ah," he said, smacking his lips and belching loudly as he sat back down on the bed, "that's what I'm talkin' bout!"

Jake continued waiting in silence. He knew there was no point in trying to get Ruben to talk if he didn't feel like it. After a few beats, Ruben rolled the empty bottle across the floor, placed his hands on his knees, and lifted his head to look at Jake. "There's a fancy disco about ten minutes from here called El Diamante … ever heard of it?"

"Yes," said Jake. "But I haven't been there. Not yet, anyway. What about it?"

"Well, I went there with Mary Lou. Cost us a fucking fortune to get in too—almost everything she earned last night with Pedro."

"I'm surprised they let you in," said Jake.

"What's that s'posed to mean?"

"Have you looked in the mirror lately?"

"Very funny," said Ruben. "The night was young. I still looked okay. Anyway, you wanna hear this or just talk about how bad I look?"

"Go ahead," said Jake. "I'm listening."

"We split up inside, right? That's how we do it. Mary Lou started dancing by herself while I took a seat at the bar, you know, keepin' an eye on things. There was this group of rich-looking Spanish guys at a table sharing a bottle of scotch. One of them kept staring at Mary Lou. A real handsome creep. Typical Spaniard: you know, dark hair, dark eyes, nice even white teeth. Pretty soon, he gets up and starts dancing with Mary Lou. Next thing I know, they're dancing real close. He's got his arm around her, and they're grinding their hips together. She wasn't just playing around, either. She was into it. I could tell."

"I don't see the problem," said Jake. "Isn't that what she's supposed to do? Pick up guys with money?"

"Yes … I mean, no, uh, I dunno," said Ruben, grabbing his hair and rolling his eyes toward the ceiling. "Anyway, I lost it. The way she was looking at him just bothered me, y'know? I got up from the bar and went out on the dance floor and shoved the guy, you know, all the while telling the guy to leave her the fuck alone."

"Uh oh," said Jake, shaking his head. "So what happened next?"

"Of course, Mary Lou wasn't happy about it. She started screaming at me to leave her the fuck alone. She even shoved me. Next thing you know, there's this big melee. The guy's friends all got up and came to his rescue. A few punches were thrown before this huge bouncer got involved and hustled me out of the club and onto the sidewalk."

"Jeezus," said Jake, "are you all right?"

"Yeah, sure. After all, most of the punches came from these babies," said Ruben, proudly raising his fists in the air. "Those rich pricks prob'ly never even been in a real fight before."

"But what about Mary Lou?"

"Like I said, I dunno. I had to skedaddle outta there. The bouncer made sure of that. I hung around for a while on the other side of the street, thinking she'd come out and join me, but she never did. We'd made a plan that if we ever got separated, I'd wait for her back in my room. So here I am."

"Jeezus," said Jake.

"You sure do say Jeezus a lot."

"What else is there to say?" said Jake, studying Ruben. "So, what's your plan?"

"I think we gotta go back there, Jake. Back to El Diamante."

"We?"

"Yeah, us! You and me. C'mon, Jake, I need you. We're in this together, right? We gotta make sure Mary Lou is okay. That's the least you can do."

Jake didn't quite understand what the implied debt was that he owed Ruben, but he knew it would be useless to argue. Whatever sense of comradeship he'd had with the man had pretty much evaporated. Still, as long as they were roommates, Jake still felt a sense of obligation toward his erstwhile partner. "Okay," he agreed. "I'll help you if I can, but I don't see how. I'll try, though. But after tonight, we're done."

"Whatcha mean, done?"

"Just that. I don't wanna be part of the Ruben and Mary Lou show anymore. It's too nuts. Nancy and I have our own thing going on, and that's about all I can handle."

"Oh yeah?" said Ruben, eyeing Jake with suspicion. "Your own thing? What's that s'posed ta mean?"

"It means she and I are a team. Business partners."

"You are now, are ya? Then where is she now?"

"She's off work. Having dinner by herself. Relaxing after a busy day. I know where she is, and she knows where I am."

"Good for you," said Ruben grudgingly. "You know somethin', though, Jake? I never would've taken you for such a faithless friend."

"Who's faithless?" asked Jake. "I just said I'm gonna go with you, didn't I? I just never signed up for all this ... chaos. Chaos seems to follow you two wherever you go. Now, c'mon, Ruben. Let's try and end this on a high note, shall we? Let's see if we can extricate Mary Lou from whatever mess it is you've gotten her into."

"She's gotten herself into, you mean."

"Whatever," said Jake.

Chapter 53

There was no question of Ruben and Jake getting inside El Diamante to look for Mary Lou. Ruben was already *persona non grata*, and Jake didn't want to spend any more of his dwindling funds to get past the doorman. Ruben had it in his head that once Mary Lou and her new friends finished partying inside the disco, they'd all leave together through the back door in order to avoid the crazy American who'd picked a fight with them earlier that evening. It was late, but he was betting they were still inside the disco, and his intuition proved to be correct. Less than twenty minutes after Ruben and Jake began staking out the back exit together, crouching against the wall beside some large garbage bins, the door opened, and four well-dressed men, as well as Mary Lou and a blonde woman in high heels, made their way toward some expensive-looking vehicles parked across the street. A strikingly handsome man had his arm around Mary Lou's waist, and they appeared to be in high spirits, laughing and talking loudly as they made their way toward the row of cars. Before Jake could say a word, Ruben leapt up and started jogging in their direction. "*Hey*," he yelled. "Mary Lou, it's me! C'mere, I wanna talk to you."

The little group of revelers froze in their tracks. Mary Lou spoke briefly to her escort before breaking away and walking briskly toward Ruben, scowling all the way. She stopped at a safe distance and planted her feet, out of earshot of the Spaniards and far enough away that Ruben couldn't lunge and grab her.

"What?" she demanded.

"Well?" he said.

"Well, what, Ruben?"

"Did he pay you?"

"No," she said. "He didn't. Not yet."

"Well, you know he's gotta pay you first, babe. That's the deal. Have him give you the money before you get in that car with him, and then you come over and hand it to me. No freebies, remember?"

"Sure," she said, "whatever you say, Ruben. Now please wait here." Without uttering another word, she turned and walked quickly back toward the little crowd that had gathered by the parked cars. As soon as she reached the man who'd been escorting her, he grabbed her arm and moved her quickly toward a red Lamborghini. Unlocking the driver's side door, he gestured for her to go around the front of the car and get in on the passenger side. Ruben started running, but it was too late. The powerful engine roared into life, and within seconds the car had disappeared down the street, leaving behind a plume of noxious gray smoke. Ruben kept on running down the street, shouting obscenities in a futile attempt to catch up with the roadster.

"Mary Lou," he yelled, shaking his fist in the air. "Get back here!"

Jake took a few steps and stopped in the middle of the road feeling his heart thump wildly in his chest. He was far more alarmed by Ruben than by what Mary Lou had done. The whole scene, to his mind, was more like an escape than an abduction. The group of partyers had simply wanted to get away from the raving maniac in the road, who finally stopped running and slowly began to retrace his steps, cursing and gesturing to himself in the balmy night air.

"That bitch," he cried, sobbing and panting, as he straggled toward the streetlight where Jake stood waiting. "Now she's really gone and done it. Fuck that bitch. FUCK HER!" His blue eyes were bloodshot, and sweat was pouring down his face. "Didn't I tell her to make sure she got the money first before she got into the car? You heard me, right, Jake? Didn't I?"

"Maybe she just couldn't, Ruben, maybe she—"

"She was s'posed to get the money first!" roared Ruben, unloading a blast of beery breath in Jake's face, "then come over here, hand me the money, and then get in the car. This way, she may never get paid."

"That's all you're worried about?" said Jake, wincing in disbelief. "What about the possibility she may never come back at all?"

"Fuck you, Jake," said Ruben, curling and uncurling his hands into fists. He began laughing aloud then—a maniacal tittering laughter that seemed to echo off the cobblestones and mingle with the hum of the power lines above their heads. "She'll come back, Jake. You can be sure of that," he said. "My Mary Lou always comes back. Oh yeah, that's for damn sure."

Would she, though? wondered Jake. The only thing he was sure of was that he no longer wanted to be in Palma de Mallorca, pretending to be a pimp or a partner or a protector or whatever you wanted to call it. The sense that this was all some kind of harmless adventure had long since passed. He could no longer pretend that he was anything but a poseur. Whatever initial Kerouac-ian thrill he'd gained from this escapade had worn off, only to be replaced by an oppressive feeling of dread in the pit of his stomach. Whatever benefit of the doubt he'd awarded Ruben up till now, based on his romanticized outlaw image, had been replaced with ill-disguised contempt for the man's cruelty and chaos and sheer stupidity. The irrefutable evidence that Ruben was an irresponsible and even dangerous partner who was willing to throw his own girlfriend under the proverbial bus had become impossible to ignore.

"C'mon," pleaded Jake. "There's nothing more we can do here. Let's go back to the hotel. We're both exhausted, and I wanna see if Nancy's gotten back yet."

"Don't you worry about that bitch," slurred Ruben, his drunkenness on full display. "She knows how to take care of herself. You said so yourself, Jake. Just worry 'bout gettin' your cut of the action when she finally gets back, 'kay? It'd just be too embarrassin' to not get paid now, dontcha think?"

"I got paid," protested Jake. "Last time I saw her. Just before she went to dinner."

"Really?" said Ruben. "Hmmmpf. Well, that's surprising. I never did trust that limey bitch."

Jake sighed. "You know something," he said, glaring at his erstwhile friend as he stumbled down the sidewalk. "You really are a prick, Ruben."

Ruben let loose another salvo of high-pitched laughter. "You sound just like Mary Lou," he said, grinning wickedly. "Now I've got two bitches on my back."

Chapter 54

Sometime later that night, Jake awoke with a start in their hotel room, stretched out fully clothed on top of his bed. For one disorienting moment, he was unable to get his bearings in the room, which was only dimly lit from the light of a streetlamp coming in through the flimsy curtains on the window. His head sank back into the pillow as memory returned, along with a subsequent feeling of nagging anxiety. Lifting himself up on his elbows, he let out a sigh just as Ruben started thrashing around on the floor nearby, mumbling to himself. Why he was on the floor and not in his bed was a mystery which Jake attributed, as he did so much of Ruben's behavior, to having one beer too many.

It seemed like eons ago that Jake had lain on this same bed, in a much more buoyant frame of mind, listening to Nancy's low, muffled voice and the muted sighs and grunts of her first client, the Danish seaman she'd met at breakfast the morning before. That was the way it was supposed to work, he reminded himself, being here in the next room, listening for sounds of duress, prepared to break down the door if need be, or at least go bang like hell on it, interrupting whatever unacceptable act was being perpetrated should that prove necessary. Fortunately for him, Nancy had the patience and the observation skills to wait until someone amenable came along, neither too drunk nor troublesome but just out to have a good time and willing to pay for his pleasure. There was always the risk that her judgment might be off, and she'd inadvertently picked up some kind of pervy weirdo, but the more he'd gotten to know her, the more Jake felt that was a risk that he could live with. Mary Lou, on the other hand, was Nancy's polar opposite, with an uncanny inclination to attract men like Ruben—macho, strong-willed, and with an underlying streak of violence. Jake was amazed at how naive they'd all been. Even Ruben. How ludicrous to imagine that their mere presence might have a moderating influence on the unpredictable forces of lust and passion, once they'd been unleashed. In the midst of these reveries, Ruben's hand suddenly appeared above Jake's mattress, presenting him with a bottle of beer.

"Here," said Ruben, his voice choked up, "this'll do ya good. Gotta keep our spirits up, right?"

Jake could hardly believe his eyes. Could the man be weeping? Ruben's cheeks appeared to be stained with tears, and his normally stoic features bore a look of unaccustomed grief. "I've lost her, Jake," he groaned, collapsing back onto the floor. "I've lost my Mary Lou."

Jake felt at a loss. How should he respond to this thoroughly atypical behavior? Was this the same guy who had no qualms about Mary Lou performing truly debasing sexual acts as long as she got paid? Trying to monitor the man's fluctuating internal guidelines for pimping was proving to be a daunting task. In fact, it was downright impossible. Ruben had set it up so that whatever Mary Lou could or couldn't do was up to him, but his judgment could shift on a whim. Jake suspected that what had set him off with the Spaniard in El Diamante was that he was simply too good-looking, which according to the original pimp plan as Jake understood it, should have been irrelevant. It was all getting to be far more bizarre than Jake had ever bargained for, but the final nail in the coffin had occurred earlier that afternoon in the bar where Jake had agreed to meet Ruben for a beer. Out of nowhere, a furious Mary Lou had stormed up to them, wagging her finger in Ruben's face. Her anger about the Pedro affair had apparently not abated.

"What is the matter with you?" she'd spat out. "You should've done something, Ruben! I kept shouting NO again and again. You had to have heard me. I know you were listening. What is the matter with you? And don't say you didn't hear me, you bastard!"

"First of all," said Ruben with an icy calmness. "I didn't hear you say anything. If I had, I would've done something, right? C'mon, babe, this is me you're talking to. And second of all, the guy left you a generous tip. You said so yourself."

"I never should have told you that," she hissed. "Next time, I'll just keep it to myself."

"Oh, so there will be a next time?"

"Just shut the fuck up," said Mary Lou. "You're not the one getting ass fucked here."

"That's show business, darlin'."

"It may be just show business to you," she railed, "but I'm the one who ends up feeling slimy."

"You'll be all right," he said dismissively. "Just go sit on the bidet in your room for a while. Why'd ya think the goddamned Frogs invented them anyway?"

That memory of Ruben, with his ruthlessly calculating and cavalier attitude, had left Jake totally unprepared for this helpless, blubbering, and vulnerable figure stretched out now on the floor beside his bed.

"I mean, for all we know Jake, he's gonna drive her out in the country somewhere and … and rape her and throw her off a cliff fer Chrissakes."

"I think your imagination's shifted into overdrive," said Jake, rolling the beer bottle back and forth on his belly.

"How did you get to be Mr. Cool all of a sudden?" snapped Ruben. "You should be worried too. No one's seen Nancy since that supposed dinner she went to at the yacht club. How many hours ago was that? Where the hell is she? I don't like it, Jake. I don't like it at all! Everything was supposed to happen right here. Here in this hotel. Otherwise, what the hell do they need us for? This is fucked up, Jake. Really it is. Who the hell knows where they are? What time is it anyway?"

"About twenty minutes since the last time you asked. Four a.m."

"Four in the fucking morning, Jake. And we don't even know where the fuck they are." Ruben's face suddenly took on a chalky appearance. "Oh God," he moaned. "Oh shit. I haven't felt this bad since … well, since I was in prison."

"Stop it, Ruben," yelled Jake at last, "you're scaring me."

"Well, you should be scared, goddammit. Haven't you been listening to a word I've said? I've lost my Mary Lou!" Ruben curled himself up in a fetal position, blubbering to himself while cradling his face in his hands. After a while, though, he began calming down, his crying subsided to a whimper, and he lay inert on the floor, issuing a snuffling sound that soon became a steady snoring.

Thank God, thought Jake, who'd settled back down on his pillow. *Finally, some quiet time to think about what our next move should be. I mean, my next move. I'm through with having to deal with this maniac.* He clasped his hands behind his head and looked up at the ceiling, gathering his thoughts. He knew he had to get away from Ruben, but also knew he couldn't leave until he found out what was going on with Nancy. Feeling helpless and confused, he began shutting out all thoughts and focused on his breathing. What else was there to do? Breathing in and breathing out more and more slowly, he gradually began to calm down. He'd just managed to achieve a semblance of a meditative state when the sound of someone trying to insert a key into the lock of the room next door reached his ears through the thin walls. Sitting up in silence, he swung his legs off the side of the bed and tiptoed to the door, careful not to disturb the snoring Ruben. Cautiously, he cracked open the door to peek into the dimly lit hallway. Standing there, looking tired but no worse for wear was Nancy, fiddling with a key in the lock. She glanced at Jake with weary surprise and smiled. Immediately placing his finger to his lips, Jake stepped out into the hallway, noiselessly closing the door behind him. He strode over to embrace her, and she turned and put her arms around him, squeezing him tight.

"Am I glad to see you!" she whispered. "C'mon, let's go inside."

"I'm so glad you're back," said Jake, once they were seated together on the edge of her bed. "How are you?"

"I'm fine," she said. Jake could see that she was more than fine. There was a kind of quiet excitement in her countenance, something he'd never noticed before.

"You really are, aren't you?" he said, relief washing over him. "So c'mon, out with it then! How was the yacht club?"

"First of all, I'm sorry, Jake, you must've been worried sick. But I have some exciting news. Can you guess?"

"Umm, you've won the lottery?"

"Close! I've met someone!"

"Wait … what do you mean?" asked Jake, feeling confused.

"Someone special. And I don't mean a client, Jake. I mean, someone special!"

"Okay now, slow down, Nance. Take your time and tell me all about it."

"His name is Manuel," she said, "and he's the captain of a yacht."

"That's fantastic!" said Jake.

"But not just any yacht," she continued. "He's the captain of the royal yacht. You know, the royal Spanish family?"

"You're kidding, right?"

"No, I'm not!"

"And you and he …?"

"Well, as you can probably tell from how excited I am," she said, giggling, "something really clicked. Like, *wow*, Jake. I've never felt this way about a man before."

"And he … feels the same way too?"

"I think so, Jake! We really hit it off. I'm not kidding. The energy between us was just … I don't even know how to explain it. It was just …"

"Love at first sight?" offered Jake.

"Yes! I know it's a cliché, but I'm convinced it was or rather is!"

"Well, that's great!" said Jake. "Where is he now?"

"He's pulling up anchor this morning and sailing to Gibraltar. I'm not allowed to be on board for that, but he'll be coming back in a week or so, and he wants to see me again right here when he returns!"

"That is amazing," said Jake, deciding to hide his skepticism. "And you just met this guy at dinner?"

"Not exactly. Look, Jake. I know I said I was just going to have dinner—no business—but as I was looking around at all these clearly well-to-do people, I thought, blimey, I can't let this opportunity go to waste, ya know what I mean? So I approached this guy, Manuel, who was sitting all alone, dressed up in his blindingly white crew outfit and cute as hell, thinking I would proposition him. I mean, why the hell not? It couldn't hurt, right? I mean, the worst that could happen is that he'd turn me down, right? Well, before I could even say one word, he asked me to sit down and join him for a drink, and you know, this almost never happens, Jake, but the more we talked, the more we began to really connect! I mean, we had real chemistry together, which is why I've been away so long."

"Yeah, what's it been, almost ten hours?"

"Has it? I've lost all track of time, to be honest. I really have. We were just having so much fun. I could've stayed with him forever. And he took me on board his yacht too! It's got everything you need for a really good time, Jake. I can promise you that! Champagne, caviar, even a sauna! All courtesy of the Spanish taxpayer!"

"So I take it the King wasn't there?"

"Of course not, Jake. He almost never is. That's the thing, you see. If things work out the way I hope they will, Manuel and I will sail around the Mediterranean together, awaiting orders from the King or someone else in the royal family. Manuel thinks he can get me a job on the yacht, ya see. He thinks there might be work for me in the kitchen, which is surprisingly modern and very well-stocked, I must say. And by the way, in case you ever run into him, I told him I'd just quit my job as a dancer on Ibiza and was looking for work over here."

Jake stared at her, his mind racing. "So, does this mean … I mean, are we …"

"Oh, Jake, of course, I've been meaning to tell you," she said, reaching into her purse. "Here, take this. It's enough for your flight back to Ibiza and a bit more as well. Now I couldn't really charge him the way I normally do, could I? Seeing as how we're, well, you know … anyway, it's not like that between us. Well, we did do it, of course, on board the yacht, and he could see I needed some money, so he gave me enough to tide me over until he comes back to pick me up next week." Nancy paused here and shook her head, her eyes brimming with tears. "I'm ever so happy about the way things have turned out, Jake. I think you must be my lucky charm! I'm quite sure this never would've happened if Ruben was in charge."

Jake stared at the wad of pesetas in his hand, nodding his head in disbelief. "Nancy," he said at last. "This is incredible news. I'm just … happy for you."

"And what about you, Jake? What will you do now?"

"I don't know … take the first flight back to Ibiza, I guess."

"But what about Ruben and Mary Lou?"

Jake explained briefly what had been going on since Nancy had been gone. "They're out of control," he said. "I really don't want anything to do with the whole scene here anymore. I can only see things getting worse, not better. It's time to cut my losses, as they say, and run."

"Well," said Nancy soothingly. "Your job was to be with me, remember? To help me out if I needed it. Ruben and Mary Lou were always a separate issue. It is a goddamned shame, though, that things have turned out this way. Do you think Mary Lou will be okay?"

"Hard to say," said Jake. "What do you think?"

"I think she's made of tougher stuff than people may think. She'd have to be to stay together with Ruben this long. Of course, anything could happen, but it's the life they've chosen, isn't it?"

"That Spanish guy from the disco knows that we saw them together," said Jake. "So I don't think he would do anything too stupid. I suspect she'll show up sometime today tired and bedraggled and get into another epic fight with Ruben. I'd rather not be around for that, though, to be perfectly honest."

"I'll tell you what then, mate," she said, slipping into heavy London dialect, "let's go next door and say goodbye to Ruben, and then I'll go out to the airport with you. It's just a short cab drive away. I'm tired, but I'm also too wired to go to bed now anyway. There's an airport restaurant where we can have some breakfast and say goodbye. Who knows if we'll ever see each other again?"

"Yeah," said Jake, feeling hugely relieved. "Who knows? But as for saying goodbye to Ruben, how about we just leave him a note. He's had a lot to drink the past few days, and waking him up now, even if we could, might not be the smartest move."

Chapter 55

J ake was back at his usual table on the sidewalk in front of the Café del Teatro, sipping a café con leche. It was still morning after the forty-minute early morning flight back from Mallorca, and once again, he had his wallet open in front of him, counting his pesetas. The whole trip had been a fiasco from start to finish, but at least he wasn't any the poorer for it. He had about the same amount of dinero that he did when he left, and that meant close to nothing. And yet he felt the slow stirring of a new optimism, as though a weight had been lifted off his chest. His self-appointed task to follow through with the desperate plan on Mallorca had been completed successfully in his mind, despite the financial failure of the operation. At least he and Nancy had managed to survive unscathed. As for Ruben and Mary Lou, they'd transformed themselves in Jake's mind from sympathetic, easy-going beachcombers to sad desperados, seemingly unable to gain any traction in life, stuck in an endless cycle of survival and dissolution. The irony of such a harsh judgement was not lost on him. He knew that he'd been teetering on the edge of just such a fate himself and was still not sure he'd escaped it. But he did feel certain about one thing; the necessity of leaving his former friends behind. Somehow that certainty allowed the sense of despair he'd been feeling about his future to dissipate, as though an onerous burden had been lifted from his psyche. He realized now that his involvement with them had been a foolish distraction preventing him from going with the true flow of his heart. He was free now to turn his undivided attention toward winning Gisela's heart. The powerful attraction he felt for her, along with his inner conviction that she felt the same way he did, would become the impetus he needed for some forward motion in his life. Whatever inevitable obstacles might arise could be overcome, he felt certain, if he just stayed the course. Her marriage was as empty as a hollowed-out tree trunk, just waiting for the first blast of true love to topple it. Gisela was waiting for him. He felt sure of that. Jake had concluded in his own inscrutable way that his fate now in life depended on his success in releasing her from the inertia of her loveless marriage to Dieter. He had only to blow on the embers of passion lying just below the surface of her too-guarded heart, and like the captive tigress it was, it would roar for him to unlock the cage.

Absently counting his coins and wondering how soon before he'd be able to see her again, he noticed out of the corner of his eye the bearded face, protruding belly, and matchstick legs of Dieter strolling into view. Sweeping up his coins and notes and stuffing them into his shoulder bag, he raised his hand and waved.

"Hey, Dieter, over here!"

His rival gave a surprisingly friendly wave in return. "I thought you'd gone to Palma?" he said, approaching the table. "That's what Gisela said, anyway. How did things turn out for you over there?"

"Not so great," admitted Jake. "You were right, as it turns out. I definitely don't have what it takes for that line of work. Big surprise, right? Would you mind sitting down for a moment, though? I've been meaning to talk to you, Dieter."

"Actually, that's quite funny, Jake. Because I've been meaning to talk to *you*!"

Just then, a waiter arrived and wearily asked what the two men would like.

"A coffee with cognac for my friend here, *por favor*," said Jake before Dieter could respond.

"How did you know?" asked Dieter.

"Know what?"

"That that's what I was going to order?"

"Gisela told me it's your favorite. With Rémy Martin, right?"

"Correct," said Dieter, smiling. "And get one for my friend here as well," he said to the waiter, who nodded and left. "Now, what did you want to talk to me about?"

Jake hesitated. "You first," he said.

"All right then," said Dieter lighting up a cigarette. "As you wish."

Jake stiffened, wondering if he was about to receive some kind of threatening ultimatum. "Go ahead then," said Jake. "I'm listening."

"Did you know she needs an operation?"

"She? You mean Gisela?" Jake felt as though he'd been body-slammed. "What? No, no, I didn't know that."

"I'm surprised," said Dieter. "I thought she would have told you."

"What kind of operation?" asked Jake.

"Something to do with her ovaries. She's had problems there for some time now. The doctors say it's finally time to go in and have a look."

Jake felt his heart imploding. "Here on Ibiza?" he asked.

"Not a chance," he said. "Back in Berlin, of course. She's flying there in a few days together with Chloe. They'll be staying in my apartment in Steglitz. It's a nice part of town. I think you'd like it."

How odd, thought Jake. *Why on earth would Dieter care if I liked his apartment in Berlin?* "Well, I'm sure I would if I were ever to visit West Berlin. I've always wanted to, actually," he confessed. "Gisela tells me I would love it. But to be honest, I couldn't even afford to get off the island right now. I'm on my last legs, moneywise."

"Especially since the pimp thing didn't work out?"

"Correct," admitted Jake. "It was quite a humbling experience, to be honest."

"And you don't have any other prospects?"

"*Nada,*" admitted Jake.

"Well then, I have another crazy idea for you to consider. I'm going to be driving up to Berlin in another week or so to be there for Gisela. How would you like to come along with me? I hate driving by myself. Especially such a long distance."

"Are you serious?" asked Jake.

"As a heart attack," said Dieter. "But I must admit I have an ulterior motive."

"Tell me," said Jake. "I can handle it."

"I have a new business I want to start up in Berlin. I need some help, and I think you might be the perfect person for it."

"Go on," said Jake, "I'm all ears."

"I've just got hold of a new portable machine that prints decals on T-shirts. As far as I know, I'm the only one who has it in Berlin. My idea is to set someone up on the sidewalk in Wilmersdorf, which is a major shopping area. I've got some great designs for decals, and I think I could sell a ton of T-shirts as a side business, but I need someone I can trust to man the machine for me. I don't know anyone who would be interested in this kind of work, but Gisela seems to think you might be. She speaks very highly of you, Jake. You speak German, which will be necessary, of course. You just have to show up for work every day. I'll show you how to get started, and I'll pay you fifty marks in cash at the end of every day. What do you think?"

Jake was stunned. *Fifty marks a day?* This seemed too good to be true. "It ... it sounds ... fantastic," he stammered. "But wouldn't I need a work permit for that?"

"Technically, yes. But I think they go easy on Amis in Berlin. After all, you guys saved our asses from the Russkies during the airlift. We haven't forgotten that."

Jake swallowed hard. Could this be for real? "What's the catch?" he asked.

"Catch?" said Dieter. "Hmmm, I guess the catch is that you'd have to go to work every day. Is that a problem for you?"

"No," said Jake, his heart beginning to pound with excitement. "Not at all. I'm definitely ready to go to work. But where would I stay?"

"Well, my apartment is quite large. And Chloe will be there. And Gisela will be there after the operation, recovering. But I'm sure we could find room for you. If you're okay with just a mattress on the floor, that is."

"More than okay," said Jake. "I'm used to roughing it."

"Oh, and Moische will be there too!"

"Moische? You mean you're stealing him from the neighbor?"

"Gisela insists. Actually, I've already made an arrangement with the neighbor to appropriate him for some cash so I won't have to steal him at all. We've all grown very fond of him, as you know, and I think it will be very good for her during her recuperation period to have as many friends around as possible. I would expect you to help take care of him too. You know, take him for walks around the neighborhood, feed him, that sort of thing. I can't rely on Chloe for that, and I may not be around all the time."

"No problem," said Jake. "Me and Moische are buds. He may be a dog, but he's also a real mensch! Will he be coming in the car with us?"

"Yes, just you and me and Moische. How does that sound?"

"I'll tell you how it sounds," said Jake. "It sounds like an answer to my prayers."

"Funny," said Dieter, "you don't strike me as someone who prays a lot."

"You're right," confessed Jake. "I don't. It's just a figure of speech."

"I know what you mean, though. Sometimes just when you least expect it, something good shows up in your life. That's what happened to me," he said, grinning, "when Gisela and I first met."

"Yes," said Jake, avoiding Dieter's gaze. "I heard about that. That was kismet indeed."

"Here's to kismet then," said Dieter as the waiter arrived with their drinks.

"Yes," said Jake, as they toasted one another. "Here's to kismet!"

"By the way," said Dieter, "what was it you wanted to talk to me about?"

"I can't even remember," said Jake. "I'm sure it doesn't matter anymore."

Chapter 56

As soon as his meeting with Dieter at the café concluded, Jake hitchhiked back to their finca to fill Carl in on the latest developments. He knew Carl would want to know what happened in Palma and he felt relieved to be able to report to his friend that his short-lived career as a pimp was over.

"But what about Ruben and Mary Lou?" asked Carl, who'd just returned from an overnight gig. "Are they still over there?"

"As far as I know," said Jake. "When I left at about five o'clock this morning, Mary Lou was still missing. She'd hopped in a car with some rich guy and took off somewhere. Ruben was too drunk and groggy to even talk, so I just left him a note telling him I was going back to Ibiza and good luck!"

"So you didn't feel like you needed to support him as a friend?" asked Carl, who, as usual, sat at the table in front of the finca strumming his guitar.

"I tried to," said Jake. "But he and Mary Lou definitely have their own little drama going on, which has nothing to do with me anymore. Ruben was pretty much on a bender the whole time I was there, getting more and more out of control. And Mary Lou, well, she's a pretty tough cookie, as you know. My guess is, she'll come back and find Ruben drunk in his room, then they'll fight and fuck like they always do. Not really anything I need to be around for. Anyway, I doubt I'll ever see them again."

"Why do you say that?"

"Because, *amigo* … now hold on to your guitar … I am going to go to Germany!"

"The fuck you are!"

"The fuck I am!"

"What? How?"

"I'm driving up to West Berlin. Next week. With Dieter!"

Jake proceeded to share the details of the conversation he'd had that morning at the Café del Teatro. Carl listened intently, his bearded face unusually somber.

"Hey Carl," said Jake as he finished his story. "What's up with you, man? You look like someone just took a sledgehammer to your favorite Martin guitar."

Carl wrinkled his nose and passed his hand over his face regaining his composure. "Well," he said with a tinge of sadness, "I guess I wasn't expecting you to leave quite so soon. That's all."

"Carl," said Jake. "It's been more than a year now."

"I know, but well, I guess I just thought we'd be housemates for a while longer. Especially after finally finding such an ideal place. Shit, it's just starting to feel like home, brother."

"It'll still be home, Carl, with or without *moi*. And you've got Renata now to keep you company."

"Yeah, that's true," said Carl managing a smile. "Thank God for that. But I'll miss our jam sessions."

"Me too," said Jake. "We did create some fine harmonies together!"
"I'm gonna miss you too, brother," said Carl in a rare show of emotion.

"Yeah, me too," said Jake eyeing his friend wistfully. "But don't go anywhere, you hear? I'm gonna come back to visit for sure! Berlin is not that far away."

"Don't worry," said Carl. "I'm right where I'm supposed to be."

"Looks that way to me," said Jake. "It's kind of like a dream come true for you, isn't it? I mean, you haven't been here that long, and already you're in a band, getting gigs, playing in hotels …"

"I know," said Carl. "And living here in this incredible finca."

"You're right," said Jake looking around him as some ravens fluttered down on the branch of a nearby olive tree. "It's really almost too good to be true. Whenever I'm here, I feel like pinching myself; it's just so goddamn peaceful and beautiful."

"And Berlin," said Carl, "that feels right to you?"

"It does!" said Jake. "Unbelievably so, in fact. Not that I have a lot of options right now. But Gisela's gonna be there, Carl. That's what really blows my mind. I can't believe how it's all coming together."

"I'm happy for you, man. Really I am. But what about Dieter? How does he fit in?"

"I know, I know," said Jake. "It's crazy! Dieter's the last guy I ever would've expected to save my ass, let alone invite me to share his apartment in Berlin. But it appears that's what fate has in store for both of us."

"Well, you'll both have something in common, that's for sure."

"Right you are," said Jake. "We'll both be there for Gisela. I told you what's going on with her healthwise, right?"

"Yeah, you did," said Carl. "I was really sorry to hear about that. I hope she's gonna be okay."

"Dieter thinks she will be, and he knows more about it than I do since I haven't had a chance to talk to her yet. But I think being in love will help pull her through in any case."

"Being in love?" asked Carl. "With you?"

"It's still early stages, bro, but I'm pretty sure she will be if she's not already."

"Wow, you're pretty cocky about it."

"I am," he admitted. "And I'm not even sure why except for this really strong gut feeling I have. I tell you, Carl, it's happening. I've never had an intuition this strong before. I think that's why every part of my being is just saying yes to Berlin."

"You don't think being broke has a lot to do with it?" asked Carl.

"Well, yeah, there is that. I won't deny it. I do need to earn some *dinero*. But I also sure as shit know I've got to be there for her. Especially now. She's gonna need me, Carl."

"No doubt," agreed Carl. "But again, what about Dieter? Wouldn't that be the ultimate betrayal?"

"Man, it's not like I'm breaking up Romeo and Juliet here. I don't think love needs any defense, do you? It's like this shining path through the woods you've just gotta follow, even if you don't know where you're gonna end up. I'm just playing it by ear. If I go up there and see that there really is something happening there between them, something like genuine love despite everything she's told me and everything I've seen with my own eyes up till now, I think I can let it go. I really do. In that case, we'll just be friends, hopefully, and appreciate the fresh start to my new life in Berlin. But if it's what I suspect it will be, then all bets are off."

"So you think it's just a loveless, sad sham of a marriage?" asked Carl.

"Well," said Jake, "you've been around them. Don't you?"

"Yeah, I pretty much have to agree," said Carl. "Still, you're playing a pretty brazen game here, bud. Be careful!"

"Thanks for the warning, Carl. But remember, 'All is fair in love.' Stevie Wonder said that, remember?"

"I do," said Carl, nodding his head. "I've gotta say, Jake. I do admire your passion."

"Well, I guess that would be one of the differences between us," said Jake.

"What's that supposed to mean?"

"Aw, c'mon, Carl. Can you see yourself just dropping everything to run off and be with a woman?"

"Hmm, maybe not," admitted Carl, looking flustered, "but you, on the other hand, haven't got that much to drop in the first place. And it seems like you're always either running away from or running toward some woman. Maybe this time it'll turn out right for you, though— whatever 'right' means, but I do wish you luck, my friend. I really do."

"Thanks buddy. That means a lot. And now I've gotta go inside outta the sun and catch me some shut-eye. Turns out pimping can really make you sleep-deprived."

"You're lucky that's all you're deprived of, hanging out with that lunatic Ruben. You were lucky, Jake. Really lucky."

"Still am. In fact, Carl, I think my lucky streak might just be getting started!"

Chapter 57

Jake was up early the next morning, eager to go to San Carlos and meet with Gisela one last time before she got on the plane to Berlin. After pulling up in the Tank, he shut off the engine and immediately heard Moische barking inside the house, a sure sign that Gisela was home. He breathed a sigh of relief when he noticed that Dieter's Mercedes was gone from the garage. He needed to speak to Gisela alone, and with Chloe still at school, he would likely get the chance.

Jake slid the patio door open and called out her name. Picking up Moische, who was so excited to see him he almost did a backflip, he walked through the living room and into the kitchen, where he gently released the dog on the floor. He found Gisela sitting at the table in front of a steaming hot mug of tea, her hair swept back in a ponytail, poring over paperwork. She wore tortoiseshell glasses, lending her a professorial air.

"Oh, Jake, hello! You'll have to forgive me. I heard Moische barking, but I'm so busy paying these bills I wasn't really paying attention."

"You look very smart in those glasses, you know," he said, smiling at the sight of her.

"I am very smart. Didn't you know?" she asked, returning his smile.

"Yes, I did, as a matter of fact," he said, walking over and lifting up her chin to plant a kiss on her lips. "It's one of the things I love about you."

Jake sat down opposite her and reached across to hold her hand. "Can you put those bills away long enough for us to talk for a minute?" he asked.

"Of course," she said. "What's up?"

"Well," said Jake, "a lot has happened. I just thought we should talk about it."

Gisela removed her glasses and squeezed his hand between both of her own. "First of all," she said teasingly, "welcome back from the crime scene. I see you survived, thank God. Dieter tells me things didn't go as planned, though."

"Well, things could have gone a lot worse," admitted Jake. "There was actually a happy ending for Nancy. I'm not so sure about Ruben and Mary Lou though."

"Please," she said. "Tell me about it, Jake."

Jake explained about Nancy's unlikely good fortune and then gave a brief synopsis of the events with Ruben and Mary Lou, emphasizing his own deteriorating relationship with Ruben.

"Well, I'm not surprised," she said after listening attentively. "You know I only met him once at the Montesol, but I got a very creepy feeling about Ruben. I could never really understand what you saw in him."

"I can see now how that must've been hard to understand," said Jake. "Although he could be quite charming in fact. You'll have to trust me on that. He and I joining forces seemed very unlikely even to me. But it happened."

"Well, I did find the whole idea very bizarre, to be honest. I never felt like you fit into that, Jake. It's puzzling to me. That's just not who you are at all," she said, giving his hand another squeeze. "But I guess you felt all this pressure to make some money. I think maybe you lost your mind there for a little while, don't you?"

"Really?" said Jake, guffawing. "Lost my mind? That bad?"

"Only temporarily, I hope," said Gisela smiling.

"To tell you the truth," he said, "that is how I felt sometimes. Like I was going crazy! I can't just blame it on Ruben's powers of persuasion, either. It was me too, Gisela. The whole pimping thing had become a kind of obsession. Ruben made it seem like some kind of big game, and I believed him. Nobody'd get hurt, he said, and we'd make some money too. That was how it was supposed to be. Just glad I came out of it relatively unscathed."

"Relatively?"

"Well, I may have sustained some damage," admitted Jake.

"Like what?" asked Gisela, releasing Jake's hand to open a new pack of Marlboros.

"Like … well, it does rattle my confidence in my own judgment, I suppose."

"Judgment about … are you talking about Ruben?"

"Yeah," said Jake. "And Mary Lou as well. I did consider us friends, you know, especially when we were hanging out on the beach at Salinas together. I looked up to Ruben too. I thought he knew things I didn't know. You know, things I couldn't know because of the way I was brought up, and the way he was too."

"Like what?" asked Gisela, inserting a fresh cigarette into her ivory holder.

"Survival stuff," said Jake. "Like how to live by your wits."

"And did you? Learn from him, Jake?"

"Sure," said Jake. "You always learn something. But I got fooled. Turns out Ruben didn't have a lot of wits to begin with."

"It took you long enough to figure that out," said Gisela.

"I guess I was naive," said Jake. "I like to give people the benefit of the doubt. Anyway, that's all behind me now. It's time to move on to better things."

"Like what?" she asked.

"Like you," said Jake reaching up to touch her hair.

"*Schön*," she said. "That makes me happy. But I'm afraid I have some bad news, Jake. Did Dieter tell you?"

"He did," said Jake. "When we ran into each other at the café. He was vague on the details, though. How serious is it?"

"Hard to say," she said, lighting her cigarette. "We won't really know anything for sure until the doctors go inside and have a look."

"Are you worried?"

"Not really. This isn't new, Jake. I've had some problems there for quite some time. I'm quite sick of it, actually. I want them to just go in there and fix it."

"Of course. And they all agree it's possible?

"I don't know about all," she said, exhaling smoke. "But yes, assuming everything goes well."

"It will!" said Jake.

"That's very sweet of you to say, Jake."

"Well, it's just … I was hoping some day we might … you know … be able to …"

"Oh, that!" said Gisela blushing slightly. "Me too."

"Really?"

"Yes, of course. I'm afraid it might take some time, though, Jake. Maybe a few more months? Are you sure you can wait that long for me?"

"Listen, the most important thing is for you to have this operation and get better. And no, I can't wait. But I'll just have to, won't I?"

"Just come here, will you?" said Gisela, grabbing his head and pulling him toward her, kissing him deeply as she slid her hand through his hair.

"Jake," she said, coming up for air. "I'm so glad you're going to be in Berlin. Now I really have something to look forward to when I get out of the hospital."

"Me too," said Jake. "Are you sure, though? What about Dieter? Sorry, but I have to ask."

"I suspect he's not going to be around that much. He has a way of disappearing whenever I really need him. He always has plenty to do there. He and a friend own a casino together. He's usually out till dawn and comes home drunk and tired and flops right into bed if he comes home at all. And then he also has business here he still has to come down and take care of."

"And you?" said Jake. "Aren't you going to want to come back here as soon as you can?"

"I don't think so, Jake. Not anymore. I know that's hard to believe, but I think I'm going to stay in Berlin, for Chloe's sake. It'll be better for her there. She can get a better education. We can't just stay here in Ibiza doing what we're doing forever."

"But I thought you loved it here?"

"Jake," she said, cradling his face in her hands, "I do love it here. And I'll always have fond memories. But there's nothing for me here anymore. I mean, I can never be free here, Jake."

"What do you mean? I thought Ibiza was all about being free!"

"I mean, I need to figure out what to do with my life. Find a profession. Be able to support myself. If you can't do that, you're never free."

"But you have the boutique," said Jake.

"Dieter's boutique, you mean."

"Well, yeah."

"But I don't want to be involved with Dieter anymore, Jake."

"You really don't?"

"No, Jake. Can't you see that? Why do you think I'm kissing you now?"

Jake felt a wave of pure happiness passing through him as Gisela embraced him. He felt her love for him in every cell of his body. Or was it merely need? Either way, it had become an irrelevant distinction. He was willing to surrender to it, whatever it was. He'd felt needed before by Joan, by Marie-Madeleine, even by Cannelle. Now, something was different. Something had shifted inside him. Whatever it was, he wanted this feeling to go on forever.

Chapter 58

A week or so later, as the ferry pulled away from the dock, Jake stood on the deck gazing at the illuminated silhouette of the old medieval town slowly receding in the distance, his heart full of a bittersweet blend of melancholy and happiness. Leaving the fabled island, at last, Jake felt a tension in his chest, like a bowstring stretched to the limit. *I've got it for sure, now,* he thought, *the Ibiza blues.* How else to describe this feeling? With its promise of beauty and pleasure, the island had not disappointed, delivering a taste of freedom and adventure, which Jake knew would remain indelibly etched on his spirit long after he'd set foot in West Berlin to begin a new urban lifestyle with its own unique set of challenges.

Dieter had booked a cabin for them both with separate berths and awaited Jake now for a nightcap at the bar before they stumbled down into the claustrophobic depths of the ferry to enclose themselves in an airless cabin the size of a broom closet on their way to Barcelona and the highway to Berlin. The outlandishness of hitching a ride with his future lover's husband to lead an unpredictable new life in a city he'd never set foot in before suddenly overwhelmed him, and he found himself bent over the rail laughing into the white frothing sea water splashing up the side of the accelerating vessel. "Life is crazy," he yelled into the wind at the top of his lungs, *almost unbearably mad,* he thought, *and maddening and sad and beautiful and unpredictable and meaningful and pointless and simply all too much!* Turning, at last, he pushed off from the rail and stumble-footed his way toward the cabin door and the semblance of safety down inside the ship's inner sanctum.

THE END